SPHINX'S
QUEEN

SPHINX'S QUEEN

ESTHER FRIESNER

Random House New York

Text copyright © 2010 by Esther Friesner
Jacket art copyright © 2010 by Larry Rostant

www.randomhouse.com/teens

Educators and librarians, for a variety of teaching tools, visit us at
www.randomhouse.com/teachers

Library of Congress Cataloging-in-Publication Data
Friesner, Esther M.
Sphinx's queen / Esther Friesner. — 1st ed.
p. cm. — Sequel to: Sphinx's princess.
Summary: Chased after by the prince and his soldiers for a crime she did not commit, Nefertiti finds temporary refuge in the wild hills along the Nile's west bank before returning to the royal court to plead her case to the Pharaoh.
ISBN 978-0-375-85657-0 (trade) — ISBN 978-0-375-95657-7 (lib. bdg.) —
ISBN 978-0-375-89331-5 (ebook)
1. Nefertiti, Queen of Egypt, 14th cent. B.C.—Juvenile fiction. [1. Nefertiti, Queen of Egypt, 14th cent. B.C.—Fiction. 2. Kings, queens, rulers, etc.—Fiction. 3. Egypt—Civilization—To 332 B.C.—Fiction.] I. Title.
PZ7.F91662Sq 2010
[Fic]—dc22 2010013769

Printed in the United States of America
10 9 8 7 6 5 4 3 2 1
First Edition

For the Trullis,
family and friends

~CONTENTS~

PART III: THEBES

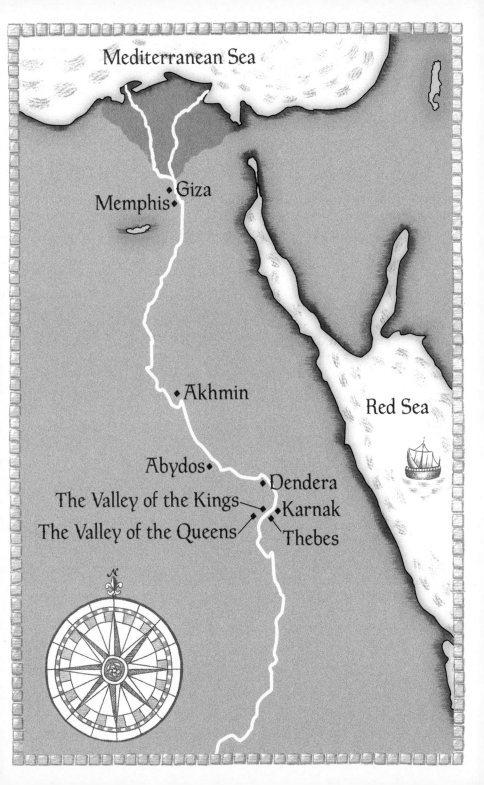

SPHINX'S QUEEN

PROLOGUE

Nefertiti . . . Nefertiti . . .

I walked in moonlight beside the sacred river, the sweet earth of the Black Land beneath my bare feet. It was still warm from the heat of the day, and the full moon lit my path. I turned my head and looked all around, but I couldn't recognize where I was. All I could see was the river to my right and a row of hills in the distance to my left, rising out of the sand. There were no cities, no lone houses, no plowed fields, no beasts or birds or insects, no sign of any life but mine.

Still a voice was there, calling and calling my name. Every syllable echoed in my ears and pulsed through my body: *Nefertiti . . . Nefertiti . . .*

It came from everywhere and nowhere, from the river, from the earth, from the hills that had grown into mountains. It filled the sky and made the moon shiver. It shook my bones.

And yet—how strange!—I was not afraid. I knew that voice. When I looked down at my feet, I saw that the path I was taking was already marked by the prints of a lion's paws. And not just any lion, no! What ordinary lion could leave footprints so big that it took three of my own strides to cross just one of those paw marks in the sand?

Nefertiti . . . Nefertiti . . .

I knew who was calling me, and I broke into a run, eager to overtake him, find him, greet him with a joyful smile.

I don't know how long I ran. There was no way to tell how far I'd gone, no matter how fast my legs pumped and my heart thudded in my chest. Though my feet throbbed and my legs ached, though sweat stung my eyes and I gasped for breath, I might as well have been running in place. The moon and the hills and the river and I were like the work of an artist's hand, carved and colored on a temple wall, forever caught in the net of a single moment. Yet even though running seemed to take me nowhere, I somehow knew that I didn't dare stop.

Faster, Nefertiti! Faster, or you'll be caught again! The voice resounded through the night. *Only I can protect you! Only I can save you! Hurry, I am waiting. I am calling. I am here!*

And just like that, the world around me changed. Suddenly I found myself in the heart of a grove of palm trees, their thick green crowns heavy with ripe red dates. They towered over me, a hot wind rustling through their fronds. My stomach rumbled with hunger for the fruit that hung so far out of my reach, but all I could do was sigh.

Yet when I stretched out my hands in a weak gesture of

longing, they were filled with sweet, sticky dates. So delicious! I savored every mouthful as I walked through the enchanted grove of palms.

The last bite was halfway to my lips when I saw him. He crouched in the shifting moonlit shadows, a mighty lion's body, a noble man's serene and handsome face. The Great Sphinx stared at me with burning golden eyes, and though his lips never moved and his tranquil expression never altered, I heard him speak my name:

Welcome, Nefertiti. Welcome, daughter. Welcome home.

I fell to my knees and stretched out my arms toward him, bowing so low that my forehead touched the earth. When I was very small, my dreams had been haunted by monstrous lions who chased me mercilessly. They always caught me, and in the moment before they devoured me, their faces changed. They became the faces of men, but men whose mouths hid the terrifying fangs of lions.

The nightmares ended when I finally told Father the reason why I always woke up screaming. That was when he told me the story of my birth, so far down the sacred river, so distant from our home in Akhmin. My mother served Queen Tiye, and when the queen traveled north, so did she, even though she was about to have a baby. Queen Tiye—Aunt Tiye, my father's sister—was used to being obeyed.

So I was born where the wondrous pyramid tombs of ancient pharaohs cast their shadows over the land and where the Great Sphinx gazed across the sacred river, his eyes forever watching the horizon for the sun-god Ra's return each dawn. But I met my first dawn in Father's arms as he implored the spirit of the Great Sphinx to be my guardian and my protector, because my mother was gone and because I think Father was afraid that I might follow her into the realm of Osiris, god and king of the dead.

Now I slowly raised my face from the earth and sat back on my heels as I looked at the Great Sphinx. I frowned. Something wasn't right. A small, uneasy feeling nibbled like a mouse in the pit of my stomach. I sat very still, but inside I was shaking. "Here I am," I said softly, trying to keep my voice steady. I wasn't used to being brave. "Why have you summoned me?"

To rescue you, my daughter. The answer rasped through the air between us like the hiss of a cobra's slithering scales. *To protect you from the one who wants to see you dead. Come nearer. See what lies between my paws. It will save you, and then you can go home.*

I peered at the Great Sphinx, but I could see nothing between his mighty forepaws—only shadows and more shadows. I stood up and took a step forward, then another. The small hairs at the back of my neck prickled. I heard a strange humming in my ears, high and thin and frantic, as if some bodiless being was trying to reach me with a warning. My lips were very dry and covered with sand so fine it was dust. The sweet taste of dates had turned sour in my mouth. When I glanced at my hands, I saw that they were stained red.

Why do you hesitate? The Great Sphinx's voice sounded different, weaker. It reminded me of a spoiled child, whining if someone dared to tell him no. *Why won't you do as I say? Why do you disobey me when I am the only hope you have of escape, of life? How can you doubt me? Why don't you trust me with all your heart?*

Why would you ask such questions? I thought, looking up into that hard, carved face more intently. *Why, unless there's something about you that you know I shouldn't trust?*

Nefertiti . . . Nefertiti . . . The Great Sphinx crooned my name in a voice that dripped with false love, thick and too sickeningly sweet to stomach. *If you don't come closer, how will you ever be able to receive the gift I have for you? Draw near and see how good I am to you, beautiful one! Come, my treasure, my prize, come. . . .*

Something stirred between the Great Sphinx's paws. I saw a glint of gold in the darkness, and then a lithe, elegant shape stepped into the light on dainty feet. Tail held high, a glittering collar around her neck, the royal cat called Ta-Miu left a trail of little paw prints like golden flowers in the sand. The star-shaped patch of white fur on her brow shone with mysterious light.

"Ta-Miu, you're alive!" I clapped my hands with joy. "Gracious Isis be thanked."

How dare *you thank Isis?* The Great Sphinx's voice was suddenly strong again, roaring his rage. *Ungrateful girl, you should thank* me! *Me and* only *me!* He scowled, and the sandstorm-pitted surface of his face cracked like a dry streambed, hard flakes scattering everywhere. A second face began to emerge from what was no more than a thin shell of stone. *Your life depends on whether this creature is alive or dead! Have you forgotten that you were the one accused of killing her? That to kill one of the goddess Bast's own children is blasphemy, a crime that carries the supreme penalty? Her blood is the ransom for your own! Thankless, treacherous girl, don't you know that I have the power of life or death over you? Still you repay my gracious kindness to you with a thousand betrayals!*

The flakes of stone were falling faster. I gasped when I saw what lay beneath the Great Sphinx's mask.

"Thutmose . . ." I spoke the name of Pharaoh's heir in a whisper, but a whirlwind whipped through the grove of palm trees, turning my voice into a roar that rivaled the false Great Sphinx's voice. My whisper became a clap of thunder that smashed what was left of Prince Thutmose's disguise and tore away the illusion embracing him. While I watched, he shrank like a green leaf left to bake in the sun. In three heartbeats, he stood before me as a young man hardly older than I. All that was left of the looming presence of the Great Sphinx was the nemes crown he wore, the blue-striped cloth adorned with the protective image of Wadjet, the cobra-goddess.

"*Now* see what you've done to me, Nefertiti!" His handsome face twisted with resentment. He knelt to scoop Ta-Miu into his arms, and his sullen expression softened for a moment when he glanced at the pretty little cat. "If you had been a normal girl, you would have *jumped* at the chance to marry me, not delay and delay and *delay.* You made me wait— *me,* the next pharaoh, the god-on-earth! Father would have named me coruler long ago if you'd married me when you were supposed to instead of wasting time with my brother, that ugly, stammering bundle of sticks and stupidity!"

"Don't speak about Amenophis that way!" I snapped back. "He's your closest kin."

An ugly smile stole over Thutmose's face. "And what is he to *you*?"

I pressed my lips together and gave him a hard look. "He's my friend," I said stiffly.

"Really?" The crown prince's sneer grew more repulsive by the moment. "Nothing more? Nothing . . . closer than that?"

"My *friend,*" I maintained. "Maybe if you'd tried to be my friend—my true friend—no one would have had to force me to marry you."

"Is that it?" Thutmose's mean smile was gone. His face darkened with rage. "Is that your nasty little secret? You want to marry him—*him!* That gawky, ridiculous, worthless—!"

I covered the ground between us in two strides and slapped the words from Thutmose's mouth. Ta-Miu gave a little squeak of surprise and leaped from his arms. "No more!" I shouted in his face. "I won't let you speak like that about Amenophis ever again. You may be stronger and handsomer and your mother's favorite, but his kindness and courage make him worth *ten* of you!"

He grabbed my wrists before the last words left my lips. "What do you know of courage, Nefertiti?" he snarled. "You're only a girl."

"Try me," I shot back, and wrenched myself out of his grasp. My hands were fists. "I'll show you how brave I can be."

He laughed, and it echoed as if we were deep in the heart of a tomb. Something hissed. The cobra atop Thutmose's crown rose and swayed back and forth, no longer a golden image of Wadjet but a living serpent. It spread its hood and gaped at me, its cruelly curved fangs heavy with venom. I gasped and jumped back.

"How brave are you now, Nefertiti?" Thutmose taunted.

My mouth went dry and my heart beat as fast as a quail's whirring wings. The cobra slowly descended from Thutmose's crown to circle his neck and slither down the length of his body. It poured itself across the sand, eyes flickering with unnatural scarlet fire. I backed away and it followed me until I felt something solid at my back. My fingertips brushed the rough shapes of stones. I glanced to either side, glimpsed the wall behind me, and knew I had run out of room for retreat.

"How brave are you now, Nefertiti?" Thutmose's mocking words rang out a second time. "Brave enough to fight? Brave enough to die?" The cobra reared up and grew before my eyes until it was as tall as I. I met its merciless stare and trembled.

And then, in an instant, a small shape appeared on the ground between us. My former slave, Nava the Habiru child, sat hunched over a papyrus scroll, her eyes intent on the strands of words, the complicated symbols of our written tongue. Innocent, vulnerable, she was completely unaware of the deadly serpent towering over her.

Nava was blind to the cobra, but it saw her. It opened its mouth even wider, as if to swallow her whole, and its fangs glistened.

I whirled around and seized a stone from the top of the wall. It was the size of a loaf of bread, but Nava's peril gave me unexpected strength. "Get away from her!" I shouted at the snake just before I flung the rock with all my might. I didn't wait to see if it hit the target; I was too busy grabbing more stones, pelting the cobra, beating it back, away from the child. It gave a halfhearted hiss, then shrank away from me, bowing its head. I could hear Thutmose yowling with frustration, screaming at the snake, ordering it to stand firm, to turn and attack me.

"How brave am I, Thutmose?" I called out in triumph. "You tell me. *You tell me!*"

And I hurled one last stone, which struck the snake right between its eyes. The stone shattered the snake like glass from snout to tail. The glimmering shards vanished before they hit the ground, and Thutmose vanished with them.

"Did you see that, Nava?" I laughed, glorying in my victory. But the laughter died on my lips: Nava was gone. "Nava?" Fresh terror seized me. "Nava, where are you? Nava! *Nava!*"

Darkness fell around me as I cried her name. All that answered me was a voice on the wind that called out again and again: *Nefertiti . . . Nefertiti . . .*

"Nefertiti, wake up! Wake up!" Nava shook my arm with her small, strong hands.

"Oh, Nava! Thank Isis, you're *here!*" The child squawked with surprise when I bolted awake on the ground beside the sacred river and hugged her as if I'd never let her go.

— Part I —
THE VALLEY OF THE KINGS

— 1 —

SUNRISE

Sunlight touched the western shore of the sacred river. I sat hugging Nava as we watched the beautiful return of light to the world. The nightmare that had disturbed my sleep on that first night of our escape from Thebes was gone. In my heart, I praised Ra, who had triumphed once more over the monsters of the underworld to steer his sun-ship safely back across the open sky.

"Are you all right?" Nava asked, gazing at me with a worried look that was much too old for such a little girl. "You were making a lot of noise. You must have had a very scary dream."

"It was scary," I replied, brushing a few stands of hair out of her eyes. "But it wasn't all bad."

"I heard you yell the *evil* prince's name." Nava pursed her lips, her small body radiating anger. She knew what Thutmose had done to me—condemned me for blasphemy, imprisoned me, tried to have me killed—and that he was the reason we'd fled Thebes the night before. "A dream he's in *has* to be all bad!"

"Not if I fought him"—I smiled—"and won."

She tilted her head. "Did you?"

"I certainly did. First he tried to fool me; then he tried to harm me, but I defeated him. And do you know why I could do that?" Nava shook her head. "Because I wasn't just fighting to save myself. You were in my dream as well, Nava, and I fought for you."

"Oh, I know I was there," she said, lifting her chin. "I heard you call my name, too. Did I help you?"

"In a way."

"Hmph. That means I didn't do *anything,* really."

"Maybe next time I'll have a dream where we fight together," I said. "And isn't it better to know that I can depend on your help when I'm *awake*?"

Nava wasn't satisfied. "I want to help you *always.* At least you dreamed that you won. I'm glad. That means we'll be safe, no matter what. Dreams don't lie, not the really important ones."

"So now you're a dream-reader as well as a musician, Nava?" I teased her gently, the way I sometimes teased my little sister, Bit-Bit. How I missed her!

Nava shook her head. "I wish I were. Dream-readers— even those who are slaves—can become very rich and important. Before she died, my mama used to tell us about one of our people, a Habiru slave who was a great dream-reader, long ago. He read Pharaoh's dreams so well that he was given his freedom, and gold, and a big house, and a princess!"

"Those must have been *very* important dreams," I said lightly.

"Oh, they were!" I was treating Nava's tale as no more than a child's fancy, but she was completely sincere. She believed every word she told me. "Mama told us that those dreams saved the Black Land from a famine that lasted *seven* years."

A wistful look came into her eyes. It was the first time I'd heard Nava talk about her mother.

I patted her shoulder. "Your mother knew very good stories, Nava. I hope you'll tell me more of them someday."

"It's *not* a story," she said, giving me a determined look. "It's the *truth*."

"What's the truth?" a sleepy voice called out weakly from the far side of our dead campfire. With groans and moans, Prince Amenophis pushed himself up to sit cross-legged on the harsh ground. "Horus spare me, but my arms and legs feel ready to break before they bend normally again," he muttered. "Ugh, what a night. Amun grant we don't have to spend too many more like it before we reach Dendera."

"How far is it from here?" I asked.

Amenophis shrugged his bony shoulders. "A few days."

"How many?" I pressed. I was concerned, for his sake. After only one night away from the comforts of Thebes, he was starting to look haggard. The fewer days we'd have to travel, the better for him.

It was an innocent question, but it seemed to make Amenophis surprisingly uncomfortable. "I—I'm not sure. I've always been brought there in one of the royal ships. It was very pleasant, sailing down the sacred river, so I never paid much attention to how long the journey took."

"Royal ships with oars and sails," I remarked. "They'd go much faster than our little papyrus boat, but it'll get us there all the same."

"Is Dendera the *only* city we'll pass?" Nava asked.

"Y-yes. I mean, I'm not sure about that, either. The last time I traveled there, I was much younger. Even though I wasn't a child anymore, Mother kept sending me into the cabin for most of the trip. I think she was afraid I'd fall into the river if I wandered around the deck. Thutmose made fun of me, called me a little lotus petal."

"*He's* the lotus petal," Nava decreed. "Not brave like us. He'd never leave the palace to help his friends." She hugged me.

"Maybe not," I said. "But he will leave the palace to come after me. If we don't know how many days' sail we've got ahead of us, we'd better start as soon as possible, to put plenty of distance between us and him."

"Do we have to go right now?" Nava asked plaintively. "I'm hungry."

I tousled her thick hair fondly. "Of course we'll have breakfast first. We'll just have it as quickly as possible." I stood up and shook dust from my dress. The cloth was already much the worse for a night spent sleeping on the ground. I hoped it would hold together until Dendera. Clapping my hands, I turned to Amenophis and said, "Which bag shall I open for us? Where's the bread packed?"

My friend began to chew on his lower lip nervously. His

eyes darted to the bags of provisions he'd carried ashore from the humble boat that had ferried us across the sacred river. I watched his fingers curl and uncurl as he silently tallied the sacks, and I saw worry creep into his eyes. "That . . . that one has bread in it, I think," he said, pointing unsteadily at one of the smaller bags. "Just take two pieces—four if they're small. None for me, please. I'm . . . I'm not hungry."

I opened the bag he indicated and took out two substantial loaves, round and golden brown. They were fresh enough to still be soft, though the rest of the bread we'd brought would soon turn so hard it would need to be soaked in water or beer before we could chew it. I gave one loaf to Nava, who sank her small white teeth into it greedily; then I tore the other loaf in half.

"Hungry or not, you'll share this with me," I said.

"No, really, I don't want it." He turned his face away, but I'd seen the longing in his eyes when he'd looked at the loaf. I could almost hear his stomach rumbling with early-morning hunger. If he wasn't famished, I was a frog.

"Then I don't want it, either."

"But you have to eat! You'll get sick if you don't."

I thrust the bread at him again. "And you won't?" Still he refused to accept it. The two of us stared at one another like a pair of goats head to head in a narrow alley, both too stubborn to budge.

"What's the matter?" Nava had devoured her bread and was now looking at us unhappily, her small fist pressed so tightly to her mouth that I could hardly understand her words. "Why are you fighting?"

"We're *not* fighting." Amenophis and I replied in such perfect unison that the silliness of our situation struck us both at once, and we burst into laughter.

Reluctantly, he stretched out his hand. "I'll eat if you will."

"Me too."

While we had our meager breakfast, I scanned the pile of sacks on shore and grew thoughtful. "Nava, would you like to help us get ready to go?" I asked casually. "You could start loading the boat. We'll help you once we're done eating." Her response was so eager I had to caution her to carry just one bag at a time. While she scrambled back and forth, stowing our provisions, I was able to speak privately with Amenophis.

"I know what's bothering you," I said quietly. "You're afraid we won't have enough food to get us to Dendera."

"Was I that obvious?" he said sadly.

"I saw how you looked at the bags. I could almost read your thoughts, tallying the food against the number of days we've got to travel and dividing everything among the three of us."

He hung his head. "I didn't want you to worry. It wouldn't be so bad if I knew exactly how long we'll have to sail. If you and Nava go hungry, it'll be all my fault."

"If any of us go hungry, it will be our own fault for starving in the middle of a feast," I replied. "Even if Dendera lies a hundred days' sailing from here, we don't need to worry about food or drink. Look there." I gestured at the sacred river. "Not even the gods could drink all of that, and it's full of fish. If the three of us go after them together, we'll have to catch *something*. It might even be fun."

"Yes, that's true." A glimmer of renewed confidence touched his eyes. "I've never fished before, either, though I have gone hunting in the marshes. I have a good eye, a good aim." In an instant, the glimmer faded. "But I'm not half as skilled as Thutmose is with the spear."

"Well, you're going to be better than he is when it comes to fishing!" I decreed.

"Have you ever gone fishing, Nefertiti?" Amenophis asked hopefully.

I had to admit that I'd never tried it. "But I *have* seen how it's done," I told him quickly to keep him in good spirits. "Father and I saw them hard at work almost every day. Some of the men used nets, and some used spears. If we can't find any wood long or straight enough to make our fishing spears, we'll hunt through the reeds until we find some that are stiff enough to hold a sharp point."

"If we do find wood, I could try to make myself a throwing stick, for hunting waterfowl." He sounded as if he were catching my enthusiasm.

"Exactly! And maybe we could also make a bow and arrow for me to use. You know I'm not a bad shot. I'm not sure if I could hit a *moving* target, but if I come across a bird that's polite enough to stand still and wait for my arrow . . ." It did me good to hear him laugh at my little joke. "As for the fish, I'm going to see if I can turn one of our food bags into a net, or a scoop, or—or *something* that'll catch them. If the first thing we try doesn't work, we'll just have to come up with a new idea, and if that fails, we'll think of another. I'm not going to give up, and we're not going to go hungry."

He smiled. "When I listen to you, I can almost believe that we'll arrive at Dendera with a boatload of fish and game."

I wrinkled my nose. "I don't think your mother would like the smell of that." I laughed, expecting him to join in, but this time he kept silent. A shadow had fallen over him again. It pained my heart to see him so downcast. Gently I reached for his hand, but he moved away.

"This is the least of our troubles," he muttered. "Fish or no fish, it doesn't matter. What have I done to you, Nefertiti? What was I thinking when I brought you away from Thebes?" His words sounded hollow and desolate.

"You were saving my life; that's what you were thinking," I replied, speaking softly so that Nava wouldn't overhear. I was becoming more and more concerned about Amenophis. Whatever was preying on his spirit, I had to make him tell me before it gnawed him to pieces inside. "If you hadn't carried me across the river, out of your brother's power, I'd be dead by the time your parents returned."

"Don't say such things." He shook his head violently. "I can't stand the thought of anything happening to you, my— my friend, my dear friend. O gods, help me!" He groaned. "Why wasn't I born like Thutmose, strong and sure of myself? It's one thing to get that little boat across the sacred river, but to steer it for *days*? I don't know if I can do it, and now I *must*."

He grabbed my hands, clasping them fiercely between his own. "What good was it to break you out of your prison if Thutmose recaptures you because I wasn't smart or strong enough to *keep* you out of his hands? I should have paid one of the palace guards to take you far away from here, far from Thebes, even far beyond the borders of the Black Land itself." He bowed his head. "But I was selfish. I wanted to be the one to save you, not some paid servant. And I dreaded the thought of never seeing you again. It's my self-ishness that's put your life at risk—and not just yours!" He cast worried eyes to where Nava was still happily distracted with loading our boat of bundled reeds.

I squeezed Amenophis's thin hands as hard as I could, so hard that I felt the bones move against each other. He gasped, shocked by the unexpected pain. "*Stop* it," I said firmly, scowling at him as hard as I could. "Stop filling your mind with these thoughts. They'll drag all three of us to the river bottom. Amenophis, look there, look at the sun, how beautiful it is, how the Aten-disk shines, chasing away the shadows and bad dreams and dangers of the night! If not for you and Nava and Sitamun, I might not be here today, welcoming the Aten's light. How can you say you were self-ish, after all you've done to help me? My friend, you're risk-ing much more than I am."

"Impossible," he replied, bewildered. "Your life's in danger—"

"And yours," I cut in. "Maybe more than mine."

He shook his head again. "No matter how much Thut-mose hates me for thwarting his plans, there's a limit to how much he can punish me. I'm his brother."

"Set was Osiris's brother," I murmured.

We both knew the story of how the evil god of the

wastelands grew envious of his brother Osiris, the beloved husband of Isis. Set killed Osiris, and in his murderous rage, he tore his brother's body to pieces and scattered them throughout the Black Land. Sweet Isis had to seek the pieces everywhere until she had them all. With her own hands, she put them back together, wrapping them into place with strips of linen, then used her magic to revive him. So Isis taught mortals the way for preserving and preparing the dead for eternity. Osiris returned to life, to reign as lord of the underworld, in spite of his brother's evil.

Osiris was a god. Amenophis was not. He wouldn't even be the god-on-earth that Thutmose would become when he inherited his father's crown. If his brother destroyed him, it would be forever.

"Thutmose can't hurt me the way he can hurt you or Nava," Amenophis maintained. "You two are at much more risk than I am, out here with only—only me to protect you. I should have let someone stronger take care of you."

I squeezed his hand again. "Does that feel weak?" I demanded. "I may like to spend my time with Henenu, learning the scribe's art, but that's not all I can do. And Nava isn't some sheltered, pampered infant. She was born a slave, and she's lived a slave's hard life. Her sister . . ." I felt a pang, remembering how Nava's sister Mahala had saved my life, and the horror that struck my heart when I heard she'd been killed for that. "Her sister's death shattered her, stole her voice, but she found the strength to come back from that ordeal. None of us are weaklings, Amenophis, least of all you! We'll protect each other."

This time my friend's smile was more certain. "I think that you'll be the one protecting us all, Nefertiti."

That made me laugh. "You expect too much from me, but thank you. Now, let's help Nava load the boat or she'll be mad at us for making her do all the work."

"Oh, I wouldn't want to feel *her* wrath," Amenophis joked.

Together we got busy carrying the last few bags to the reed boat, then set Nava in the prow and launched our vessel back onto the sacred river.

How fortunate we were to be sailing downstream! We didn't have to fight the current—no easy task without a sail to steal the wind. All we had to do was steer. Nava kept her seat in the prow of the boat, Amenophis guided us from the stern, and I sat midway between the two of them, enthroned in a nest of provision bags. How very different from the way I'd come to Thebes, riding with my family amid the luxuries of my aunt Tiye's regal ship. But except for wishing that Father and my second mother, Mery, and my sister, Bit-Bit, were still here with me, I wouldn't have traded places with my then-self for a double handful of gold. *Then* I'd been as much of a captive as Nava, being dragged to a marriage I didn't want to a boy I'd learned I could never love. *Now* I was free.

As the sun rose higher, the river came to life. Flights of egrets rose out of the reeds when our little boat came too close for their liking. Their plumage made white streaks across the bright blue sky. Little green herons peered at us curiously for a moment from the shallows and then went back to feeding. Sometimes I thought I saw the darting brilliance of a kingfisher's wings, and once, Nava came scrambling over the food sacks to tug my hand and point eagerly at the magnificent sight of a falcon with outstretched wings. He rode the heavens with kingly calm, without the frantic wing-beating of lesser birds, as if the sky itself balanced on the tips of his golden-brown feathers. Without warning, he folded his wings and plunged to snatch a fish from the river. The ripples of his strike lapped against our boat as he flew away to enjoy his silvery, squirming feast.

We weren't the only ones sailing on the sacred river— how could we be? This was the heart and spirit of the Black Land, the realm of the god Hapy, whose timely floods renewed the fields and fed us. Our small boat was one of countless others, watercraft of all sizes, some under sail, some driven by oars, some carried along by both. Upstream and downstream, the peacefully flowing water was a wonderful confusion of people, ships, livestock, the sweet scent of spices or incense wafting from a merchant's vessel, the lively music of the boatmen's work songs, the cry of a baby, the laughter of a child.

I marveled at the spectacle and power of the sacred river. Not so long ago, I'd stood helpless in the house of Isis, back in Akhmin, while the goddess's chief priest took cruel joy in telling me that Mahala was dead. The slave girl had saved me from drowning, but for his own malicious reasons, the priest declared that she'd cheated Hapy of his chosen sacrifice. No doubt he'd seen to it that she was given to the river-god in my place.

And yet here was Nava, sailing happily, fearlessly, along

the same waters that had claimed her beloved sister. I quietly gave thanks to Isis for having healed the little girl's heart. Nava was so at ease on our boat, as though she'd been born to the life of the river. She was captivated by everything she saw. She even pointed out a bank where a raft of crocodiles lay dozing, baking their scaly backs in the sun. One of the biggest of them sprawled lazily, his deadly jaws gaping wide while a tiny brown bird hopped here and there, picking bits of food out of the monster's teeth.

"What a brave little thing," I said, putting one arm around Nava's shoulders. "Just like you."

"He's not brave," she told me. "He's smart. He knows the crocodile won't snap him up. Then who'd clean the monster's teeth? Look at him! He's safe and he knows it."

That was true. I saw how the speck of a bird went on with his business, helping himself to the leftover scraps of less-lucky creatures. There was a bold quality to his hops and flutters that made it seem as if he were swaggering, telling the whole world, "Oh, yes, this is a fine crocodile, isn't it? One of the biggest, the strongest, the best hunters. And he works for me."

I don't know how far we'd traveled when I asked Amenophis to steer our boat back to shore along the western bank.

"Why?"

"You've been at the oar for a long time, that's why," I replied. "Just look at how high Ra's boat has risen! You must be tired."

"I'm fine," he countered, but his appearance told a different story. I saw a slight trembling in his legs, and his grip on the oar wasn't just tight but desperate, as if it was holding him upright more than he was holding it. "We have to go farther. If not, my brother will—"

"We'll go farther, but not if we don't take the time to rest a bit along the way," I said calmly. "You have to remember that if—*when*—your brother comes after us, he's only a man, not a hunting hound. He can't track us by scent or sight—not now. I can't see the towers of Thebes from this far down the river. Can you? And just look at how busy the river is! We're one small boat among many, small enough to hide in the reeds if he does come sailing up to us."

"I—I guess you're right," Amenophis admitted. "And if we go ashore now, maybe we can find a village, get a few more loaves of bread, a real fishing spear—"

"As long as we're careful about how we bargain for them," I told him. "You'll have to act like an ordinary person. If not, they'll remember you, and if Thutmose sends messengers up and down the river, asking people if they've seen a regal-looking young man—"

"Oh, I don't think my brother would describe me as regal-looking," Amenophis said, rubbing the back of his shaved head sheepishly. "He'd just tell his messengers to ask folks if they'd seen a scrawny boy, a little girl, and a beautiful—"

"Are you going to land this boat or not?" I said quickly. "My legs hurt from being folded under me for so long. If I don't stand up and use them, they'll probably fall off when we *do* come ashore."

"I'm sorry, I'm sorry." Amenophis babbled more apologies as he turned the reed boat's prow toward the western riverbank. We were fortunate to find a stretch of shore where the reeds didn't grow too thickly and where landing wasn't difficult. A few date palms clustered together a short distance inland. They were small and had sickly-looking trunks—nothing like the magnificent trees of my dream—but there were a few fistfuls of fruit hanging below their green crowns. Nava exclaimed in delight when she saw the fruit. As nimble as a little monkey, she scrambled up one tree after another to pluck their sweet harvest and bring it down to share with Amenophis and me.

We ate the dates and enjoyed the shade of the trees. "We should stay here a while longer," I said. "The sun's at the top of the sky, and we haven't got a drop of oil to protect our skin. If we're not careful, we'll burn or, even worse, be heat-struck."

Amenophis began to argue with me, urging a quick departure, but I stood my ground. "For all you know, your sister Sitamun has covered our tracks for us. She's a very smart woman. Think about it: Thutmose discovers that we're gone and starts raging through the palace, demanding to know who's responsible for our escape. I wouldn't put it past Sitamun to act guilty on purpose, just so he'd turn on her and demand a confession. Oh, she would pretend to know nothing about it, but she'd pretend badly, until finally she'd make a great show of breaking down and telling him that we ran away *up* the river or that we didn't even sail away at all, but took a chariot and—"

Amenophis chuckled. "Thank the gods that Henenu taught you how to write. You were born to weave stories the way other girls are born to weave linen. But you have to watch out for the loose threads, my friend. If there's no chariot or horses missing from the stables, that puts an end to *that* tale."

"Hmph." I'd gotten caught up in my own story about Sitamun's cleverness, and I didn't like having it picked to pieces. "Well, then, do you want to find fault with the part about her telling Thutmose we've gone *up*river?"

"Why would we want to sail in that direction? Everything important to our safety lies *down*river from Thebes: my parents in Dendera, yours in Akhmin, Lord Osiris's most sacred city, the refuge of Abydos—"

I threw my date pits at him and turned my back. "You know everything, don't you? But you don't know enough to get out of the midday sun."

I was in a foul temper. The time we'd spent on the river had cramped my legs badly, just as I'd suspected. I hated sitting there while Amenophis did all the work. I didn't want him to overburden himself, but even more, I didn't want to be just another piece of baggage, hardly more than the sacks holding our supplies. Why couldn't I put my hands on the oar, do my share, use my own strength to save myself and my friends? It wasn't fair.

As I sat there, hunched over like an old woman in the marketplace, Nava crept around to peer up into my face. "Don't be mad at Amenophis, Nefertiti," she said. "It's still a good story, even if he's right about the parts where you made mistakes."

Nava had the gift for coaxing smiles out of stones. "Is this how it's going to be? You and him against me?"

"Well, it *is* his boat," Nava said quite seriously. "I like sailing in it. I don't want to walk all the way to Dendera."

"Good point," I said, grinning. "Neither do I." I looked back at Amenophis, who was trying not to laugh out loud at Nava's reasoning. "What about it, my friend?" I said. "May we still share your royal watercraft?"

Amenophis stroked his chin as if considering grave matters that might affect half his father's kingdom. "Hmm, I don't know. You *did* throw date pits at me. But you also amused me with your story. All right, you can get back in the boat."

"No, no," I said, hanging my head dramatically. "I don't deserve it. I've insulted you; I must be punished. Let me take the oar and steer the boat between here and our next resting place, and let me continue to trade places with you—steersman and passenger—all the way to Dendera. It's the least I can do to make up for such a terrible offense."

My friend snorted and smothered his laughter with a bony fist. "Do you know how to manage a boat?"

"Did *you,* before last night?" I countered.

"When we went duck hunting in the marshes, I paid attention to how our servants mastered the boats."

"And I've been paying attention to how you've been doing it. So unless you think I'm dull-witted or a bad student—"

"She's *not,*" Nava spoke up, giving Amenophis a fierce glare that dared him to say otherwise. "You *know* she's not!"

Amenophis raised both hands in surrender. "If I say yes, it will be a sin that will weigh down my heart when I stand before Lord Osiris's judgment in the afterlife. Ammut the

Devourer of Hearts will have me for sure! You can take the oar, Nefertiti, except . . ."

"What?"

"You need to do something about that." He gestured at my dress. "It's too long. You could trip while steering the boat and fall in the river. The gods forbid it, but—but it *would* tangle your legs and drag you down."

His words called up awful memories. I suppressed a shudder as I stood up and stuck out my hand. "That's easily fixed. Give me your knife, Amenophis. Please."

He watched in fascination as I began slicing my dress off at the knees. Nava wanted to help, but Amenophis's knife was large and keen-edged; I felt it wouldn't be wise to let the child use it. Still she persisted. I was so distracted, constantly trying to make sure she wasn't getting too close to the blade, that I made a very awkward, uneven job of shortening my dress. When I was done, I blew out a great breath of relief and tied the cutaway material around my waist. It might come in handy.

"Thank you." I gave the knife back to Amenophis and swung my legs experimentally. "Do you think I made it short enough?"

"I guess so." Amenophis sounded uncertain, and he was staring at me in the strangest way. "It's—it's really a shame that you had to ruin your dress. You don't *have* to help at the oar."

"I'll have other dresses," I told him. "But how many chances will I have to master a boat on the sacred river? Besides, did you even *look* at my dress until now? It was already tattered along the hem, halfway to rags."

"I thought it was beauti—nice," he said so softly that at first I wasn't sure if he'd said anything at all.

Nava and I stepped back into the boat, and Amenophis pushed away from the bank. He'd agreed to let me guide our vessel, but he insisted that he be the one to get it out onto the water and bring it ashore. I didn't argue about it, but I did make a silent vow to observe exactly how he launched and landed the craft so that I could do it myself another day. As much as I wished he'd trust me to do more, I felt it wasn't worth any further objection. It was more important that we reach Dendera quickly than that I win an argument.

As soon as we were well away from the shore, Amenophis and I traded places, edging past one another carefully. We had to hold on to each other as he moved toward the middle of the boat and I headed for the stern. How strange it was—his hands were so cold when they clasped my shoulders that I could feel the chill even through what was left of my dress.

"Are you all right?" I asked.

"Fine." He wouldn't look at me. "I'm—I'm only trying to keep my balance."

"Me too," I said, reaching the stern and picking up the oar. Lowering my voice so that Nava wouldn't hear me, I added, "I've fallen into the river once in my life. That was enough."

Now he *did* look at me, his face sharp with worry. "Can't you swi—?"

"Shhh!" I nodded toward the prow, where Nava was sitting, and gestured for him to speak as quietly as he could.

Neither one of us wanted the child to overhear a conversation that might conjure up tragic memories.

"Can't you swim?" he repeated in a whisper.

"I can stay afloat." *When I'm not weighed down by heavy jewels and a long dress,* I thought. "And you?"

"Father's best huntsman insisted on teaching Thutmose and me how to swim before he took us on our first waterfowling trip. I should teach you and Nava."

"I'd like that. You'd be a good teacher." My words made him beam with pleasure.

My first turn managing our boat went well. I made only a few small mistakes—coming too close to one of the larger ships on the river, scraping the bottom of our vessel when I accidentally veered us into a stretch of shallows—but they were soon corrected, with no harm done. By the time we made camp for the night, I'd had two more chances to show my skill with the oar, and I was sure I was getting better at it.

"A good day's work!" I said as we shared our dinner.

That night, I slept without dreams, good or bad. I awoke refreshed, even though it was so early that Ra's brightly shining boat still hid its golden prow below the horizon. There was a light mist on the river, soon banished when the eastern sky began to kindle, then to glow. I walked down to the river's edge, drawn by the light. A lone blue lotus floated on the ripples that lapped against the shore, and I knelt to touch its delicate petals with my fingertips.

"How wonderful," I whispered, and I thanked the gods for giving us a new day.

I was seated in the middle of the boat as we began that

day's voyage. It was still very early, and there weren't many other boats on the water. Nava began to sing a merry tune, clapping her hands to keep the beat. It was a work song, something I'd heard slaves sing when they had a long, tedious job to do. The words were simple and repetitive, the melody brisk and lively. I had no trouble joining in. Even Amenophis raised his voice in song. How lighthearted we felt, how free!

"Look there, Nefertiti!" The happy song had vanished from Nava's lips. She sounded afraid, far more afraid than when she'd seen the crocodiles. Her small hand shook as she pointed to the eastern shore of the sacred river. A herd of hippos lolled in the water, their huge heads turning lazily to watch us as we floated by.

I crept forward slowly until I was close enough to lay a comforting hand on her shoulder. "I see them, Nava," I said softly. I tried, but I couldn't stop my voice from quavering. Who wouldn't be afraid of those massive beasts? Only a fool or a foreigner who had no idea of how dangerous a hippopotamus could be. Their enormous bodies looked too bulky to move easily, but that was an illusion. "Shhh, it's all right; we'll be past them soon."

"Yes, don't worry," Amenophis chimed in. "See, they're all the way across the river. They're feeding. There's no need to be—"

The water to the left of the prow erupted with a roar that drowned our screams, and our boat of bundled reeds flew wildly as the lone hippo rose from the depths to destroy us.

— 2 —

THE LAND OF THE DEAD

The hippo's square jaws gaped, his terrifying tusks dripping with water and foam. His breath enveloped us in a wave of heat and the smell of rotting greens as his bellow of blind rage dinned in our ears. Nava shrieked and dug her fingers deep into my skin. While Amenophis and I had been whispering shaky reassurances to the little girl, we'd kept our gazes on the herd of hippopotamuses lolling on the eastern bank. We'd neglected to turn our eyes west, even for a glance. If we'd done that, perhaps we might have spied two wickedly flicking ears just above the waterline, a pair of tiny, spiteful eyes watching us, even a telltale trail of bubbles on the river's surface.

We hadn't, and now it was too late. The solitary beast attacked.

I grabbed Nava even tighter than she'd seized me and scrambled backward in the boat, dragging her as far from the raging creature as possible. The boat pitched and tossed crazily under my feet. I heard Amenophis calling my name. From the corner of my eye, I caught sight of him raising the big steering oar and swinging it at the hippo. The wooden blade bounced off the monster's shoulder as if it were a fly. I watched, my blood as cold as the deepest night, as the hippo turned and snapped his jaws shut on the oar so forcefully that he nearly yanked Amenophis into the river before he crushed the wood to splinters.

Then, as suddenly as he'd attacked us, the hippo sank back beneath the river. I dropped to my knees, hugging Nava, looking up into Amenophis's ashen face. My heart was thumping so loudly I thought that it would overwhelm my labored, panting breath.

Just as I drew a long breath of fresh air into my lungs, the beast burst from the water a second time, only a hand's breadth from the stern, and plowed headfirst into the side of our boat. Our vessel heeled steeply as we all struggled to keep from sliding overboard. Panic began to choke me as I clawed for something, anything, to save me from the water. Slivers of reed slid under my fingernails as I fought to hang on to the boat with one hand and to Nava with the other. Sky and water teetered before my eyes for one heart-stopping instant, and then—

Then a fresh bellow from the beast, a second blow to the boat, and our watercraft turned over, spilling us into the river along with everything aboard. As the water closed over my head, Nava's small hand slipped from my fingers. I kicked my feet frantically and broke the surface, hair plastered across my eyes. My ears were filled with the sound of brutal crunching as the hippo demolished our capsized boat. He tore the bundled reeds into flying, floating debris mouthful by mouthful in a mad, mindless riot of destruction.

"Nava! Nava, Amenophis, where are you?" I called, desperately scanning the water. The river's current was carrying me along, away from the rampaging animal. I used my hands the way I'd used the oar, steering myself toward the shore. My head throbbed with prayers: *O great Hapy, lord of the sacred river, save them! Lady Isis, loving and gentle, powerful and wise, bring them safely out of the monster's jaws!*

My legs began to ache and tire. I thought that I was near the bank, but no matter how energetically I kicked and paddled with my hands, the land didn't seem to get any closer. My neck grew stiff from the effort of keeping my head above the surface, and I choked when a wavelet slapped me across the face, filling my nose and mouth with water.

Blinking my eyes rapidly to clear them, I cast heartsick looks everywhere, seeking one glimpse of Nava, of Amenophis, of any sign that the sacred river had spared them. All I saw were three great boats with sails set to catch the wind that would carry them upstream. Some nobleman was traveling south to Thebes or beyond with his family or followers. Laughter and loud music drifted to my ears from the brightly painted ships. I shouted for help, but no one aboard those magnificent vessels heard my voice over the beat of the drums and the jangling of the sistrums. If my cries reached them at all, they must have sounded as faint as birdcalls on the wind.

Every kick I made to stay afloat became more and more difficult. Weariness was a rope lashed around my ankles, relentlessly dragging me down, and despair at seeing no sign of Nava or Amenophis turned my heart heavy as a stone. Something bumped into my shoulder. I turned my head and saw a big bundle of reeds, part of the wreckage of our boat. I threw my arms over it and let it carry me along, but I was too numb with gloom to rejoice over this unexpected, life-saving gift of the river.

Hugging the reed bundle, I was able to rest until my legs recovered enough for me to resume kicking. Every hope I'd clung to since the hippo's attack was gone, swallowed up by the river, whose banks and surface showed no sign that Nava and Amenophis were still in the land of the living. My face was wet with river water, wetter with tears, but sheer stubbornness made me go on, fighting to guide my tiny float to shore.

At last I felt the blessed sensation of muddy ground underfoot. I staggered out of the river, through shallow places where papyrus plants towered over my head. Water-fowl heard me coming and took flight, squawking angrily. I let the bundle of reeds bob away back into the current, and I sprawled on the bank, my cheek pressed to the warm, wel-coming earth. I took one deep breath before my chest tore open with loud, inconsolable sobs for everything that had been wrenched away from me.

"Nava, little Nava . . . Amenophis, my friend, my dear, brave . . . Oh, gods, why?" I howled, and beat my hands against the ground. "Why, why, *why*?"

I don't know how long I lay there, crying out my sor-row. In the end, grief stole the last scrap of my strength and I fell into a deep sleep. There were no dreams. When I awoke, Ra's great sun-ship was well on its way to entering the gates of the underworld, past the western horizon. Beyond that gate lay darkness and the giant serpent, Apep, whose one purpose was to devour Ra and his ship, leaving us to perish in an endless night. It was no wonder that so many of Pharaoh's royal ancestors had ordered their tombs carved into the rocks of the sacred river's western shore. This was the land of the dead.

I pushed myself up and sat back on my knees, gazing at the sun. My throat felt raw, and my palms were red, badly scraped and stinging. I tucked them under my arms and hugged myself, taking deep, steadying breaths.

Dendera . . . The name slipped into my mind unbidden. *I can't stay here. If I don't move, I'll die. If hunger and thirst don't kill me, I'll shrivel to dust in the sun or be found by some hungry beast that prowls the night. I must get up. I must go on. I have to reach Dendera.*

"Dendera," I whispered. "Yes. Nava and Amenophis risked—lost—their lives to save me from Thutmose's plotting." Fresh tears trickled from my eyes. I wiped them away and stood up. I knew with all my soul that if I didn't go on, stand before Pharaoh, let him know the injustice that his crown prince had committed in his name, there would be more than my life at stake. Could someone like Thutmose be trusted to rule if he worshipped his own desires and scorned the goddess Ma'at's holy truth? The gods would avenge it; all of the Black Land would suffer.

Pharaoh Amenhotep has many sons. A wicked, insinuating doubt disturbed my thoughts. *Many, but only two are Tiye's children. He adored her enough to raise her to the position of Great*

Royal Wife, even though she wasn't nobly born. She still holds power over him. How will he react when he hears one of his favorite sons has been accused of so much wrongdoing and learns that the other died trying the save the accuser? More important than that, how will she *react? Who will suffer then?*

I clenched my hands, even though it made the pain worse. *"No!"* I shouted, stamping my foot. Wings whirred up out of the papyrus thicket, but I didn't see the birds I'd startled with my outburst. "No, no, no!" I shook my head violently, my eyes squeezed shut, as if that would banish the evil whisper that I knew came from my own weakness. "I won't turn back. I won't run away."

Why not? it came again, cajoling. *Pharaoh has many sons, but you have only one life. Why gamble it when you could live it? You have a scribe's skills, and cleverness, and you can dance as well as many of the girls who earn their bread by entertaining at banquets. Forget Dendera. Seek your fortune somewhere else, far from Dendera, from Thebes, from the royal court, from—*

"Not from the gods," I said quietly. "Not from Father, Mother, Bit-Bit, all that I love. Even if I'm punished for Amenophis's death, I'll see them again. No matter how enraged and vengeful Aunt Tiye will be, even she's not cruel enough to deny me that." I opened my eyes. "And even if she is so pitiless, I'm still going to Dendera." I knew that I was alone on the riverbank, talking to the air, but it gave me courage.

The sacred river showed itself in lingering flashes of brilliance through the green thickets of fringe-topped papyrus plants. There were more boats sailing along its deep blue surface now, though none of them steered a course close to my side of the wide water. Would one of them come to help me if I could hail them loudly enough, or would they just sail on, indifferent?

Even if a boat answered my call, could I blindly trust my fate to whomever took me aboard? If all men's hearts were good, upright, and honest, Lord Osiris wouldn't need to keep ever-hungry Ammut at his side when he judged the dead. *Better to walk than take that chance,* I decided, and took the first steps of my renewed journey.

I headed inland first, seeking a clearer way, one where I wouldn't have to push aside the plants that grew so thickly at the water's edge. I was overjoyed when I happened upon an irrigation canal. Its banks would be well maintained, providing me with an easier path. It might also lead me to the farmers who used it to raise their crops. In any case, I'd never go thirsty as long as I could dip my hands into its sweet water.

Water alone wouldn't sustain me. The western bank of the sacred river was where the sun sank into the dark land of many dangers. It was the place where generations of our pharaohs, their families, their highest-ranking and most honored nobles were entombed, an empire of the dead. The living dwelled here, too, but this side of the river wasn't as thickly settled as the other. How far along the canal would I have to travel before I met another human being? If I was going to reach Dendera on my own, I had to find other people or I'd starve.

And what will you do once you find them? Oh, that horrible voice of doubt, haunting me! *How will you persuade them* to give you anything to eat? You're no one to them, a stranger, a grubby beggar from who knows where!

Mery—my second mother—always gave bread to any beggar at our door, I thought, fighting back against my own misgivings.

She could afford to be charitable! She wasn't a farmer's wife with a brood of children to feed. It's easy to give away a loaf of bread when you've got five on the table, ten more coming out of the oven, and thirty jars of grain in the storeroom!

I shook my head again, as if that would force out my troubling thoughts, and walked faster, following the line of the canal. As I strode along, I muttered prayers: "O Isis, have mercy. Let me meet another human being soon. I don't dare stray too far from the river. If I lose my way and there's no one to help me find it again . . . Goddess, please, don't let that happen. Guide me. Help me. Hear me!"

But if the goddess heard my words, she gave no sign. Daylight was fading, and the track of the canal wasn't bringing me any closer to finding a peasant's home or even a boy sent out to herd goats for his family. Hunger dug deep into my belly. How grateful I would have been for a mouthful of bread, even if it was as hard as baked clay! I paused, torn between following the canal a little longer or giving up on my search. The land was silent except for the chirr of insects and the distant cries of birds. *Not even a dog's bark,* I thought. I took a deep breath through my nostrils. *Not even the smell of a cookfire.* That decided me. Reluctant but resigned, I turned my back on Ra's sinking sun-ship and headed toward the river.

I don't know if I walked faster because of the coming night or if I'd simply taken a shorter route than following the irrigation ditch, but it felt as if I'd taken less time to return to the sacred river than to leave it. As I neared the water's edge, I heard the sound of raised voices. Moving cautiously, I crept closer until I saw two men loudly arguing as they waded through the shallows, hauling a boat between them. It was a larger version of the one the rogue hippo had destroyed, except this one was laden with baskets brimming with the feathered bodies of dead ducks and other game birds. One of the men looked much older than the other, perhaps his father. I hoped he wasn't. No son should fling so many curses and complaints at his father's head.

"Why I have to listen to you, you worthless frog skin! It's more my hard work than yours that's filled this boat! Stupid old bag of bones, you're already blind in one eye and the other's halfway gone. I'm the one who killed all these birds, and you think you can claim *half*?"

"You couldn't kill 'em if you couldn't find 'em," the older man replied just as hotly. "You're a poor excuse for a hunter. You'd waste your days sticking this boat into every patch of reeds on the river and praying to Lady Neith for luck. And that's the only way you *would* find your quarry. The gods might've stolen the light from my left eye, but my right's still sharp enough to read the game signs and know where the birds are."

"Pfff! Sharp as *mud,* you mean. You nearly steered us onto a bank full of crocodiles!"

"No such thing! Tell a few more whoppers like that, boy, and you won't have to worry about Ammut gobbling up your heart. Your mother'll do the job first. Trust me, I know my sister's temper when it comes to liars."

"Ah, Ma's not that bad," the younger man replied with a snort.

"Oh, no? How d'you think I *really* lost sight in this eye?"

The two of them laughed over that and the harsh mood was broken.

I watched them secure their boat and build a small fire using whatever they could scrounge that would burn. I stayed where I was, hidden in a stand of dead reeds. Hapy had withdrawn his waters from them and left me thankful for a hiding place where I could wait out the night. I was close enough to the hunters' fire to discourage any wild beasts from bothering me. As for encountering any crawling things—insects, lizards, or serpents—I'd have to pray to Isis for protection and take my chances. I was too afraid to risk letting them see me, though when they began to eat their modest evening meal of bread and cheese, my empty stomach complained stridently that some risks were worth taking. I fought back the aching emptiness, folded my arms around me, and squatted down in my nest of reeds.

I didn't think I'd fall asleep where I sat. I honestly expected that my fears and sorrows wouldn't let me nod off, especially after that who-knows-how-long slumber I'd had earlier that day after crying myself into collapse. But in spite of all that, fatigue stole over me, body and mind, and sleep followed.

I awoke to the sound of a loud crash and found myself flat on my back in the dead reeds, staring up at the moon and stars. When I'd fallen asleep, I'd *really* fallen, toppling backward, rattling and crushing the plants around me. Before I could take a breath, I heard the old man shout out, "What's that? Who's there?" and saw shadowy hands shove aside the few reeds left standing.

"Well, look at this, Uncle!" The young man's expression was hard to read in the dark, but it seemed he could see me well enough. His hands shot out and grabbed my wrists, yanking me to my feet and hauling me out of the reeds to the side of the fading fire. "You might know where the ducks nest, but I've caught something better." He laughed. I hoped it was a friendly laugh; it *had* to be!

"Who is that?" The older man squinted at me. Even in such faint light, I could see the thick white film covering his left eye, though the other one looked as keen as he'd claimed. "Who are you, girl? What's happened to you? You look as if you've been fighting jackals bare-handed!"

I glanced down at my ragged dress, my scraped and filthy arms and legs. I could only imagine what my face and hair must look like after all that had happened to me that day. "I—I—" I bit my lip. "I was on the river and a hippo destroyed my boat." It wasn't exactly a lie; it was only part of the truth. *May Ma'at forgive me.*

"You look it," the older man said, clicking his tongue in sympathy. "When did it happen?"

"This morning. I've been walking ever since. I'm trying to get to Dendera." I clasped my hands, hoping fiercely that the next words out of the older man's mouth would be an offer to take me there.

Instead, I heard "Pretty little thing, aren't you?" from

the nephew. He chucked me under the chin with his roughly callused hand and grinned before he kissed me so hard that our teeth clacked together.

I didn't think about what I did next; I just did it. I made a fist and punched him so hard in the center of his chest that his head made a loud *thunk!* when it hit the ground. When I heard that, I spun on my heel and dashed away.

I didn't get far. The older man's right eye *was* clear and good: He caught me before I'd gone ten strides. He might have been wrinkled, with gray stubble covering his cheeks, but he had a lifetime of hard work behind him, and it had left him strong. He ignored my kicking feet and flailing fists, seized me around the waist, toted me back to the fireside over one brawny, scarred shoulder, and dumped me between a covered basket and a sagging waterskin.

"Are you looking for that hippo to finish the job of killing you?" he said, one corner of his mouth quirking up in amusement as he stared down at me. "Or would you rather step on a cobra in the dark and do it that way? Now listen, girl, you're safe with me. Safe with *us,* or I'll know the reason why." He gave his nephew a short, sharp glare. The younger man was sitting up, rubbing the back of his head and looking sheepish. "You'll forgive the lad: He can't help it; he's a jackass. Me, I *break* jackasses. Understand?"

I nodded slowly. "Thank you, sir."

" 'Sir'?" His laugh was as loud as that cursed hippo's bellow. "Who *are* you, with such fine manners?" He dropped to one knee and grabbed my hands, studying the palms. "Hmm. Soft enough, under all these hurts. Funny *here,* though." He ran one fingertip over the toughened spots on my right hand. They'd come from long practice with reed pens and brushes as I worked to master the scribe's art. "Whatever work you do to earn your bread, it's nothing *too* hard. Care to tell me?"

He sounded kind, but I was afraid to say more in case I said too much. "My name is Nefertiti" was all I answered. And then, because the pain in my stomach forced the plaintive words from my lips, I added, "I'm so hungry!"

"Well, of course you are, girl! Here, get something in your belly." He stuck his hand into one of the baskets and put a small, round loaf of bread in my hands. I gobbled it as if I were a starving dog, nearly choking on the crumbs.

"Easy! Take it easy, girl! You could use a drink with that." He fetched the big waterskin and helped me hold it while I drank. It didn't taste like pure water, and I said so when I thanked him for it.

He chuckled and turned to the younger man. "How about that, Idu? She's a clever one—no fooling her." He winked at me. "There's some beer in that. A man likes his beer, but it's too thick to carry in this"—he slapped the waterskin—"unless you skim it carefully first and water it down. My wife used to be skilled at doing that, but she's gone now, gone for years. I've had to fend for myself for too long." He hung his head, looking miserable.

I patted his hand. "I'm sorry."

"Thank you, girl; you've got a good heart." He put one arm around me and squeezed my shoulders. It was a little too tight for a simple, friendly gesture. I felt uneasy, but before I could say anything or shrug free, he let me go. "All right, you've eaten my bread, and Idu here will tell you that I never give something for nothing."

"*That's* true," the younger man grumbled. "Half the ducks that my throwing stick brought down—"

"Hush, boy. The girl knows a joke when she hears one; don't spoil it with your sour-faced muttering." He turned from his nephew to me. "How about *now* you tell us who you are? We'll call it fair exchange for that bread you devoured."

"My name . . . my name is Nefertiti," I said. I prayed that I wouldn't have to tell him too much more than that. *This man might believe in my innocence, take pity on me, and help me reach Dendera, or he could drag me to Thebes, imagining the reward Thutmose and the Amun priests would give to get me back. May Ma'at shield and forgive me, I won't lie, but I can't tell him the whole truth.*

"A good name—it suits you. But I find it hard to believe that such a lovely girl with such a pretty name would be sailing the river on her own. You haven't got the hands for it." He focused his good eye closely on me. "*Were* you traveling alone?"

I burst into tears. I couldn't help it. The older man's question was a magician's spell that called up the ghosts of Amenophis and Nava. Their beloved faces smiled wistfully at me from the starry arch of the night sky. The bread I'd just eaten became a burning stone in my belly as I sobbed and sobbed. "My friends—" I said at last, rubbing roughly at my tear-wet face with the heel of my hand. "I was traveling with them, a young man and a little girl. We were trying to reach Dendera—" I broke down again.

"Why? Was your little one sick? I've heard great things about the healing powers of Hathor's shrine. Ah, what a shame, losing your husband and daughter like—"

"For the love of Amun, Uncle, stop *jabbering*," Idu yelled. "Can't you see you're making it worse for her with all your prying? If she's lost her family—"

"My *friends*," I said, making the effort to speak through my tears. "They were my friends. He isn't—wasn't—my husband, and she was—was—" I lost the battle and wept, my forehead pressed against my updrawn knees.

"Hmph! *Whose* jabbering set her off this time, eh?" I heard the older man say.

"I—I'm sorry," Idu replied in a small voice. "But did you hear what she said? A young man, a little girl? Didn't we—"

A slap rang out sharply. I raised my head to see the older man on his feet, glowering at Idu. The young man cupped his cheek and stared back at his uncle in shock. It was obvious what had just happened between them. "You shut your mouth or you'll *walk* home!" the older man raged. "Don't forget who owns the boat! Maybe the same hippo that killed this poor girl's friends can finish the job on you."

"But—"

The older man darted to the beached boat and came back swiftly, brandishing the knobbed throwing stick hunters used to bring down wildfowl in flight. He brandished it at his nephew. "I can still see well enough to use this on *you*."

Idu made a face but didn't press matters. "Yes, Uncle. Sorry, Uncle." He moved away into the shadows beyond the fading fire, where he squatted with his back to us.

As soon as Idu backed down, his uncle's attitude changed radically. He dropped the throwing stick and went over to speak with his nephew. I couldn't hear exactly what passed between them, but I did catch the older man's coaxing, persuasive tone. At first Idu objected—a voice raised in anger is unmistakable—but his uncle's went from cajolery to something far darker, judging from the way he almost growled. Was he threatening him? If so, it was effective. For the second time that night, Idu surrendered; he let his beaming uncle bring him back to the fireside.

"There, we're all friends again," the older man declared, well satisfied that things had worked out his way. "Nefertiti, I promise that I won't trouble you with any more questions tonight, and Idu promises he truly won't bother you with any more of his unwanted . . . attention. How does that sound?" I nodded. "Good, good. Now *your* part of the bargain is to promise that you won't shed any more tears until morning, all right?"

"I'll—I'll try."

"No, you have to give your word. We'll help you honor it. No more questions *and* we'll keep your mind on other things. I know some fine songs, and Idu's mother taught him plenty of stories. We'll stay merry until we fall asleep, and in the morning, we'll see to it that you get where you're going safely."

I thanked him and Idu sincerely. "It's a bargain; you have my word."

We seemed to be at peace with one another, but I could still sense the tension between Idu and his uncle. It was there even when the older man began bawling a harvest song so badly that it was clear he was clowning. He followed it with a comical song about why the baboon had a red behind, and this time he carried the tune beautifully, letting the words and not his performance make us laugh. True, Idu was laughing, but it didn't sound natural. I wondered why.

After his uncle was finished with the baboon song, Idu told a few stories about the adventures of the gods and about brave princes who were dogged by dreadful curses. They were stories familiar to every child I'd ever known, but a familiar tale can still be entertaining if it's told well.

Idu did *not* tell his stories well. His heart wasn't in the task, and he spoke in a monotonous way that reminded me of an ox's plodding steps.

When he was done with his third tale and about to begin a fourth, I spoke up. "Let me tell one now, please. All I've done since I've met you kind people is take and take. I want to make you a gift, even if it's just a story." With that, I began to tell them one of the tales that I'd made up myself, many years ago, to amuse my little sister, Bit-Bit. It was called "The Princess Who Danced on the Moon," and when I came to the part where the handsome prince sees the princess singing and dancing, I got to my feet and acted out her part, clapping my hands and lifting my voice, caught up in the enchantment of my own words.

When I finished, Idu's uncle cheered his approval. "Ah, Idu, you should learn the way to tell a tale from this girl! Nefertiti, I'd rather listen to one of your stories than ten of his. Now I know why you're headed for Dendera: You're going to serve the goddess as a singer and dancer in her holy temple. Am I right?"

"It would be the greatest honor to dance for Hathor," I replied, choosing my words with the greatest care. "I doubt it's one I deserve."

"Nonsense! The goddess would be lucky to have you. Anyone, god or mortal, would call you a little treasure." His good eye twinkled, and he grinned so wide that I could see every badly worn-down and broken tooth left in his mouth.

"Stolen," Idu muttered so low that I only caught that single word.

"What did you say, boy?" The older man's grin vanished.

"I'm tired," Idu said in a sullen voice. "I've had enough songs and stories. I want to sleep."

"Hmm, not a bad idea. We'll make an early start in the morning."

We all stretched out on the ground and soon slept.

My dreams were vague and confused. The sacred river swirled through them, becoming plumes of smoke one moment, bundled serpents the next. I was calling out something to someone, but I couldn't hear my own voice, only the distant sound of a harp playing a melancholy, wandering tune. *Nava's harp* . . . I tried to run toward the sound, but the smoke and the serpents and the sacred river tangled my feet. I opened my mouth to scream as I fell, but I couldn't make a sound. I couldn't breathe. I couldn't—

"Shhh. Don't be afraid. I won't hurt you." Idu lay on top of me, one hand covering my mouth. His face was concealed by the darkness. I squirmed wildly and made a smothered, squealing sound; he only tightened his grip, pressing the insides of my cheeks painfully against my teeth. "Stop that. You have to believe me—I *won't* hurt you, Nefertiti. I swear it. May Ammut eat my heart if I'm lying. Listen, there's something important I need to tell you, something you have to know, but I don't want Uncle to hear me. Promise you'll be quiet?"

I scowled, but I nodded and stopped struggling. Gently he released my mouth and pushed himself back onto his knees and helped me sit up. His breath was warm on my ear as he drew near and whispered, "They're alive, Nefertiti. Your friends are alive."

— 3 —

LINES DRAWN ON SAND

"They're ali—?" My astonished words must have sounded too loud for Idu's liking, because he clapped his hand over my mouth again and pulled me away from the dead fire and his uncle's snoring form. Scrambling and stumbling, he hurried me down the riverbank, past the boat, and to the far side of a lone palm tree that stood at least a bowshot away from our campsite. Once there, he let me go and leaned against the scaly trunk.

Idu tilted his head back and let out a sigh of relief. "Thank the gods that Uncle's a deep sleeper. Still, you shouldn't have done that. He'd beat me bloody if he knew I told you about your friends."

"He's been so kind to me, why wouldn't he want me to know that Nava and Amenophis are alive?" I was so confused that my head spun and my stomach turned over. I wanted to believe Idu's blessed words, but I was afraid that he'd made some horrible mistake. I didn't know if I could bear another heartbreak. "And how—how do you know this?"

"First tell me this, Nefertiti," Idu replied. "Is your friend Amenophis a tall, scrawny, gangly young fellow? Thick lips, a long face, kind of ugly?"

"He's *not* ugly." I leaped to Amenophis's defense so hotly that it made Idu snicker.

"And he's *not* just a friend to you, either, is he?"

My face flushed and I refused to respond to the taunting question. "So you really did see him?"

"If that's what he looks like, I did. He was with a little girl—not a lot of meat on her bones, foreign-looking. We sailed past them yesterday. They looked badly roughed up, but if they'd escaped a hippo attack, they were lucky not to look worse. My mother's cousin lost an arm to one of those monsters, and he bled to death. Anyway, the two of them were walking along the bank, following the flow of the river, and every few steps they called out a name—*your* name. Uncle heard it, too, so unless there are two girls named Nefertiti wandering lost around here—"

"Oh, Idu, *thank* you!" I flung my arms around his neck and hugged him. "You did see them! They *are* alive! Isis bless you forever! And if they were headed downstream on foot, we can probably catch up to them today, except . . ." A worrying thought crossed my mind. "Idu, you still haven't told me the reason for all this secrecy. Why didn't your uncle tell me he'd seen my friends, too? Why did he let me suffer?"

"Because he doesn't want you to find them again," Idu said grimly. "And he won't take you to Dendera. He plans to get you aboard our boat this morning and make up as many stories as it takes to persuade you to come home with us. He'll claim that the ducks we've caught need to be cleaned and preserved or they'll rot. Once he's brought you to our house, he'll find one reason after another to delay your departure. He'll wheedle you to be patient with a poor old man; he'll promise a hundred times that he *will* take you to Dendera . . . tomorrow. But he won't let you go. Nefertiti, he intends for you to become his wife."

My jaw dropped. "He can't be serious."

"He was serious enough last night when he told me his plan. He told me that if I didn't help him, if I told you about how we'd seen your friends, then the first thing he'd do when we got home was throw my mother and me out of his house. And it is his house, just as that's his boat. He calls Mother his sister, but they're only related by marriage. My father—his brother—left us nothing when he died, so we've had to depend on Uncle's charity ever since. He's mostly good-hearted, except when he really wants something. Then he's ruthless." Idu lowered his eyes. "He wants you."

I touched his forearm lightly. "And thanks to you, he won't have me. But . . . will you be all right, you and your mother?"

"That's up to you. I'm going back to camp, and you're going to run as far and fast as you can. When Uncle wakes up, I'm going to be as shocked as he is that you took off. The only way he'll ever know I had anything to do with your escape is if he catches you and you tell him."

"That won't happen," I said firmly. "Good-bye, Idu. I wish I could reward you for the gift you've given me."

He shrugged away my thanks. "My father didn't have

much when he died, but Mother told me he always had a clean heart. That's what I want to have when it's my time to stand before Lord Osiris. Just *move*. Head away from the river to start, then swing back when the sun's about *that* high"—he pointed across the river—"just to the top of those trees. See them?"

I peered into the fading darkness and saw the fringed shadows of more palms on the eastern shore. "Yes, I do."

"Good. That's when it'll be safe for you to come back to the riverside. Uncle will have given up looking for you by then, maybe sooner; trust me. He's a practical man, and he knows that if we waste too much time hunting you, the birds we caught yesterday won't be fit to eat. Hmm, speaking of food, there's a red-striped basket in the boat. If you can be quick and quiet, you might take a peek inside it before you go." He gave me a conspirator's grin. "Maybe take *more* than a peek. After all, a girl who would run away from the old man who was so nice to her, well, she'd probably help herself to some of his bread, too."

"I don't want to steal, Idu."

"Then don't steal. Just take two or three little loaves. That'll be my share, and I'm glad to give it to you."

Idu went back to his place by the dead fire, and I did what he'd told me. I used the strip of cloth I'd cut from my dress to cradle the bread loaves and turned my back on the sacred river. I moved as fast as I could, but I also moved with an eye to places where trees or tall plants would hide my passage. I didn't want to go too far from the river, because I had no idea how far downstream Amenophis and Nava might be, and I didn't want to loop around and miss them.

As I ran, I wondered if that was what had happened the other day, when I followed the irrigation canal. While I'd veered off to the west, my dear friends continued straight down the river, and our paths failed to cross. That mustn't happen again! I cast anxious looks to the east, eager to see the shining face of Aten's sun-disk high enough in the sky. I groaned when I realized I'd hidden my tracks too well and that the grove of trees sheltering me also blocked my view.

I'm sure *that enough time's passed,* I told myself. *It* has *to be safe for me to go back now.* I rushed toward the river.

I reached the shore in a spot where the water was shallow and the round pads of blue lotus floated on the surface. Their fragrance entranced me, reminding me of our beloved garden at home. As tempting as it was to slip into memories, I forced myself to be alert to the here and now, scanning the river for any sign of Idu and his uncle. Praise Isis, there wasn't a trace of them, and I was able to turn my attention to seeking my lost dear ones.

I looked upstream, across the river. Once again, the sacred waters were teeming with boats and ships, but if I strained my eyes, I could just make out a last glimpse of Thebes, the city's great buildings no more than slivers of gold in the distance. From there, I let my eyes move slowly along the eastern bank, trying to find some familiar landmark—even if it was only a remembered grove of trees—that would let me gauge where I was. I concentrated, trying to recall the sights I'd seen in the moments before the hippo attacked us and what the far shore had looked like from the hunters' campsite.

I'm a little farther down the river from where I was last night,

I told myself. *That is . . .* I think *that's where I am. Idu said he saw Nava and Amenophis moving downstream, but he didn't tell me if he and his uncle were sailing in the same direction.* I thought about it some more. *A reed boat has no sail. It can't catch the wind and go against the current. Idu's no weakling, and his uncle's not that old; he's got a farmer's hard muscles. Still, I doubt they had the strength to get that boat upstream with only one oar. They'd've been exhausted! So maybe they began their hunting trip by bargaining with the master of a larger ship for a tow upstream; then they just rode the current the way we did, which means*—my eyes swept the river again—*they'd have* passed *Nava and Amenophis going downstream, and that means my best chance of finding my friends again lies* that *way.* With that confident thought, I turned my steps south, backtracking against the flow of the sacred river.

My certainty lasted as long as my first burst of energy. I'd been walking since before Ra's sun-ship had showed itself fully above the horizon, and I hadn't had a lot to eat since the day before. I thought of Amenophis's worries about making our supplies last and only allowed myself half of one of the small loaves Idu had encouraged me to take. It wasn't nearly enough to satisfy the rising hunger I felt.

When hunger gnawed at my belly, doubt gnawed at my mind. *Is this really the right direction? What if they're downstream? What if they've turned away from the river? What if they came across a friendly boatman and crossed back to the eastern shore? What if they've returned to Thebes? What if, what if, what if . . .* Tears of exhaustion prickled the corners of my eyes, but I pressed my lips together and wouldn't let them fall. I knew that as tired and hungry as I was, if I wept now, it would stop me in my tracks and I'd lose precious time.

I'll only go upstream as far as those trees, I decided, picking out the farthest thicket I could see. *Then I'll turn around.*

The grove of palms didn't seem to be such a great distance from where I stood, but as I approached it, I saw that the riverbank along my way was a series of obstacles, large and small. In one place, I pushed aside a clump of reeds just in time to see a huge bull crocodile drowsing right where I was about to tread. I retreated and made a large circle around him. Next I encountered a deep channel—the silted remains of an abandoned irrigation ditch—and had to watch my step climbing into and out of it. My bare feet sank into the warm mud well past my ankles, holding me back. Insects swarmed around my head, biting my face and arms viciously. When I couldn't stand the cruel itching anymore, I had to stop and slap more mud onto the bites for relief.

I was just stumbling back onto my feet when I heard a distinct rustling from a stand of green bulrushes. The plants grew thickly all the way to the water, completely covering the bank. The only direct route for me was to beat a path through them, but what were they hiding? What was making that sound? It was too loud to be the movement of a bird. Could it be another crocodile or, worse, another hippo?

I should go around again, I thought, but my heart sank at the idea of yet another wearying, time-devouring detour. *Or maybe—maybe I should go as close as I can and see if there's anything there that I need to avoid. If I'm careful—*

Then I heard another sound through the rustling in the bulrushes: the soft sound of a child's tears.

I plunged into the reeds heedlessly, joyously, my arms sweeping them out of my way left and right. How foolish I was, and how far beyond listening to the lonely, abandoned voice of reason that begged me to slow down, to mind my footing, to question whether I was sure I'd heard those small, miserable sobs or if it was an illusion. I had no more time or desire for questions; I was caught up in knowing that my happiness lay just a few steps ahead of me, hiding among the rushes.

And, yes, it was true! There they were, my friends, my dear ones, there! Amenophis crouched in the reeds, holding a weeping Nava close to his bony chest. The two of them looked scrawny and almost as filthy as I felt, and yet to my eyes they were more beautiful than the first nightmare-banishing rays of the glorious Aten. I shouted their names with all the joy in my heart.

For an instant they stared at me, as if my voice had turned them both into stone. Then a wonderful smile bloomed over Nava's face. "Nefertiti! Oh, Nefertiti, you're alive! You're alive!" She leaped away from Amenophis and became a small, swift, happily shouting whirlwind, striking me so hard that I staggered and fell in a heap among the rushes. She swarmed over me, her eyes bright, hugging me so tightly that every breath I managed to take was a victory. "You're *alive*!"

"And so are you," I said when she loosened her embrace enough to allow it. "Oh, my little one, so are you." All at once, stupidly, I was crying again.

"Why are you crying? What's the matter? Are you hurt? *Stop* it, Nefertiti. Please." Nava's voice rose anxiously. "What's wrong?"

Amenophis answered for me, standing between Nava and me so that he could give a hand to each of us and help us stand again. "Nothing's wrong anymore, Nava. Sometimes people cry because they're so happy, it's too powerful to control. Look, I'm doing it, too." He touched his long, thin fingers to where tears were cutting channels through the grime on his cheeks. "Welcome back, Nefertiti." He spoke solemnly, but his lips parted in a radiant smile. When he opened his arms to me, I stepped into his embrace and rested my head on his chest as naturally as if I were coming home.

"Me too! Me too!" Nava tugged at our arms until we included her in our hug. It was just as well: If she hadn't broken the strange spell between Amenophis and me, I don't know if I'd have found the strength to let him go.

How strange, I thought. Even with Nava clamoring for attention between us, the beating of Amenophis's heart still lingered in my ears. I looked into his tired, homely face, only to have him quickly drop his eyes and turn from me, looking toward the river.

"When we get to Dendera, I'm going to send a messenger back to Thebes to bring every piece of gold I own." He spoke softly, as if talking for himself alone. "I'll give it all to the gods who brought you back to me—to us. Hapy will have a share, because his sacred waters didn't take you from us, and Ra, because his light guided you to us, and Isis, because I know she's dear to you." He spared me a smile so shy and fleeting that I wasn't sure I'd seen it. "And Hathor, because Dendera is her holy place, and—"

Nava tugged at my hand and beckoned me to bend over so she could whisper to me. "I don't have any gold, so I'm going to make a new song and sing it as part of my prayers. Not for your gods, though—for mine. Will you mind?"

I kissed her brow. "Not if your god won't. If you like, I'll give you a pair of gold earrings to offer him, along with your song."

She looked at me narrowly, as if trying to judge if I was making fun of her or not. Nava had spoken to me many times about the oddly solitary god that she and her Habiru tribefolk worshipped, a god without a shape, without a face, and without any name except the One. "Do you think my prayers won't be acceptable without gold?" she asked, so very stern for someone so very young.

"No, of course not," I reassured her. "We're together again, and we're not going to lose one another anymore. I think that giving thanks for that is the important thing, whether to Isis or Hapy or Hathor or the One, with or without gold."

"Maybe you should tell that to Amenophis," Nava said. "Otherwise . . . well, you heard him. He's going to give away *all* his gold, and then what will he do?"

I laughed. "Good idea. We wouldn't want him to return to Thebes as a beggar"—I looked down at my bedraggled dress and my mud-smeared arms and legs—"even if all three of us look like beggars right now."

We came up behind Amenophis and each took one of

his hands. "You know, the gods will hear you even if you come before them empty-handed," I murmured. "Otherwise it would be a waste of time for poor people to pray at all. Or do you believe the gods are like their priests?"

"Don't mock the gods, Nefertiti." Amenophis's prominent jaw was set in a forbidding expression. "Not now, not after how wonderfully they've blessed us. If you knew what I felt when I thought we'd lost you! The moment that hippo threw us all from the boat, my mind went cold. I wasn't human anymore. All I could hear was your voice calling out to me: 'Save Nava! Save the child!' The hippo was still raging through the water, bellowing, trampling, smashing everything, but all I heard was your voice, and all I saw was Nava, flailing in the water. I fought my way to her, got her to hold on to my shoulders, and swam to shore."

"He told me to hide behind a big tree, in case the hippo came on land," Nava put in. She was trembling with remembered terror. "Then he went back into the water."

"Back?" I couldn't believe it. "What were you thinking?" He didn't bother responding to my question. We both knew the answer: *I had to find you.*

"There's no sense in your worrying about that now," he said. "You can see that no harm came to me. *Or* to Nava," he added. "I didn't leave her alone on the bank for too long. When I couldn't spot you in the river, I returned to her and we took the long way around the stretch of shore where that beast was still wallowing. When we came back to the water, we began our search."

"We looked and looked for you, Nefertiti," Nava said. "We never stopped. I didn't sleep, or eat, or—"

"Nava . . ." Amenophis spoke in a warning tone, but he was smiling at the little girl's powers of exaggeration.

"Wellll . . . we did sleep. But not a lot! And we ate fish. I caught one all by myself!" She looked very proud.

"That's true," Amenophis said. "I wish you could have seen her, Nefertiti. She's a little osprey, this one. She waded in the shallows, watched patiently, then . . . splash! She dropped onto her prey with both hands and came up clutching a fish that was more than half as big as she is." His severe, chiding manner was gone, and I was pleased to see it go.

"Careful, Amenophis," I joked. "Ma'at doesn't make special exceptions for fishing stories. Nava, dear, I hope I will get to see you catch many more fish before this journey's over. You'll be able to feed us much better than I. All I've got to share with you are these." I reached into the cloth sling at my waist and handed my friends Idu's gift of bread. They greeted the small loaves as if they were the finest roast meats at Pharaoh's table. I was hungry myself, but watching them tear into the bread comforted me nearly as much as having a full stomach. While they ate, I told them of my own adventures since the hippo's rampage.

I ended my tale by saying, "You don't need to be concerned about me showing proper respect to the gods, Amenophis. I know what a great debt I owe them for saving me from the hippo, the river, and the old man's schemes. Even so, meeting one person with a heart as kind and honest as Idu's is worth ten rescues, and I owe the gods thanks for that as well."

"I didn't mean to scold you, Nefertiti." My friend

looked and sounded deeply sorry. "The gods have my thanks, but if I could, I'd give my gold to that young man instead of to them as a reward for all he did for you."

"For us," I reminded him. "He steered me onto the right path, the path that brought us back together."

"And not one instant too soon. We'd given up hope. Nava and I were about to go back to Thebes. I was going to place her in my sister Sitamun's household for protection and then surrender myself to Thutmose. I didn't care how harshly he'd punish me." He sighed. "I didn't care about anything anymore."

"Then I'm doubly glad I found you when I did," I told him. "You must never lose heart, Amenophis. Even if I'd never come back to you, you shouldn't give up. What your brother tried to do to me wasn't right—it was an offense against Ma'at—and it was made worse by the fact that he had the priests of Amun in on the plot with him."

"Priests!" Amenophis exclaimed bitterly. "They're so fastidious about keeping their bodies clean and pure for the gods, but what does that matter when they value wealth and power more than truth?"

"Then you should learn from their bad example and live better," I said. "Your brother's wrongdoing wouldn't vanish just because I did. It would still be your duty to turn him back to Ma'at's way so that one day he'll be worthy to wear Pharaoh's crown. Even if I died, you would have to—"

"Don't say that again, Nefertiti." Amenophis's eyes pleaded for my silence. "I promise that I'll do as you say—be brave, go on, help my brother be a better man if I can—but don't make me think of losing you ever again."

"Anyway, you're not fair to Amenophis," Nava piped up. "He wasn't going to give up on *anything* until he saw those men. That's why we were hiding here."

"What men?" I asked.

"Soldiers," Amenophis said, stone-faced. "Armed men from the royal palace. I recognized at least three of them, but there were more, maybe six. We were only a little way upstream when a kind breeze brought me the sound of their feet pounding the ground behind us. Who would need to go running along this side of the river? No one sends messengers to the dead." He looked southwest, to the golden cliffs that guarded the valley where so many pharaohs lay entombed.

"They weren't messengers to anyone," Nava said. "They all had swords, Nefertiti—I saw them!—and some of them had bows and quivers full of arrows. They were hunting us." She leaned her head against me. "Amenophis dragged me into the rushes before they could see us, but we got to see them when they ran by." She put her arms around my waist and clung tight.

"I didn't know they were soldiers at first," Amenophis said. "I just knew that there was no good reason for a group of men to be racing along this side of the river. The peasants who farm here are too busy working their land. That leaves the men who work on constructing and adorning the royal tombs, and their settlement must be farther downstream or we'd've encountered it."

There are also the men who rob *those tombs,* I thought. *But they wouldn't be running along the bank, in a group, in broad daylight. Those jackals stick to the dark places and the dark hours. Great*

Lord Osiris, let your might protect the dead from their greedy and impious hands!

"The gods were gracious to us," Amenophis said, continuing his story. "I got a good look at the men when they jogged past our hiding place, but they didn't see us. I thought it might be safe to go on after they were well away. Then I looked again, to the river, and saw—"

"Boats!" Nava broke in. "I saw them, too. Not just the boats we saw when we were on the river together. Those boats got out of the way when *these* went by, all full of men carrying more weapons, and one boat even bigger than that, with a sail and—"

"Thutmose," Amenophis said. "He'd send his men ahead in small boats, but he'd never set foot on any ship that wasn't worthy of Pharaoh. Having others cast nets and set snares for us won't satisfy him. He has to be part of the hunt or he won't be able to triumph in the moment of our capture."

"Then he won't enjoy anything," I declared, speaking with a calm certainty I didn't wholly feel. "There won't be any capture, and the only triumph will come when he sees us standing safe and secure beside your parents in the holy presence of Hathor herself."

— 4 —

THE FACE OF SET

Amenophis and I conferred for some time after that, planning our next move. It was clear that we would have to shift our path to Dendera away from the river. The chance of encountering another one of Thutmose's patrols was too great. We didn't know how many men he'd taken from Thebes, but knowing him, he hadn't skimped. He'd use them as his beaters—servants who moved together noisily through the vegetation, driving the frightened creatures straight to the waiting hunter.

"Thutmose has thrown a wide net, but we'll find a way to slip through it," I said. "He doesn't know that we lost our boat and our supplies, so he's probably keeping his eyes on the river. If we turn toward the mountains—"

"Do you mean the sacred valley of the tombs?" Amenophis shook his head. "Not unless we can eat and drink thin air."

"We won't go *into* the valley," I said. "We'll just go west for a bit. And we won't do it unless we find a working canal. I followed one before. We'll have plenty to drink." *And maybe we'll have something to eat, too,* I thought. *Maybe we'll be luckier than I was at finding people working the land nearby.*

"A canal!" Amenophis clapped his hands. "Of course, it's the perfect answer! We can drink our fill and catch fish much more easily than in the river. Our little osprey will be delighted." He smiled at Nava, who was taking a nap in a nest of bulrushes while we planned.

"Fish?" Why hadn't I thought of that when I was on my own?

"The irrigation ditches are full of them. You're brilliant, Nefertiti."

Brilliant? I said nothing, and if he mistook my embarrassment for modesty, I wasn't going to correct him. I could have followed that irrigation ditch to the wilderness of the Red Land, starving at every step when there was plenty to eat only a stone's throw away!

I held fast to my shamed silence even after Nava woke up and we all waded into the river up to our knees, washing ourselves as clean as possible before resuming our journey. It was just as well—this was no time for idle conversation. Amenophis took charge, cautioning us to keep our voices low if we felt we had to speak, to follow a path that gave us the greatest concealment possible, and to keep our eyes and ears open for the first hint of Thutmose's men seeking us by land or water. I listened to him, amazed at the changes that had come over him. Was this the shy, stammering boy I'd first met in the royal palace at Thebes? There'd been nothing princely about him then, yet now he sounded masterful.

My heart beat faster, but our situation gave me no time to reflect on what I was feeling.

"Stealth will save us," Amenophis said. "It won't be easy, moving through the shoreline plants, but once we find a canal feeding from the river, we'll go quickly alongside it and get to more open land. My brother can't send an entire army after us, you know." He spoke earnestly, trying to encourage us. "Father might have given him the right to rule Thebes in his absence, but the palace is full of watchful eyes. Thutmose knows that everything he does is being observed by nobles and other important men. Even with the priests of Amun on his side, he can't charge ahead with mad commands. He must walk wisely, or he could find himself so far out of Father's favor that not even Mother would be able to repair the situation."

"I wonder how many men he *does* have seeking us," I said.

"Several small patrols on each side of the river, I'll bet." Amenophis rubbed his chin. "Maybe half a dozen boats riding the water. Again, he doesn't know that we've lost our boat, so he has to cover all the possibilities."

"He's probably sent men ahead to Dendera, too," I suggested. "They'll be on the lookout for our arrival."

Amenophis nodded in agreement. "Trying to catch us before we can let my parents know we've come." He frowned. "How will we get around them?"

"Let's worry about that when we're close enough to see the city's gateway," I said. "One step at a time, right?"

So we set out on our interrupted journey with no boat, no food, and nothing suitable for carrying water. The only tools we had were Amenophis's knife and a tiny bow drill for kindling fire. How I thanked Thoth, god of wisdom, for my friend's foresight in remembering to bring such a thing and for choosing one small enough to be carried in a pouch at his waist. Thanks to his prudence, that mad hippo hadn't left us completely helpless.

We decided that we'd travel in the hours when the light was fading or not yet fully born. Amenophis wanted to carry Nava on his back, but she protested being treated like a baby. Sometimes the little Habiru girl acted so grown-up, sometimes so young! What a shame that we'd never know how old she truly was. On the day she was born, her former master must have been pleased to possess a new piece of property, but the only people who'd care *when* she had come into the world were her family. As far as we knew, all of them were gone. Now Nava trudged along between Amenophis and me, doggedly keeping up with the prince's long strides. I never heard one word of complaint from her.

The day waned, and the number of boats on the sacred river dwindled with every step we took. Soon we saw only the shining surface of the water, as empty and untouched as it must have looked on the first day of its creation. The tall palm trees on the western bank stroked shadowy fingers over the river and the land. The song of insects along the shore changed tone as those who roamed by daylight gave place to their night-flying cousins. Everywhere the birds were settling down to sleep. Earlier that day, we'd raided their nests for eggs to eat, though we all would have preferred to have something meatier in our stomachs.

I shaded my eyes to see how Ra's great sun-ship

touched the mountain peaks shielding the royal tombs. The sky spread out banners of crimson and gold to greet the god as he descended into the underworld. All the land was preparing for night when we finally encountered the mouth of an irrigation canal.

"At last!" Amenophis exclaimed, starting to follow its path away from the river.

"Hadn't we better stop for the night?" I said. "It's going to be too dark to see where we're going."

"There's still plenty of light."

"For how long? Amenophis, we won't be able to get far once it's dark. How will we find a safe place to spend the night? Better to rest here now, where we *know* we'll be sheltered by the river plants."

"It's better to get as far from Thutmose's men as we can while we can," he argued. "Let's go."

I pressed my lips together and folded my arms. *One moment I'm admiring how commanding he's become; the next I'm ready to shove him into the river because he's commanding* me! *Sweet Isis, give me patience.*

Amenophis met my stubborn look with one of his own, but he couldn't outlast me. "Oh, all right," he finally said, holding up his hands in surrender. "We'll sleep among the rushes if you're too afraid to go on."

I started to protest, then bit my tongue. *This is the best place for us tonight; I know it,* I thought. *I don't care if Amenophis believes I'm afraid; as long as he and Nava stay safe, I don't care if he calls me seven kinds of coward!*

We found a place where the reeds didn't show the same juicy green as their neighbors because the ground humped up, lifting them farther from the water. I moved as quietly as I could, pushing down the faded plants until I'd made them into a crude mattress for us.

"It looks like a nest!" Nava declared. She settled into the center of it happily.

"Too bad it doesn't hold more eggs," I said. It was a joke, but one made on an empty stomach.

"Are you hungry, Nefertiti?" Amenophis didn't wait for me to reply. "So am I. You two wait here; I'll try to find us something to eat." He vanished into the surrounding greenery before I could stop him.

Nava and I curled up together to await his return. He was away for a long time. I watched the patch of sky overhead lose more and more light until I saw the first pale sprinkling of stars. Nava and I had been passing the time by whispering stories to one another. She told me many of her people's tales, including the wondrous story of how it all began when the One first spoke to a Habiru man in the Land of Two Rivers. In exchange, I told her stories about Isis and the child Horus and all the adventures they had while fleeing the wicked god Set. Her eyes always lit up with delight when I got to the scariest parts.

"You know, Nava, I don't remember having such a taste for bloodcurdling stories when I was your age," I remarked.

"I'm sorry you can't remember things," she replied. "You shouldn't worry about it—that happens to old people."

I had to laugh. "What I meant to say—to ask—is *why* do you like hearing such frightening things?"

She shrugged. "Because they're not real. And because I know they're going to be over." She cast worried looks into the rushes surrounding us. "Not like now, waiting for Amenophis to come back. Do *you* know how much longer he'll be gone, Nefertiti?"

"Oh, not much longer," I said, forcing myself to sound confident. "Now whose turn is it to tell a story?"

As Nava was in the middle of telling me about a disobedient woman who was turned into salt, the rushes rattled and Amenophis dropped to his knees beside her. He smiled as he extended his cupped hands.

"More eggs!" Nava was overjoyed.

"Not as many as I'd like, but they're better than nothing," he told us. "Don't eat them until you've smelled them. There wasn't any sign of the mother bird near the nest; if they've been abandoned for several days, they might be rotten."

I took one of the tiny eggs from his hands and cracked it delicately with a fingernail, then peeled away a shard of shell and sniffed. "They're good." I downed it in one gulp and cast my eyes over the remaining eggs, counting them to myself.

Amenophis saw what I was doing. "Here, have another. There were six of them to start, so we each get two." He handed out our portions and pretended not to notice when I pressed my second egg into Nava's hands. I, in turn, did the same when he shared his scanty meal with the little girl.

"I have something even better than eggs to share with you," he said when we'd finished—which didn't take long. "I found a house not too far up the canal!"

"A house!" Nava and I exclaimed as one. Visions of bread, beans, the simplest foods all danced before my eyes, more beautiful than the finest feast. "If we offer to help the people with their work, do you think they'd share—"

"There were no people." Amenophis shifted awkwardly. "I'm sorry, I should've been more accurate: I found a deserted house beside the canal. A—a ruin, really. The roof's gone, as are two of the walls. I—I got your hopes up for nothing. Forgive me."

"Two walls are better than none," I said. "We can see it for ourselves tomorrow. But is that why you took so long coming back to us? Because you were exploring in the dark?" I frowned at him. "You could've fallen into the ditch! And what if you'd stumbled across some night-prowling beast?"

He flinched so much that I imagine I must have looked just like Aunt Tiye at her sternest. "It wasn't—wasn't dark," he countered. "And I had to search out the way ahead. *You* didn't want to go on because you were afraid of trying an unknown path, so I looked into it."

I gritted my teeth and took a deep breath. I'd told myself that it wasn't important if he thought I was a coward. I'd told myself it didn't matter.

Oh, I was so very, very wrong!

"Afraid?" I snapped. "If I was so afraid, would I be *here*? No, I'd be in the royal palace at Thebes, eating roast quail and honey cakes, dressed in the finest linen, with gold around my neck instead of mud and insect bites! If I was as fearful as you seem to think, I never would have stood up to my aunt Tiye. I'd be safe, I'd be fed, and I'd be *married to your brother*!"

Amenophis was slack-jawed at my outburst. His stammer returned in full force as he tried to apologize, but I was a captive of my own anger and refused to listen to him. Instead, I lay down on the flattened rushes, curled onto my side, and ignored him. I heard his repentant words trickle away into silence, then Nava's small voice whispering, "Why is Nefertiti so mad at you?"

"I said something that hurt her feelings," he replied, speaking in such a low, miserable voice that I could barely hear him. "It was wrong to do that, and what I said was wrong, too. She's never been a coward, not for as long as I've known her. I was the one who was afraid of my own shadow."

"You're not like that now," Nava said. I could picture her sitting beside Amenophis, taking his hand and gazing at him with steadfast eyes. "And I'll bet *she* wasn't always brave."

He chuckled softly. "I can't picture that, but I think I'd like to. Even if I only *imagined* her as someone who might need me as much as I need her, it would—it might let me think I had a chance to say—to tell her—"

"But she does need you," Nava cut in. "For finding food. Thank you for the eggs."

This time he laughed louder. "At least I'm good for something. Now sleep, Nava. We'll have to be up early."

The next morning, we were awake well before dawn and began our march inland, along the irrigation ditch. We moved as fast as caution would allow. Shadows still blurred the ground, and we didn't want to take a tumble into the canal. Nava scurried to keep up with Amenophis's long stride, and I brought up the rear.

I intended to keep my eyes on Nava at all times, but I

couldn't help letting my gaze stray. A morning breeze carried the scent of smoke and the faint sound of human activity from downstream. I paused for a moment and looked back.

We were clear of the reeds, and there was only flat land with a few widely spaced stands of trees before me. In full daylight, we would have a completely clear view all the way to the river. As things were, I *thought* I saw the solid outline of a large tent surrounded by a scattering of smaller shapes.

Thutmose's encampment, I thought. *Those must be his men, still sleeping.* I sighed, thinking of how they all had breakfast waiting for them. *Stop that,* I told myself. *Stop pining for what you can't have and start walking. And walk faster, or they'll see you as easily as you see them. Go!*

"Nefertiti?" Amenophis spoke my name hesitantly. He came back to see what was keeping me. "What are you looking at?"

"Nothing," I said curtly, and barged past him along the bank of the canal. By the time the Aten showed his bright disk, we'd reached the ruined house that Amenophis had discovered the night before. As he'd said, there was no roof left on the place, but the two walls that still stood were tall enough to hold a wedge of blessed shade. We settled down and slept for a while.

I woke up with Nava shaking me gently by the shoulder. Her hand felt damp and cool. "Look at what I did," she crowed, presenting a fat tilapia for my inspection.

"When did you catch this big fellow?" I asked.

"A little while ago. I woke up, but you and Amenophis were still sleeping, so I went down to the canal and—"

"Splash?" I said, remembering how Amenophis had

described Nava's first catch. "You really are a little osprey," I said, admiring the fish.

Amenophis rolled over, sat up, and yawned. "What's going on? Did I miss something?"

"Not if you can build us a fire," I told him. "We've got food!"

"As soon as we eat this one, I'm going back down to the canal to catch more," Nava announced.

"I'll go with you," I said. "Maybe you can teach me your fishing secrets. Then we'll have twice as much to eat. Amenophis, why don't you make a cookfire while we're gone?"

"Gladly," he said. "There are some sycamore trees nearby. With luck, I'll be able to gather plenty of wood." He stood up and started away from the ruins.

I caught up to him in four strides. "Nava can start fishing without me. Could you use some help?"

"Oh, yes!" My offer delighted him, but he looked a little doubtful as well. "I'm forgiven for—for saying you were—"

"I *was* afraid," I said. "Afraid something had happened to you. I couldn't stand the thought of it, especially so soon after we found one another again."

He lowered his head. "I'm honored that you care about me so much. I've never had such a—such a friend before."

Is that what we are to one another? I thought. *Is that all?* But I had no answer to my own question, only a strange feeling that danced away from me whenever I tried to give it a name.

We reached the place where the sycamores grew. The

trees were dead, and an abundance of fallen twigs and small branches littered the ground. We were able to gather more than enough wood for a cookfire in a very short time. I left Amenophis squatting over his bow drill and a handful of tinder and went to help Nava catch more fish in the canal.

"Do you smell that, Nava?" I said as we stood in the water, waiting for the telltale flash of scales. I sniffed loudly and smiled. "Smoke! Amenophis has the fire going. Soon we'll be able to eat the—"

A horrible shout of pain snatched the words from my mouth. I clambered out of the irrigation ditch in an instant and rushed back toward the ruined house. I was so unnerved that I didn't think to look back and see if Nava was following until she raced past me, both of us calling, "Amenophis! Amenophis! What's wrong?"

We found him sitting with his back to one of the tumbledown walls, his right leg drawn up onto his left thigh. He was growling his way through more curses than I'd ever heard in my life, even from the sailors who'd wandered the streets of Akhmin. He stopped only when he became aware that Nava and I were standing over him.

"Look out," he told us. "It might still be out in the open, so watch your step."

"What—" I began. Then I saw the reddening wound on his foot. I fell to my knees for a closer look. There was only one mark, not the fearsome double track of a snakebite. "A scorpion," I said, feeling the old dread rising in my throat. When my sister, Bit-Bit, was very young, I thought she'd been stung by a scorpion while in my care. One of the crueler gods must have enjoyed my terror, but a kinder one took that opportunity to bring Henenu, the scribe, into my life. It had all been a big mistake—Bit-Bit hadn't been stung after all, just frightened into tears—but this time there was no doubt about what had happened to Amenophis.

"I got the fire started, and I was about to prepare the fish for cooking," he said. He clenched his jaw for a moment, struggling against pain. "I'd put it over there"—he gestured at the other wall, where the tilapia lay in the shadow—"to keep it out of the sun. I think the creature must have its nest in that crack at the bottom. I didn't even notice it was there until it scuttled over my feet. I jumped and . . ." He nodded to his wounded foot.

"What color was the scorpion?" I remembered the question Henenu had asked me years ago. The answer was vital: Brown scorpions didn't have the power to kill humans, but white ones did.

"Brown." He summoned up a wobbly smile. "Not very big, either. I shouldn't be carrying on like this. You'll think I'm a child."

"Not many children know the kind of words you were using," I replied dryly. "You should make a thanks-offering to the goddess Serket that you didn't disturb one of her white scorpions. Until then, let me see what I can do for the pain."

There wasn't much to be done except pour cool water over Amenophis's foot. Nava and I ran back and forth to the canal, carrying water in our cupped hands. Amenophis put on a brave face, saying that we were spoiling him, but I could see he was still suffering. When we ate our fish, he only picked at his portion. Later that day, when Nava managed to catch another, he left his share entirely untouched.

"I think I'd rather sleep than eat," he said. "My father's chief doctors all agree that sleep is the best healer."

It's bad now because it's a fresh wound, I thought. *It'll be better tomorrow.*

My comforting thoughts were shattered that night when Amenophis's moans woke me up. He was biting on his knuckles, trying to mute the sounds of pain, but it wasn't working. I knelt by his side and touched his forehead. It was hot.

He opened his eyes and looked up at me. "I'm sorry. I didn't want to disturb your sleep."

"Don't worry about that. How bad is the pain?"

"It's probably not that bad. I'm making a fuss over nothing." He used brave words, but his voice rasped, and even by moon and starlight, I could see his chest rising and falling far faster than normal.

I fed more wood to the embers of our dying fire and examined his foot. The site of the scorpion's sting looked swollen, though I couldn't tell if it was also discolored or if the darker area was just dirt. I shivered as I remembered the words I'd read in one of the papyrus scrolls Henenu had had me copy, a physician's account of dealing with wounds: *When the flesh turns dark, if nothing further can be done to turn the infection, the darkness of death will follow.*

Infection . . . I closed my eyes, trying to picture more of that unknown doctor's words. Had he spoken of a remedy for such things? I couldn't remember. My thoughts kept straying back to my home in Akhmin, and the face of my second mother, Mery, floated like a veil before me, obscuring my memories of the physician's scroll.

She was in the kitchen, looking at a wound that one of our younger slaves had gotten while cutting meat. *Thank the gods, this isn't too bad. A little cleansing, a little honey, a strip of fresh linen, and you'll be fine. And eat some honey, too, just to be sure you heal inside and out. I don't think you'll object to that, will you?* Mery smiled kindly.

Honey! Sweet, wonderful honey. Its purifying, protecting, healing powers for treating all sorts of scrapes and cuts were used not just in our household but everywhere, from the humble homes of the poor to the palace of Pharaoh himself. I'd been so appalled at the possibility of Amenophis dying that the obvious cure had slipped from my frantic mind. Now I could reassure myself that his wound was still fresh enough for a good application of honey to help it heal and banish any demons of infection that might try to invade his body. All I had to do was find some.

All I had to do . . . As if it were that easy! The same cruel god who'd laughed at my panic over Bit-Bit so many years ago was probably holding his aching sides and weeping with mirth tonight. Where was I going to find honey? We were in the middle of nowhere, as far as I knew, far from any hope of help, far from any people, except—

I stood up and went to wake Nava. "Dear one, Amenophis needs you," I said.

"What's the matter?" Her voice trembled. "Is he dying?"

"No, the gods forbid it, but he does have a fever. Take

this"—I tore off a small rag from the already ruined hem of my dress—"and soak it in the water and put it on his forehead. Be sure you take a little fire to light your way. I don't want to come back and find out that you fell into the canal."

"Come back?" she repeated, growing more agitated by the moment. "Where are you going?"

"I have to get something to heal him," I said, keeping my words calm. "Honey. Bees sometimes make nests in dead trees, and I saw some dead trees earlier today, while you were fishing."

"Oh." She nodded. "Good luck. I'll take care of him for you. Come back soon."

"I'll try," I said, taking a small brand from the fire to light my way.

As I walked through the night, backtracking along the path we'd taken next to the irrigation ditch, I was beset by guilty thoughts. *Holy Ma'at, forgive me for what I've done. Everything I said to Nava was true, but some lies are like scorpions; they hide themselves in the words we choose not to say. But I had to do it, even though I will suffer for this when my heart is judged. If Nava or Amenophis knew what I'm really going to do, they'd move the mountains to stop me.*

I don't know how long I walked before I saw the dots of fire in the distance. Thutmose's encampment was in sight. I extinguished my makeshift torch and moved on, letting the moon and stars and those campfires guide my ever-more-careful steps.

When I determined I was close enough to risk being seen, I got down on my belly and studied the scene before me. Everywhere I looked, I saw men sleeping on the ground, their gear within easy reach. There were no sentries. Why would there be? Though these soldiers were escorting the crown prince of the Black Land, they did so in the heart of Pharaoh's realm. Prince Thutmose could sleep safer here than in Thebes, where the royal palace often hummed with the schemes of power-hungry men and women.

Sleep safe, Thutmose, I thought, my eyes on the lone tent that stood some distance away from the common soldiers' encampment. *Sleep safe and sleep deep until I'm gone. O Isis, lend me your magic! Give me the keen eye of your son Horus to let me find what I seek in Thutmose's tent. And seal his eyes with slumber as heavy as clay until I'm far away.* I paused for five heartbeats, gathering my nerve, then crept forward.

The goddess heard my prayer. I was able to work my way silently around the campground where the men slept and slip into the big, square tent. It was almost perfectly dark inside, though my eyes were able to pick out the shape of the field bed where Thutmose lay. It stood directly across the tent from the doorway where I now crouched, waiting. The slow, regular breath of a man enjoying peaceful sleep and pleasant dreams filled my ears. Could he really have no regrets about hunting us so ruthlessly? He'd condemned me to die, and on top of that, he'd tried to destroy me before the lawful sentence could be carried out. He'd never made a secret of how deeply he despised his brother, and he'd probably relish coming up with a merciless punishment to inflict on Amenophis for the crime of helping me. Did none of this trouble his soul?

I wish I knew, I thought, gazing at the dark form resting on the field bed. *And if it's true, I wish there were a way to draw all that venom out of your heart. I don't like you, but you're Amenophis's brother, and he loves you in spite of everything. For his sake, I wish I had the power to heal you, Thutmose.*

Once I was convinced that Thutmose was sleeping soundly, I tucked the door cloth a little to one side so that a small spill of light came into the royal tent. It was enough to let me see what I sought: the sturdy shape of a wooden chest set against the tent wall to my left. I moved toward it on hands and knees, my prayers now begging the gods to grant me the skill and luck to open it without making a sound.

If there was any honey to be found in this camp, it would be here, among the prince's things. This was no formal military expedition—more like a hunting party, traveling light for maximum speed—so there'd be no doctor along to look after the men. That meant no doctor's kit, but it didn't mean Thutmose would travel without basic remedies, in case of accident or emergency. He valued his own life too highly for that. A jar of honey and a roll of linen to dress wounds were as basic as could be.

I laid my hands on the lid of the wooden trunk.

"Rrrrrr?"

The musical rumbling of an inquisitive purr took me by surprise. I gasped as my hands touched a warm, furry, living shape. Two luminous, bright green eyes met mine for an instant before the cat perched atop Thutmose's travel chest leaped right at me. I tumbled backward, holding in my cry of alarm. My small attacker dropped gracefully into my lap and began kneading my legs, purring ever more loudly. Tiny claws pricked my flesh through the thin layer of my shabby dress until I couldn't take any more. I picked up the cat and set it on the ground before getting back onto my knees to lift the lid of the chest.

Two strong hands shot out from behind me to grab my wrists, and a well-known voice spoke softly in my ear, "What do we have here? A thief?" I was forcibly turned around, my back pushed painfully against the hard edge of the wooden chest. "Who are you . . . girl? You're a brave one, daring to rob me. What shall I do with you? Hmm. Maybe I should let my soldiers decide that. Come." He hauled me to the doorway of his tent and flung back the door cloth. By moonlight and starlight and firelight, I saw Thutmose's cold, handsome face once more, and he saw mine. If I live to greet endless dawns, I will never forget the cold-blooded, gloating sound of his laughter, low in his throat, as he recognized me.

"Nefertiti." He pressed his mouth to mine hard enough to erase all doubt: It was a conquest, not a kiss. "Welcome home."

— 5 —

THE HUNTERS AND
THE HUNTED

He yanked me away from the door, back into the darkness of his tent, and shoved me to the floor. "Listen closely," he whispered. "I don't know which god I have to thank for bringing you here, and I don't care. Unless you popped out of the earth under this tent, you've seen where you are, less than a bowshot away from *my* soldiers. I'm going to light a lamp, and if you make *one* sound or try to take *one* step out of this tent while I'm doing it, all I'll need to do is shout *one* command and they'll have you. Understand?"

I nodded, then realized he probably couldn't see the gesture in the dark. "I do." My throat felt as though I'd swallowed a double handful of sand.

I felt a slight stirring in the air as he moved past me, then heard him curse as he fumbled for something. A brief while later, a spark in the darkness bloomed into a petal of flame and Thutmose's face showed clearly in the light. He set aside the small fire drill and lifted the oil lamp he'd kindled, bringing it to where I sat, unmoving, on the ground.

"Good girl," he said, patting my cheek hard enough to make me wince. "Now, then, care to tell me why you're here?" I bent my head and wouldn't answer, not even when he grabbed my chin and jerked it up, compelling me to look into his eyes. "Silence? Maybe you're only a dream. But, no, if you were a part of my dreams, you wouldn't look this bedraggled or smell so bad." He laughed at his own jibe, but when I refused to react to it, his mouth became a small, hard line.

"Why have you come here, Nefertiti? Giving up? And where is my brother? Your surrender's useless without his. I won't return to Thebes until I have both of you. He's supposedly the reason I'm out here. A royal son of the Black Land can't simply disappear into the night without the palace, the temples, and all the city calling for a massive search and pursuit. I should thank him for giving me the excuse to hunt my true prey. It's not the crown prince's business to chase down an escaped prisoner, even one condemned for blasphemy. If I declared openly that I wanted to go after you, not even my loyal Amun priests would accept that without questioning me. Me! When I rule the Black Land, they'll learn that only *I* will ask the questions." His eyes narrowed. "And I will expect answers."

I maintained my silence, watching the angry flush rising to his face, seeing his hands tighten into fists. I braced myself for the first blow.

With a loud meow, the same cat who'd startled me before came bounding out of nowhere to land in my lap. It was astonishing to hear such mighty purrs coming from such a lithe and slender body.

Thutmose's hands relaxed. His whole attitude softened, and he looked at the cat with the affection and tenderness I'd seen him give to only one other living being—Ta-Miu, the innocent she-cat I was accused of killing. I remembered the bloody bits of evidence that had been brought to my trial and felt sick at heart. Did Thutmose hate me enough to have given up the one creature he loved in order to see me killed?

"Well, Nefertiti, you seem to have a new friend," he said in a good-natured way. It sounded false. "Pretty, isn't she?"

"Very." I began to stroke the cat's back, to her delight. Then I scratched her neck under the fine gold and turquoise collar she wore. Thutmose's unknowable heart had found a replacement for poor Ta-Miu all too easily.

"Ah, a word at last!" Thutmose snickered. "I was afraid that you'd wandered into the savage Red Lands and the vultures ate your tongue. Is that what happened to Amenophis? Is that why you won't talk about him? He's dead. The fool risked his life to save yours and lost his own. What an idiot! And now you think you'll dodge the blame for his death by refusing to talk about it. You'd abandon his unburied body like a mongrel dog's, starve his souls, deny him his place in the afterlife, just so you can—"

"He's *alive.*" I spoke softly, but in truth I wanted to shout those words in Thutmose's face. I didn't dare, not with his men outside. "And I would never abandon him, *never,* alive *or* dead."

The momentary glimpse of a kinder, more human

Thutmose vanished. "It's true, then. You love him. You insulted me, cast me aside, refused to help secure my path to Father's throne, and all because you love him."

I could have denied it. The words *He's only my friend and nothing more* were halfway to my lips. I could have spoken them. I'd said them before, so easily, so simply.

For the first time, I couldn't.

I looked Thutmose in his hate-filled, hurt-filled eyes and said, "Yes. I love Amenophis. With all my heart, I do." The cat in my lap purred louder, as if she approved.

"Love . . ." Thutmose turned the word to poison. "It makes no sense. You're as beautiful as he is ugly. What can he give you? I will have the throne. I will wear the double crown. I will be the god-on-earth. He'll be nothing. Even if . . . if there were a way for your blasphemous crime against the goddess Bast to be erased and forgiven, if you were free to marry Amenophis, you two will still be outcasts. I'll see to that! Do you think I'd allow the worthless pair of you to lead royal lives once Pharaoh's regal crook and flail are in my hands? The Red Lands can have you both, forever."

"If that's what the gods decide for us—" I began.

"Don't you listen? It's already so. As god-on-earth—"

"Your royal *father* is the god-on-earth," I said firmly. "Are you as eager for his death as you are for your brother's?"

My words struck Thutmose hard. I saw a flash of remorse in his expression as he realized what his rash words implied. "I didn't . . . I didn't mean it that way. I don't want anyone dead," he murmured. "Not even you, Nefertiti. Not even after all the ways you've hurt me. All I ever wanted was to have you for my wife, the way Mother had it all planned, but you spoiled everything. Why did the gods ruin such a beautiful creation by filling it with so much defiance and stubbornness? They're as much to blame as you for making me treat you this way."

Did I see tears in his eyes? Did that mean there was still hope for him? I knew very well that the royal palace could be a woefully unhealthy home for its children. Its high walls and countless rooms bred plots the way rotten meat bred flies. Thutmose's mind carried the scars of always living in the shadows of uncertainty, fear, and suspicion. Aunt Tiye hadn't helped matters by raising him to think he could only be Pharaoh or nothing. If he could be reclaimed even now!

I leaned forward to offer him a comforting touch, but before my hand could reach his, the little cat decided I ought to be using it to pet her some more. She slid her sleek head under my palm and butted it so imperiously that I had to smile.

You are *Bast's true daughter,* I thought as I stroked her head. She closed her eyes in bliss when I massaged her whiskery eyebrows with my fingertips. *May the goddess give you a safer life than poor Ta-Miu.* As if she could read my thoughts, Thutmose's new pet gave a small mew and pushed her head against my hand again, harder.

"I believe you, Thutmose," I said gently while I rubbed the cat's head. "You do care for your family; you don't want to lose them. Neither do I. We're kin, remember."

"Kin who keep secrets from one another," he responded glumly. "You wouldn't even tell me if my brother was alive or dead."

"That's because I thought you wanted him dead. I was afraid that if I gave you any bit of information, you'd use it to hunt him to his doom. I was wrong; I'm sorry. You want to know why I came here tonight? To save him. Listen." And I told him about how Amenophis had been stung by the scorpion and now lay sick and feverish. What I didn't tell him was where his brother lay. My heart believed that Thutmose held no life-threatening grudge against Amenophis, but my mind whispered, *Remember Set! Tread cautiously,* and I heeded the warning.

When I was done speaking, Thutmose raised one eyebrow. "Honey?" he said, bemused. "That's all you wanted?"

"To fight the infected sting, yes," I said. "Do you have any?"

"Of course." He nodded at the wooden chest. "I have a casket of such things in there, packed toward the top. You'd have found it and been long gone if I hadn't heard that scuffle you had with *this* little demon." He reached out his hand to pet the cat, and I drew back my own hand to let him.

Then I drew a sharp breath. My fingertips were stained brown, and in the place where I'd been rubbing the cat's head, a patch of smudged white fur was now visible. The edges of the blaze were still obscured by whatever stuff had been used to conceal it until this moment, but I could see enough of it to recognize the shape of a star.

"Ta-Miu!" I was so dazed that I could hardly speak that name above a whisper. The little cat lifted her pointed chin as though acknowledging this startling truth.

I turned a furious face to Thutmose. "This is Ta-Miu,

isn't it? She's not dead. She was never killed, never even harmed!"

"You sound disappointed," he replied coldly. "Do you think I'd let anything happen to my dearest one?" He scooped the cat from my lap and held her close, whispering loving nonsense in her ears.

The full meaning of what I'd discovered fell over me like a mountain of sand. I felt that I was about to choke on my rage. "You knew this," I rasped. "When you pretended to feel pity for me at my trial, when you listened so earnestly to the false testimony brought against me, when you so *reluctantly* let me be condemned to death for killing Ta-Miu—through all of that, you knew that there was no crime. There never had been; Ta-Miu was alive, unhurt, and hidden away so that you could use her 'death' to destroy me. And *you* would rule the Two Lands? Ma'at forbid it—that would be the real blasphemy."

Thutmose dropped Ta-Miu and slapped my face so hard that I almost knocked the lamp over when I sprawled on the floor. He snatched it out of the way and held it high. "Ma'at doesn't listen to a grubby little upstart who doesn't even know how to act like a *real* woman. So you've discovered my secret; so what? All I need to do is hide her away again. Your accusations won't be anything more than the terrified raving of a condemned criminal. Your word against mine, the word of Pharaoh's heir?" He laughed.

I sat up on my knees and bowed my head. I knew he was right. In that moment, he held all the power. I was his captive. All I had left to sustain me were words.

Slowly I raised my eyes and looked around the tent. Was this going to be my new prison until we started back for Thebes in the morning, or was he going to summon one of his men and have me tethered outside, like an animal? The oil lamp's flame revealed more of Thutmose's hunting gear than I'd been able to make out in the dark. There was the bed and the chest, but now I could also see several smaller boxes stacked against the other wall, and the prince's magnificent bow and quiver full of arrows propped in one corner. A low-seated folding stool was set beside the small, round table near his bed. A goatskin bag for carrying drink lay beneath it, and the remains of Thutmose's evening meal were still scattered on the tabletop.

"More silence?" he snapped at me, lowering the lamp. "I'm tired of these games. What are you staring at?"

"Food," I answered honestly.

"*That's* what's on your mind? Not your life, not your fate, but *food*?"

"You've made it quite clear to me that my life is over and my fate's decided," I replied evenly. "Why shouldn't I think about food? I'm hungry."

He snorted. "Leave it to Amenophis to carry you off in a grand, romantic escape and never think about providing for you. Did he think you could feast on love?"

"He brought food," I said. "We lost everything in an accident on the river."

Thutmose sauntered over to the little table, set down the lamp, and gathered up the remains of his meal. He was probably going to toss them at me as if I were a begging dog, but some remnant of kindness in him made him reconsider. Instead, he opened one of the small boxes and took out a stack of flat, heavy breads. "Here." He let them tumble into my lap. "You probably would have eaten the *honey* instead of bringing it to my brother."

He crossed to the big chest and took out the casket he'd mentioned. I stuffed pieces of bread into my mouth as I watched him kneel beside me to unpack rolled strips of linen bandages, tweezers, and a flint-bladed knife. There was also an assortment of stoppered clay jars and flasks, their contents marked in the wax sealing them. He picked up the one labeled *honey* and held it out to me. "You might as well," he said.

"What are you talking about?" I looked at him suspiciously.

"You might as well eat it. Go on. It won't turn that bread into honey cake, but it's still good."

"Is there more?" I eyed the now-empty casket and scanned the clay containers, but their markings showed that they held other remedies—coriander, paste made from willow bark to ease pain, henna, poppy juice to bring sleep, several flasks of the same castor-bean oil that was now burning in the clay lamp. "You're making fun of me, Thutmose. We need this honey for Amenophis."

"No, we don't." Thutmose's face was unreadable. "I've been thinking things over, Nefertiti. What good will it do to bring my brother back to Thebes? He rebelled against the lawful decision of Pharaoh's justice. All your fault, of course, but that doesn't change the fact that he's a traitor."

"For what? For helping me live long enough to prove my innocence?" I lunged forward so suddenly that Thutmose jerked back. My hands hit the ground painfully hard, one worse than the other. The fat handle of the small flint knife made a hard lump under my palm. "Your parents won't stay in Dendera forever, Thutmose."

"They won't need to," he shot back, struggling to recover his dignity. "You'll prove nothing to anyone. The river will have you before my boat reaches Thebes, and the underworld will have my brother. A shame that my men and I won't be able to find him." He smiled at the evil lie.

"You said you didn't want his death!"

"I don't. My heart is pure, free of his blood. I won't touch him."

"No, but you'll leave him to die in pain, from fever and infection."

Thutmose was unmoved. "Better that than to die a traitor's death. You see how much I care about my brother? I'm only doing this to spare him."

I couldn't take my eyes off Thutmose's face. There wasn't a hint of sarcasm in his voice or his features. *He believes what he's saying,* I thought, aghast. *He believes it. His mind's become as twisted as a knot of serpents. Lady Isis have mercy on him!*

"Aren't you afraid I'll tell the soldiers where to find their prince?" I asked in a low voice.

"Their *prince* is here," he said haughtily. "And if you say one word to them about Amenophis, you'll regret it."

"I can't be condemned to *two* deaths." I defied him to argue with that.

"One for you." He drew out the words, savoring them. "One for your family."

My hand curved protectively around the flint knife. It was so small, so very small, a blade meant for delicate work to save a man's life. Yet it was also big enough to end one.

Could I do it? I thought. *Could I use this knife against this twisted, miserable boy, spill his blood, kill him? He's wanted to kill me for a long time. He'd kill my family without a second thought. He talks so casually about leaving his brother to die! No. I can't do it. It would make me as bad as he is. Worse than he is: My mind is clear and sound. I wouldn't even have the excuse of madness.*

But I must do something, or his madness will become a wildfire that consumes all that I love.

"You win, Thutmose," I said. "I won't tell your men about Amenophis. If the gods are kind, he'll recover from his fever and return to Thebes on his own. I'm only sorry I won't be able to see your face on the day he comes back to court and tells Pharaoh everything."

"Pfff! Everything? Nothing. Without proof, his words will be no more than the rantings of a lunatic. His actions will only confirm that. Running away with you—"

I grabbed one of the flasks of castor-bean oil and smashed the clay neck with the hilt of the flint knife. With one smooth motion, I cast the contents over Thutmose, and before he could react, I did the same with a second marked flask. He was gaping as I dashed past him, but he still retained enough presence of mind to try to stop me. I jabbed his hand with the knife. The wound would be small but enough to keep him at bay until I reached my goal.

"Look at me, Thutmose," I said grimly, holding the

burning oil lamp in front of me. "I want you to look into my eyes so that you know I'm not afraid of you."

"You're not afraid; you're crazy," he said with disgust, cradling his bleeding hand. "My men will—"

"You won't call them." I took a step closer to him. "If you do, I swear by every god that lives, I'll set this lamp to your oil-soaked clothing and skin. I'll do it! You'll be in flames before the first soldier comes through that doorway."

I glared at him, striving to look as menacing as possible. He had to believe that I'd fulfill my threat. I had to make myself act as though I'd turned into a creature as heartless as he, or everything would be lost. *O Thoth, lord of wisdom, sometimes you use your powers for trickery, too. Lend me your divine skill to mislead my enemy! Turn my face into a mask of ruthlessness as frightening as Thutmose's own!*

Thutmose's face paled. He held up his hands in surrender. "All right, Nefertiti. Go in peace. I won't try to stop you. Take the honey, take bandages for my brother, take anything you like."

"I'm not a fool, Thutmose," I said. "If I leave you like this, I won't have gone twenty steps before you rouse your men." I waved the lamp at the remaining jars and flasks from the medicine casket. "Pick up the poppy juice," I told him.

It took him some time to find the right jar. He couldn't take his eyes off me and had to keep picking them up, one after another, so that he could glance at the writing on the seals. Finally he found the clay vessel that held the sleeping potion. He scraped off the wax seal, removed the stopper, and raised it partway to his lips.

"How—how much should I take?" he asked.

I had no idea, but I hazarded a guess. "Two mouthfuls."

"Are you sure? Too much, and I might never wake up again."

I had the same concern. I didn't want him dead, just sleeping too deeply to call for his men. However, I couldn't let him know I cared if he lived or died. I took a step closer, brandishing the lamp. "I won't argue with you anymore, Thutmose. I'll just give you a choice: Drink or burn."

He drank.

The moments that followed left my nerves scraped raw. It seemed as if the poppy juice would never work or that I'd ordered him to take too small a dose. Then I saw his eyelids begin to droop, his whole body begin to slump.

"May I—please, may I—?" He nodded feebly to his bed. His words were slow and slurred. I nodded, and he lay down. I hovered over him, heard the rhythm of his breath, and just to be sure, I pinched his arm. He didn't stir. There could be no doubt of it: He was wrapped in the spell of sleep.

I put the lamp down and began searching all the chests in the tent as fast as I could. I took clothing, food, and half the contents of the medicine casket. My ragged dress was left in a heap on the floor, replaced by a pair of Thutmose's linen kilts that I fastened together to make a decent garment. Two goatskin bags went over my shoulders. I didn't know what sort of drink they held, but anything would be welcome. Just as I was about to steal away, my eyes lit on Thutmose's bow and quiver. As soon as I secured the arrows so that they wouldn't rattle against each other, I left.

I had no light to guide my steps as I made my way from Thutmose's encampment. I couldn't risk taking the oil lamp and having some restless soldier catch sight of it. I had to make do using the moon and stars and memory. Once I reached the canal, my road was easier.

I returned with the faint light that comes before true dawn. I found Nava and Amenophis where I'd left them, in the shelter of the ruined house. As soon as she heard me approach, Nava turned her tearstained face in my direction.

"Where *were* you?" Her mournful greeting tore my heart.

"I'm sorry, I couldn't help it," I said. "Will you forgive me? Look at what I have for you." I opened one of the sacks I'd stuffed with food from Thutmose's tent and filled her hands with bread.

While she ate, I knelt beside Amenophis. He seemed to be resting comfortably, and his skin was no longer flushed, but I had to lay my hand on his forehead to be sure.

"Where were you, Nefertiti?" He half opened his eyes, and a wisp of a smile lifted the corners of his mouth.

"Nowhere I want to go again," I replied. "Your brother's tent."

"What?" Now his eyes flew wide open. "Is *that* where you went last night? Did you lose your mind?"

I told him the simple truth: "I wouldn't have gone if I'd had any choice about it. I was afraid that if I didn't find something to treat your fever and that scorpion bite, I'd lose you." I cocked my head and studied him closely. "Maybe I was too reckless. You seem better. You don't feel hot anymore."

"I have Nava to thank for that. I don't know what

helped more—all the cool cloths she kept putting on my head or all the prayers she offered to her god. You know, I asked her *why* her people had only one god, and she said she wasn't sure, but she thought it was because if a god was supposed to be able to do anything and everything, why would you need more than one?" He laughed. "She may have a point."

"Well, how powerful *were* her prayers?" I asked, looking down at his foot. I'd hoped for a happy surprise, but the swelling looked no better and daylight let me see the deep purple discoloration surrounding the sting. I could hardly stand the sight of it.

"Oh, Amenophis!" I cried in sympathy. "Can you move it?"

"Yes, but I'd rather not. Last night when I *had* to get up to—you know—I accidentally put a bit of weight on it. The next thing I knew, the whole world flashed white, then red, then black. I must have fainted, because I woke up with Nava dribbling water all over my face."

I wanted to throw my arms around him and beg the gods to let me share half the burden of his pain. *And how will an outburst like that do him any good?* I asked myself. *He'll just feel guilty for having caused you so much grief. Forget tears— do something useful.*

I planted my hands on my thighs. "We'll have to do something about that. If we're not far away from here soon, Thutmose will catch up to us. I wasn't thinking about covering my tracks when I came back here, and if any of his men are good hunters, they might be able to pick up my trail. Nava!"

"Mmph?" The Habiru child answered me around a mouthful of bread.

"Please bring Amenophis something to eat, too, and let me have those goatskin bags. If we're fortunate, at least one of them is full of wine. I remember Mother using that as well as honey to clean wounds."

I gave thanks when I discovered that though the larger of two goatskins held watered beer, the smaller did hold wine. Together, Nava and I bustled about, assembling all the rest of the things I wanted to use for treating Amenophis's sting.

When we were done, his foot was clean and comfortably swaddled in linen bandages. He regarded it with a wry smile. "It's too bad that only men can serve as embalming priests in the House of Beauty. You've done a marvelous job of wrapping my foot."

"Don't praise me until you've tried putting weight on it again," I said. "The people brought to the House of Beauty are all done with feeling pain. Here, put your arm around my shoulder and let's see."

With me helping him stand up and Nava helping him keep his balance, Amenophis took a few tentative steps before joyfully declaring that his foot no longer hurt.

"Well, not *too* much," he added when I asked him to swear to it. "But it's really much better. I can walk on it, I promise! And you don't need to support me like this; I can get around on my own."

"I hope you're right," I said as Nava and I lowered him to the ground. "We'll leave this place as soon as we've eaten."

"Now? But it's almost full daylight."

"Your brother knows we're near. It's no use trying to hide from him anymore. Now we have to outdistance him."

"Then should we waste time eating when we should be moving?"

"I think—I hope—I bought us enough time for this meal. Thutmose's hunters won't come after us until he commands them, so unless he gives them orders in his sleep, we're safe."

Amenophis looked doubtful. "Look at the light, Nefertiti. Thutmose must be awake by now. My brother has never slept late in his life."

"He will this morning," I said with a self-satisfied smile. And while we enjoyed our first adequate meal in days, I told Amenophis and Nava what had happened in Thutmose's camp.

"Would you *really* have set him on fire, Nefertiti?" Nava asked, her eyes as round as drinking cups.

I could not lie. "I don't know. I would never *want* to do something like that to any human being, but when so much was at stake and I had so few choices . . ." I sighed. "I never want to face a decision like that again."

We finished eating and took stock of our new supplies. Nava and Amenophis were happy to have clothing that wasn't half dirt, half rags, though it took some clever folding and tying to get one of Thutmose's garments to fit Nava. Once she was outfitted, I sent her to the stand of dead sycamores to see if there were any fallen branches that Amenophis could use for a staff. The only one that came close to being the proper length was still too short for him, but it would have to do.

"I'll be as curved as a shepherd's crook if I lean on this too long," he joked as he tried it out.

"Do you want me to look for a different one?" Nava asked eagerly, and scooted away before we could stop her.

"I don't think you'll have to worry about getting a bent back from using that staff," I said. "You can't walk very far, even with something to lean on."

"You're right." His face fell. "Nefertiti . . . I think you and Nava should go on alone."

"What? No!"

"I mean it. If we stay together, I'll hold you back and my brother will catch us all. But if you leave me behind, you'll have a better chance of reaching my father. He's the only one who can help you against my brother. Don't worry about me; I'll get myself to Thutmose's camp and turn myself in. The official reason for his search is to find me, right? Well, once he has me, that's that; he'll have to go back to Thebes."

"Thutmose believes there's nothing he *has* to do except have his own way in everything," I countered. "He'll find some excuse to continue the hunt, and if he has you"—I closed my eyes—"he has me."

"What are you say—"

"Nefertiti! Amenophis! Look what I found!" Nava's high, sweet voice demanded our attention. The Habiru girl came running toward us with a small, familiar creature bounding playfully at her heels.

"Orow!" Ta-Miu declared as she outdistanced Nava and leaped to the top of one tumbledown wall.

"Bast witness this, she must have followed me!" I cried. "Why would she do that?"

"You're nicer than the bad prince," Nava said. "She knows that."

"Rrrr." Was that the cat's way of telling us she agreed with the child?

"Not even the priests and priestesses of Bast can explain why cats act as they do." Amenophis scratched Ta-Miu on the white blaze marking her brow. The star shape was much sharper; the cat must have been washing herself. "But I think Nava's right. This is good, Nefertiti. If we have Thutmose's cat—the cat you 'killed'—we have the proof that will clear your name and make my brother pay for all his wrongdoing. It's no longer just our word against his."

I stood beside him and rested my cheek on his shoulder. "This is a sign from the gods. They've sent us Ta-Miu to help us restore Ma'at's balance of truth when we speak to Pharaoh. If you let Thutmose have you now, it's the same as throwing the gods' gift back in their faces."

He bent his head over me, and I felt his breath on my hair. "I can't walk fast or far until my foot has healed. It will be my fault if Thutmose catches up to us and we lose Ta-Miu. Won't that be the true waste of the gods' kindness? Are you so sure this gift is meant for us, Nefertiti?"

"Amenophis . . ." I turned my head so that there was only a fingertip's breadth between our faces. "Amenophis, I—I feel—" Why couldn't I tell him the words that had come to my lips so readily when I spoke to Thutmose? *I love Amenophis. With all my heart, I do.* He had been the awkward one when we'd first met, but now it was my turn to be gawky, clumsy, tripping over my words the way he used to trip over his own feet. *He's grown up since those days,* I thought. *He's more sure of himself, less timid, more—more of a* prince. *And I'm the timid one. Dear Isis, why is it so hard to say such simple words as* I love you? *If Amenophis has found the way to be bolder, why can't I?*

But all that I could manage to do was turn my head away from him again and say, "If it was meant for me, it's meant for us. I won't accept it any other way. If you can't travel fast or far, then we'll have to choose a path that offers us plenty of places to hide from Thutmose until you're fully healed. *Then* we'll race to plead my case before your father."

He rubbed his chin. "Places to hide . . . I might have an idea about that." He sounded confident, but his expression was uncertain. "Not even my brother would imagine us taking refuge there. You're right: The important thing is that we keep Ta-Miu with us."

I clasped his hand. "The important thing is that we stay together."

— 6 —

THE SERVANTS OF BAST

This is not a tomb, I told myself as I sat with my back to the cool stone wall and looked out over the deserted, moonlit landscape. *It's* not. *It's a cave, an ordinary cave, not something made by human hands, not a sacred place, not consecrated to the dead.*

It was the same recitation I made to myself every night since we'd come here, to a place so close to the great valley of tombs that it might as well have been a part of that august royal burial ground. I don't know why I felt the need to go through such a ritual. There was no need to convince myself that we'd taken refuge in a cave and not . . . elsewhere. We *were* in a cave—that was Ma'at's own truth. We would never have committed the sin of trespassing on a tomb, even if it was one that was still under construction or, worse, one that had been despoiled by thieves.

But the place of the royal tombs cast a long, invisible shadow. It was impossible to turn my eyes in that direction and not picture what lay hidden there. The dry riverbed valley where so many of Amenophis's ancestors were at rest drew my imagination with its mysteries and made my heart tremble in awe. The steep, rocky paths that climbed its cliffs wound their way past an unknown number of hidden burials. The bodies of kings, princes, men of power, and their families were preserved for eternity in carved stone rooms piled high with all the luxuries and treasures they would need to enjoy the afterlife. Their safety had been guaranteed by generation after generation of priests who sealed those tombs with potent spells and curses on anyone impious enough to break those seals and take those treasures. The whole valley seemed to echo with all of the threats and warnings that had followed the royal dead into the heart of the mountains.

This is not a tomb, I repeated over and over again in my mind. *Isis, shining goddess, you are my witness: We've done no wrong in coming here. We'll be gone as soon as Amenophis is well enough to travel again.*

But when would that be? We'd reached this cave two days ago, after a fear-driven march. None of us had slept well on the road. Amenophis pushed himself too much, trying to get us away from the flat land surrounding the abandoned house, away from the possibility of Thutmose's guardsmen spotting us too easily. A healthy man would have found the pace tiring, and Amenophis was still sicker than he'd admit. He didn't speak up when his wounded foot began hurting more and more. He wouldn't let me touch him, not even to hold his hand, for fear that if his fever had come back, I'd discover it. Now he lay stretched out on the floor at the back of our cave, drained to the bone. I heard him toss and turn, groaning in his sleep, and covered my face with my hands, feeling helpless.

"Nefertiti, are you crying?" Nava squatted in front of me and leaned against my updrawn knees.

"No, dearest," I said, looking up. "I'm just tired. See? No tears."

She glanced back into the cave. "I think he's getting better. His foot's not swollen anymore, and it's the right color." She looked at me. "So why won't he get up?"

"I don't know. It could be that he just needs to rest more. He needs to rebuild his strength." I remembered the scrawny boy I'd met in the royal palace. Amenophis had the look of someone who'd been battered by childhood illnesses. He'd already shown that he could be as strong and commanding a presence as his brother, but the ghost of past ailments lingered near him.

I stood up and walked into the cave. We had no light because we had no fuel in this barren place, so I had to feel my way and do my best to remember where I'd stored our things during daylight. I located our last bag of provisions by touch. The only food we had left of what I'd carried away from Thutmose's tent was some bread that was now as hard as the rock walls around us. What would become of us if Amenophis still couldn't move after the last crumb was gone? The goatskin bags had been drained days ago, refilled when luck led us past a natural stream, and now were nearly empty again. I'd put them near the mouth of the cave, next to Thutmose's bow and quiver so that they'd be easy to find, but I had no idea where to look for more water.

"Murrr." Ta-Miu wound her sleek body around my ankles in the dark. The cat was the only one of us who seemed to have no worries about finding another meal. For a pampered pet who'd been born and raised in a palace, she was quite the talented huntress. Whenever she left the cave, she always returned with some luckless rodent in her jaws. Sometimes she even laid the bodies at our feet, as if trying to teach her hunting skills to a trio of very stupid kittens. *Why do you furless fools sit there looking so hungry when the world out there is full of all this wonderful food? Go on! Get it! Do I have to do everything for you?*

"It may come to that, Ta-Miu," I said, stroking her back. "How many jumping mice would you say I'll have to pounce on to feed all of us, hmm?"

"Less than you think," Amenophis called from the deeper darkness. "You can have my share."

I crawled toward the sound of his voice. "If I do resort to catching mice for our meals, you'll eat them," I said, finding his hand in the darkness. "The only thing wrong with you now is hunger. If a diet of mice is what it takes to cure you, I'll feed them to you with my own hands."

"Yes, O Hathor, great healing goddess. You speak and I obey."

"You shouldn't mock the gods, Amenophis."

He sighed. "You're probably right. We can't afford to have them angry at us. I was only joking, but if I've offended the lady Hathor, I'll make a generous offering when I ask for her forgiveness."

"It sounds as if you're offering her a bribe." A trace of

bitterness touched my words. "And if the servants of Hathor are anything like your brother's tame Amun priests, they'll be happy to tell you the exact price that will buy the goddess's pardon." I clicked my tongue, tsk-tsking impatiently. "Sometimes I wish I worshipped Nava's god. All she has to offer the One is song, but that seems to be enough."

"It would be more pleasant to visit the shrines without feeling like we were entering the marketplace," Amenophis admitted. "Still, Nava's god is very strange. We spoke about the One while you were in Thutmose's encampment. She says her people don't have images of him because he doesn't even have a face."

"The Aten has no face, either, only the burning disc of the sun. Does that mean we shouldn't give thanks for the light?"

"I'd give thanks for some light now." Amenophis sounded downcast.

"Why don't you promise the Aten a gift greater than anything that's ever been given to the other gods?" I joked. I couldn't light our refuge, but I could lighten the mood. "If this cave fills with sunlight, we'll know the priests are right: The only way to reach the gods' ears is to fill their laps with offerings."

"*Now* who's mocking the gods?" The sound of Amenophis's chuckle made me smile. "But the priests might be right. My family builds huge temples to glorify the gods; we heap their shrines with treasure. Nava's people offer only words of prayer and songs of praise. Tell me, Nefertiti, who rules the Black Land." He was too good-hearted to say *And who lives here enslaved?* but he must have been thinking it because he added, "How powerful can one lone, faceless god be?"

"Only you could turn our talk from mice to gods," I said.

"Ah, so you've uncovered my scheme to distract you. Now I'll have to eat mice after all. Don't forget to skin them first. We can use the hides to make you a nice pair of sandals."

I laughed. "You always know how to cheer me, Amenophis. No wonder I love you."

"What?" His startled question echoed in the cave.

Oh, gods, how had *that* slipped out of my mouth? I wasn't ready to say such things to him, not yet! Not yet!

"If you won't eat mice, I guess I'll have to find you something else, you ungrateful thing." I chattered like a stork clacking its bill, trying to bury his question in a rockslide of words. "You have to eat much more than bread if you're going to be able to walk out of here. We need more water, too. I'll have to find a source. Maybe I ought to watch Ta-Miu and follow her wherever she goes. She could lead me to more prey than mice. Would you stoop to eat a lizard, O great prince? Think about it because I might not give you a choice. Mmm, lizards . . ." I smacked my lips clownishly and scuttled out of the cave before he could say anything more.

Nava was sitting in the moonlight just outside the cave mouth with Ta-Miu in her lap, lost in her own thoughts. I bent forward to touch her shoulders. "What do you see out there, little one? Or are you dreaming with your eyes open?"

Nava misinterpreted my question. "Do I *have* to go to sleep now? The night's so pretty, and look at how the moon shines!"

"It is bright, isn't it?" I knelt and carefully poured the last of the water from one bag into the other, then slung the empty one over my shoulder. Thutmose's richly decorated quiver joined it. Last of all, I picked up the royal hunting bow. "Wish me luck, Nava."

"Where are you going?" Her voice went high with fear.

"Dear one, don't make this hard. I have to go. We need food, but we won't live if I don't find us some water. Don't worry, I'll be very careful and I won't get lost."

"You will if you go too far," Nava said mournfully. She made a sweeping gesture at the scope of the deserted landscape. It did look as if the barren hills went on forever.

"Don't you trust me, Nava?" I asked with a confidence I didn't fully feel. "If I could find my way through the royal palace, a few trails won't confuse me. If I wonder which way to go, I'll climb to the top of the nearest cliff. I won't be able to miss spotting this cave from up there."

"In the dark?" The child was unconvinced. "We don't have a fire. How will you see us?"

"Look, we have two fires." I indicated the green glow of Ta-Miu's eyes.

Nava was a smart girl and refused to be sweet-talked, but I couldn't argue the matter with her anymore. Putting on Aunt Tiye's air of command, I told her that whether or not she believed my promise to return, I *had* to go. "I *will* find my way back," I told her. "Because I'll know that *you* will be waiting."

"And Amenophis," Nava added.

"Yes. Always." Amenophis's voice sounded low in my ear. I whirled around to face him. "I heard what you said, Nefertiti," he told me. "I only said 'What?' because I wanted—I *want* to hear you say those words again."

I set the hunting bow aside and let my arms slide around his waist and rested my head on his chest. It was the most natural thing in the world for me to do. "I love you." I couldn't raise my voice above a whisper. I felt as if the two of us were standing in the presence of something greater, more humbling, more mysterious than the Great Sphinx of my dreams.

"I can't—I can't believe it." The words rasped from his throat. "How can this be real? You're so lovely, and I'm nothing but— Ow!" He jerked to one side, and both of us looked down to see Nava's ferocious scowl. "Did you just *pinch* me?" Amenophis demanded.

"I had to," Nava told him. "You were going to say something stupid. I'm *happy* that Nefertiti loves you. Why do you want to ruin it with a lot of silly questions?"

Amenophis inclined his head solemnly. "Your words are wise and true, O little biting flea. I'm going to tell my father to make you one of his counselors."

"I accept," Nava said just as solemnly, and the three of us burst into laughter.

With a kiss from Nava on my cheek and an even sweeter one from Amenophis on my lips, I left the cave to find us food and water. I kept my word about walking carefully. I really had no other choice: My feet were sore from all of the marching we'd done to reach our hillside shelter.

Scratches and blisters crisscrossed and dotted the soles of my feet. I would have given the best jewels I owned for those mouse-fur sandals Amenophis had joked about.

At first I retraced the narrow trail we'd used to reach the cave, descending the hill. *If I can backtrack on this path, maybe I can find that stream again. We came across it the day before we found the cave . . . I think. Or was it two days' walk before that?* I paused and surveyed my surroundings. *I should be going uphill, not down,* I decided, tilting my head back to look at the top of the nearest cliff. *From up there, I'll have a better view. I might see some greenery—that is, if it would* look *green by moonlight.*

All of those days on the march had made me stronger. I wasn't even breathing hard when I got to the summit. The moon was not full but still shed generous light over the land. I remembered the story Mery told to Bit-Bit and me about how the moon was one of the eyes of the god Horus, the hawk-headed son of Isis and Osiris. It held less light than the sun because wicked Set had struck it cruelly when Horus fought him to avenge Osiris's murder.

O Horus, give me a hawk's keen eyes tonight! Let me see the way to bringing fresh water and food back to save my dear ones. I prayed from the heart, my arms and face raised to the starstrewn night sky.

What was that in the distance? I gazed into the silvered dark, and a cluster of squarish shapes drew my attention. I caught my breath: houses! They were houses! I hadn't seen them right away because they were small, humble dwellings built out of mud bricks. Even in daylight, their color would blend in with the land.

Who lives out here? I wondered. *There are no fields to plow, no crops to harvest. I don't know how far it is to the sacred river.* Then I remembered where I was: in the land of the dead, where the rulers of the Black Land needed workmen close at hand to create and adorn their houses of eternity.

When I'd lived in the royal palace, I often heard two of my maids talking about their families. One of them spoke about a cousin of hers, a master painter whose wall paintings were highly prized: *"Pharaoh himself has commanded him to decorate the walls and ceiling of the royal tomb! We're all very proud of him, but it's such a shame that all his best work is sealed away. We were very close as children, so I miss seeing him, but he has to live across the river in the village of the tomb workers. I hear there are almost forty families out there, maybe more, and their houses are made of whitewashed brick, all very fine. Of course, when he's called to work on a wall painting, he has to spend his nights in—"*

—a simple house like one of those, I thought. *Not as fine as his home in the village, but closer to the valley of the kings.*

I started down the rocky slope, turning my steps in the direction of the houses. Would I find them occupied or empty? I prayed that the houses sheltered enough tomb craftsmen for there to be plentiful supplies of food and water on hand. I prayed even more fervently that there would be few enough workers around so that I could avoid them easily. How could I explain my presence if they discovered me? How would they react if I told them I was seeking food and water for Amenophis? "So you say Pharaoh's son is just on the other side of that hill, starving in a cave? Oh, yes, we believe you—that happens every other day around here!" They'd think I was a lunatic. Then they'd turn me in to the authorities. I had Thutmose's bow and arrows for protection, but how could I use them against innocent, honest men?

What other choice do I have except to be a thief? I thought sadly as every step I took brought me closer to the rough brown walls.

Shame at what I was about to do made me careless. I was less than ten paces from the doorway of the closest house when voices from just around the corner took me by surprise. They rang out loud and clear, though sometimes they went from low, threatening growls to sharp, indignant tones. I dropped into a crouch and listened attentively. There were at least three distinct speakers, all of them male. Should I try to get away before the speakers knew I was there?

"—beg of you, don't force me to do this! What you're asking is sacrilege. It will destroy my soul!"

I turned to stone, transfixed by the sound of that piteous voice. Then a reply came, and the casual callousness of the second speaker made the hair rise at the back of my neck.

"No one is forcing you to show us the way to Lord Iritsen's tomb, Samut. Go home and keep your soul pure."

"And what about my son?" Samut wailed. "What about my precious child? Where have you hidden him?"

"Keep your voice down, Samut. You'll rouse a witness."

Jackals' laughter filled the night. "What witness?" A third voice, nasal and shrill, sneered. "This place is deserted. The workers are all back in the village, waiting for their next round of tasks. Why d'you think we're here, having our little . . . *talk* with Samut?"

"Please—" Samut sounded on the point of tears or madness. "*Please* give me back my boy. His mother is dead; he's my only child. Listen, you don't need to rob Lord Iritsen's tomb. I have some jewelry and a gold image of Lord Osiris as big as my middle finger. You can have that. You can have anything else I own. Come into my house and take whatever you want, but please don't make me despoil the dead!"

"Did you hear that?" the nasal-voiced one cried with mock joy. "A gold statue as big as his middle finger! Who needs old Iritsen's rooms full of treasure if we can have *that,* hey? And you know how we're going to reward your generosity, Samut? We're going to give you what you want: You'll have your son back tomorrow." I could picture the ugly grin twisting the speaker's lips as he toyed with the heartbroken father. "Most of him."

"*Monster!*"

I heard a scuffle, curses, then a merciless beating, and Samut moaning with pain. Suddenly it stopped and the cold voice declared, "All right, that's enough. You don't teach a man to hold his tongue by breaking his jaw. If we snap his bones, who's going to show us the way to that tomb?"

"He wasn't the only one who worked on Iritsen's burial," the nasal voice whined. "Why don't we just get rid of him and his brat and find someone else to get us inside?"

"Because I don't want to waste any more time, that's why! You know how long it took to get that little boy to trust me enough so he'd come away peaceably? Hey, you! Samut!

I'll keep it simple for you: Either you come back here to-morrow night, ready to take us into Iritsen's tomb, or you can start carving out one for your boy."

I slipped into the shelter of an empty house as the four tomb robbers strode past my hiding place. When they were well away, I went looking for Samut. He was lying curled up on his side, tears pouring from his eyes, his face and body bruised and bleeding. One eye was already swelling shut, but he could still see me kneeling by him.

"Gracious Isis, why have you come for me?" he whispered. "Am I dead?"

"Nava, if you keep on eating like that, you'll get sick." I tried to take away the figs that the Habiru child had piled in front of her, but she threw her small body over them protectively and looked at me as if I were the most heartless person in the world. All her fuss disturbed Ta-Miu, who had been enjoying a piece of dried fish. The cat decided I was to blame for her interrupted treat and uttered a sharp, scolding mew.

"See?" Nava proclaimed. "Even Ta-Miu thinks you're wrong."

"Ta-Miu doesn't have to nurse you through a belly-ache," I replied.

"Let the little one eat." Samut sat cross-legged on the floor next to me and gazed wistfully at the child. "My boy loves figs, too."

Amenophis swallowed the mouthful of fresh bread he'd been chewing. "You'll share a plate of figs with your son again soon," he said. "You'll see."

Samut sighed. "You're a very kind person, young master.

You mean well, but what can you do? There are too many of them for you to—"

Nava tugged at my elbow and whispered, "Why is he calling Amenophis 'young master'? Does he know he's a prince? Did you tell him?"

"I didn't even tell him our names," I whispered back while Samut and Amenophis continued speaking. "And he hasn't asked."

Nava's brows knitted. "Isn't that strange?"

"He just might be the sort of person who respects another's privacy. He probably thinks that we must have a good reason for not letting him know who we are. It doesn't bother him too much because we've proved we're not enemies."

"Oh." The Habiru child nodded. "Because you took care of him, right?"

"I didn't do that much—just cleaned him up after that awful beating he got and bandaged a few of the worst scrapes. If he calls Amenophis 'young master,' he's just showing respect. You didn't argue about it when he called you 'young lady,' did you?"

She giggled and tried not to look *too* pleased with herself.

"—and I *am* strong enough to help you find your boy." Amenophis's voice rose, drawing my attention back to his conversation with Samut. "I'm in your debt for all this"—he indicated the food that Samut had given us so freely—"and I *will* pay it back! When you meet with those two vermin tomorrow night, I'll be waiting with that bow and pick them off. Osiris will be sitting in judgment over their hearts before another dawn."

"It's not that simple, young master," Samut said. "There are three of them, not two. They've hidden my child in a cave like this, somewhere in these hills, with their third partner holding him captive. He'll be watching from hiding tomorrow night when I'm supposed to meet the other two, back at the empty houses, and he'll have my boy with him. He'll only bring him out into the open once I've given those sacrilegious beasts what they want—the location of Lord Iritsen's tomb and help breaking into it. If an arrow were to come out of nowhere and kill one of that man's partners, my son would be—would be—" He covered his face and sobbed.

Amenophis laid one hand on the weeping father's back. "That won't happen, Samut. I'll find another way."

"*We* will," I said. "Whatever course we decide on to save Samut's son, I'll be a part of it."

Samut lifted his chin and spoke to me in a faltering voice. "Oh, no, my lady, I couldn't allow such a lovely girl to endanger herself!"

I smiled at him. "Not so long ago, you didn't think I was a girl, lovely or not."

He struggled to smile back. "If only you *were* Lady Isis. You could use your magic to make short work of those criminals."

"Yes, if only. Maybe that would teach them to fear the gods."

"Oh, but they do fear the gods, my lady!"

"Tomb robbers who fear the gods? They have a strange way of showing it," Amenophis broke in.

"It's true, young master." Samut bobbed his head. "You

see, I know these men. We grew up together, all of us the sons of tomb workmen. We were even friends once." He sighed. "But they chose a bad path and became notorious rogues. They went swaggering through our village, refusing to learn their fathers' honest trades, making fun of those of us who did. Finally they ran off, and the next any of us heard of them was word that they'd gone north, to seek their fortunes in Per-Bast."

"Bast's holy city? Why would they travel so far?" I asked.

"I don't know. Maybe it was the only way to outdistance some trouble they'd stirred up closer to home. Sometimes a traveler would bring messages to their families here— simple words, letting their mothers know they were alive and well—but when the travelers were asked for details, they always talked about how surprising it was to meet three men so devoted to the goddess of the city. My former friends might be criminals who scorn and defy the other gods, but they are Bast's devoted worshippers."

"That's not so odd," Amenophis said. "Lady Bast is a goddess of love and pleasure, but she's also a terrifying avenger of wrongs, like Sekhmet."

Nava gave me a puzzled look. She was still too young to know all the gods of the Black Land, so I explained, "Sekhmet is the goddess of war. You've seen her images. She's a woman with the head of a lion."

"And Bast is a cat, like Ta-Miu," Nava said, nodding. She stretched out her hand to scratch Ta-Miu's ears. "I wish you could go punish those bad men," she told the pretty creature.

Her words struck me like cold water dashed in my face.

My eyebrows shot up, my mouth fell open, and all I could say was, "Oh!"

Amenophis noticed and said, "Nefertiti, *what* are you thinking?" So I told him; I told everyone.

"No, no, my lady, you mustn't," Samut said, shaking his head violently. But there was a faint trace of hope in his voice. He was desperate for some way to save his son, and so far, what I'd suggested was the only plan that wouldn't worsen the child's situation if it didn't work.

My fate, if it failed, would be another story—a grim one—but I would take that chance.

"What other choice do we have?" I asked Samut. "And I won't be doing this alone. Each of you will have a part in it. I know I can rely on you." I looked at Nava. "Now the gods have entrusted all of us with the opportunity to save another life. I can't turn my back on it. Stand with me again, my friends." I stretched out my hands. "Please."

Nava was the first to leap up and grab my left hand. Amenophis got to his feet somewhat more slowly and took my right.

"You make it impossible for me to say no to you, Nefertiti," he said.

"You can always tell me no," I replied with a half-smile. "But I won't always listen."

"I wouldn't have it any other way. Now tell us what we have to do."

We worked hard all day, preparing ourselves for the night to come. Samut looked ready to collapse from exhaustion. It was his job to bring us the supplies we needed to make my plan succeed. He had to make several trips back and forth to his village to do so without raising questions among the other workmen and their families. We all knew the value of keeping things secret. No decent person would allow the violation and pillage of a tomb. If the villagers learned about the would-be robbers, they'd react without thinking and attempt an open attack. No need to guess what would happen to Samut's son then.

With this in mind, we were all startled to see Samut returning to our cave accompanied by a sturdy, plain-faced woman. He introduced her as Kawit, the sister of the nasal-voiced tomb robber.

"She's looked after my son many times since my wife died," he told us. "I'm very thankful for that." There was more affection than gratitude in his voice when he spoke about her. I wondered if she noticed. "She's the only one who thought to ask me about where he's been."

The woman snorted. "We live in a village full of people who care only about the doings within their own four walls. Of course I asked about the child! If I were married, I'd pray to the gods every day to bless me with such a sweet boy. And a fine answer I got, once I bullied it out of this one." She jabbed Samut with her elbow. "That brother of mine is the only family I've got left alive, but he's always been trouble. When he ran away with those nasty friends of his, I praised the gods. Now I hear he's back like *this*? To rob a tomb and condemn his heart to eternal death? I'll push him off a clifftop first!"

"You know we can't make any open moves against those men," I told her.

Kawit snorted again, louder and more eloquently. "You think I don't know that? Samut tells me you three are nothing but a bunch of deep, dark secrets. You're welcome to keep 'em, but you'd best know you're not the only ones with the wit to keep your mouths shut. Here." She was carrying a big basket that she now shoved into my hands. "He told me what you've got in mind. You'll be able to use what I've brought, and you'll use me, too, or I'll know the reason why!"

Oh, I *liked* her! "Samut's a lucky man to know you, Kawit," I said. "I hope he realizes that."

"Who cares?" she grumbled, but I saw her blush.

With an extra pair of hands, our preparations went much faster. Samut was free to go back to his home and rest so that he'd be completely alert for what awaited him. We were ready to set out well before sunset. Kawit led us from our cave on the hike into the valley of the dead. Our goal lay halfway up the side of one of the cliffs. It wasn't a formidable march—even little Nava was able to cover the distance easily while carrying a highly uncooperative Ta-Miu— though it was a struggle for Amenophis. He did his best to keep pace with the rest of us, but I could tell he was still weakened from his scorpion bite and forcing himself to go faster than was comfortable for him.

"Do you want to lean on my shoulders?" I asked.

He reacted as if I'd caught him committing a crime. "You have enough to do," he said, sweat beading his brow with every painful step. "You're carrying the bow and arrows *and* that heavy basket of firewood *and* a flask of oil; you aren't going to carry me as well."

"Stubborn," I snapped.

"Look who's talking," he snapped back.

"Are you two married?" Kawit's question slapped the two of us into embarrassed silence for the rest of the march.

Amenophis balked when he saw the place where Kawit brought us. "It's a tomb!" he cried, looking deep into the shaft cut into the cliffside.

"It's not a tomb yet," I said. "Not until someone is laid to rest inside."

"It's true," Kawit said. "And look, this one's hardly begun. The stonecutters haven't even started to carve out the chambers, only this entryway. It's nowhere near to being finished, not like the one being prepared for Pharaoh, may he live forever."

Amenophis looked pained. It must have been a chilling thought to realize he was standing in the valley where his own father would be buried. I didn't blame him for not wanting to think about such things, even if Pharaoh Amenhotep would ascend to eternal life among the stars. His son would still miss him when he was gone.

We went into the new tomb and settled down to wait. Kawit shared bread and fruit with us while the sky darkened outside. We'd kindled a fire at the very back of the passageway and laid out the torches we'd want for the night's work. We kept the blaze small so that its light could be mostly blocked. If the tomb robbers saw any sign to make them suspect our presence, it would be all over for us and, more importantly, for Samut's son.

When we finished eating, we each took our places for what was to come. Nava scooped up Ta-Miu and popped her into the covered basket Kawit had brought. The woven reed lid muffled the regal cat's yowls of indignation. Meanwhile, Kawit began painting my face.

"How do I look?" I asked when she was done. Earlier, with her help, I'd restyled my clothing, tying and tightening the fit of the fabric so that I looked as if I were wearing a sheath. Nava used the same paints that Samut had provided to turn the plain linen into an exotic display of stripes—red and blue and green—like nothing any ordinary girl would wear. My hair was adorned with the one piece of jewelry Kawit owned, a multicolored bead necklace. It wasn't costly, but the beads were large, shiny, and would catch the light nicely. "Do you think I'll be convincing?"

"Your face is all red," Nava said. "And your eyes look much bigger, like an owl's."

"Hmph! An owl wouldn't have such beautiful eyes, even ringed by all that red paint," Kawit said. "Don't insult my work. I learned from my father, and he was one of the best tomb painters ever. If there was any fairness in this world, I'd be able to do his job now that he's gone."

"You look . . . formidable," Amenophis said, gazing at me. "Beautiful, yes, but—"

"Formidable is much more important than beautiful," I cut in. "Especially tonight."

We all took our places. Kawit filled a small clay pot with embers and a cloth sling with precious wood to keep them alive. Nava followed her out of the tomb, carrying four thick sticks with rags bound to their ends, and I followed Nava to have one last look at the board where we were about to play out a most perilous game.

"Remember, we'll be keeping watch for them from up there," Kawit said, pointing to the top of the cliff directly above the mouth of the tomb. "We'll drop a handful of stones when we see them coming."

Once Nava and Kawit were gone, Amenophis and I had nothing to do but wait and sometimes check on how well Ta-Miu had settled into her basket. We sat together with our backs against the passageway wall and spoke in whispers when we spoke at all. We were too tense to exchange more than a few words, mostly small, nervous questions: Was I comfortable, was his foot bothering him, was that the sound of rocks falling or just our imaginations? When we actually heard Kawit's signal, the handful of pebbles she dropped to alert us to Samut's approach, it sounded as loud as if a monumental temple pillar had toppled to the ground.

"It's time," I said, groping for his hand and squeezing it. "Wish me luck. Better yet, beg Ma'at to forgive me."

"Why do you need her forgiveness?"

"Because what I'm about to do is either a lie or blasphemy or both."

"You don't believe that and neither should the goddess. We're fooling evil men to save the life of a child. If Ma'at can't see the good behind that deceit, how wise can she be? Good luck, Nefertiti." He planted a clumsy kiss on my cheek and then made a disgusted sound when he tasted the paint on my face. I smothered a laugh, but it broke the tension. I stood up, slung Thutmose's quiver over my shoulder, grabbed the bow with one hand, swept Ta-Miu out of her basket with the other, and waited just within the entrance of the tomb.

I saw three shapes coming across the valley floor from the direction of the workmen's temporary houses. They moved quickly, the one in the lead lighting the way with a small torch. I strained my ears to catch any trace of their conversation, but they maintained silence until they began the climb up the rocky path to where I waited.

Abruptly the torch stopped moving. "Hey! What do you think you're doing, Samut?" a cold voice growled. "Get going."

"Not until you let me see my son."

"We'll let you see him in *pieces* if you keep acting like a donkey."

"For all I know, he's already dead!" Samut cried bitterly. He was playing out the strategy we'd practiced. What courage it took for him to say those words! "If you want me to take you one step closer to Lord Iritsen's tomb, you'd better give me proof that I'm risking my soul for a good reason."

The cold voice chuckled. "Fine, why not?" I heard a shrill whistle from below, followed by the sound of a child's frightened scream. I paid sharp attention to the direction of that cry. The third tomb robber must have been trailing his comrades with the boy in tow, and he now lurked close enough to overhear whatever passed between them and Samut. "Good enough?" the cold voice asked. "Or do you want to see if we can make him cry *louder*?"

"No, no more, please. That was all I wanted. Tell me— I'm just asking; I don't want to make trouble—tell me, when will I *see* him?"

"When *we* decide." The cold voice fell like a mallet.

"Hey!" The familiar nasal voice of Kawit's brother. "What are you talking about? Weren't we going to give him back his kid as soon as he got us into the tomb?"

"Now you're on *his* side?" There was an unspoken threat in those words.

"No, but . . . come on, it's *Samut*. We used to be friends."

I could hear the scornful snort clearly on the night air. "You're an idiot. That's why no one asked you when we made our plans. It's been decided: He'll take us into the tomb, and then he'll wait until we've got what we came for, and *then* we'll let him have the brat back. Or do you want him taking the boy and running back to the village to sound the alarm? Do *you* want to die for this?"

Samut spoke up. "Please, there's no need to argue. All that matters is my son's return. Look there, up the slope. That's the tomb entrance. I came out here earlier today to break the seals so you can get in faster. We'll go on now."

We'll go on now. I cast a glance behind me to where Amenophis knelt beside our small fire. I hugged Ta-Miu to my chest and whispered, "Promise you won't leap out of my arms, my sweet one, and tomorrow morning I'll give you the biggest fish you ever saw." I inhaled slowly through my nostrils, offered a prayer to Isis in my heart, and sprang out of the tomb with a shout loud and wild enough to echo through the whole valley of the dead.

I felt a surge of heat at my back and knew that Amenophis had poured oil onto the fire. A cry from the slope below told me that the tomb robbers had seen the flare as well. Ta-Miu struggled in my grasp, but I held on to her firmly as I strode forward and struck a pose I'd seen many times in statues of great Sekhmet, showing the lion-headed goddess going forth to destroy the enemies of the Black Land.

"Oh, gods, what's that?" Kawit's brother's twangy voice was shrill with panic. He froze where he stood.

"I—I don't know." The one who'd spoken so callously to Samut was suddenly a fearful child again, shaking in his bed in the dark. I glared downhill, and he began to back away. "It looks—it looks like—"

I let Thutmose's bow drop to the ground and used both hands to lift Ta-Miu to the star-filled sky. The little cat yowled and hissed furiously. I heard some scrabbling from the clifftop and knew that Nava and Kawit had dumped the pot of embers onto the fuel they carried up there. With fire behind me, fire above, and a enraged cat in my hands, claws slashing the air, I let the full impact of my silent presence strike home.

"It's a demon, that's what it is!" Kawit's brother yelled.

"No, no, look! See what she has in her hands? A sacred cat!" The other would-be thief fell to his knees.

"I warned you!" Samut exclaimed, filling his own voice with a convincing note of pathetic terror. "I told you that we'd all suffer for your blasphemy! Didn't I carve the story of Lord Iritsen's life on the walls of that tomb? Didn't my own hands chisel out the curses that would fall on the heads of any who dared to disturb the rest of Bast's most beloved servant?"

On cue, I took another step forward and clasped Ta-Miu to my chest. From below, we must have looked like a sacred image of the goddess and her sacred creature. There wasn't enough light for the villains to notice how frantically the cat was squirming, and I held back the urge to yelp with pain when her claws dug into my skin through my garment. I lacked a cat's head to make the impression complete, but the red paint covering my face must have turned it into a bloody mask.

A chorus of blood-chilling yowls resounded from the clifftop and the passageway behind me. Nava, Amenophis, and Kawit were putting their whole hearts into their part of the performance. I saw the robbers shrink back and heard Samut undermining what was left of their courage with his own horrified whimperings. I wished that there was something I could say to urge them into flight, but it had been my idea that I stay silent unless it became absolutely necessary for the "goddess" to speak. A closed basket can hold a honey cake as easily as a cobra. Let the thieves' own imaginations and uncertainties feed their fears. I saw the wisdom of my plan working as the men continued to back away. The next step was Nava's.

The Habiru child's sweet voice rose in song from her hiding place at the top of the crag behind me. Her true talent was the harp, but she also had a gift for setting words to melodies. In this case, finding the right words was no challenge:

"Free him, free the child, return him to his father or feel the wrath of Bast, her curse, your doom! Your hearts will be torn to pieces by her claws; your bones will crack between her mighty fangs; she will devour their marrow; she will lap your spilled blood from the stones!" Somehow, hearing such horrible things set to delicate music, all sung in a child's innocent voice, made them infinitely more terrifying. "Free the child or the lady Bast will hunt you by day and by night. She will slash the flesh from your bones! Return him and leave this place, never to return, or she will turn your eyes into lumps of salt. She will burn your bodies to ashes in the fires of her fury. She will—"

Really, Nava was having a little *too* much fun. At least her taste for bloodcurdling stories had turned into something we could use.

And, oh, how well it was working! Kawit's brother began to blubber for mercy. His partner stood like a stone, teeth chattering. Samut continued to do his part to build the illusion, falling to his knees, prostrating himself, and begging "Bast" to spare him. Meanwhile, Nava kept up her litany of all the deliciously awful ways the "goddess" was going to punish the would-be desecrators of Lord Iritsen's tomb, interwoven with orders for them to release Samut's son and go away.

The thief who'd turned to stone was the first to crack. "Holy Lady Bast, compassionate one, have mercy, forgive me, and I'll do exactly what you say! This whole evil adventure wasn't my idea. I never wanted to come here and do this! I'm your devoted servant, your *slave.* I'll bring the brat—the boy to his father immediately, I swear!" He started to move in the direction from which the child's cry had come such a short time ago.

"What in Set's name do you think you're doing?" A new voice boomed in the night, and a burly man came out of the shadows dragging a small, weeping child along behind him by the arm. Samut's piercing cry of relief at seeing his son

alive and well was cut off abruptly when he saw the man put a dagger to the little boy's throat. "What's wrong with you stinking cowards? Here we are, about to get our hands on more treasure than you hollow-heads ever dreamed of, and you're shaking like dry reeds? Pissing yourselves on account of a *girl*? Are you crazy?"

"You're the crazy one!" Kawit's brother yelled. "What *girl* looks like that?" He gestured at me with trembling hands. "What *girl* appears in the middle of the night, in the land of the dead, with a sacred cat attending her? Her face in bathed in blood! She summoned up the fires of the sun!"

"Ha! Sounds like the fires of the sun cooked your brains, if you ever had 'em." The burly man sneered. "I see a girl and a couple of campfires. The gods know why she's got a cat with her, but—"

"The gods *do* know!" the cold-voiced man cried. "And I'm not sticking around to get punished for *your* stupid scheme." He sprinted away before the big man could say another word.

"And I curse the day I ever let you talk me into getting mixed up with this unholy business," Kawit's brother whined. "You've brought the vengeance of Bast herself on us! Let the boy go!"

"I don't take orders from mice." The third thief yanked Samut's son by the arm, making the child squeal in pain. Samut started toward him, but the dagger's point moved closer to the boy's neck and a warning hiss from his captor froze the father in his tracks. "If I don't head back to Per-Bast with a basketful of gold from that tomb, I'm leaving this valley over the bodies of this brat, his father, *and* that so-called goddess up there. You hear me, girl?" he shouted, turning his head sharply in my direction.

I dropped Ta-Miu before his eyes reached mine. As the cat leaped away, I swept one arm down to pick up the hunting bow, plucking an arrow from the quiver with the other. An instant was all I needed to pull back the bowstring, aim, and let the shaft fly. It whizzed through the darkness and struck him in the shoulder with such force that he lost his hold on Samut's son and staggered back, dropping his dagger. Samut snatched his child into his arms and ran.

"I hear you!" I shouted back at the writhing, sobbing villain who had dared to threaten a helpless child. "Now you hear *me*!"

-Part II-
DENDERA

~7~

A Prince in Dendera

With his son safe at home once more and back in Kawit's care, Samut summoned every able-bodied worker in his village to sweep through the surrounding countryside and capture the would-be tomb robbers. They found two of the three soon enough—the cold-voiced one was discovered hiding in a dry streambed, and the one I'd hit didn't get very far before the men tracked him down by following the scattered drops of blood from his wounded shoulder. Samut told us how the two of them had been marched off to Thebes for judgment.

Kawit's brother remained unaccounted for.

"She has him hidden in her house," Samut told us when he came to our refuge the next morning. "She's going to send him back north to Per-Bast as soon as they stop searching for him. I think that this time he'll try to make a different sort of life for himself once he gets there."

"He might succeed if he finds better companions,"
I said.

Amenophis wore a long face. "He's as guilty as the
others of abducting your son and of beating you. How can
you let him go free?"

Samut looked sheepish. "He was the youngest of those
three, and a weak-willed soul. Even when we were growing
up together, he was always too eager to be everyone's friend,
too willing to do anything in order to be accepted. And he's
Kawit's kin; she still loves him, even though she says she
wants to break his head open and stuff some common sense
into it. I can't stand the thought of how heartbroken she'd
be if Pharaoh's officers took him into custody. Let him have
a second chance, for her sake; that's what I say."

"It's *wrong*—" Amenophis began.

I laid my hand on his forearm. "It was Samut's son in
danger. If he can forgive Kawit's brother, can't you?"

We spent that day enjoying more of the tomb worker's
generosity. He brought us plenty of food and drink, as well
as a new dress for me, one that had belonged to his late
wife. There were even treats for Ta-Miu, the fish I'd promised her.

"I wish I could entertain you properly, in thanks for all
that you've done for my boy and me," he told us. "Why can't
you come out of this place and stay under my roof?"

"We have our reasons," I replied. "Please don't insist on
hearing them. I can swear by any god or goddess you choose
that we've done nothing wrong."

Samut bowed low. "Forgive me, my lady. I'm a fool who
puts his nose where it doesn't belong. Of course you've

done no wrong! I only asked because I yearn to do something more for you, to show my gratitude."

"Do you have a boat to take us to Dendera?" Nava asked pertly.

Samut had no boat, but he saw to it that we did soon enough. He left us on our own for most of the day, and when evening came, Kawit was the one who brought our food and more.

"Make yourselves ready," she said, setting down her basket. "My Samut—I mean, Samut has arranged for you to travel onward." The covered basket that held our evening meal also contained a razor, a container of kohl, and a tiny flask of scent.

I pounced on the kohl with a happy cry. The black powder was more than just a way to make our eyes look larger; it protected them from the glare of sunlight and kept insects at bay, too. "It's been ages since any of us painted our eyes! No wonder mine feel so tired. Come here, Nava, and let me do yours for you; then do you think you can do mine?"

"Allow me to do that for you, my lady," Kawit said. "But first, let me fetch some water and I will shave your head for you, young master." She inclined her head to Amenophis. "Samut regrets he doesn't have any fine clothes to give you, but if you smell important, people will treat you better." She handed him the vial of perfume.

"I couldn't take this from him." Amenophis raised his hands. We both knew how costly such a thing was and how precious the flower essences must be to our friend Samut. Why would a tomb worker spend his hard-earned livelihood on such a thing if he didn't pine to own it? Every human soul I ever knew was happier if he or she could find some small touch of beauty to adorn their lives—a jewel, a hair ornament, a brightly colored belt, or this dab of sweet scent. "And why would he think I'd need to . . . smell important?"

"You're going to Dendera, aren't you? Samut said to me there's got to be a reason for you three to head there now, when Hathor's festival's making the whole city rejoice. Folks feel more generous and forgiving at such times." She got a knowing, conspiratorial look in her eyes. "Maybe even the same folks who don't want you two to marry, hmm?"

Sweet Isis, she thinks we're love-struck runaways with disapproving parents! I thought. I was about to correct her when a second thought crossed my mind: *Oh, dear. That really isn't so far from the truth.* I could just imagine Aunt Tiye's reaction when she found out that Amenophis and I were more than friends. It was as if Thutmose's unfounded, jealous suspicions had been so strong that they'd become real. And what would my own parents have to say about it? If I ever fought my way free of Thutmose's false, vicious charge of blasphemy and could reclaim a normal life, how would Father and Mery react if I married Amenophis?

My cheeks turned hot. Marry Amenophis? Wasn't I rushing things with such childish dreams? He said he loved me, but the Black Land was filled with songs and stories about young men and women who fell madly in love only to go their separate ways when love faded away. How could I know if his heart yearned for us to be together always? I was building a future out of sand.

In the end, Amenophis accepted the gift of perfume to please the giver, and neither he nor I bothered to correct Kawit's romantic notions about us. We didn't have the opportunity. The sturdy woman let us know that we were going to be moving out of the cave, like it or not, in the dim time before the next morning's dawn. "Samut's been busy working for your benefit, running up and down the riverbank, seeking a boat whose master is willing to take on some passengers," she informed us as she scraped the stubble of travel from Amenophis's head. "It cost him his best necklace, the pretty blue one that he loves, but he was glad to do it. He kept talking about how you were the ones responsible for bringing him back his only *real* gem."

She paused and lowered the razor. Her eyes were moist with tears. "And that's true. You saved that sweet little boy, may the gods bless you forever. Samut's got a heart that's much too trusting. If he'd consented to help those ruffians on his own, he'd've done it believing that they'd give him back his son and leave them both alone after. But my brother told me that their ringleader—the pig you stuck so neatly with that arrow, my lady—he'd've murdered them both as soon as Samut gave him the way into Lord Iritsen's tomb. My brother told me he didn't want any part of that trickery—said that a bargain's a bargain—but he knew his leader well enough to know that any objections would buy his own death."

"An honest thief," Amenophis muttered ironically.

Kawit heard, and slapped his newly shaved skull. "You save that sharp tongue of yours for making a proper life for this pretty lady," she scolded. "She's much too beautiful to be dragged down by a man—a boy, more like it—who can't provide her with bread, or a roof over her head, or—"

"I pray daily that the time will come when I can give her all of that and more," Amenophis said solemnly.

He was a little too solemn. Kawit thought he was being sarcastic again and slapped his head a second time.

We said our farewells to Kawit that night and were roused from sleep the next morning by Samut's urgent summons. The grateful tomb worker led us away from the land of the dead, back to the lush verge of the sacred river. A medium-sized sailing vessel was waiting for us in the shallows. There were only five men on board, and they were already getting the ship set to sail. The master of the ship stood at the stern, supervising his crew. Samut hailed him and we were curtly ordered to come on board. Samut took Nava on his back, leaving Amenophis and me to wade out to the ship on our own. I had to tie up my new dress so that it wouldn't snare my legs. Samut's late wife had been a much larger person than me, so there was a lot of linen to get out of my way. It made clambering onto the ship difficult, but not impossible. Once I was aboard, I leaned over the side so that Samut could hand me the covered basket where Ta-Miu was once more curled up, sleeping peacefully while her human servants did everything to maintain her comfort. Then and there, I decided that if the gods ever allowed our souls to return to the world, I'd ask Isis to let me come back as a cat.

By the time the dawn was a pink and golden sliver in the east, we were sailing downriver, waving good-bye to

Samut. The voyage to Dendera didn't take long at all. We had the current on our side, an experienced shipmaster and crew, and the blessing of Hapy. If not for the fact that the ship was a merchant vessel that had to stop twice along the way to receive and deliver cargo, we'd have been in Dendera that same day.

As it was, we approached the dock of Hathor's favored city next morning, early enough for the air to be fresh and filled with the sounds of celebration. We heard the first strains of music, the clapping of many hands, and the clamor of voices raised in joyous song long before our ship was tied up and we were allowed to land.

"Just look at that," the shipmaster said, hands on hips, head shaking in disapproval. "Scarce three souls on the dock. No need to ask where the rest have gone. This festival makes the city crazy. Dancing in the streets, music, flowers everywhere, and palm wine until your head spins!" He frowned fiercely, then broke into a smile and winked. "I can hardly wait."

I turned to Amenophis and sighed happily. "*That's* a relief. All that fretting we did was for nothing. It looks like your brother didn't station his men around the city to keep us from reaching your parents after all."

"He might've realized he didn't have enough soldiers for the job," Amenophis replied. "Or else he tried it, but the lure of the festival was too much for them and they sneaked away. Whichever it was, I'm relieved. I had no idea how we were going to handle the situation if we had encountered them."

"Oh, that's easy," Nava asserted. "If anyone tries to stop

us, Nefertiti can stick *them* full of arrows, too!" She hadn't stopped crowing about my skill with the bow since the instant I'd saved Samut's child.

"Nava, I did not stick that man full of arrows, and I would *not* want to do that to anyone else," I said. "The only reason I shot him was to make him drop his dagger before he hurt the little boy."

"But you'd do it to save *us,* wouldn't you?" She appealed to me with her eyes.

"Only if there was no other choice. And today there is, so no one's going to be shooting anyone else, understand?" I gave her a crooked grin. "Don't look so disappointed."

Amenophis's mouth grew small with concern. "Let's not speak too soon. Thutmose might have decided that it's easier to keep us from reaching my parents by planting a fence of his men around them instead of around the entire city. If that's the case, what will we do? Try to sneak past them?"

I took Nava's hand before the overeager child could grab my bow and offer it to me. That was becoming her solution to everything. "No more of that, Nava. From here on, we're letting Amenophis have the bow and arrows. A girl carrying such weapons would attract too much attention in the city. I'm not going to use the bow, and we're not going to use stealth. Stealth wasn't what saved Samut's boy. We acted boldly then, and we have to act boldly now. A thief sneaks into the house he wants to rob, but the owner strides straight through the door. That's his right; he belongs there. He's *supposed* to go in! Who'd even think to stop him? And who's going to dare stop a royal prince from seeing his parents?"

Amenophis surveyed his travel-worn clothes ruefully. "I don't look all that princely."

"If your clothes don't tell people that you're a prince, act like one! Stand like one! Speak like one!"

Amenophis took Samut's perfume vial from his belt and dangled it before my eyes. "*Smell* like one?" he joked.

"If that's what it takes."

We thanked the shipmaster and his small crew for their kindness to us on the voyage to Dendera, then set out to find Amenophis's parents in the city. He'd taken my advice to heart and was no longer acting like just another polite young man. When he said good-bye to the shipmaster, he did it with such a regal air of command that the fellow actually bowed to him without thinking! My hopes rose. *If he can keep this up, we're sure to succeed. Let the whole city of Dendera know that a prince is coming to rejoin his parents, and no one will stand in our way, not even Thutmose's most loyal soldiers!*

"Let's go to the temple," I said. "That's where we'll find your parents. If they're not taking an active part in the rites, surely they'll be watching the priests make the offerings and listening to the temple musicians singing and playing to honor the goddess."

"Good idea," Amenophis said, nodding. "Even if they're not present at the ceremonies, they'll be staying at the guesthouse inside the temple grounds. It's a miniature palace, very luxurious. I remember that's where we stayed the time I came here as a child."

"Do you think you can lead us there, then?"

"Maybe." Amenophis sounded only a little doubtful. "It was years ago."

"You don't have to know the way," Nava said, cradling a purring, docile Ta-Miu in her arms. "If today is Hathor's festival, *lots* of people will be going to the temple. We can just follow them."

I laughed. "Leave it to you, Nava."

Nava was right, of course. If we were going to find Pharaoh Amenhotep and my aunt, Queen Tiye, Hathor's temple would be the place. Pharaoh was the god-on-earth by his own decree, a pronouncement he'd made to remind the priests that he was the ultimate authority in the Black Land. The so-called servants of the gods, especially the priests of Amun, had been growing more and more wealthy and influential over the years. Pharaoh's decision to name himself god-on-earth was his clever way of putting a leash on them, and they didn't like it.

What better place to find the god-on-earth than in the house of his sister-goddess Hathor at the time of her festival? He would show himself at his finest to the people of the city—clad in the richest garments, adorned with brilliant flashes of gold, wreathed with gracefully ascending trails of the sweetest incense from distant Punt—and the priests would be cast into the shadows.

It would also provide an effective distraction from the real reason that had brought Amenophis's father to Dendera, namely to seek Hathor's help in restoring his health. Pharaoh had not been well for some time, a fact that had to be hidden from everyone except his closest kin. The land was only as strong as the one who ruled it—everyone I knew grew up believing that. A weak pharaoh meant a weak land, a land where the sacred river failed to rise, the soil became barren, the crops refused to grow, and the people starved. It could also mean a land that would fall easy prey to the armies of our enemies. Pharaoh *must* stay strong!

But what would happen on the day when Pharaoh's strength failed for the last time and his spirit rose to dwell among the stars? Thinking about that ill-omened day made Aunt Tiye half mad with worry. It wasn't just that she loved her royal husband—she did, and would have loved him even if he hadn't been pharaoh—but also that when he did go to meet Osiris, who would rule after him? Aunt Tiye would sooner die than lose the power she wielded as Pharaoh's Great Royal Wife. If another woman's son somehow managed to take Amenhotep's throne when he died, that would be the end of Aunt Tiye's status. She was determined that this would *not* happen and that the next ruler of the Black Land *must* be her older son, Prince Thutmose.

Must and *must* and *must,* with never any room for argument because that was the way Aunt Tiye had decided things were going to be. She was a very determined woman. She took nothing for granted. The chances of Thutmose succeeding his father looked almost inevitable. Even though I had good reason to dislike him, I couldn't deny that the prince was handsome, intelligent, and fascinating. His father trusted him enough to have given him charge of governing Thebes in Pharaoh's absence, but Aunt Tiye wouldn't be able to sleep easily until the great red and white double crown of the realm was placed safely on her favorite son's head.

Her obsession with securing Thutmose's inheritance had been the source of all my own troubles. If not for her insistence on making me Thutmose's wife, this festival day would have found me at home in Akhmin with my sister, Bit-Bit. Together we'd be singing songs of praise to Hathor and draping her statue with flowers. Every so often we'd drop the tune to lick our lips as we imagined the wonderful feast my stepmother Mery was preparing for us. How we'd laugh if we caught one another doing that!

Instead, here I was in Dendera, pushing my way through the crowds of people choking the streets near Hathor's temple. It was very difficult breaking a path through so many merrymakers. Besides the goddess's sincere worshippers and those people using the sacred festival as an excuse for wild revelry, there were also all of the shopkeepers and street vendors eager to sell their wares. I couldn't tell if the man offering me a honey cake wanted to share a treat with a fellow worshipper in a friendly way or wanted me to buy it. The problem was, neither the merchants nor the ordinary celebrants would take no for an answer. Every step we took had to be fought for, as though we were wading through the thick, fresh silt of the riverside when the waters of the Inundation sank back, leaving their treasure behind. Arms waved all around us, like a bewildering thicket of windblown reeds.

I began to perspire from the effort of making any progress at all. Besides struggling to move forward, I had the triple distraction of keeping track of Nava, holding tight to Ta-Miu's basket, and trying to keep Amenophis in sight. He had taken my advice seriously and was carrying himself as if he were someone extremely important, someone to whom an ordinary city dweller should show reverence.

It's working! I thought proudly. *They're all falling back as soon as they see that commanding look in his eyes. He's like the old images of past pharaohs, the ones that show them trampling their enemies. See how wonderful he looks, how impressive, how— Uh-oh, how am I going to catch up?*

Amenophis had mastered my advice too well. He was far ahead of us. The person he was pretending to be was too important to bother looking behind him to see if we were still there. I'd noticed the same behavior among the nobles and other high-ranking officials in the royal palace at Thebes: They expected their slaves and servants to keep up with them no matter how fast the pace or how many parcels, scrolls, fans, stools, or other items their followers had to juggle. If they couldn't keep up, it would be their problem— and probably their punishment as well. But that wasn't any concern of the big, important man they followed.

Suddenly I was very glad that I had to *tell* Amenophis to behave like that. It wasn't a natural part of who he was. I called for Nava to stay close beside me, got a better grip on the cat's basket, and used my shoulder to shove our way after him.

When we caught up to him again, I was breathing hard and sweat was pouring down my face, my back, and my legs. "Slow down, for the love of Isis," I said, shifting Ta-Miu's basket to my other hip. "We almost lost you at least five times. All I can say is that it's a good thing you're so tall and that Kawit reshaved your head."

"Why, so you can follow the glare?" He grinned and ran one hand over his hairless skull.

As hot as I was, I began to wonder if I'd be happier with my head shaved, too. I loved my hair, but I could always get a wig. Nearly all of the palace women wore them.

"Very funny," I said. "And very true." We both laughed while the mob of singing, clapping worshippers swirled around us. "I think you should carry this for a while." I indicated the basket.

"What?" he cried in mock indignation. "The idea! A royal prince does not go through the streets carrying baskets."

"Then take Ta-Miu out and carry her in your arms," I said. "Holding a sacred cat will serve to make you look even more regal."

"Regal, scratched, and bleeding." He was enjoying himself. "But are you sure you want me to bother? Look, there's the main gateway to Hathor's temple. We're here!"

I made him wait a little longer before we approached our final goal. I wanted to inspect him, to be sure that we'd done everything we could to make him look like the prince he was. Aside from his frayed clothing, he had the bearing and presence of a prince. We were as ready as we were ever going to be.

We broke through the crowd massed before the temple gateway and marched in single file up to the men stationed there. By the looks of them, they were young priests, not soldiers, which gave me hope and puzzled me at the same time.

They aren't Thutmose's men! If he still wanted to keep us from seeing Pharaoh, this is exactly where he'd put them. Has he given up? Has he decided we are no longer a threat?

I shook my head. That seemed unlikely. Thutmose saw *everyone* as a threat. *Pharaoh gave his older son the authority to rule Karnak, to uphold the balance of Ma'at, but we're here to tell him that the prince used his power to* twist *justice, not to preserve it. Once I testify, once I show Pharaoh that Ta-Miu lives, it will prove that Thutmose isn't fit to rule the Black Land, now or ever. And then what will he have left? It will be the end of everything for him.*

I stood in Amenophis's shadow as he approached one of the priestly doorkeepers, drew himself up even taller, and looked down his long nose as haughtily as he could without bursting into self-mocking laughter. He was so effective at playing the part of someone with every right to enter the temple gates that the young priest began to bow to him at once, without bothering to take in the ragged, ill-fitting clothes or the wear and tear and grime of travel. I should have been happy, but all I could do was ask myself again and again, *Why is Thutmose letting us get so close to Pharaoh? Why isn't he trying to stop us anymore?*

Those questions were still echoing in my head when the young priest stepped to one side and motioned for us to enter the gateway. I could see the respectful, almost fearful look he fixed on Amenophis as he walked by without deigning to give the "lowly" doorkeeper even a passing glance. I, too, transformed myself into the superhumanly dignified "goddess" I'd played to save Samut's son and glided after Amenophis as gracefully and haughtily as I could. Nava came last, carrying Ta-Miu. I couldn't look behind me to check if the child was acting with the dignity of a prince's servant, but there was no need to be concerned: The cat had enough poise for them both.

Across the temple threshold, we found ourselves in a great courtyard where a smaller, more exclusive crowd stood in rapt attendance as a group of young women performed an intricate dance for the goddess. The jangle of sistrums blended with the singing of hymns to the goddess of love, motherhood, and joy. Hathor's statue gazed down at the dancers with her alluring, secret smile. A gold sun-disk was framed by the curving cow horns crowning her head, and the space between her feet was heaped with fragrant blue lotus blossoms. Trails of incense rose from burners surrounding her gorgeously carved image. It was all so entrancing, I nearly forgot to breathe.

"What do you think you're doing?" A harsh voice broke the goddess's spell. We saw a blustering, double-chinned man come bearing down on the young priest who'd let us in. His clothing was a richer version of the door-keepers' priestly garb. "Where do you think this is, your father's butcher shop? Is that why you let every stray cur in Dendera come in?"

"Lord, my father didn't have a—" the young priest began.

The older servant of Hathor didn't let him finish. A sharp slap ended his protests before he turned on us. "Get out of here, you chaff," he barked. "Leave before the righteous anger of Hathor destroys you for daring to set your filthy feet inside her holy house!"

"Watch what you're saying, Djau," Amenophis said slowly. "My father was not pleased with the last reports he heard about you. You are a priest of Hathor only because this was your father's position, and he was a good man, but more than one of your fellow priests has complained that you spend more time worshipping your belly than your goddess."

I don't know if my eyes went wider than the priest's or the other way around. Both of us were goggling at Amenophis, but it was Djau who asked the question foremost in my mind: "How—how do you know my name? How do you know so much about me, about the reports—the *lies*—my enemies have sent to Pharaoh?"

"Those reports came before Pharaoh's eyes in the royal palace at Thebes, and he saw fit to speak about them with his counselors. But the descriptions of your greed and gluttony were described so amusingly that he decided to share them with his family as well."

Djau looked ready to shatter. "In Hathor's name, *who are you*?"

Amenophis's heavy lips turned up in a lazy smile that was frighteningly like his brother's. "If you were half as wise as your father, you wouldn't need to ask that. Didn't you just hear me speak of my father? Who else can I be but Pharaoh's son?"

"Pharaoh's . . . son?" Djau's chins trembled. He looked as if he was debating whether to run away. "But that—that can't be." He looked Amenophis up and down and back up again. "It can't," he finished lamely.

"Can't?" The lazy smile vanished. Amenophis became

a lion ready to destroy his prey. "Why not? Because of how I look to your ignorant eyes? If you had ever gone even *half* a day's journey away from the feasting table, you would understand why I look like this! If you used the brains in your head instead of just the tongue and teeth, you would ask yourself, 'What possible cause would be so vital that Pharaoh's son leaves the safety and comfort of his palace and faces the hazards of travel?' I call on all of the gods to witness my words: I have come to Dendera for nothing less than a matter of life and death, an unholy violation of Ma'at's sacred truth! *Now take me to my father!*"

"Y-yes, my prince." The priest held up his hands and bowed stiffly. "This—this way." He tottered off and we followed. The eyes of every worshipper in the courtyard were turned away from the goddess and fixed on us as we crossed the open space and entered the shaded passageways beyond.

As soon as we'd left the courtyard behind us, Amenophis fell back a few paces to walk beside me. "Well, how was that?" he whispered with a wink and a self-satisfied smile.

"Not bad. You convinced *that* one." I nodded to where the plump-faced priest was hurrying along as though starving hyenas were on his tail. "I'll make a real prince of you yet," I teased.

"And with Hathor's blessing, I'll make a real princess of—" Amenophis didn't get to finish what he was saying. There was no need: We both knew what the next word out of his mouth would be. My heart fluttered and I blushed, but the sweet joy of that moment lasted only for a breath before it was snatched away from me.

We had come to an inner chamber of the temple where light streamed down from high, narrow windows, bathing the colossal image of Hathor in radiance. I counted at least six priests in attendance, some singing the praises of the goddess, some perfuming the air of her sanctuary, some chanting prayers. At her feet was a heap of treasure—alabaster vessels, intricately painted wooden caskets overflowing with gold and silver jewelry, boxes fragrant with precious incense, bales of leopard pelts to clothe the goddess and her servants. To one side of these kingly offerings stood Pharaoh Amenhotep himself, his hands raised in an attitude of worship. Beside him stood his favorite queen and Great Royal Wife, my aunt Tiye.

But to the other side of the pharaoh's sacrifice stood Thutmose, with a leering, knowing smile on his face that turned my blood to water.

"Welcome back, Nefertiti."

~ 8 ~

TWISTING THE FEATHER

The priests fell into uneasy silence as Thutmose crossed the space between us in three strides. His eerie, disturbing smile remained as unchanging as a statue's except for the moment when his gaze fell on Ta-Miu. I was holding the cat to my chest, and when he closed in on us, I automatically turned my back to protect her from being snatched out of my arms. To my surprise, Thutmose made no move to reclaim his beloved pet, though I did see a fleeting instant of longing in his eyes when he looked at her. His right hand also seemed to move as if it had a will of its own, slowly reaching out to stroke the cat's silky fur.

With the swiftness of a sword's slash, the moment was over. Thutmose jerked back his hand, recovered his cool, mocking attitude, and acted as if the cat weren't there.

"Hathor's power is great," he said, tasting every syllable as if it contained a hidden core of honey. "I came to Dendera in order to tell my father and my lord face to face about your crimes, Nefertiti. It was a great burden to me, beloved. You were my promised wife, the beloved niece of my noble mother, Queen Tiye, Great Royal Wife of—"

"Enough, Thutmose," I declared, making my voice fill every corner of the chamber. "No more lies, not here, not in the goddess's own house!" I turned quickly to place Ta-Miu in Nava's arms, then walked past Thutmose to bow before Pharaoh himself. "Mighty lord, wise king, god-on-earth, hear me," I said. "I have much to tell you if you will only give me permission to speak." I bowed low to him and waited.

"Stand, Nefertiti," he said. It was a gracious invitation rather than a royal command. "Stand up so that I can see you. It's been too long since these eyes have enjoyed the sight of so much beauty. Say anything you wish to me, only please, don't be so formal and worshipful. Coming from you, my dear, it makes me feel much too old, too close to my . . . elevation. The stars can wait. I'm still just a god-on-earth, you know, and I'd like it to stay that way for a long time to come."

I obeyed, feeling a new stirring of hope when I heard the warmth in his words. Pharaoh Amenhotep was a great lover of beauty, especially beautiful women, and he had many wives and companions besides Aunt Tiye. They, in turn, were the mothers of many children, any one of whom might be named heir to the throne if Pharaoh willed it. That was one reason Aunt Tiye decided I had to be Thutmose's bride: She knew her husband's tastes and guessed correctly that if the prince had a wife whose looks could win his father's favor, Thutmose's place as Amenhotep's successor would be assured.

"I rejoice to see you looking strong and well, my lord," I said, and I meant it with all my heart. Pharaoh had always been kind to me; I had no quarrel with him.

"And I am happy to see you looking so . . ." His voice trailed off. A perplexed expression twisted his features as he took his first really close look at me. I must have been quite a sight: borrowed, ill-fitting clothes, travel-battered feet, hair that hadn't been near a comb for many days, face that still showed a few stubborn specks of red paint from my goddess disguise. "Er, so you're *feeling* well?" he concluded lamely.

I inclined my head slightly. "My lord Pharaoh, you honor me with your concern. I am well, but what good does it do me to be healthy when I'm condemned to die on a false charge of blasphemy?"

"*What?*" He spun to confront his older son. "What is the meaning of this?"

Thutmose held his ground. "Father, I keep no secrets from you. You heard what I said just now: I came here to tell you everything about this unhappy business, but I haven't had the proper chance to do it. Hathor's powers have restored your health; I would die before I'd interrupt your thanksgiving offerings to her with such wretched news. I know the tenderness of your heart and how this girl took advantage of your goodness. I didn't want you to hear about her treachery from a mere messenger. But now . . ." And he began to recount his own version of my alleged crime and of his brother's treachery in helping me escape from "justice."

What followed in that chamber of Hathor's house was

like a clash of armies. I had never seen a great battle, but I had read many accounts of them. First came the wild uproar of the charge, the riot and confusion as chariots and foot soldiers crashed against one another, the deadly hiss of thick swarms of arrows launched into the sky. Then the tumult faded, rose here and there across the field, faded again as the course of combat changed, fresh troops pouring into the fight here, exhausted or annihilated combatants dropping out of it there.

My own fight for true justice put more than two armies onto the battlefield. Amenophis added his voice to mine when I testified about what Thutmose had done to warp the truth, laying false charges at my feet. Aunt Tiye took her older son's side, shrilly accusing Amenophis of disloyalty to his brother when she wasn't blaming me for bringing the whole situation down on my own head. Thutmose said nothing more after his initial words sparked the raging fight, but it was obvious that he was merely biding his time, like a seasoned commander who waits to see which way the battle is going before sending his men forward at exactly the right time and place to seize victory.

As for Pharaoh, he had the look of a man caught between a blazing fire and a starving crocodile. From time to time, he would bark a command for everyone to speak in turn rather than shouting all at once. Other than that, the god-on-earth was unable to rule the fray. The priests of Hathor huddled together, not because they were frightened by the regal conflict, but because they were enjoying it. They might as well have been peasants watching two of their drunken friends caught up in a brawl. They did everything but cheer and make bets on the outcome. Throughout it all, I stood by Nava, taking her and Ta-Miu under my arm to keep them safe and to lend the Habiru child courage. She might have enjoyed tales of violence, but when the real thing threatened to erupt before her eyes, she was only a scared little girl.

At last the battle wore itself out. A bristling, prickly silence ensued. I felt as if we all stood amid the ruins of a house that had been torn to pieces by demons riding a sandstorm. I stooped to take Ta-Miu from Nava's keeping and held out the cat for Pharaoh to see.

"My lord, see for yourself what I have here. We've wasted too much anger in this room, throwing accusations and blame back and forth and ignoring the only thing that matters: I was charged with having killed this cat, Ta-Miu, and using her blood to make wax images for the purpose of putting a curse on you and Prince Thutmose. Yet here she is, alive and well! Even more important, here you are, in the best of health, thank the gods. If there has been no killing and no curse, there can be no crime committed and no punishment for it. I am innocent, and the proof of it is here."

Pharaoh put out his hands, wordlessly requesting that I let him hold Ta-Miu. He examined the little cat thoroughly, from the tip of her tail to the top of her head to the place on her brow where the white star shone. Fingering her collar, he turned a stern face to Thutmose.

"I know this cat," he said. "I remember the day that I gave her to you. This collar was my gift as well. I was deeply pleased by how much you loved her. Frankly, my son, there were times that I wondered if your heart would ever learn *how* to care about another living creature."

"You think I don't care about you or Mother?" Thutmose sounded genuinely hurt, but I also noticed that he made no mention of Amenophis or his sisters.

Pharaoh sighed. Had he noticed it, too? "You are *obliged* to love us, as your parents and as rulers of this land. But there is no force that compels you to love this small cat, and yet you do. Or you did. If you love something truly, you don't *use* it; you don't manipulate it or turn it into a gaming piece, moving it here or there to serve your own desires."

"You're right, my father," Thutmose said. His voice was submissive, but I saw the way his eyes narrowed when he looked at his mother. There was more cold accusation in that look than in all the false charges he'd brought against me. "Ma'at herself would recognize the truth you speak about love. But she would also affirm that I am right when I say Nefertiti is *still* guilty of acts of sacrilege and blasphemy against the gods."

"Thutmose, have you lost your mind?" Pharaoh's scowl was terrible to see. "Do you *hear* your own words? You claimed she killed your cat and used its blood to cast evil spells on us, yet *here* is the cat and *where* is the evil magic?"

With the swiftness of a cobra's strike, Thutmose sprang forward and grabbed Nava by the wrist. Before Amenophis or I could stop him, he dragged the stumbling, wailing girl in front of Pharaoh and forced her to her knees. "*Here* it is, my father!" he declared, pointing at her while she wept with fright. "Here is the proof of Nefertiti's crime."

"What is this?" Pharaoh demanded. "What are you thinking of, bullying a child this way?"

"This 'child' is a Habiru slave, one who worships a god without a face, a god who has no known shape, a god of smoke and shadows. What better god for someone whose hands are steeped in the darkness of sorcery?"

I couldn't bear any more. I rushed to scoop Nava into my arms. She wrapped her thin legs around my waist and buried her head against my shoulder, clinging to me so hard that her fingers dug into my flesh painfully. "This is nonsense!" I shouted. "Madness! To call this harmless little girl a sorceress—!"

"Not her," Thutmose said calmly. "You."

"My son, think about what you're saying." Aunt Tiye moved to place one steadying hand on his arm. It was the only time I'd seen her confident, determined face soften so much. She was no longer a queen or Pharaoh's powerful Great Royal Wife. She was only a mother concerned for her child. "If you and Nefertiti have quarreled, let us help make peace between you. Whatever she has done to fill you with such a thirst for vengeance, this is not the way to make her sorry or to teach her to show you the love and respect she owes her future husband."

"By Osiris, it's true," Thutmose mused aloud. "You'd marry me to a scorpion if you thought it would help me get the throne."

Aunt Tiye drew back her hand and slapped him. One of the priests of Hathor had the bad luck to gasp. The queen whirled on him in a fury. "Leave us!" she commanded. "Take your miserable carcasses somewhere else or I swear by your own goddess that I will squash you like the gape-mouthed, goggle-eyed frogs you are!"

Some of the priests didn't wait to be given a second order. They ran from the chamber. Only Djau and two others remained behind, hesitating. "My—my lord Pharaoh," he quavered. "My lord, we were in the middle of the litany. I cannot go. Hathor will be insulted."

"There, there, you stay," Pharaoh reassured him. "My Great Royal Wife knows better than to insult the goddess who heard my prayers for renewed health. Isn't that right, Lady Tiye?" My aunt closed her mouth and glowered at him.

He gave his attention back to Thutmose. "My son, when I left Thebes, I gave you the power to rule there in my place. I've always intended for you to follow me onto the throne of the Black Land. From the time you were small, you showed nothing but the brightest promise. Your teachers admired your cleverness. The men who taught you how to drive a chariot, to hunt, to use the sword and spear and bow, all were happy to tell me how strong and skilled you were. You were always a pretty child, and when you grew up, I could see for myself how handsome you were. No pharaoh could have asked for a more perfect heir."

I looked over the top of Nava's head to where Amenophis stood hearing all this. It must have been hard for him to listen to his father pouring so many praises onto his brother's head. Pharaoh hadn't spoken one word against his younger son, but Amenophis had spent most of his life in Thutmose's shadow. Other people had let him know that he wasn't as handsome or as strong or as destined for great things. If two different foods are set on the table before a guest and he only eats from one of the dishes, smacking his lips and loudly insisting it's fit for the gods themselves, does he really *need* to say "This is tasteless, worthless, only fit for dogs" about the dish he ignores?

"*Perfect . . .*" Pharaoh repeated the word bitterly. "A perfect illusion. Thutmose, if you can see a crime where there is no victim, sorcery in this child, sacrilege in this young woman, treachery in your own brother, then all of your other gifts and talents are dust and sand. You cannot govern with justice if your vision is warped and your mind is ailing, and I cannot give the crown of the Black Land to a prince who sees monsters."

Thutmose lowered his eyes. "Father, will you hear me out? Or would you rather judge me without *all* the evidence?"

"Go on." Pharaoh's voice was tense.

"There is one truth you haven't been told: I was not the one who charged Nefertiti with sacrilege and blasphemy. When we return to Thebes, you can call for witnesses, including your own vizier, who will swear to this. Ha! Why wait? Amenophis himself was there. Well, brother? Can you deny what I've just said?"

Amenophis spoke reluctantly. "I didn't know that she was being brought to trial until it was almost too late. When I arrived, I learned that the evidence against her was a ripped, bloodstained dress and the testimony of our half brother, Meketre."

"Exactly!" Thutmose slapped his palm with his fist. "Meketre accused her, not I! And there was something odd about the boy's testimony. It sounded too practiced to be real, as if he were reciting a lesson he didn't fully understand."

"That was *your* doing!" I exclaimed. "Your plot, helped by the priests of Amun. You told Meketre what to say; you sent your own doctor to give me a potion that clouded my mind and slowed my tongue so that I couldn't defend myself, and when I tried to write an explanation—"

"If it was my plot, Nefertiti, why would I be plucking it to pieces now?" Thutmose asked lightly. Before I could respond, he added, "Father, look at this girl. Isn't she the most beautiful creature you've ever seen? Can anyone help falling in love with her? The one who wins her for his wife will think he's the luckiest man alive. The *weak* man who wins her will spend the rest of his days living in fear that he'll lose her again. He'll pay any price to keep her, give her anything and everything she wants, even if what she wants is mastery of the Black Land itself!"

I tried to object, but Pharaoh raised his hand, bidding me and everyone else present to remain silent. "I don't believe that you are a weak man, my son," he said.

"Neither does Nefertiti," Thutmose replied. "That's the problem. She came to Thebes destined to be my bride, but she came with greater ambitions than that. I loved her at once, but she soon saw that I would never love her blindly, drunkenly enough to let her rule me."

"And through you, to rule the Black Land," Pharaoh mused. "I understand." He glanced at his Great Royal Wife and nodded in a thoughtful way that made my aunt look nervous.

"But I never wanted—" I began.

"You will let my son speak." All the warmth and kindness was gone from Pharaoh's tone and face. I bit my lip and was still.

"I don't know what I did or said to make her realize that I would be her husband but never her slave. I do know that she found someone she could command with her beauty, someone who had never imagined a girl who looks like this"—he pointed at me—"could love a boy who looks like *that*." He couldn't keep the scorn out of his voice as his finger swung around to indicate Amenophis.

"Thutmose, you shouldn't speak that way about your brother," Pharaoh chided.

"I hear you, Father," Thutmose said docilely. "Forgive me; I'm still wounded by how coolly Nefertiti abandoned me for Amenophis and by how easily he welcomed her attention without a second thought that she was his own brother's promised bride." He put on the mask of a heartbroken lover, but I remembered the truth behind the mask. He had never loved me. He had only wanted to marry me because his mother assured him it would get him the crown.

"My son . . ." Pharaoh sounded weary. "My son, I sympathize with you, but it's a common thing for girls and boys to let love make them do cruel things. Sometimes they don't even realize they're hurting others. What you've described to me is no scheme against you."

"Isn't it?" Thutmose spoke with sudden, fierce intensity. "Then why has she used every bit of her powers—beauty, cunning, ambition—to make me look like a madman in your eyes? *Why?* So that you will set me aside and give the crown to my brother—her devoted, doting slave!" He ticked off point after point on his fingers: "She conspires with Amenophis, who's like wax in her hands. Together, and with the help of that brat"—he jerked his chin at Nava, who cringed tighter against me—"they created and planted all the evidence of Ta-Miu's death. I would give a double handful of gold to know how they forced Meketre to be a part of their scheme. Bribes? Threats? Both? They manipulated me so that I had no choice but to condemn her, but before the sentence could be carried out, she escaped! She cast a sleeping spell over her guards with the help of her Habiru brat—"

"What *spell*?" I snapped. "It was a potion in a jug of wine!"

Thutmose ignored the interruption. "My love-struck brother helped those two flee across the river, but not before they whisked Ta-Miu from her hiding place and took her away with them. Now they're here, claiming that Ta-Miu is living proof of Nefertiti's innocence when her true purpose is to prove that I'm not fit to rule! Father, *you* chose me to govern Thebes in your absence. *You* proclaimed that I was as capable as you to see that justice was done. Everything that Nefertiti has done to overthrow me strikes at *you*. The people will hear—the peasants, the merchants, the soldiers, the nobles, the priests—and they will ask if Thebes was given into the hands of someone who condemned a guiltless girl for a crime that never happened. Then they'll ask, 'Who put someone so witless in power in the first place?' "

Without warning, Thutmose dropped to his knees and prostrated himself at Pharaoh Amenhotep's feet, then raised his head and said, "I love you because you are my father. I respect and obey you because you are my king. But I worship you because you are the god-on-earth, as great as Amun himself! To doubt the power and wisdom of the gods is blasphemy. My lord—and you, holy priests of Hathor—in your wisdom, what name will you give to the crime of plotting to make a living god look like a fool before all his people?"

The priests' response rang through the chamber at once—"Blasphemy! Blasphemy! Blasphemy!"—and every one of them was glaring at me with loathing and malice. They hadn't even waited to draw a breath before attacking me or to spare an instant's thought considering whether Thutmose's words held truth or air. To question the gods was to question the men who made their living from the gods, like dogs under a rich man's table. Amenophis's objections were drowned out by their shouts. Nava yowled in panic. Aunt Tiye burst into tears, wailing that it would kill her poor brother when he heard what his daughter had become.

Only Pharaoh remained calm. With Ta-Miu still in his hands, he restored order with a low but audible command. "My son, I confess that your words have left me on a tangled path in a strange land. I find it hard to believe such things about this girl"—he nodded in my direction, then sighed—"but I also find it hard to doubt your word. You are my son and the heir to my throne. You were raised to honor Ma'at's sacred balance from the start."

"So was I," I said softly. Pharaoh's sorrowful face turned toward me. "So was I, my lord," I said more firmly. "Great one, my father is one of your most trusted servants. My first mother died while attending your Great Royal Wife. My family is loyal to you—so loyal that if I am found guilty of the schemes Prince Thutmose describes, they would be the first to call for my death. My lord, you are the god-on-earth. Let me put my fate in the hands of your sister goddess, Ma'at, whose Feather of Truth stands in the balance against every human heart!"

"How do you propose to do that, Nefertiti?" Pharaoh asked.

"By returning to Thebes and from there to the great sacred place, Karnak. I will stand before the goddess herself—"

"In the Palace of Ma'at," Pharaoh finished my thought for me. He was smiling again, though it was a melancholy smile. "Yes, of course, I should have thought of that myself. An oath of truth in the presence of Ma'at, in the heart of her house—so be it." He raised his voice and proclaimed, "We leave tomorrow! Make everything ready for our departure. Find worthy lodgings for my son Prince Amenophis, for the lady Nefertiti, and for . . ." He cocked his head at Nava, who had stopped crying but who still hung on to me like a baby monkey to its mother. "Well, Nefertiti, if this little one is your slave, I must say you are the most tolerant mistress in all my kingdom."

"Nava is no longer a slave," I said. It felt good to reveal a happy truth. "I gave her freedom before I left Thebes. She is . . ." I paused. What was Nava to me? No longer a slave but not a servant, either. We were too close for that to be the right name for her. A friend? Yes, but more than that. "She has become my sister."

I thought I would die then and there, squeezed to death by all the hugs, deafened by the cries of joy, and robbed of breath by all the kisses from the Habiru child in my arms.

As Pharaoh had commanded, we left Dendera for Thebes the next day. The festival of Hathor still filled the streets, but Pharaoh and Aunt Tiye had finished their service to the goddess, so there was nothing to prevent them from departing. The priests all hastened to assure their most generous patrons that Hathor was completely satisfied with the rich thanksgiving offering now carefully stored in the treasure rooms of her sanctuary. They came down to the dock to attend the departure of the royal ship, all the while throwing flowers, waving palm fronds, and chanting, "Hathor smiles! Hathor smiles!"

I stood between Nava and Amenophis, watching the ship's crew set the sail, feeling the resistance as the captain turned the vessel's prow upstream, against the current of the sacred river. The gorgeously painted sail caught a helpful breeze and bellied out strongly. The god Hapy, who ruled the river, was strong, but his power was tempered by the authority of Shu, who commanded the favorable winds. With his help, we would reach Thebes soon.

Once again I found myself a passenger aboard a royal ship. As I rested my eyes on the dark blue waters, I thought back to how Aunt Tiye had taken me on board her own splendid vessel from my home in Akhmin to a new life as the betrothed of Prince Thutmose. How my little sister, Bit-Bit, had envied me! I was going out into the wide world to a future as a princess, married to the young man who was certain to become the next pharaoh. And when that happened, I would be his queen! I would live out my days having every wish fulfilled, with only the most gorgeous clothes, the finest jewels, the most luxurious surroundings. Poets would praise me and artists would make my face eternal!

I had to laugh. What childish dreams those were. Bit-Bit had no idea of the reality that had been awaiting me. If Isis were merciful, the day might come when I'd see my dear little sister again and be able to tell her about everything that had happened to me since we parted. Would she envy me then?

I glanced away from the sacred river and met Amenophis's eyes. He was gazing at me with the strangest smile on his homely face. "Why are you staring at me like that?" I asked. "Is there a smudge on my cheek? I don't see how that's possible: I had the most wonderful bath last night. I've been scrubbed and oiled and scented and had my hair washed and plaited and decked out with these"—I flicked the gold charm weighing down one of the countless tiny braids framing my face—"until our escape and adventures seem like nothing more than bad dreams."

"Was it a bad dream when you said you loved me?" he murmured.

I moved closer to him and gave him a kiss. It was the best answer.

Well, maybe not for everyone.

"Amenophis, get *away* from that girl!" Aunt Tiye swept down on us like a hawk on a baby hare. Her dainty hand clamped onto his bony wrist and she yanked us apart. She glared at me as if wishing her eyes could riddle me with flaming arrows.

"Good morning, Aunt Tiye," I said sweetly. I knew exactly how to pitch my voice in order to annoy her most. I had a death sentence hanging over my head, a future that might be written in blood or dust, and a cunning, ruthless prince for an enemy, but I couldn't let fear devour me. If I could steal a bit of laughter by teasing my manipulative aunt, I'd scoop it up with both hands.

"Don't you play the tame, dutiful little lady with *me,* you sly thing. Oh, how I curse the day I asked Ay to let me bring you to Thebes! You were nothing but an ungrateful, wayward, obstinate block of stone from the first, and now you've made things as bad as they could possibly be for everyone, including yourself. A *normal* girl would have bowed her head and let her life be guided by people old enough to know the best and wisest course to take. But not you! You're like a she-goat that kicks over the milk bowl just for spite. It wasn't enough that you spurned the *crown* prince"—she glowered at Amenophis when she said that—"but you plotted against him with his own brother!"

"Aunt Tiye, none of that is true," I said, trying to be heard without shouting above her. There had been too much of that in Hathor's house. "Those wild schemes Thutmose described are inside his own mind."

"That's just what you *would* say." Aunt Tiye looked ready to spit at me. "Anything to tear him down. Well, it won't work! When you stand in the Palace of Ma'at at Karnak and take the oath of truth, you won't be able to cover your deceptions with clever words. The goddess will look into your heart and give us all an unquestionable sign that everything you've said against my Thutmose is a lie!"

"Or not," Amenophis said under his breath.

His mother heard and shot him a look like a spear point. "There is only one reason that I haven't ordered you to be punished for all you've done to betray your own brother: I pity you. Yes, I pity you with all my heart. What chance did someone like *you* ever have to resist this girl's charms? She could ask you to fetch her a bull hippo's tusk from a living beast and you'd kiss her hands and rush off to meet your death singing! With or without magic, she's turned your head. I only hope that when she's gone, you'll be yourself again."

"I don't think you understand the way things are between Nefertiti and me, Mother," Amenophis said, his voice level. "Without her, there *is* no me. We speak with two mouths but only one voice. We look at one another with eyes that don't see beauty or ugliness, only love. She is my heart, and the wings that will lift me to the stars when I go to meet Osiris. Nothing can part us." He shook off his mother's grip and held me in his arms.

Aunt Tiye had little use for any act of defiance, even one as gentle and loving as this. She shoved her way between us and elbowed me away. Turning her back to me, she focused all her anger on her younger son. "If you knew how stupid you sound, you wouldn't clutter my ears with such babble. Or maybe you would. You were never very bright. A piece of cheese could outwit you. That's why you have a mother to look out for your best interests and to keep you from making a complete idiot of yourself. Since you haven't got the good sense that the gods gave to geese, I'll save you from your own folly. You are forbidden to see or speak to this girl again, from this moment until she has offered her heart to Ma'at!"

"No, Mother," Amenophis said. His long jawline was tight, and there was a smoldering threat in his eyes. "You haven't got the power to give me such orders anymore. I won't leave Nefertiti."

"Not even if your father commands it?"

"He never gave any such command. It's yours!"

"It *will* be his." Aunt Tiye looked smug. "I can promise you that. Your father knows and respects my good judgment. You little whelps aren't the first two to be—what was that *clever* way you put it?—'two mouths but only one voice'?"

"There *is* no voice that can keep me from her."

"Will you defy Pharaoh himself?"

"For her, yes."

"Very well." Aunt Tiye shrugged in such an exaggerated way that it was obvious she didn't mean surrender. "It's not my job to enforce the will of Pharaoh. That task will fall to other women and men, guards and servants and slaves. They will bear the responsibility for removing you from *her* influence. Of course, you can always confront them, tell them that you are a prince! *You* don't have to listen to the words of underlings. *You* will walk right past them to be with her. They won't be able to stop you. They wouldn't dare." She smirked.

"And so they will be punished for failing to fulfill their

job, and since that job is to enforce a direct order from Pharaoh himself, the punishment will be accordingly severe." Aunt Tiye showed us her teeth. "But I wouldn't worry about it too much, if I were you. They're only little people. Why should you care what becomes of them, as long as you get your own way?"

Amenophis and I looked at one another. There was no need to speak; we knew she'd played a winning game against us.

"Ma'at will triumph," he said to me. "And on that day, I will be with you again."

I nodded, then kissed him. I didn't let him go for a long, long time.

~ Part III ~
THEBES

— 9 —

VISITS AND SECRETS

Amenophis and I didn't see one another for the rest of the voyage. He was kept confined in the curtained shelter in the middle of the deck, and I was forbidden to enter it. I didn't mind too much—it was better to be able to stroll around the ship at liberty and watch the changing sights of the shore slip by—but I felt bad for him, pent up in such close quarters. The chamber held every comfort—the best food and drink, soft cushions, game boards to pass the time—but not freedom.

I saw Thutmose frequently. It was impossible to avoid him. The royal ship was big, but not that big. Whenever I caught sight of him, I held my ground. I'm sure he would have enjoyed our encounters more if the sight of him made me run, shudder, sneer, turn my head away sharply, any kind of reaction, but I refused to let him think he had the least effect on me. I looked at him the way I'd look at a palm tree on the riverbank, my eyes merely acknowledging that, yes, there it was, and that was as much attention as it deserved. At first he wore a nasty grin each time our eyes met, but it quickly withered when I let him understand that he was nothing to me now. Soon *he* was the one who ran or looked away if we chanced to cross each other's path.

When the royal vessel docked at Thebes, a suitable welcome awaited us. I think that the priests of Hathor must have sent runners or chariot drivers ahead to the south the instant that Pharaoh's ship left Dendera. The god-on-earth was greeted by a procession of musicians, dancers, fanbearers, priests of many gods in all their ceremonial finery, and, of course, his highest-ranking counselors, including the vizier. Pharaoh and his Great Royal Wife walked from the ship to the palace in splendor over a carpet of flower petals. A canopy was held above their heads by four Nubian servants carrying the jeweled and gilded poles. I was still on board the ship, and from the height of the deck, I could see that the top of the canopy was decorated with a brilliant picture of Horus in the form of a hawk with outspread wings of blue, red, and gold. The two princes followed their parents, their heads shielded by painted cloth sunshades. Thutmose was carrying Ta-Miu. The little cat who had caused so much trouble had been restored to her former owner back in Dendera, before we left the temple of Hathor. I was surprised at how much I missed her.

There was no such courtesy as a formal welcome nor such comfort as a sunshade for Nava and me when it was our turn to debark. On Pharaoh's orders—more likely the orders of Aunt Tiye—the vessel's master kept us on board until the royal procession was out of sight, then turned us

over to the four guardsmen who'd been waiting for his summons. They looked bored and they smelled as if they'd been
passing the time with a jug of beer. As we walked up the
road to the palace, they traded crude jokes and used language that a child of Nava's age had no business hearing.

"That will be enough of *that*," I told them crisply after
the man to my left finished an extremely vulgar story with
an even worse gesture. "If you can't keep your tongue out of
the dung heap, don't speak at all."

"So *you* say," the man replied with a grunt worthy of
any pig. "I'll talk how I like, when I like, where I like. You
may look like a fine lady, but we heard all about *you*. What's
worse, a little rough talk or spewing lies? And in Hathor's
house, too! I'm bringing my kids with me to the Palace of
Ma'at when you head there to try blabbing your way around
that goddess. Her feather won't balance out a deceitful heart,
no matter how pretty a face goes with it; you wait and see. I
want my kids to be there and witness what Ma'at does to
you. My wife says fire'll shoot right out of the earth and
burn you alive. I figure it'll just be the earth splitting open
under you and dropping you into a pit of snakes or scorpions or . . . well, *something* nasty."

"Maybe I'll just get turned to salt," I said, and gave Nava
a wink that made her giggle. The guard scratched his head
in puzzlement the rest of the way to the palace.

I was given my old rooms in the women's quarters,
but my former servants were gone. In their place were
two scared, skinny, self-conscious girls who didn't look
much older than me. They refused to give me their names
and avoided speaking to me at all unless it was absolutely

necessary. I presumed that Aunt Tiye had handpicked them because they were the two palace servants who would serve me the worst. They were the clumsiest girls I'd ever seen. They tripped over their own feet, dropped things, and stepped on the hem of any garment they carried.

I didn't mind having servants who were not much better than having *no* servants. Nava and I were used to taking care of ourselves. The girls discovered that they had fewer and fewer chores to do and promptly took advantage of it. When they weren't breaking, tearing, or losing things, they were sleeping in corners or—so Nava told me—stealing off to the kitchen to flirt with the younger cooks.

The only time that those two managed to act like real servants instead of failed jugglers was when Princess Sitamun came to visit me. I sent the girls to fetch refreshments, all of which promptly landed on the floor when one tripped over the doorsill and the other let the wine flask slip through her hands.

My friend surged to her feet and gave the slip-fingered girls such a harsh tongue-lashing that it seemed as though sweet-natured Sitamun had shed her skin, revealing Aunt Tiye at her most scathing. The maids squealed in distress, raced away to bring us more food and drink, then dashed off to hide in some dusty corner until my guest was gone.

"Whew! I didn't know you had that in you, Sitamun," I said, with nothing but admiration for the plainspoken princess.

Sitamun pursed her lips primly and raised one eyebrow. "Hmph! If you don't tell servants what to do in a way that says *or else,* they'll sit around all day eating dates and spitting the pits in your eye."

"They don't do that," Nava said. "They don't do *any-thing.* We take care of ourselves."

"What? That's not acceptable! Nefertiti, I know that you're being kept here as a prisoner until Ma'at's high priest says the goddess is ready to hear your plea, but you're of noble birth! A princess! You shouldn't be doing servants' work."

I laughed. "I'm only linked to the nobility because of Aunt Tiye, not by birth, and if you ask her, she'll tell you that I'm the fool who threw away my one chance to *become* a princess! So I guess I'd better get used to doing my own work, because once my trial before Ma'at is over, your mother's going to send me home on the fastest ship she can find."

"Then I know someone who'll be on that ship with you," Sitamun said with a subtle smile. "He's told me every-thing. I'm very happy for you both."

I lowered my eyes. "Even if—even *when*—I'm free again, what's going to become of him and me? Your mother hates me for not living my life according to her choices. She'll have Amenophis walled up alive before she'll let us be to-gether."

"Then you'd better learn how to use a chisel."

Even Nava laughed at Sitamun's joke. "I don't care if those girls don't help us," the Habiru child announced. "I like it better this way, with them hiding from their chores all the time. It keeps them away from us, and that means they can't go tale-bearing about who comes to visit and what they say."

"What a smart little girl," Sitamun said. She handed Nava a plump fig as a reward. "Tell me, O daughter of Thoth the wise, how would you make sure that those two stayed far away from these rooms for a long time?"

Nava chewed the fig while she thought this over. At last she replied, "Can I have another fig?" Sitamun passed her the entire plate. Between bites, the child said, "I'd give them a big, complicated job to do, but it would have to be something they couldn't do in these rooms, or even in the women's quarters."

"Laundry!" Sitamun exclaimed. "Do you have any pleated linen sheaths, Nefertiti?"

"I had at least two," I said. "I haven't bothered to see if they're still where I stored them."

"Never mind if they're not; I'll send you a basketful of mine, and you can pretend they're yours. Do you know how long it takes to wash and bleach and repleat those things? Your maids will be gone for half a day!"

"A whole day," Nava said. "Half a day to do the work, half a day to do whatever they want, but they'll *tell* you they were working the whole time." She ate the last fig contentedly. "They'll think they fooled you. It will make them very happy."

Sitamun leaned her head closer to mine and grinned. "Oh, *do* let's make them happy, Nefertiti."

I narrowed my eyes. "What are you up to, Sitamun?"

She only smiled.

The basket containing Sitamun's badly wrinkled linen

sheath dresses arrived in my quarters the following morning, and I turned it over to my maids. I never said the dresses were mine, just that they needed to be washed and the pleats refreshed.

"This will take us a long time, mistress," one of them said.

"A long, long time," the other added.

"Take the whole day, if you like," I said casually. "I don't think I'll need you for anything else until tomorrow morning."

"Oh, we'll be done before that," the first one said.

"*Maybe.*" The second one moved close to her companion, and I thought I saw her pinch her. "We want to do a *good* job, don't we?"

"Oh. Oh, yes!" The first maid bobbed her head like a bird banging a snail on a rock. They both had the most ridiculous smiles on their faces.

Either they're madly in love with the idea of doing laundry or they've got plans, I thought, trying not to smile back. *Half the day making a mess of those dresses, the other half—and part of the night, I'm sure—seeing those boys they like from the kitchens.* I felt the ache of envy. *Even maidservants are luckier than Amenophis and me. They're free to see their sweethearts.*

Later that same morning, after the maids were gone, I received word from the Palace of Ma'at that my trial before the goddess would take place the following day. I felt my stomach sink while I listened to the royal messenger who brought the news. I knew I was innocent, but I had spent enough time in Aunt Tiye's world to know that much too often, innocence was not enough. Her son Thutmose had been raised in that unhealthy atmosphere of intrigue, and he'd learned all its wicked lessons. With the skill of a master potter at his wheel, he'd transformed the raw clay of my words and the evidence that should have cleared my name into the twisted shape of fresh accusations.

Nava sensed my unease. The little girl became especially attentive since the messenger's announcement, always at my elbow, always trying to cheer me or distract me. She filled the day with lively chatter, fetched me special treats from the kitchen, braided and rebraided my hair, and got me involved in a storytelling contest, all to keep me from thinking about what awaited me.

Now that we were back in the palace, she'd been able to lay her hands on the harp she'd left behind. When the day began to fade into the starry glory of night, it was a comfort to sit beside her in the courtyard outside my rooms and listen to her sweet, clear voice raised in song while her fingers drew melody from the strings. Music holds its own magic. Soon its spell laid hold of me, and I was able to put all thought of the next day's trial out of my mind. While Nava sang and played, I stood up, left my worries in my wake, and began to dance.

Oh, how long had it been since the last time I'd enjoyed the rapture of dancing? Too long, much too long. I'd forgotten how good it felt. *This must be what it's like to fly,* I thought, my bare feet scarcely touching the ground. I spread my arms like a hawk's wings, turned my face to the stars, closed my eyes, and let my imagination send me soaring over green fields and towering golden cliffs, white cities, and the eternal blue miracle of the sacred river. I wished that

Nava would play her harp and sing her songs forever. I prayed to Isis and Hathor to let me dance forever.

A foolish, beautiful prayer, a prayer I knew would have to go unanswered. It was better that way: My feet moved swiftly in the dance, but was I dancing or trying to run away?

I stopped. Nava noticed and dropped her hands from the harp strings. "Don't you like this song? I know others I could play for you instead."

"It's all right, Nava," I told her. "You're a wonderful musician, but I'm done with dancing for today. Another time."

"Are you sure?" She looked worried. "I want you to be happy!"

I knelt beside her on the floor and put my arms around her as comfortably as her harp would allow. "I am happy, Nava. I'm just a bit concerned about tomorrow, but that's natural. It doesn't touch my happiness."

The child began to cry. "I wish I could be happy," she said. "But all I can do is think about what might happen to you tomorrow and then I—" She sobbed.

"Shhh, hush, little one, cast away those thoughts. Doesn't your god defend truth, too? If we pray together, then the One and Ma'at will both be on my side."

Nava sniffled and shook her head. "There can't be both of them together. The One . . . is the *One.* Please don't hit me, Nefertiti; it's true."

I was taken aback. "Why would I hit you for saying something like that, Nava?"

"*He* used to," she replied, looking at her knees. "My old master, the priest of Isis. He did it every time he heard

Mahala and me singing praise songs for the One. He got so mad! He'd turn red all over his bald head and call us ugly names and he'd beat us. He said he didn't care what kind of useless gods his slaves prayed to, but we should do it quietly, where *real* people wouldn't have to overhear such nonsense. He was angry because some of our prayers and songs say that the One created everything and watches over everything and that we don't need any other gods."

"I see. *Not* the sort of thing a priest of Isis wants to hear in his goddess's own house. Maybe he was afraid that if enough people overheard you, they'd start thinking that they should worship the One as well. Instead of going to the temple of Hathor to pray for health and the temple of Thoth to pray for wisdom and the temple of Bast to pray for love, they'd only have to go to one place and make one offering. It would certainly be more efficient." I was joking, trying to distract the child from unhappy memories, but she took me seriously.

"That's not why we worship the One. Nefertiti, you shouldn't talk about your gods that way."

"Don't worry, little one. I don't think they'll punish me for saying such things. If the gods were as petty and vengeful as some of their priests, they'd have wiped us from the earth long ago. I fear the gods—I mean that I revere them—but I'm not afraid of them."

Nava shook her head a second time. "Not the gods—their priests. Like the one who—who—" Tears began to trickle from her eyes. The old, brutal, pitiless pain of her sister's death was back, tormenting her tender heart. She thrust her harp away so hard that it crashed to the ground

and the wood split, the strings jangled. I tried to hold her,
but she curled herself into a ball and rocked back and forth,
mourning her loss anew.

I let her cry herself out until all she could manage were
a few hoarse sobs, then silence. *Was it always this way?* I
thought as I stroked her back and pulled her tousled hair
away from her hot, tear-wet face. *Did the servants of the gods always serve their own desires first?*

I didn't want to believe it. I couldn't: Father often told
me of the time when he and the grandfather I'd never
known had served the patron god of Akhmin, Min himself.
Father was filled with tales of how he and Grandfather and
the other priests of Min had used the offerings to ease the
lives of Akhmin's poor, not to fatten themselves. I turned
my thoughts to conversations I'd overheard between Father
and my second mother, Mery. Whenever the town cele-
brated one of the great festivals, they were always open-
handed with the sacrifices they brought to the gods' altars,
and it gave them pleasure to talk about those priests and
priestesses who turned this bounty into charity.

"Did you see our new Amun priest today, Mery?" Father's
words whispered in my head. *"He was personally overseeing the
distribution of grain from the temple storehouse to the widows of
the city."*

"I wish they were all like that, Ay." The memory of Mery's
gentle voice brought tears of homesickness to my eyes.

*"I think most of them are, my beloved. I think that the vir-
tuous, honest priests and priestesses outnumber the corrupt servants of the gods. It's just that we tend to* notice *wrongdoing more
than goodness.*

"I suppose that's for the best," Mery replied. "If we notice it, we can put an end to it."

Father's sigh was a wisp of smoke. "We can . . . if we have the strength to do it."

I sat cross-legged and pulled Nava into my lap. Sometimes she seemed like a wise old woman in a child's body, but at moments like this, she was as fragile and defenseless as an infant. I would never know how old she was. She'd been born a slave, and some households didn't bother noting the ages of their human property except as *too young to earn her keep yet* or *ready to breed more children for us* or *too old to bring a good price if we sell her.* Her age didn't matter to me, only that she was in need of someone to shield her from harm.

What will become of her if tomorrow goes badly for me? I thought. My heart beat faster. *At least a slave has a master who wants to protect his valuable property—to feed and clothe and shelter what belongs to him. But if I'm gone, Nava will have nothing and no one. Amenophis! I have to write a letter to Amenophis, telling him to take care of her. It mustn't wait!*

"Nava, dear, there's something important I need to do right away. You have to help me. Can you get up?" I murmured to her.

She lifted her chin, wiping her nose on the back of one hand. "Yes. I'm all right now. I'm sorry I cried." She stood up and I did the same. "What do you need?"

"Papyrus and a scribe's kit. Do you remember where I put mine? Is it still in these rooms?"

"I think you had it with you when the bad prince locked you away," Nava said.

I slapped my brow with one hand. Of course! How could I forget the night when I'd used my stone palette to save myself from the poisonous serpent Thutmose had sent to kill me? I'd never look at a scribe's gear the same way again.

"Well, when you bring me the papyrus, see if you can borrow a kit, too. I need to write a letter."

"Who are you writing to?"

"Amenophis."

"Oh." Nava gave me a penetrating look. "Is it a *love* letter?"

"Why should you care about that, you nosy kitten?" I told her lightly. "Do you want to help me, or do you want to spend the rest of the evening asking me questions that are none of your business?"

"I'll help," Nava said. "But I don't know how you're going to see that he *gets* the letter. I'll bet the queen has him tied up like a dog somewhere, with a whole *army* of guards around him."

"Or"—a familiar, plain, much-loved face showed itself in the archway leading to my courtyard—"or she could have made the grave mistake of assigning the two greediest men in the palace to watch over me."

"Amenophis!" I was in his arms so fast that I slammed him against the frame.

"Shhh, not so loud, dear one," he said, kissing my brow. "Some of the palace guards are greedy and some are gullible, but none of them are deaf."

"Come with me," I said, taking him by the hand and leading him into my rooms. I had kindled one oil lamp at sunset, and now I asked Nava to light more. There weren't enough chairs for the three of us, so we knelt together on the ground, as we'd done so many other nights on the road. How good it was to see his face again! I cupped his cheek in my hand and sighed happily. "You're so handsome."

He laughed. "And you are very brave to say such lies when you're about to appear before Ma'at in the morning."

"If it's a lie, Ma'at will read it in my heart, and if Ma'at can read my heart, she'll know that it's not a lie." I kissed him softly. "I'm glad you're here. What did you use to bribe your guards? It must have been an incredible amount for them to risk the punishment Aunt Tiye will give them if you're caught out of your apartments."

"That's between the guards and my liberator—my *temporary* liberator. I had nothing to do with it. My jailers are busy performing a 'very important' task for a royal princess who somehow couldn't manage to find one other soul in all the palace to do it for her. She's a very righteous young woman, that princess, and *deeply* scandalized by how my behavior has offended our exalted mother. So not only were my guards richly rewarded for serving Pharaoh's daughter, but they also know their miserable prisoner won't stray in their absence, not when his own sister is keeping a stern, disapproving eye on him."

I gasped in admiration. "Sitamun! Was she always so shrewd?"

"She's our mother's daughter." He shrugged. "I think it's something in the blood. It almost makes me afraid to imagine what our daughters will be like, Nefertiti."

Our daughters . . . I pressed my hand to my mouth. I

didn't know whether to laugh for joy or weep, because the idea of being Amenophis's wife and the mother of his children seemed like such an impossible dream.

No! No, it will not *be impossible!* Fierce, defiant thoughts flared like falling stars through my mind, my heart, my spirit. *There has to be a way for this to happen. We love one another, and we've gone through so much, survived so many dangers. Oh, Amenophis! When I first met you, you were such a gawky, timid boy! You could hardly say a word without stammering. Now look at you: brave enough to be my defender, to stand up to your brother, to defy your mother! And what about me? I remember when I was the shy girl who only wanted to be left alone with my music, my dance, my pens. We've changed. We've helped each other become brave. We're warriors, you and I, and the battle isn't over. Amenophis, we will win it, together.*

Little Nava tapped my arm, bringing me back to the moment. "Why are you so quiet?" she asked. "Don't you *want* daughters?"

I lowered my hand and clasped hers. "Of course I do. They'll be the luckiest girls in Thebes. Do you know why?" The Habiru child shook her head. "Because they'll have *you* for their music teacher."

"Me?" Nava's face shone brighter than the flickering light of the oil lamps.

"No one else. Will you do that for us, little one? Live in our home and teach our children how to play the harp and sing?"

"I broke my harp."

"We'll get you another one, then. And your own room, and new clothes, and—"

"Nefertiti . . ." Amenophis's solemn voice cut the thread of happy dreams I was spinning. "Beloved, we must speak about tomorrow before we talk about anything further in the future. We don't have much time. I have to get back to my quarters—"

"And my maids will be trailing back here *some*time tonight," I concluded. "But what's there to say about tomorrow? I'll be ready early, I'll dress my best—to show honor to the goddess—and I'll speak the truth. But what happens after that?"

"After that . . . Ma'at herself will speak."

Something in Amenophis's tone put me on edge. "How will that be done? Will the priests cast stones, or bones, or papyrus stems?" All these were things I'd seen done in the temples of Akhmin, methods that priests and priestesses used to divine the will of the gods. I'd also seen such things done in the marketplace by magicians, or common fortune-tellers. One temple was famous for the accuracy with which their priests could read what the gods had planned for the future from the patterns made by tossing a handful of black beans onto a white cloth. Another claimed that all the secrets of life and death were visible in a few drops of oil scattered on the surface of a bowl of water. The gods had always had many ways to let their worshippers know their rulings. "Which will it be?"

"None of those," Amenophis said. "I told you: The goddess will *speak*. Her priests say that Ma'at's own voice will come out of her house for all to hear."

I was awestruck. "I've heard that there are temples where the gods do speak directly to the people, but I never

dreamed the Palace of Ma'at held such a wonder." Then I
noticed the odd look he was giving me and I had to laugh.
"Oh, Amenophis, do you think I'm *that* gullible? I know it
can't be the *real* voice of the goddess. It's likely going to be
one of her servants, but the effect must be astounding."

"It is. Ma'at's will is heard through her largest image,
the one that stands just within the main temple chamber. I
have been present a number of times when she's 'spoken,'
and I've seen how the accused react when that voice booms
out of the sanctuary. That's why I came. I wanted to forewarn
you so that when you heard Ma'at's voice, you wouldn't be
frightened. I want Mother and Father and everyone who's
there to witness your trial to be able to say that you heard
the goddess speak and were unafraid. People remember
such things; they make an impression."

"Why do I have to impress anyone?"

"Because it will look better. After it's all over, you don't
want anyone to be able to say 'Did you *see* how high Nefertiti jumped when the goddess said that she'd told the truth
about her innocence? It was as if the girl didn't expect to
have her name cleared. Maybe she's not guilty of those
crimes, but could she be up to some other mischief? Oh,
she'll bear watching, that one!' "

I laughed. "Is that how you believe people think?"

"That's how I *know* they think in the palace. I want you
to be found guiltless once and for all. I want you to be free
to live your life again, without having to watch every step or
dodge gossip."

I crossed my hands in my lap and looked down at them.
"I wish I was free, Amenophis, completely free. If I was, the

first thing I'd do would be to leave this palace, leave Thebes, and go back to Akhmin—"

"Nefertiti!"

"With you." I took his hand in one of mine. "Both of you." I took Nava's hand with the other.

"At least you'd be able to do that much." He nodded at Nava and drew his hand out of my grasp. There was such yearning in his eyes. "How can we ever be together? My mother doesn't like having her plans spoiled. She'll spend the rest of her life spoiling yours—ours."

"There must be a way," I said. "I'll find it. I won't give up until I do. Sitamun's smart; she can help me. Amenophis, we *will* be together." I grabbed his hand a second time and squeezed it so hard he winced.

"Maybe you can make your mother so mad at you that she'll tell you to go away forever," Nava said. "Or maybe you'll save her life from something scary, like a cobra or a lion, and after that she'll be so grateful, she'll let you do anything you want. Or maybe Pharaoh will have bad dreams, and you'll be the only one who can tell him what they mean, and he'll let you marry Nefertiti as your reward. Or maybe—"

Amenophis chuckled. "One thing at a time, little bird. Right now the only reward I want is to see Nefertiti standing brave and beautiful before Ma'at's shrine when the goddess declares her hands are clean, her name is stainless, and her heart is light as the Feather of Truth."

"That too," said Nava, looking so serious it was funny.

He had to leave soon after that. We stole a kiss when Nava wasn't looking, then another when she was. She squeaked and covered her eyes, which let us have a third kiss before Amenophis said good night and left us.

"I don't understand why you do that," Nava said.

"You don't have to," I replied. "But you *do* have to help me pick out the dress I'll wear tomorrow. If I'm going to hear the voice of a goddess, I want to look my best."

We laid out all of my nicest gowns on the bed along with the finest necklaces, bracelets, and earrings I owned. I might never become a princess, but Aunt Tiye had seen to it that I'd look like one, back in the days when she thought I might still marry Thutmose. Nava and I were busy debating which necklace looked better with which dress when we heard heavy footsteps in the courtyard.

Probably the maids, back with those dresses, I thought. *I hope they didn't mangle them too much, even if Sitamun does have plenty of others.* "One of you bring more lamps!" I called out without a glance at the entryway to my rooms. "I want to see if you did a good job."

"There is only one of me," Henenu replied. "And I think you'll discover I've done an *excellent* job indeed."

Nava was faster than I. She rushed across the room to embrace our friend and teacher, the dwarf scribe. I had to hug the two of them together. The joy of our reunion brought more light into my rooms than a hundred lamps.

"So you *are* real, my dearest girls," Henenu said, his broad face one big smile. "May Amun be thanked, I didn't believe I'd see either one of you again until it was my time to travel to the next world. Can you see me trying to give you two your writing lessons in the Field of Reeds?"

"You couldn't do that," Nava said. "I won't go there."

"Hmm. Well, yes. You're so skilled at reading and writing our language that it's easy to forget you're not one of us. Nefertiti is a very good student, but if you continue your studies, I think you could follow in my footsteps and become a royal scribe. That would make me very proud."

"I'd like that, too," Nava said. She kissed his cheek. "Are you hungry?"

"What a good girl," the scribe said. "Why, yes, I am. How thoughtful of you."

"Good, because so am I. Nefertiti, can I go to the kitchens and bring something back?"

"I don't know what you'll find there at this hour," I said. "Except the maids, probably. But, yes, go. I'll just sit here with Henenu and be embarrassed that you're a better host than I."

"I wouldn't be if I wasn't hungry," Nava said, and ran off.

"What a good child," Henenu said, glancing after her. "And a fortunate one as well. The gods must favor her. She always seems to do the right thing."

"If that's meant to chide me for not having offered you refreshments—"

"Oh, no, not at all! I meant that if she hadn't suggested fetching us something to eat, I would have had to come up with an excuse for getting her out of here so that you and I could speak privately."

My brows drew together. "What do we need to talk about? I'm glad to see you again, Henenu, but what are you doing here at this time of night?" I asked.

"As I said, privacy. This is the only time I knew I could

visit you without two unwanted pairs of eyes and ears present to spy on us, or two sets of rather clumsy feet ready to go bearing tales to the queen. Luckily I have the word of *another* lovely student of mine that your maids are busy elsewhere. I would have come earlier"—he gave me a sly look—"but that same young lady also told me someone else would be here, and I didn't want to intrude." He patted my hand. "I'm very happy for you and Amenophis, my dear, and I hope to be happier yet. May Ma'at steal the voice of that treacherous priest and truly speak tomorrow."

"Treacherous?" My stomach knotted. "Henenu, what are you talking about?"

"Tomorrow, when you stand before the goddess in the Palace of Ma'at and make your plea, the goddess will speak to—"

"I know that. Amenophis told me what to expect, so I wouldn't be startled when I hear her voice. I know it's only one of her priests talking through her hollow image. Henenu, how do they decide what the goddess will say?"

"Most of the time, the priests do all they can to learn the facts behind the cases brought to the goddess's house. They send trusted men to ask questions, to investigate everything they can discover about the person who comes into Ma'at's presence for judgment, and then they do their best to reach a fair ruling."

"Then I have no worries about tomorrow. What a relief! I can't wait to tell Nava. She's spent all day trying to ease my spirit. When the priest speaks—"

"A priest who wants Pharaoh's favor, Nefertiti."

"Even better!" I saw his grim expression, but it made

no sense to me. Why look so gloomy in the face of so much good news? I blithely ignored it. "Pharaoh likes me; he knows I'm guiltless. The only reason he's putting me through this trial tomorrow is because Thutmose gave him no choice. If the priest of Ma'at wants to please Pharaoh, the goddess will free me before I finish taking my oath!"

"Not if the pharaoh he wants to please is the pharaoh to come."

Henenu plunged a needle into my heart. My whole body felt suddenly numb. "It can't be. Ma'at's priests serve in the house of truth! How could Thutmose corrupt them?" I cried out in betrayal and anguish, but I already knew the answer: The gods were not the same as the servants who spoke for them. Thutmose already had the powerful priests of Amun on his side. They'd helped him engineer my false conviction, because they looked forward to the day he'd rule the Black Land. Then he would remember how well they'd served him and reward them for it. Were the priests of Ma'at no better? Would they sell the voice of truth itself if it meant riches and other royal benefits would come to them in the future?

"So I'm about to put my life in a scale weighed down by lies." I stared into Henenu's eyes. "Does Amenophis know?"

"The royal family has always known, as have some of us who are easily overlooked when loose tongues wag." Henenu dropped his voice in shame. "Only the common people are kept ignorant. The temples that use special statues of the gods—statues that can be made to move and talk—have the most hope of influencing the people. Sometimes they share this power with the pharaohs, when it benefits them both. There are times when the love and reverence the people have for their ruler aren't enough to keep them docile and obedient: times when crops fail, when the sacred river doesn't rise properly, when there's plague in the land, when taxes grow heavy. At those times, when angry mutterings begin to rise against the god-on-earth, the voices of the other gods are used to proclaim terrifying threats against any who aren't entirely loyal and devoted to Pharaoh. They ignore the people's justified complaints and silence them by filling their hearts with awe and dread." He smiled at me sadly. "Have you never noticed how much easier it is to control a man who's always afraid?"

I clenched my hands. Lies! So many lies, and in the house of truth! Did no one else feel as sick at heart as I did, knowing this? "Why do we let such abuses go on, Henenu?" I cried. "Why do we build so many shrines to so many gods if every one of them is just another storehouse for hollow images and falsehood? Too many of their servants act like rival packs of mongrel dogs, fighting over scraps in the street. And why didn't Amenophis tell me the whole story when he came to prepare me for Ma'at's voice? Why has he lied to me, too?"

"Sweet girl, he loves you." The scribe's words were placating and sympathetic. "You told me he wanted you to be brave. How would you be able to face tomorrow if he'd told you that your fate was already decided?"

"*You* didn't have any problem telling me about it," I said bitterly.

"I see you through clearer eyes than he does, Nefertiti," Henenu said. "He can't look at you without wanting to build strong walls around you to keep the dangers and ugliness of the world away from you. He loves you because you're a strong young woman, not a delicate little flower petal, but he still wants to cup your life in the palms of his hands. Haven't *you* ever wanted to shield someone you love?"

I had to say yes. Ma'at knew it was so; Ma'at, the *real* voice of truth in my heart, and not in the trickery-haunted shadows of some self-serving temple. "I think I'd do the same for him if he stood in my place tomorrow," I said.

"You know that's not all he's prepared to do, if his brother has his way with Ma'at's verdict," Henenu said, resolute. "You have many friends, Nefertiti. We will not let you suffer for crimes you didn't commit. You escaped from an unjust verdict once before; we'll help you do so again. We'll spirit you out of the Black Land altogether. You and Amenophis can make a new life for yourselves. Sitamun and I will see to it that her brother leaves Thebes with treasures worthy of a prince. I'll go back to Akhmin and arrange for your whole family to follow you wherever you decide to go, whether south to Nubia or north to the kingdoms of the Mitanni, to the great trade city of Byblos, to the lands of the Canaanites—"

"No."

"No?" he repeated. "Well, you could also travel to Punt, if you'd rather—"

"No, Henenu, don't give me any more choices like that. I've made one of my own: I will not run away again. My innocence is true, whether or not the priests of Ma'at have sold themselves to Thutmose, and I will defend it. If the voice of the goddess proclaims me guilty, I will reveal that there is an even greater sacrilege taking place in the house of Ma'at herself."

"My dear, what good will that do? You'll be silenced where you stand."

"Then I won't stand still. I'll run into the temple. I'll push the hollow goddess from her pedestal, and if I don't have the strength to do that, then I'll find the hiding place of the priest who filled Ma'at's mouth with lies and I'll drag him out of there, into the light. Let the shining face of Aten destroy the shadows that hid him!"

My voice rose and I was breathing hard, but I couldn't help myself. If someone overheard me, so be it. I was already condemned. What else did I have to fear? I realized that all my bold intentions for storming Ma'at's shrine were as empty as the goddess's image; I'd be seized by guardsmen before I could fulfill a single one. Still, I wouldn't accept my unjust fate without a battle. Thutmose's wicked plans might pull me down, but I would never bow my head to them. I would never surrender.

"Nefertiti, calm yourself, I beg you." Henenu's sturdy, capable hands held mine firmly. "Such fierceness. When did my little Seshat become the lion-headed Sekhmet, ravenous for blood and war?"

"No blood, Henenu," I said. "No blood and no war: justice. That's all I've ever wanted. Since I won't get it tomorrow, will you at least give me something else?"

"I already have something that I—"

"Give me your word," I said, interrupting whatever he was trying to say. "Make me a solemn promise that after tomorrow, you'll bring Nava to my family in Akhmin.

Amenophis would take care of her, but I don't want her to stay here. This place will hold too many bad memories for her." Another thought struck me. "Oh! But Akhmin will hold worse ones. Henenu, you have to help me find another place for Nava to go, somewhere she'll feel safe at last, loved, somewhere she'll find a new family to cherish her."

"I can't agree to do that for you, Nefertiti." The scribe shifted his weight and took a small roll of papyrus from the leather case at his belt. He unrolled it so that the writing was plain for me to see by the oil lamps' light and weighted down the ends with his hands. "She needs no new family. Her sister is alive."

— 10 —

THE VOICE OF MA'AT

"She's alive! She's alive! Oh, Nava, your sister, Mahala, is alive!"

The instant that I heard Nava's small feet cross the threshold to my rooms, I leaped up and rushed to greet her with the wondrous news. Henenu's revelation had gone to my head like the strongest wine ever poured, dazzling and dimming my senses at the same time. All I wanted to do was dance and clap my hands and laugh out loud like a madwoman.

I was too ecstatic to realize what a shock I was giving to the little girl. She dropped the bowl of fruit she'd brought us and shook so hard I heard her teeth clatter in her head. All she could say was "I'm sorry, I'm sorry, I'm sorry," over and over, until the words became a heartrending whimper that ended in a howl.

"Nava, please, no, I'm the one who's sorry!" I cried, hugging her. "Don't cry, I beg you! This isn't the time for tears. I'm telling you the truth. Mahala is alive. Listen, listen, let Henenu tell you. It's not a dream."

The dwarf got to his feet and walked slowly to where I was frantically trying to undo the harm I'd done with my unthinking eagerness. He bent over and picked up a handful of the sweet, spicy fruit of the doum palm from the shards of Nava's bowl. "If this *were* a dream, child, no one would be able to make me share these delicious treats with you." He pressed them into her trembling hand. "Here. I don't need them. What I have to tell you fills my mouth with honey every time I repeat it. But you must stop crying. Your tears are too salty and the doum fruit will taste bad."

Nava gulped for breath, then began to chew on the fruit, all the while staring at Henenu like an owlet. I led her to the one chair in the room and coaxed her to sit in my lap.

"Ah, this is good." The scribe knelt on the floor once more. The papyrus holding the glad news about Nava's sister had rolled itself back up in the recent uproar, so Henenu smoothed it out and slapped his thick thighs with satisfaction. "If I live forever, I'll never get tired of looking at this scrap of beaten reeds and ink," he said. "And I'll never get tired of remembering how it came to me. When you two fled Thebes, I missed you very much, you know. It was just Princess Sitamun and me at lessons, while you were gone. She's an intelligent young woman and a good scholar, but she knows so much already that our lessons were only practice, practice, practice, writing the words she'd already learned. It wasn't as much fun as teaching you new things, but it did give me some extra time to pursue a matter that had been on my mind. Your sister had a reputation for being a very talented girl, true, Nava?"

Nava nodded. "Mahala was the best music-maker in our master's house; he said so himself. She played the double-flute so well that he used to send her to the homes of important people to entertain their guests when they had parties."

"For a price, no doubt," I said.

"Oh, no doubt about that at all," Henenu responded. "We three are all from Akhmin, so we know what a good place that is for gossip, right, girls? Well, maybe you're too young to know about such things, Nava, but trust me, it's true. Our people love to talk. Rumors thrive like rats in a grain jar. Luckily, so does news. Ever since I heard about your sister's fate, little one, something about the whole business didn't sit right with me. She was a *valuable* slave, and the high priest of Isis has a reputation in Akhmin for being a man who doesn't part with his treasures easily."

I agreed. "I was horrified when I first heard what he'd done with her, but afterward, when the shock dulled, I had a hard time believing it. The high priest wanted to punish me and my family—Father rejected that man's proposal for me to marry his son—but if he really ordered Mahala's death, he'd be punishing himself worse."

"Apparently he saw it that way, too," Henenu remarked. "I wanted to settle my doubts about this one way or the other, so I wrote to my family and asked them to keep their eyes and ears open, to seek out the biggest busybodies in Akhmin, and to ask discreet questions. Shortly before you came back to Thebes, I had my answer." He tapped the papyrus. "The high priest of Isis had *not* thrown away what he could sell for a good price. He owed a large debt to one of his colleagues, a servant of the creator-god Ptah at Memphis. Mahala was that payment."

"Memphis!" I often had heard Father speak of that city, once the foremost in the Black Land until our rulers turned their favor to Thebes. My parents had sailed past Memphis when they accompanied Pharaoh Amenhotep and Aunt Tiye on their northward pilgrimage to visit those monuments. It was my mother's last voyage. "That's so far away!"

"Yes, far enough from Akhmin to make it seem as if Mahala truly had vanished from the land of the living. But as my mother always says, a gossiping tongue is long enough to reach from the earth to the moon." He made a wry face. "And she ought to know. She was the first to hear this." He tapped the unscrolled papyrus again. "Nava, be glad: Your sister is still playing her music in this world."

Nava beamed, her face now streaming with tears of joy. She clapped her hands and exclaimed something in a language I didn't understand. Even if the words were foreign to me, I would have wagered my life that she was saying a prayer of thanksgiving to the One she worshipped.

I gave her a hug and set her on her feet as I stood up. "Dear one, do you remember the casket where my best jewels are kept?" I asked her. "I want you to bring it to me, please." She looked puzzled, but obeyed.

"Nefertiti, if you're thinking of giving me a reward for this news, I assure you, it's not necessary. This news *is* my reward," Henenu said gravely.

"I'm not giving you a reward, my friend," I replied as

Nava returned with the gilded and painted wooden box. "I'm giving you a task." I opened the lid and took out the pieces, one by one. Each was exquisite, a gift for the girl who had come here to become crown princess of the Black Land, and someday queen.

That girl was gone. Why should her jewels remain?

I placed the box in the scribe's hands and knelt before him, my hands raised as if praying to one of the gods. "I beg of you, Henenu, take all this and use it to travel north to Memphis. Bring Nava with you. Find the priest of Ptah who owns her sister and buy the girl her freedom. Leave at once—tonight, if you can, or before dawn tomorrow. Please."

"So soon?" Henenu's eyebrows shot up. "But, Nefertiti, tomorrow is—"

"*Please,*" I repeated, and looked meaningfully from him to Nava and back. The scribe was a wise man. He understood my unspoken plea: *Don't let her be here tomorrow when I stand before the goddess of truth in the house of lies. If the worst happens, I don't want it to poison her new happiness. Remember what you asked me only a short while ago? "Haven't you ever wanted to shield someone you love?" I want to shield her, Henenu, more than anything and with all my heart!*

The scribe rose from the ground and stowed his precious papyrus. "Well, my little friend, it is a long way to Memphis, but it won't get any shorter if we stand around here. Run and bring anything you might want for the journey, and we'll begin nosing about the palace and the city for news of any ships heading north. I know a couple of clever young scribes-in-training who won't mind helping their old teacher with this. You and I will be on the river by dawn."

"I—I don't want to leave Nefertiti," Nava protested.

"Don't you want to see your sister as soon as you can?" I asked.

She looked miserable. "But *you're* my sister, too. You said so."

"And I meant it. You will always be a sister to me, Nava." I kissed her brow. "I love you. Nothing will ever change that. But Mahala needs you more than I do now. You were all the family she had. She wasn't even given the chance to tell you good-bye. How long has it been since she had any news about what became of you? Her new master wouldn't know and her old one didn't care. Go to her, Nava. The moment she sees you again will be an even greater joy and blessing to her than the moment you tell her she's going to be free."

There were more tears between Nava and me and many more hugs and kisses before she gathered up her few possessions and left with Henenu. I went into the courtyard and looked at the sky. Although no one was with me, the presence of all those who cared about me, loved me, missed me, surrounded me like a cloak of starlight. The fragrant shadows whispered with the ghostly echoes of Father calling me his little kitten, Mery proudly telling the neighbors what a fine dancer I'd become, Bit-Bit's giggles, Henenu's praises, Sitamun's friendly advice, Nava's song, and Amenophis's tender words of love. I was by myself, but I was not alone.

Let tomorrow come. I was at peace.

I don't know when my maids returned that night. I was in my bed, sleeping deeply. I woke up to find myself covered with at least eight of Sitamun's badly laundered and pleated gowns. I suppose they wanted to make sure that I couldn't miss the evidence that they'd actually accomplished the task I'd given them the day before.

I got out of bed and took one of my own dresses from the storage chest against the wall. It was a simple, old-fashioned thing, the linen clean and unpleated. I started to look for my jewelry, then remembered that I'd given all of it to Henenu and Nava, to redeem her sister. The only piece that remained was a strand of blue clay beads that had been overlooked in a corner of the chest. The string was frayed, but I tied it around my neck anyway, all the while laughing at my own vanity.

You're going out to greet what might be your last day alive, but you just couldn't *show yourself without some pretty trinket!*

Hush, I told myself. *It's not for me; it's out of respect for the goddess.*

After all you've learned, do you still believe *there's a goddess of truth and justice? Or a god of wisdom? Or of love? Or are they all just empty images that dishonorable mortals use to deceive and control others?*

I don't know. But I do know that even if all the gods and goddesses were to vanish from the Black Land tomorrow, I would still want to believe in truth and justice, wisdom and love. There is something greater than me in this world—a source of life, a comfort in darkness, a light that doesn't fail. I can't prove it by pointing to a statue and saying, "There. That's where it lives. That's what holds the light." But I feel it; right or wrong, I feel it and I am grateful. Does it matter if I lift my hands before the statues of Ma'at and Thoth and Isis or if I lift my heart before Nava's faceless, bodiless, homeless god, as long as I give thanks somehow?

Thanks! The bitter voice of doubt inside me was back. *If you can give thanks for anything after today, it will be a miracle.*

I don't need miracles, I thought. *I need justice.*

One of my maids came stumbling into the room, wiping sleep from her eyes and yawning like a hippo. "Oh, you're dressed," she said. "I guess you don't need me for anything."

"You can bring me some breakfast," I said. "And have your friend gather flowers for me. I want a wreath of blue lotus for my hair."

"Umm . . . I don't think she knows how to make a wreath. Me neither."

"What a surprise," I said with a half-smile.

At least the girls were capable of fetching me a hearty meal and of filling a basket with flowers. I wove my own wreath and had one of them hold the mirror when I placed it on my hair. The braids little Nava had made for me were still neat and shining, so all I needed to do to complete my preparations was paint my eyes and put on sandals. Then I went out into the courtyard to wait.

A group of four guards came to escort me to the Palace of Ma'at. None of them wanted to look me in the eyes. My step was light as we marched through the palace halls and out into the streets of Thebes. At one point, the leader of my armed escort asked if I felt equal to the walk to the temple or if I wanted to ride there in a chariot.

"Only if I can drive it myself," I said, and did my best not to laugh at his shocked expression.

So we walked. The sun was still low in the east, and the sacred river was the deep blue of lapis lazuli. One of the necklaces I'd given to Nava was gold set with those precious stones, one of my favorites. I pictured her and Henenu, already on the river, sailing north to Memphis. A kind breeze brought me the green scent of reeds and tassel-topped papyrus plants, and I said a quiet prayer for their safe journey.

"My lady, don't you worry; it'll be all right," one of my guards mumbled so quietly that I almost didn't hear him. "Someone like you, so beautiful, you'd never do any of that stuff they're saying you did."

"How ugly do I have to be to be guilty?" I whispered back, joking. He turned red and clamped his mouth shut. "Oh, dear, I'm sorry, I didn't mean to insult you," I apologized in hushed tones. "Thank you for wishing me well." He remained silent.

I had glimpsed the Palace of Ma'at before this day, but I had never really *seen* it. Karnak teemed with temples. In the past, before Thutmose revealed his true nature, he'd taken me to view the sacred city. My eyes were filled with the sight of so many different buildings, statues, and monuments that they all became a jumble in my mind. If anyone had asked me, "Did you see the Palace of Ma'at?" it would be like showing me a field of wheat and asking me if I'd noticed one particular grain.

Now I took note of it, gazing up and to either side as we entered the temple grounds. The way to the Palace of Ma'at was flanked by two sets of pylons—those gigantic paired walls whose only purpose was to remind the worshipper of mountains. Their faces were decorated with towering images of the rulers who had ordered their construction and the gods who blessed such devout pharaohs.

"They say the temple was built by that outrageous woman Hatshepsut." My mind whispered the memory of Thutmose's words when he'd pointed out this place in passing. *"After her husband died, but before his heir was old enough to rule the Black Land, she dared to declare herself pharaoh! She dressed like a man while she held the crook and flail and scepter and tied on a false chin-beard when she wore the crown. Can you imagine that?"* I remember how he'd preened when he added, *"It didn't last; I am named for the pharaoh who followed her unnatural rule. He restored the way things are supposed to be and erased her name and image from all the monuments."*

Erased, but not forgotten, I thought as we walked between the second set of pylons. I'd heard others speak of her—Hatshepsut, daughter of one pharaoh, wife of another, a woman with the fearlessness to ask why *shouldn't* she govern her own land just because she wasn't born a man. They said that she'd ruled wisely and well. Her reign brought peace and prosperity to the Black Land. The Thutmose who succeeded her brought war. I imagined her carved and painted story glowing beneath the layers of concealing plaster and the clumsy chisel blows that a petty, vindictive king had used so futilely, trying to unmake the existence of a heroic woman.

Walk with me, O Queen, O Pharaoh! I prayed. Lend me your courage.

We left the pylons behind as we came into the main temple building. I saw a courtyard filled with people—nobles, court officials, representatives of the other gods, their wives and the slaves and servants attending them. To one side stood a platform shaded with an elaborately painted

and fringed canopy. I turned to face it and bowed low to
Pharaoh, his Great Royal Wife, and the sons and daughters
she had given him. I couldn't think of her as Aunt Tiye in
that moment, nor could I look up and see Sitamun as my
friend, Thutmose as my enemy, Amenophis as my beloved.
They had all come so splendidly arrayed, so dazzling and so
dignified that they seemed to belong to some other world.
There was also such an air of solemnity, grandeur, and significance lying over the house of the goddess that for a moment I forgot what I'd been told about the trickery at play
within these walls. I could almost believe that when I testified
to my innocence, it *would* be Ma'at herself who answered.

My guards stepped back, joining the other soldiers positioned to keep watch over the crowd. A priest came forward and beckoned me to follow him. I was brought to
stand inside a circle of white feathers, facing the dark entryway to the goddess's shrine. The chatter of the crowd dwindled and was gone. The stone walls surrounding us held
nothing but a silence.

"Mew!" A cat's strident cry pierced the stillness, making
the crowd murmur nervously. *Thutmose has brought Ta-Miu
with him,* I thought. *He's so smugly certain of how this will
turn out that he's flaunting the very evidence of my innocence.* I glanced back at the royal platform and saw him
looking at me with a hyena's grin. He was *tasting* my doom.

I might not be able to escape your jaws, Thutmose, I thought
resolutely, *but let's see if I can't break a tooth or two for you before that happens.*

I turned to the priest and saluted him with reverence.
"Shall I speak now?" I asked.

He looked pleased that I'd asked. "First we will invoke the goddess with prayer and song. I will let you know when you should address Ma'at. Know, Lady Nefertiti, that this is not a court of law. You are not here to plead a case but to submit to the verdict of the goddess. She is immortal and all-seeing: She knows every step that brought you into her presence, and she has witnessed every act and every piece of evidence that will decide your guilt or innocence. All that you will do is call out to her for judgment."

I bowed my head. "When the time is right, I will call out for justice," I said. I don't think he heard the difference in my words.

The priest gave me a benevolent look that might have been sincere. "The prayers and songs of praise are long. Would you like me to summon a fan-bearer to attend you, or some slaves to hold a sunshade over you?"

"No, thank you. I'm standing in the presence of the goddess. Let her see that I'm strong enough to stand on my own."

The priest looked confused for a moment by my response. I think he was expecting me to be a different sort of girl, one who clung to others for help, one who fled from the harsher parts of life. I had endured much worse than having to stand unprotected under the Aten's life-giving rays, especially so early in the day. If the ceremony were taking place under the unforgiving blast of noon, I would have accepted the priest's offer of a fan *and* a sunshade. I was strong, not stupid.

I felt every eye upon me as I stood there, hearing the priests chant the praises of Ma'at, listening to the hymns glorifying the goddess who weighs every human heart. I stood as tall and dignified as I could, keeping my eyes on the gateway to the goddess's house. *Where are you, little priest?* I mused. *Are you already hiding inside the image of Ma'at, or do you have some other way to make your voice speak for her? What will you say when I finish speaking? Will you demand my death here and now, or will you merely proclaim my guilt and leave the details of my punishment to others? Will you roar with divine rage against me or sigh with regret over my "crimes" before condemning me? And when this is over, will you be proud of what you've done?*

My legs grew stiff from standing so still for so long. Many of the people in the crowd shared my discomfort; I could hear them muttering and fidgeting. No matter how beautiful the poetry and songs offered to the goddess, they were long. If there was one prayer in everyone's heart, it was for the priests to be done with all this and get to the event that everyone had come to see.

All at once, partway through yet another hymn extolling Ma'at's beauty and virtue, a muffled clamor went up from the platform where the royal family sat. I heard Sitamun's voice cry out, "Oh! He's fainted!" and then confusion fell over the entire courtyard. Singers and musicians stumbled through a few more notes before stopping their song. Priests barked commands to slaves and servants, sending them scurrying in every direction. It was impossible to see what was happening on top of the royal platform, though plenty of people stood on tiptoe, straining for a glimpse of the goings-on in the shadow of Pharaoh's canopy. One elegantly bejeweled nobleman tried climbing onto the shoulders of one of his servants, only to have the two of them tumble to the ground. Guards formed such a tight fence around the royal platform and maintained the barrier so zealously that the high priest of Ma'at had to bluster at them for a long time before they'd let him through. The spectators jabbered and babbled and made useless demands to be told what was going on. Two of the ladies present fainted, too (probably just to be part of the fuss).

At last we saw the high priest descend, followed by two muscular servants. They were very well dressed, unlike the humbler garb of the temple servants, so they were probably part of the royal entourage. With their hands linked to form a human chair, they carried the limp body of Amenophis between them. A third man walked behind, supporting the prince's lolling head.

"Hmph. Well, I'm not surprised," someone in the crowd remarked just loudly enough for me to hear. "He's been a bit of a weakling since he was a child."

A weakling? I thought with scorn. *If you only knew! I'd like to see how you'd fare on a journey like the one he and I shared. But, oh, Amenophis, where's your strength now? Was it the thought of what awaits me that stole it from you and struck you down?* My right foot stirred and took a step forward, unbidden. I was about to run after the servants who were carrying him away. I could feel desperate words rising to my lips: "Wake up! Come back! Don't leave me! I can't face this without y—!"

My panic-stricken thoughts died abruptly, as though one of the huge granite blocks of Hatshepsut's stolen monuments had dropped on top of them. I forced myself to breathe calmly.

That's not true, I thought. *I* can *face this on my own. I am Nefertiti. I must.* And I remained standing as though carved from stone while the hubbub surrounding Amenophis's collapse died away and the priests resumed their service to the goddess.

At last the singing and the music stopped, the prayers ended. The priest who'd brought me into the circle of feathers came forward and announced for all to hear that, with Pharaoh's royal consent, the lady Nefertiti would speak. I heard Pharaoh Amenhotep's familiar voice respond, "So let it be done." He sounded so sad.

I licked my lips, which had gone terribly dry, cleared my throat, and spoke: "O Ma'at the Beautiful, the Changeless, Lady of the Hall of Judgment, I am Nefertiti, and I come into your house to ask for your eternal gift of justice. Your law holds the world in balance. You sustain the sun. You are the Perfect Measure of the heart after death. Measure my heart now, O Ma'at! Place it in the scales against the words that have been said against me and declare which one contains your sacred truth!"

My words were done. I'd said all that I could say. Silence settled over the courtyard like a layer of dust. No sound broke it, not even the creak of a leather sandal as its wearer shifted his weight, not even a cough or a sigh. Every eye, every ear was focused on the gateway to the goddess.

"O Nefertiti, daughter of Ay!"

The voice that boomed from the heart of Ma'at's shrine was resonant and powerful, but pitched strangely high. *A man trying to imitate a woman's voice,* I thought, and resigned myself to hear the hidden priest's verdict. I heard gasps and murmurs from the crowd to my left and right, and a low, indistinct rumble from the royal platform.

"Silence for the Lady of the Twofold Truth!" Ma'at's chief priest swept away every sound like a housewife chasing crumbs from her table. "Hear the goddess!"

"Nefertiti, I have seen your deeds and heard the words spoken against you." The magic of deception was strong— the voice from the temple made the short hairs at the back of my neck rise up even though I knew it came from someone as human as myself. "I have set my Feather of Truth in the balance against the charges of sacrilege and blasphemy brought against you. See, I have weighed your heart! Let no one deny my enduring truth." The voice paused for a moment, or for what might have been a hundred years, then said, "You are wrongfully accused. You are guiltless. You are free!"

I gasped and my legs crumpled under me. I fell to my knees in the circle of white feathers, while all around me the people cheered.

"Treachery!" A shriek from beneath the royal canopy tore through the sounds of rejoicing. Thutmose stood at the edge of the platform, his face dark with demonic rage. "Filth! Traitor! You declare her *innocent*?" He leaped from the platform and for a moment was a black shape against the sun. He landed in the courtyard with a cat's grace, but with a serpent's death-cold eyes. A dagger flashed from his belt to his hand. "I'll teach you what happens to those who betray me!" he shouted into the shadows of the shrine, and plunged in.

The crowd burst into cries of dismay and horror,

appalled by the prince's impious act. To their eyes and ears, he had committed acts of sacrilege worse than any of the charges laid against me. He had smeared Ma'at's holy name with atrocious insults. He had drawn a weapon in the house of the goddess!

"Stop him!" Pharaoh Amenhotep barked commands to every guardsman present. "Seize him, bring him out of Ma'at's house now!" His men raced to obey.

I was on my feet when they dragged Prince Thutmose back into the courtyard. Two of them held him by the arms, but he still had the dagger clutched in his hand. Some of the other men bore the marks of it—shallow cuts and slashes—and were keeping their distance. He was still their prince, and they hadn't found the nerve to disarm him. He thrashed in his captors' grip, spewing threats and curses. He poured abuse on the heads of all the men who'd hauled him out of the temple, swearing he'd remember every one of their faces, and on the day that he was crowned pharaoh, he'd call for their deaths. He raved so fiercely that the guards holding him turned pale and exchanged uneasy looks. The crowd fell back as the guards hesitantly steered him toward the platform where his father stood waiting, his whole body trembling with rage.

Then Thutmose's head swung toward me. His lips curled back, and in a voice that came from a place of endless, all-consuming darkness, he growled, "This is your doing. You wretched girl, you've destroyed my life, but I'll end yours!"

With an unexpected twist of his body and two vicious slashes of his dagger, he was free of the guards who held him. As they staggered back into the arms of their fellow soldiers, their hands pressed to the wounds his blade had opened, Thutmose leaped straight at me.

I didn't pause for any thought—I spun on my toes and ran. My skirt held me back, so I pulled it high and dashed away. The nobles who had come to witness my trial screeched and fled, but fear confused them and they wound up milling crazily in the courtyard, bright petals caught in a whirlpool. I dodged in and out among them with Thutmose after me. I heard grunts and screams in my wake. I prayed that all he was doing to clear his path was shoving the innocent aside. I ran faster and knew I was outdistancing him when I heard his foul curses receding behind me.

Then I heard him cry out in fury and frustration, "No! Let me go! She's *mine*. Release me, or your life will pay me back for hers! Ah, you dog, you dare to take a prince's dagger? I'll still make you bleed—"

One of the temple singers, a motherly priestess, came up behind me and gathered me into her arms. "It's all right now, Lady Nefertiti," she said. "See? You're safe." She gently pried the bunched-up fabric of my dress from my rigid grasp, smoothed it back into place, then turned us both around to view the courtyard. Thutmose was once more in the grip of his father's guards, except now he was without his weapon. They brought him to the foot of the platform where his father waited.

"Take him away," Pharaoh said. His voice was drenched in a bitterness and grief that broke my heart.

— 11 —

HATHOR'S GIFT

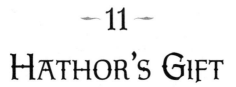

The rest of that day became a blur for me. I know that someone must have brought me back to my rooms, because that was where I was when my maids lit the lamps and offered me dinner.

"You must eat something, mistress," one of them said. "You didn't touch a bite of your midday meal."

"Is Amenophis all right?" I blurted. Now that I was back in the waking world, I was suddenly struck by the fact that I had no idea what had become of him after he'd fainted. *How could I forget to ask such a thing?* I thought, miserable with self-reproach.

"Ameno—? *Prince* Amenophis?" The two maids exchanged an uneasy look. "We heard that he fell ill this morning, but nothing more."

"We could go find out, if you give us permission, mistress," the second maid said. I couldn't tell if she was sincerely willing to serve me or just avid to have a fresh excuse to run back to her sweetheart in the kitchens.

"That would be good. You are free to go. Come back as quickly as . . . when you can." I was too worn out from the morning's ordeal to care about the honesty or duplicity of another girl in love. "Thank you."

"Mistress?" Her expression changed from eagerness to concern. I must have looked dreadful. "Mistress, I promise you, I'll be back *very* fast. And when I come back, would you . . . would you like the two of us to prepare a bath for you? I can bring some fragrant herbs to scent the water."

The maid who'd insisted I eat something answered for me. "Yes, do that! A bath is just the thing she needs. And don't you dare take all evening finding out about the prince. The news must be old by now; everyone will know it. You *don't* need to get it from the kitchens," she concluded meaningly.

The second maid didn't wait to hear more. She was gone and back again before I'd eaten the last of my dinner. "I have good news, mistress," she announced with a smile. "Prince Amenophis is well. It was only a mild fainting spell. He looked healthy and fit when he accompanied his royal parents back to the palace. It's even said"—she lowered her voice to a whisper—"it's even said that Pharaoh himself had to reprimand the prince for looking *too* well."

"That makes no sense," I objected.

"They say that Pharaoh was made so wretched by what his eldest son did in the Palace of Ma'at that he spent the rest of today snapping at anyone he saw who didn't wear a face long enough to trip over. They say that finally he shut himself up in the heart of his chambers and wouldn't see anyone, not even his Great Royal Wife. They say that she beat on the doors with her fists and shouted at him to let her in, but he refused. They say she looked like a wild thing, and—"

"That's enough," I said curtly. "I am tired of what *they* say. All I wanted was news of Prince Amenophis. He's better; I'm content. The two of you are free for the night."

"But, mistress, your bath—" The news-bearing maid offered up the basket of herbs she'd brought me.

I took it from her hands and set it aside. "These will keep. I'll bathe in the morning. For tonight, I want to be alone."

"We are here to obey your wishes, mistress," the first maid said. "But we were also told—"

"To stay near enough so that I didn't try to escape?" I finished her sentence for her with a wry smile. "You haven't been doing a very good job of that, have you?"

The two of them looked embarrassed and nervous. "We didn't think you *would* try to escape," the first maid said. "You are—forgive me, mistress, but it's true—you are only a girl. How would you be able to come up with a successful way to get out of the palace? And if you did manage that, where would you go? How could you survive?"

"I'd die," the second maid said plaintively. Her eyes were wide with all her unspoken fears of what lay beyond the palace gates.

"And yet you must know that I did escape, once before," I said. "What did you think of that?"

"Oh, that someone took care of everything for you."

The first maid shrugged. "You're so beautiful, mistress; people must be pushing each other aside for the chance to serve you and keep you happy."

I had to laugh. If only that were true! "Well, you don't have to fret about watching me anymore. You know that I've been proved innocent. I can come and go as I like. So can you."

"Oh, *yes,* mistress!" they exclaimed in joyful chorus, and left me in a flurry of promises to bring me a wonderful breakfast and a morning bath so luxurious that Lady Hathor herself would envy me.

In their haste to be gone, they left behind my dirty dishes. I sighed and carried them out of my rooms, not wanting the crumbs to attract vermin. I was in the courtyard, wondering if I should take the things all the way back to the kitchens or only leave them a reasonable distance from my quarters, when two men surprised me. One had the humble look of a servant, and he carried the burden of a covered basket as if to prove it. The other was dressed more richly and carried only a delicately made oil lamp shaped like a leaping gazelle.

"You there, girl! Do you belong to these rooms?" the lamp-bearer demanded.

Apparently I was looking humble enough to be taken for a servant, too. I suppose my freight of dirty dishes didn't help dispel the illusion.

"Yes, sir," I said with a little bow. His mistaken assumption amused me, and I had a great hunger for laughter that evening.

"I don't want to disturb your mistress. She has endured much today, poor lady."

"True, she isn't herself right now," I said.

"Small wonder! The goddess Ma'at appeared before everyone and declared that Lady Nefertiti was not only innocent of all wrongdoing, but also that the evil Set himself was at the bottom of the plot that had dragged such a pure and lovely girl through untold suffering!"

"Not *Set*." I was glad to have the chance to gasp in amazement; otherwise I would have burst out laughing.

"The Evil One and none other." My elegant visitor nodded vigorously. "What's more, the dreadful god of the Red Land also appeared in person and tried to destroy Lady Nefertiti with a flaming spear! But blessed Ma'at's sacred Feather of Truth became a wall of shining light around her and Set was vanquished."

"Oh, *my*." I opened my eyes as wide as they would go. "You must have been *terrified*."

"Er, no." The man looked sheepish. "I regret to say that I wasn't there. But I have it on the very best authority that everything happened exactly as I've told you. What's more, I bring the proof of it." He made an imperious gesture for his attendant to come forward with the basket. "This is for Lady Nefertiti from the god-on-earth, the Beloved of Amun, Lord of the Two Lands, the almighty Pharaoh Amenhotep himself. You shall bring it to her and tell her it is hers to keep forever."

The servant and I performed an awkward dance as he tried to hand me the basket while taking the dirty dishes from me at the same time. It was a miracle that we didn't drop everything. I stared at the woven lid and wondered what could be inside. The temptation to lift the lid and peek was strong, but I knew it wasn't something a mere "maidservant" could do in front of Pharaoh's messenger.

Then the basket meowed.

"A *cat*?" I exclaimed.

"The *royal* cat, called Ta-Miu," the man corrected me. "The very cat whose life was proof of Lady Nefertiti's innocence."

"But—but she's Prince Thutmose's cat!"

"Not anymore, apparently."

"Why would Pharaoh do such a thing?"

The man gave me an exasperated look. "You *are* an impudent little creature, acting as if you've got the right to question Pharaoh's commands. Lady Nefertiti must have her hands full, trying to get you to behave like a proper servant. You'd better learn to be quick, silent, helpful, and obedient or you'll find yourself looking for work somewhere else. Now go do as you're told."

I bowed my head over Ta-Miu's basket. "I live to make Lady Nefertiti happy."

"Ah, that's the way to be!" He chucked me under the chin. "You do have a pretty face, girl. I like you. You know, I'm a rather important person in this palace—entrusted with messages by Pharaoh himself. If you could . . . *like* me, I'd see to it that you got a job with even more prestige than waiting on Lady Nefertiti, better food, new clothes, easier work—"

"Oh, sir, I couldn't," I replied. "I know for a fact that if

I . . . *liked* you"—I twisted my mouth as if I'd just bitten into something sour enough to make my teeth ache—"that wouldn't make Lady Nefertiti happy at all!" With that, I dashed back into my rooms, leaving my visitor gape-jawed and his servant stuck with my dirty dishes.

I carried the basket into the inner chamber of my rooms, set it on my bed, and removed the cover. Ta-Miu looked up at me and complained about the shameful disrespect she'd been forced to suffer.

"Yes, yes, I know," I said, trying to make myself heard over a strident, unending series of meows. "You are the divine child of Bast, and I should be grateful for the privilege of serving you." I lifted her onto my lap and stroked her fur. "Except I'm going to be a very bad servant, at least until morning, because I haven't got any food in my quarters and I'm really too tired even to think of going to the kitchens now. Will you ever forgive me, O exalted feline?"

"That will depend on how many fish you lay at my feet tomorrow, O worthless human!" said a weirdly pitched, throaty voice that came from the room beyond my bedchamber.

I jumped to my feet in alarm, sending Ta-Miu leaping from my lap to hide herself under the bed. "Who's there?"

"You tell me," said Amenophis, smiling as he crossed the bedchamber threshold. "Today I've been many different— well, not *people*." He struck a stiff, dignified pose and intoned, "You are wrongfully accused. You are guiltless. You are free!"

The verdict of Ma'at! "*You* were the voice of the goddess?" I cried. "But what happened to the priest Thutmose bought? The one who was going to use Ma'at's mouth to condemn me?"

"You knew about my brother's plot?"

"Henenu told me."

"I see." He looked dejected. "I would have done the same, Nefertiti, but I thought if you knew what Thutmose had in mind—"

I stepped into his embrace and took a swift, sweet kiss from his lips. "Hush. I understand why you kept some secrets from me. Henenu helped me see your reasons."

"Bless him for that," Amenophis said. "I was afraid you'd be mad at me for hiding things from you."

"Just see to it that you never do so again," I told him. "Now, how did you deal with Thutmose's hired priest?"

"By hiring men of my own," he replied. "Did you see them? They were the ones who carried me away when I 'fainted.' As soon as we were well away from the courtyard, in a deserted part of the temple, I enjoyed an extraordinary recovery. I led the way as we stole through the inner corridors to reach the room where the 'voice' of Ma'at hides. Father showed it to me once, when I was still a child. It's very small—not more than a cubbyhole with a speaking tube that leads to Ma'at's wooden image—so the job usually falls to one of the youngest, smallest, scrawniest priests. When my men yanked open the door, he took one look at them and crawled out without a fight. I took his place, and you know the rest." He grinned. "No one else will, though. My men made it clear to the little priest that his silence and his health are now partners. And they'll never say one word about what happened. I sealed their lips with well-earned gold."

His smile withered. "It's always gold, gold and influence. Thutmose buys the goddess to destroy you, I buy her back to save you, but the real voice of Ma'at is gone. Was it ever there? If the gods have any real power, why do they stand by and allow us to buy and sell their voices? If Ma'at is the goddess of truth, why does she remain silent and permit so many lies to flourish? I am just as guilty of profaning her holy truth as the priests my brother bribed. I impersonated Ma'at herself, speaking in her name: If that was sacrilege, why didn't she stop me?"

I lifted my face to his. "If she had stopped you, what would have become of me?"

He kissed me, and his kiss was far more lingering than mine had been. I wished I could drown in it. When he drew back to speak again, I gave a little sigh of longing.

"Maybe the gods know better than we do when to keep silent," I said, resting my head over his heart. "Maybe— maybe the goddess sees what we can't, a greater truth."

"I love you, Nefertiti," Amenophis said softly. "I don't know of any greater truth than that. Do you think that's what Ma'at read in my heart when I pretended to be her?"

"If she did, then she must have forgiven you."

We kissed again, and I felt my blood turn to honey, warm and sweet. My senses danced, and all the fears and uncertainties and revelations of the day blew away like the dust of the Red Land's wild wastes. We were alone in my rooms, and I was powerless to tell whether knowing this made me eager or afraid. When our lips parted, he murmured, "I should go."

"Don't."

His long-fingered hands, once so clumsy, brushed my hair away from my face. "Even in the lamplight, you shine like the sun, Nefertiti. When I kiss you, it's like bathing in the fire of heaven. What an incredible gift of love Hathor has given me to cherish in you. I've never felt like this. I never knew I could."

"And I—" I choked on all the words I wanted to say. There were too many things I needed to tell him, and not enough time, not if we lived for a hundred years. "I want you to—"

A cascade of flickering flames invaded my bedchamber, oil lamps held high in the hands of a small army of harried, fearful serving women. Their eyes darted here and there, as if they didn't dare to look at us but didn't dare to look away. Then their ranks parted and a blazing coal of pure fury hurled itself upon us.

"Get *away* from her!" Aunt Tiye's nails dug deep into Amenophis's shoulder. She pulled him back so hard that it seemed she was trying to fling him to the floor. "Is *this* what you do? Fly to *her* like a vulture to carrion? There's not enough gold in this palace to reward the man who warned me about where to find you!"

"You don't need to be 'warned' about my comings and goings, Mother," Amenophis said evenly. "I'm not a prisoner."

"But your brother is! And here I find you, in the arms of the one to blame for that. Have you no loyalty? Don't you understand that she's destroyed our lives? Your brother was my one hope to secure this family's future! Now what's going to happen to us? Because of her, Amenhotep has turned his face away from his own son! I've beaten my hands bloody against his doors and he still refuses to let me in. If I could only talk to him, I could make him see that Thutmose was not himself today. He was—he was sun-struck, that's what happened. It affected his mind, but only for a little while, except *she* took advantage of his momentary weakness to make him look bad in Pharaoh's eyes. I don't care how slyly she played it or who helped her, Thutmose can't possibly be held responsible for what he did today! We might as well punish you for fainting like some weak-blooded girl. My husband must be made to see what really happened in the Palace of Ma'at. He loves the boy. He might be swayed to forgive him. He could—"

"Mrrrr?" Ta-Miu stuck her head out from under my bed.

You would have thought she was a viper from the way Aunt Tiye reacted. *"What's that?"* she shrieked, pointing at the cat with one shaking finger. "Why is she here? Ah! You stole her, didn't you?" she snapped at me. "You took the one comfort my poor child had in his unfair captivity!"

"I didn't take Ta-Miu," I said, trying to stay calm. "She was given to me."

"Liar! After all you've made him suffer, why would Thutmose give you his most precious—"

"Thutmose didn't give me this cat," I said. It was all I wanted to say. Even though she had reviled me, I felt a lingering pity for my aunt. She had built her life on the goal of seeing Thutmose become the next pharaoh. If I told her the full truth about why I now had Ta-Miu, it would devastate her.

Aunt Tiye was a smart woman. She didn't need me to

tell her anything more. I saw the blood leave her face. "Pharaoh." I could only nod.

I expected her to tremble, to weep, to wring her hands. She knew what this gift meant: If Pharaoh could take away his eldest son's dearest companion, his heart had turned cold to him. Thutmose had angered his father beyond words, beyond hope of reconciliation.

Again, I underestimated her. This hard-eyed, determined woman from a commoner's household had used her beauty, charm, and intelligence to rise from the ranks of all of Pharaoh's women—the highborn, the beauties, the daughters of foreign kings—to become the Great Royal Wife of the mightiest man in the Two Lands. Her small hands had held power that the most nobly born men in Pharaoh's court only dreamed of. She would not let it go without a fight.

"So, my husband favors *you*." Her eyes glittered as she gazed at me. "Of course he does. I knew he would from the first moment I saw what a beauty you'd become. Before your trial, he told me how much he hoped that the goddess would declare your innocence. I've even heard my own servants whispering that he's so pleased with the verdict that he ordered a thanksgiving offering for her temple. One of his best sculptors will make an image of the goddess to be covered in gold leaf and sent to her shrine accompanied by a train of slaves bearing chests filled with treasures." She glared so angrily at the women who attended her that their lamps' flames shivered like their own reflections in a troubled pool.

"I am grateful for Pharaoh's kindness—" I began.

"Be *quiet*. Let me think." She pressed her fingertips together and closed her eyes.

"Mother?" Amenophis tried to touch her shoulder, but she jerked away from him.

Her eyes snapped open. "I said *let me think*! I'm doing this for you, too, Amenophis. I only wish you were smart enough to appreciate it." She scowled at him. "But you're not, are you? No, you proved that when you got yourself mixed up with this girl, running away with her, pouring her lies into your father's ears. Why? Did you envy your brother because he was going to have a beautiful wife? If that's what you wanted, you could have come to me. I would have found you *someone*. Even someone pretty. What sane man *wouldn't* give his daughter to the brother of our next pharaoh? You could have lived out your days at ease in your brother's court, your every desire fulfilled. Instead, you hated him, you undermined him, and you won't be happy until you've ruined him!"

O gods, I thought. *If this is how she sees Amenophis now, what will she say if she knew what he did in the Palace of Ma'at this morning?*

"Mother, you're wrong," Amenophis said in his steady, quiet voice. "I don't hate my brother. He's the one who thinks I'm his enemy. I love him, in spite of all that he's done—"

She slapped his face. "He's done nothing wrong. *Nothing!*" The sea of little oil flames around us trembled anew at her shrill cry of denial.

Amenophis took a deep breath and continued. "I love my brother. It would make my spirit fly on falcon's wings if

I could see him contented, healthy, free, and back in our father's favor."

"Would it?" A small, disturbing smile uncoiled itself across Aunt Tiye's mouth. "Then I am going to make you very happy, my son." She leveled one finger at me again. "Your name is cleared, Nefertiti. You are free to come and go anywhere you like in the royal palace and in the city of Thebes. Come to my rooms, when you can. You're my dear niece, after all, and I haven't seen as much of you as I'd like. We must get to know one another better, dear child."

"Yes, Aunt Tiye," I said cautiously. *What is she up to?*

"Good. I look forward to our conversations. Come tomorrow. I will expect you to share breakfast with me."

This was no invitation but an out-and-out command. I bowed my head, consenting. There was no sense in rebelling against her demands just for the sake of rebellion. I had the feeling that Aunt Tiye would give me enough cause to stand against her soon enough.

I was right. I wished I'd been wrong.

"May I come, too, Mother?" Amenophis asked. "I think that you and I need to speak about why I acted as I did, helping Nefertiti escape from the palace."

"Oh, that." She waved his words away. "I don't care to hear your excuses and explanations, and you've made it clear that you don't care about me at all."

"Mother, you know you're wrong."

Amenophis, that is the worst thing you can possibly say to her, I thought. *Aunt Tiye lives in a world where she is* never *wrong.*

"Is that so?" She wore a tiny, brittle smile. "*Do* you care about me, my son? Do you still have room in your heart for the woman who gave birth to you, raised you, wanted only what was best for you, or is it filled with nothing but my niece's image?"

"I do love Nefertiti, Mother. The gods would punish me for lying if I denied that. But I love you, too."

"Ah, love. You love her, you love me, you love your brother, and I presume you love your royal father as well. *Is* there any end to all the love you claim to feel, Amenophis?" She was taunting him openly, but he ignored her sarcasm.

"I hope not."

"Do you know what love *is,* my openhearted son? It's being willing to place the needs and dreams and happiness of the ones you love ahead of your own. It's the reason a mother will take bread from her own mouth and starve rather than let her child go hungry."

As if you *ever went hungry for anyone,* I thought, watching my aunt closely. *Why can't I look at you without thinking of a snake slowly coiling itself into a deadly ring just before it strikes? Oh, Amenophis, she's your mother and I know you do love her, but still—be on your guard!*

"I understand, Mother," he said. "And I'm glad you said that, because it means *you* will understand why Nefertiti and I want to—"

"And you, child?" Aunt Tiye turned sharply to me, cutting off her son's words as brutally as if she had a naked sword in her hands. "Does your heart have room to love anyone but this boy?" She couldn't keep the contempt out of her voice when she spoke of Amenophis. I wanted to shake sense into her, force her to see the worth of her second son, but all I could do was grit my teeth and endure.

"Don't pretend there's nothing but devoted friendship be-tween you. That might explain why he risked his life to bring you to Dendera uninvited, but not the *spectacle* I saw when I entered this room. And I was not the only one to see it. Here are my witnesses."

She spread her hands to include the maidservants sur-rounding us. The poor girls exchanged nervous looks. I wondered if they ever enjoyed a single unanxious moment, working for the Great Royal Wife, or if their days were spent forever balancing on the point of a needle, teetering over an abyss.

"I wouldn't dream of pretending I don't love Ameno-phis," I said. "I'm not ashamed of it, nor of what you saw."

"Mmm-hmm." Aunt Tiye stooped to pick up Ta-Miu and scratch the cat between her enormous ears. "This crea-ture has no sense of shame, either. A room, a rooftop, a darkened street, they're all the same to her." She put the cat down again. "But that wasn't what I asked you. Who else do you love, Nefertiti? Truly love?"

"My family," I said readily. "You know that. I miss them."

"Oh, dear, and I thought *we* were your family." Aunt Tiye put on a false look of hurt feelings. I decided to follow Amenophis's lead and act as if she'd spoken to me honestly.

"I mean my family that's not here. I haven't received a single word from them since I got here, and I haven't been allowed to send them any news."

"Where did you get *that* notion? You used to send them messages all the time, before your little . . . adventure. If there's anyone who's keeping news from my brother Ay and the rest of them in Akhmin, it's you alone."

How did you know about how frequently I used to write to them? I thought. *How, unless your agents were the ones who intercepted my messages?*

"Then who's to blame for my hearing nothing from them?" I asked.

She shrugged. "Oh, who knows? Maybe that sort of neglectful behavior runs in Ay's part of the family. Like father, like daughter, or the other way around. Some people prefer to avoid writing letters. They'd rather hear the news about their loved ones from the source itself." Aunt Tiye's lips stretched into a crocodile's smile. "How would you like to go back to Akhmin, Nefertiti?"

"With all my heart!" The words were out of my mouth before I could stop them. Even as I proclaimed the truth, my head rang with exasperated thoughts: *Fool! Idiot! What have you done? You've let that woman see your weakest spot, and you've given her the spear to pierce it!*

Maybe I'd made a horribly wrong move, but I couldn't help myself: The thought of returning to Akhmin, of seeing Father and Mother and Bit-Bit again, filled me with longing. I wasn't like Aunt Tiye, living a life of endless strategy and calculation. I prayed I never would become such a person.

"Such passion!" Aunt Tiye laid one hand to her bosom. "My dear, you should have said something. Akhmin isn't that far away. Now that there's no further need to keep you shut away in these rooms, you should be able to go visit your parents and that adorable little sister of yours. I'll see to the arrangements myself. It will make a lovely wedding voyage."

I saw Amenophis's face light up with hope, with joy, and I wanted to cry out, "No! You're listening to her words but you're hearing her say what you want to hear! Don't you understand her yet? When she says *wedding voyage,* she doesn't mean you and me, she means—!

"How wonderful it will be, dear Nefertiti," Aunt Tiye spoke on, enfolding me in a hug that felt like strong ropes binding my arms to my sides. "A royal ship laden with gifts for your family, musicians playing love songs on the deck, incense perfuming the sail! And then, your homecoming. What a vision that will be! I can hardly wait to see Ay's face when his beautiful daughter comes home as she was always meant to be: crown princess of the Two Lands, wife of Prince Thutmose, my beloved son."

— 12 —

SHADOWED HEARTS

Amenophis's anguished cry seared my heart. I thrust my arms straight out to the sides, breaking Aunt Tiye's loveless embrace, and jumped away from her as if she were made of knives.

"Are you *insane*?" I shouted at her. All thought of the respect I owed her as my aunt and my queen was gone. She was nothing but a jackal with foaming fangs she wanted to sink into my throat and steal my last breath of life. "Have *you* been sunstruck or has your mind been shattered? After everything that Thutmose has done to me!"

"*Nothing . . .*" The word was a warning growl deep in her throat, but it sounded as if it came from the depths of an eternal night. "My son has done *nothing wrong.*"

At least she didn't try to slap me. I would have slapped back, and the gods know where that would have ended.

"How can you say that?" I protested. "As soon as you and Pharaoh left for Dendera—"

"Nefertiti, no more." Amenophis cupped my shoulders with his hands, speaking softly but urgently. "It's no use arguing with her about what's in the past between you and my brother. Speak to her about *now*."

I saw the wisdom in his words and nodded. "Aunt Tiye," I said, pulling back my shoulders and standing as firmly as I'd done that morning in the house of truth. "Aunt Tiye, the only wedding voyage I will make is when I marry *this* man." I clasped my beloved's hand in mine and raised them high for her and all her attendants to see.

My aunt regarded the two of us coldly for a long time. My bedchamber filled with silence as we waited to hear what she would say to my open act of defiance. Then, instead of speaking, she made a curt gesture to her maids and they filed out of the room, out of my quarters entirely, leaving the three of us alone with the few lamps my maids had kindled before I'd sent them away. One of these had already run out of oil and was no more than a blackened wick sending up a thread of smoke in the shadows. Two remained, petals of fire wavering against the dark.

"Little girl, save your breath," my aunt said at last. "You can argue, fight, weep, curse, even bring the voices of a *dozen* gods to speak for you. The result will be the same. You will marry Thutmose or you will marry no one."

"What's the matter with you, Aunt Tiye? Why are you still trying to do this to me? The game is *over*. You can't win. You said yourself that Thutmose won't inherit the throne because he's lost his father's favor."

"And you have gained it. I have stood outside my husband's rooms, pleading with him to reconsider his actions against our boy, to understand, to forgive him and restore him to his rightful place as heir to the double crown. He wouldn't open the doors. But if you were to go to him and declare that you realized that Thutmose was—was under a spell, or ill, or *something* to excuse his actions this morning, those doors would open. And if you then told Pharaoh that you repent all your foolishness and want nothing more than to accept Thutmose as your husband, your words would become the wings to lift him to the place he belongs—onto the throne of his ancestors. Marry my son, Nefertiti, and undo all the harm you've done to him, to me, to your family."

Her reasoning made twisted sense: If I could forgive Thutmose for everything he'd done and tried to do to me, his father should be able to forgive him anything, even profaning Ma'at's shrine with a bared weapon and vile speech. Even so, how could she believe I'd ever be a willing part of such a plan?

I sighed deeply. "Aunt Tiye, I'm not the one who's done any harm to our family. I never wanted to leave Akhmin, to come to Thebes, to live in a palace, to wear a crown. I certainly never wanted Thutmose's father to turn his back on his eldest son. If Pharaoh will consent to see me, I'll go to him and ask him to take Thutmose back as his son, even if not as his heir, but that is *all* I'll do."

"Little enough," Aunt Tiye snarled. "Worse than nothing. Amenophis!" Her head whipped in his direction. "You claim to care about me, and you say you want your brother's happiness. Show it! Make this stupid girl do what's needed to restore Thutmose to his rightful place. You can do it. She loves you."

I never saw such a look of dismay and disillusion on Amenophis's face as I saw then. "If that's how you think, Mother . . ." He shook his head slowly. "My poor, poor father."

"What are you babbling about?" Aunt Tiye spat the words in his face. "Go! Get out of my sight!"

"I'm not leaving you alone with Nefertiti," he replied.

"Why not? Afraid I'll hurt her?" Aunt Tiye sneered. "If *that's* what you think of your own mother, rest easy: I'm leaving, too."

"I never said I was leaving at all."

How Aunt Tiye's eyes flashed with rage when he said that! "Then stay with her, and may Ammut devour both your hearts for this treachery." She strode out of the room.

I reached up and kissed Amenophis's cheek. "I'm so sorry, my dearest one. I wish she'd turned all of her anger against me before she said such awful things to you."

"She couldn't help herself, Nefertiti," he replied. There was a great weariness in his voice. "She loves Thutmose too much to see him the way others do. And what's worse"—he paused for a breath—"so do I."

His words robbed me of the power to speak. All I could do was stare at him, my mouth open, numbly asking myself if I'd misheard him. "How . . . ?" was all I could muster. "How?"

"How can I say that, after all you endured today?" Amenophis made a helpless gesture. "I can't explain it. It's not as if he was ever kind to me. There were moments when I sensed he wanted to treat me differently, except he didn't know how." He shook his head. "Maybe I just imagined those times because I craved them so much."

Or maybe they were there, I thought. *Maybe Thutmose did want to be a true brother to Amenophis, but someone made him afraid to try. Oh, Aunt Tiye, if this is what your love has done to your firstborn, I'm glad you held it back from your second son!*

Amenophis held me close. His eyes brimmed with sadness. "I must speak honestly, even if you come to hate me for it. I can never forget what Thutmose tried to do to you, but—forgive me, Nefertiti—I still love my brother."

"Then love him." I cradled Amenophis's face in my hands. "And may the day soon come when he loves you." We shared another kiss, but I was the one who ended it when I realized I was trying to stifle a yawn.

"Poor Nefertiti." Amenophis chuckled and brushed my chin with one fingertip. "You're tired, aren't you?"

It was the truth. My legs were beginning to feel like wilted flower stems. Suddenly all I wanted to do was go to bed and sleep for days. "Sorry . . ." I tried and failed to smother a second yawn.

He kissed the top of my head. "Rest well, beloved," he murmured into my hair, and left me.

I shed my dress, blew out the two remaining lamps, collapsed onto my mattress, and dove into sleep.

The next morning, I was wakened by Ta-Miu's cold little nose touching mine. The cat mewed loudly, wanting to be fed. I called for my maids and was pleasantly surprised to find that they'd not only brought my breakfast already, but had also included a dish of fish and cold chicken for the cat.

After I ate, the girls escorted me to the bathing room in a nearby part of the women's quarters. While I washed myself with sweetly perfumed cream, they took turns pouring jugs of water over me until I felt deliciously clean again.

I was just dressing when a messenger from Aunt Tiye showed up. It was a maidservant—perhaps one of those who had attended her last night when she stormed into my bedroom. She could scarcely look at me while she delivered her mistress's words.

"Hail, Lady Nefertiti. I am commanded to bring you to my most excellent royal mistress, Queen Tiye, Great Royal Wife of Pharaoh Amenhotep, Lord of the Two Lands, god-on-earth, master of—"

"What for?" I didn't need to hear all of Pharaoh's grand titles. "Why does she want to see me?"

"Uh! That is, she was expecting . . . um . . . You should have—you had to . . ." My interruption had thrown off the poor girl's memory. "I mean, um, you were supposed to be there for breakfast!"

Strange, I thought as I followed the maidservant through the palace halls to Aunt Tiye's apartments. *I forgot all about that invitation. Even if I'd remembered it, I wouldn't think she'd still want to see me after what I said to her last night.* It was all very perplexing, but I soon shrugged off my puzzlement. I was too taken up with enjoying my restored freedom. How nice to be a part of the bustling world of the palace that lay beyond the women's quarters! How interesting to see the grand variety of people swarming in and out of the reception areas, the offices, the storerooms. So many different faces, clothes, jewels, to say nothing of the stunning combination of smells—food, perfume, sweat, spices, even the sudden sharpness of an animal's presence when we crossed paths with a noble leading his tame cheetah through the halls. *What would Ta-Miu make of you, my pretty one?* I thought.

Some of the faces I passed were familiar. I was deeply pleased to receive warm greetings and cries of "Welcome back, Lady Nefertiti!" from several people. At one point, I nearly bumped into Pharaoh's vizier. His momentary frown at being jostled disappeared the instant he recognized me.

"Ah, Lady Nefertiti! May the gods be praised that all went well for you yesterday. The memory of your first trial still disturbs my dreams. I never did believe you were guilty of such terrible offenses. Now that everything's been settled, I'm going to see to it that the boy who gave false testimony against you is punished. Meketre probably won't get everything he deserves—he's still one of Pharaoh's lesser sons, even if he's a wicked little liar—but I'll do what I can."

"Please, let it pass," I said.

The vizier was surprised. "You don't want anything done to the boy?"

"I don't want revenge against a child." *Especially not a child who was only someone else's tool,* I thought, recalling how badly Meketre had stumbled over his testimony and how closely the Amun priests had shepherded him throughout. *He was forced to work for the priests, the priests worked for Thutmose, and even Thutmose worked for another. Has he ever lived free of Aunt Tiye's power? Has he ever had the chance to ask himself whether he wants to be pharaoh, or have her wishes left no room for any of his own?*

Aunt Tiye had a sumptuous meal waiting for me in her

apartments. The bread was fresh and warm from the ovens, some of the loaves stuffed with savory onions, and there were bowls heaped with honeycombs, baskets of fruit, and platters of cheeses. She greeted me as if our clash of the night before had never happened, and even set a wreath of flowers on my head with her own hands. I wished her a good day, thanked her for the food, and spent the rest of the meal waiting for her next attack. It never came.

"Hasn't this been nice, Nefertiti?" she remarked as she escorted me to the door of her apartments. "We must do it again soon. I'm sorry it can't be tomorrow, but I've had such a splendid note from my beloved lord, Pharaoh Amenhotep, saying that he wants my company all day then." She blushed like a young girl.

"Did he? Oh, Aunt Tiye, I'm so happy for you!" I meant that sincerely. It pained me to think of the family remaining so shattered by what Thutmose had done. I didn't want to marry him, and I didn't want him to become our next pharaoh—if he couldn't govern his own passions, how could he govern the Black Land?—but I did want to see him reconciled with his father. If Aunt Tiye was going to spend the whole day with her husband, I was sure she'd use her persuasive wiles to bring that about.

"What a good girl you are," she said, patting my cheek a little too briskly. It stung, but I said nothing. Surely it was an accident. "And what do you think you'll be doing for the rest of today and tomorrow?"

"Oh, I'm—I'm not sure," I replied.

But I was, and my expression must have betrayed my thoughts because she said, "You're going to seek out

Amenophis, aren't you? Of course you are." She smiled and gave me a sharp push across her threshold into the hall. *"Good luck."* The words sounded as hard as her laughter at my back when she slammed the door behind me.

There was no servant waiting to guide me back to the women's quarters from Aunt Tiye's apartments. I had to find my own way, and it took a good deal of time, even though I asked directions. By the time I got back to my own rooms, my maids had disappeared yet again. There was no one to carry a message for me to Amenophis. I couldn't do so myself. In all the time I'd lived in the royal palace, I'd never found out where his rooms lay, though I had a vague idea.

Should I go to that part of the palace and ask? I thought, then discarded the notion. I longed to see him, but if I went running after him like that, it would give the countless wagging tongues throughout the palace a fresh source of gossip.

I don't care what they'd say about me, I told myself. *I just don't want* him *to be embarrassed.* A sudden, telltale warmth flushed my cheeks, forcing me to admit, *Who am I fooling? I care what they'd say about me, too. I'll write out a message for Amenophis and get one of the other women's servants to deliver it for me.*

It was all so easy. I didn't have any close friends among Pharaoh's junior wives and his other female companions, but nearly everyone knew me. I'd come into their midst as the promised bride of a royal prince, I'd gained notice when I happened to uncover a deadly plot by two of the women, and I'd become notorious when I was dragged away to stand trial for Ta-Miu's "death." Now I'd returned, victoriously acquitted by the word of Ma'at herself. Who *didn't* know my name? And who hadn't heard the story of how grateful Pharaoh was to see me exonerated?

In the women's quarters, Pharaoh's good will was worth more than gold. As soon as I approached one of the younger junior wives with my request for writing supplies and a messenger, every other woman within eavesdropping distance flooded me with pens, paints, papyrus, and offers to lend me the services of their smartest, swiftest-footed maidservants. My note was on its way before midday.

There was no answer. The girl returned looking downcast and handed back my letter. "I'm so sorry, Lady Nefertiti. When I reached the prince's apartments and announced I had a letter for him from you, I was told that he'd gone away. I asked where he was and when he might return, but all I got was a slap and a scolding about minding my own business." She looked at her feet. "Forgive me; I've failed you."

I forced her to look up again. "You've done no such thing. I'm the one who's sorry that Prince Amenophis has such churlish servants. When I see him next, I'll be sure to tell him to teach them better manners. They had no right to strike you. If I write another letter, will you carry it for me?" She looked hesitant, so I quickly added, "Not to Prince Amenophis—to the household of Princess Sitamun."

This time the messenger returned happily, her mission fulfilled, a reply from Sitamun in her hands:

> *Dear friend, I don't know what to tell you. I have no*
> *idea where my brother Amenophis is. I sent him my own*
> *note and the servant who carried it to his apartments*

received the same reception as your messenger, except for
the slap. Perhaps that was because I sent one of my
strongest manservants and not a defenseless girl. Slap or
no slap, no one in my brother's household would say
where he'd gone or when he might come back. Come see
me and we will speak more about this. Sitamun.

I had the girl turn around and take me to Sitamun's rooms. I found my friend walking in her garden, watching a flight of egrets cross the sky. After we exchanged a kiss in greeting, she had me sit beside her on a bench that viewed a small lotus pool. Here I told her everything that had happened in my bedchamber the previous night.

"So much for you to endure in one day!" she exclaimed. "And to enjoy." Her smile was genuine. "I'm very happy for you and Amenophis."

"Your mother's not," I said. "She's after me again to marry Thutmose."

"I heard. And this time she's got even more pressing reasons to force things along. I'll never understand how her mind works. It's brilliant and frightening at the same time. Father would be more likely to pardon Thutmose if he saw irrefutable evidence that you'd done so."

"There's no better proof of my forgiveness than marrying the man who tried to kill me," I said bitterly.

"Forgiveness or revenge." Sitamun was joking, though there was a grain of truth in the jest.

"At the cost of being his wife for even one day? No, thank you. Even if I knew I'd be able to make him pay for everything he's done to me, *that* price is too high."

"No need to pay it, then. You've got a *much* more pleasant way to punish him at hand." Her eyes twinkled. "I can't wait for the day when you and Amenophis live as man and wife!"

"I'll have to find him first." It was my turn to joke, but I couldn't quite manage to free my words from the uneasiness that was beginning to gnaw at me. I remembered the disturbing note in Aunt Tiye's voice when she'd wished me "good luck." It still troubled me.

I'm being ridiculous, I thought. *I'm reading too much into an accident of tone. She didn't mean anything more than what she said.*

But I'd spent enough time with Aunt Tiye to know that there was seldom only one face to what she said or did.

"Find him?" Sitamun's carefree voice plucked me out of my worries. "Not before he finds you, I bet. Then you'll come running to me, complaining that he's not giving you a single moment alone!"

I scared up a weak smile. "You're probably right. It's just that I'd like to see him soon, to make sure he's all right. Your mother said some deeply hurtful things to him last night. Every time she spoke as if Thutmose were her only son, I wanted to throw water in her face."

"Is that all you wanted to do? I've wanted to do worse to her for years. She's always acted that way toward Amenophis. It's awful, I hate it, and it's not what he deserves."

"It's not what any child deserves."

Sitamun squeezed my hand. "I thank Hathor for bringing you into Amenophis's life, dear Nefertiti. Listen, why don't you come back here this evening? I don't know what he's up to, but instead of you chasing after him all day, I'll see to it that he's here to join us for dinner. It will be a lovely time, just the three of us." She winked and added, "To start. I'm deathly afraid that I'm not going to be feeling well and I'll have to leave the two of you alone. I hope you'll forgive me."

"Poor thing, you can't help it," I replied as gravely as I could before the two of us burst into giggles.

I went back to my rooms and spent the day resting, dreaming, fussing over Ta-Miu, and enjoying the gift of peace. I took a little time to search my belongings for something that would be a fitting gift for the maidservant who'd done so much for me earlier in the day. I settled on a precious vial of rare perfume. If the girl didn't want to use it herself, she'd be able to barter it for something equally valuable.

After I found her and rewarded her, I lingered in the women's quarters to play with the children and to chat with their mothers. One of Pharaoh's junior wives was a good harp player; another had a sistrum whose delicate metal disks made the most beautiful jingling sound when she rattled them. Still others were famous for their singing voices, and so I soon found myself dancing in line with six young women, a handful of excited toddlers, and someone's pet dog. It was joyous, exhausting, and wonderful.

My heart was high as I made my way back to Sitamun's apartments that evening, but my elation slipped away the instant I saw her face. "He's not here," she told me.

"That's all right, we can still enjoy our dinner together," I said. I didn't want her to feel as though she'd let me down over something out of her control. "Did he mention if he could come tomorrow night instead? We could eat in my rooms. My maids will probably break half the dishes, but if you bring some of your servants to help them, it might not be *too* bad."

"Nefertiti, he won't be there. Unless something happens to intervene, you won't be meeting Amenophis again. She's seen to that."

I didn't need to ask who "she" was. My flesh went cold.

"He's all right," Sitamun went on quickly, seeing the look on my face. "She hasn't done anything to hurt him. She'd never do something so unnatural. No matter how angry she gets or how much she prefers Thutmose, she always remembers that the rest of us are her children, too."

"But she's imprisoned him, hasn't she?"

"Not even that. Not exactly. How could she justify such a thing? She knows that word of it would fly to Father's ears. She's too sharp-witted to risk doing anything that would anger him further. But she doesn't need to shut Amenophis in a room in order to keep him away from you."

"So that was what she meant when she wished me luck in finding him," I muttered.

"What?"

"Nothing. Tell me, Sitamun, how is she doing this?"

"Today it was by sending him a message before dawn, telling him that there was hope she could repair the breach between Father and Thutmose. Father loves banquets, so she planned a magnificent one for tonight to soften his mood. She told Amenophis that she was terribly sorry for any hurt she'd caused him last night and wanted to make it up to him. That was why she was going to entrust all the arrangements for the banquet to him."

"Perfect." I had to admire Aunt Tiye's cunning. "Amenophis couldn't say no. It's a chance to prove how much he wants to reestablish peace between his father and brother and show his mother that he does care about her. But, Sitamun, how did you come to learn all this?"

"My messenger returned from Amenophis's apartments with the bare bones of the story. I was sure there had to be more to it, so I let all my servants know I'd be very generous to anyone who could bring me more information. My household butler is a very reliable, truthful man with excellent contacts among the other royal servants. He told me everything I've just told you, and more." She gave me a sympathetic look. "Amenophis isn't here tonight because he's a guest at the feast he spent all day organizing. And he won't be free tomorrow, or the next day, or the next, because our mother has suddenly discovered how highly she values her younger son and has already prepared an endless list of tasks that require his 'help.'"

"She can't keep him busy forever!"

"Don't make a wager on that. She's a resourceful woman. I hear that she was so pleased with the arrangements he made for tonight's banquet that she couldn't stop praising him. He was like parched ground, drinking up every drop of her new kindness and thirsting for more."

I shook my head. "I don't care how many tasks she gives him or how long she intends to play this game; I'll play it longer. Aunt Tiye might think she'll make us grow indifferent to one another if she keeps us apart, but I know Amenophis loves me. I trust his heart."

"And he can trust yours," Sitamun said. "Meanwhile,

let me help the two of you. Don't give up trying to see him, but find other ways to touch his life." She smiled. "Weren't you Henenu's best student?"

"More likely that honor belongs to you, or even Nava," I said. "Besides, I don't have my scribe's kit anymore."

"That's easily fixed. I'll send you one before midday tomorrow; then you can write a letter to Amenophis."

"I wrote letters home. They never got there. Or if they did, *someone* made sure I never saw the replies. When I sent a letter to Amenophis's door today, the girl carrying it was told lies and given a smack for her troubles. I'm sure we can thank Aunt Tiye for that, too. What makes you think she'd allow *any* of my letters to reach Amenophis?"

"Because they won't be *your* letters," Sitamun said. "They'll be mine."

"Oh. Then I guess I'll have to be even more careful about what I say when I write them." I blushed, and she laughed at me.

It seemed like a good plan, or at least the best one we could devise until Sitamun or I came up with a better one. As she had promised, she sent me a new scribe's palette and a box of pens and brushes, along with a generous supply of papyrus. I spent a lot of time composing my first letter to Amenophis, doing all I could to make it seem as though the words came from his sister, not from the girl who loved him as dearly as breath.

It was a challenge—a very time-consuming, irritating challenge. What good was it for me to have the freedom to go anywhere in the palace or the city when my words were still enslaved? And what could I do about it? Aunt Tiye had robbed me of my most precious treasure, the gift of choice, the gift that the gods themselves put into our hands when the world and all its possibilities were new.

At least I didn't have to lose more time over making a perfect copy. Sitamun offered to transform my scribbled sentences with her own pen so that our messenger could swear by Ma'at or any other god that he was delivering "a letter from Princess Sitamun to her royal brother, Prince Amenophis, written by her own hand."

When the first reply from Amenophis revealed that he knew exactly who had composed "Sitamun's" letter, we all felt very clever. It amused me to see how readily he fell into the spirit of our plot. Even so, he didn't break away from the series of errands and assignments Aunt Tiye kept heaping in his lap, although he saw plainly that they were keeping him from being with me. It was good to know that his eyes had been opened, yet I felt some sadness, too.

He sees the truth, and the truth is that his mother isn't drawing him closer because she loves him as he deserves, but because she wants to use him. Then and there, I promised myself that if we ever were able to break away from Aunt Tiye's web, I would give him a family where the love was as unconditional as the Aten's light, favoring no single person over another, embracing all.

The days passed uneventfully for me. My life in the women's quarters was pleasant but bland. The only change that seemed to touch my existence was that the list of people I missed so badly was growing longer—my family, my friends, and those who had become as dear as family to me. Every morning I woke up hoping to hear that Nava and

Henenu had returned from Memphis after successfully buying Mahala's freedom, but no word came. I had to comfort myself with the thought that they had undertaken a much longer journey than our voyage to Dendera and that once they reached Memphis, they might not be able to make a bargain with Mahala's owner right away. All I could do was wait and pray. Sometimes I implored Isis for help, but once I found myself looking up into the morning sky, my face to the sun, and asking the One to bring them home.

I'm praying for Nava and Mahala, I thought as the Aten's light bathed my face and its warmth soothed me. *Is it wrong to make that prayer to their god?*

There was just one part of the day that filled me with excitement. I lived for the moment when Sitamun's servant would come to fetch me to her rooms with one excuse after another—I had to see her new wig, she wanted my opinion about which dress to wear that night, or she was blending perfumes and had some to give me. The real reason was always the same: Amenophis's letter had arrived and it was time for me to write my reply.

One afternoon, while watching me bent over the papyrus, Sitamun said, "How long will you let this go on, Nefertiti? May the gods forgive me for asking such a question, but do you and Amenophis intend to wait until Mother is *dead* before you live your own lives?"

"We don't need to wait that long, Sitamun," I replied, grinning. "Only until she grows tired of pounding at yet another closed door and looks elsewhere for a way to make Pharaoh favor Thutmose again—or if not favor him, at least forgive him."

"Hmph. Why should she? She pounded at Father's closed door long enough and it opened. The two of them are like newlyweds these days."

"Then maybe she can use her renewed influence over Pharaoh to gain what she wants for her elder son."

"If all she wanted was a reconciliation between those two, she'd have it by now. And from what I hear, she's also halfway to persuading Father to reconsider Thutmose as his heir. The palace is buzzing with talk of a trial period where they'll share the duties of ruling the Two Lands."

"This is the first I've heard of it," I said. "I should leave the women's quarters more often."

"The news always goes through the women's quarters, Nefertiti," Sitamun said, her expression so serious it made her look old. "It just never reaches you. Don't you see what she's doing? One by one, she's cutting the strands that link you to others. For some, she doesn't need an excuse. Even if they envy her or hate her, no one from the women's quarters would dare to thwart the Great Royal Wife. If she lets it be known that no one is to give you any important information, your neighbors will fill your days with a flurry of mindless chatter about hair, dresses, and cosmetics, but no useful news."

"Then it's lucky for me I have you, Sitamun," I said. "Now tell me something useful." I ran my fingers through my tiny braids and teased, "Does this hairstyle look pretty enough with this dress, or do you think it would work better if I put on some more cosmetics?"

She threw a cushion at me.

It wasn't until later, when I was back in my own rooms,

that I recalled Sitamun's ominous words about Aunt Tiye: *"If all she wanted was a reconciliation between those two, she'd have it by now."*

What else does *she want, then?* I wondered. *And why does she need* me *to get it?*

I resolved to ask Sitamun that very question the next time I saw her, but it slipped my mind until some seven days later. I'd dismissed my maids and was in my courtyard, anxiously watching the sun fade from the sky. It was almost evening, and I'd had no word from Sitamun. This wasn't usual. Amenophis never let one day pass without writing to me. My mind began to conjure up all sorts of bizarre reasons for this unnatural silence. All of them were horribly dramatic and involved hideous disasters. Any peep of common sense in my head was outshouted by countless ridiculous possibilities. When Sitamun's servant finally presented herself at the entryway to the courtyard, I swept down upon her like a rockslide.

"There you are! I was afraid that . . . I thought . . . Has anything . . . ?" I saw the look of badly reined-in panic in the girl's eyes and forced myself to regain some self-control. "You know that your mistress and I are close friends. She's shown me such kindness every day that I'm afraid she's spoiled me. When you didn't come until now, I became concerned that there was something wrong with the princess. I forgot that she has many other things in her life besides me. If she can't see me today, that's all right. Tomorrow will do. She's well?"

"Lady Nefertiti . . ." The girl's voice shook. Instead of responding to my question, she bowed very low before me and handed me a scrap of papyrus. When she straightened her back again, all she said was "Please give me leave to go back to my mistress. She hasn't stopped crying all day."

"Crying? Why? What's the matter?" Fear shot back through me and I crushed the papyrus between my hands.

"*Please,* my lady, let me leave." The servant looked on the brink of tears herself. "I'm not even supposed to be here, but my mistress got down on her knees to me—to me!— and begged me to do this. If I'm discovered, I'll—I'll be whipped and taken away from the princess's household and—and—and—"

"Go, go!" I cried, waving the crushed papyrus frantically. "You were never here."

She didn't wait for another word from me, and I didn't wait to see the last flash of her heels as she fled from the courtyard. I spread the papyrus so roughly that it tore, but I could still read my dear friend's message, scrawled in haste, stained with tears:

My dear friend, I thought I could do more for you and Amenophis than help pass messages between you. I went to Father to let him know how dearly you loved each other and how Mother had built walls between you. I thought that if he knew, he would overrule her and bless your marriage. At this point in the letter, the lines were so badly smeared that it took me several attempts before I read the words: *I did not know at first that he was not alone.*

I pictured the scene in Pharaoh's apartments—Sitamun pleading for his support; Aunt Tiye overhearing her own daughter chipping away at her plans; the moment she revealed her presence not as Sitamun's mother but as Great

Royal Wife, the god-on-earth's beloved. She'd have no trouble coming up with a plausible way to make Sitamun look foolish. She had more influence over Pharaoh than his daughter could ever hope to possess. With tender whispers and oh-so-reasonable explanations and many loving kisses, Aunt Tiye would guide her royal husband like a master of chariots. Sitamun would never have a chance against her.

And afterward, she'd make Sitamun pay the price for what Aunt Tiye could only see as treachery.

She has forbidden me from seeing you anymore and has taken steps to make sure we will not even be able to exchange letters. May the gods protect my loyal and devoted servant who brings you this, because it must be our last message. I wanted you and Amenophis to have something better than one letter a day exchanged between you. My foolishness has cost you even that. Be strong, Nefertiti, and forgive me.

I sat on the bench in the moonlight, Sitamun's last letter in my lap. Aunt Tiye had cut another thread that anchored my life to those who cared for me. No way to contact Amenophis, no further visits with my true friend Sitamun, certainly no letters to or from Akhmin . . .

And what about Nava and Henenu? She knew the scribe was my friend. She was too smart not to suspect that the Habiru child was special to me. What would she do to them when they came back from Memphis? Would I even be allowed to *know* they'd returned? I felt like a beetle buried in the sand beneath a great battlefield, knowing nothing about the kingdoms being lost and won somewhere over my head.

I had never been so alone.

— 13 —

THE BUILDERS OF WALLS

In the days that followed Sitamun's last letter, I learned that it is possible to live in the midst of crowds and still be as isolated as if I were standing on the peak of the great pyramid called Khufu's Horizon. All around me, the women's quarters bustled with life—wives, companions, children, servants, slaves, pets, and the royal overseers whose duty it was to govern this world-within-a-world. It was nothing to me. Chatter wasn't the same thing as being able to *talk* to someone else. Being caught up in a crowd of other human beings wasn't the same thing as belonging.

I did try to make things better for myself. Since I was cut off from my old friends and those I cared about, I decided I'd create new ties where I could. It was all a dismal failure. Whenever I tried to strike up a new friendship, I was met with pleasant conversation, smiling faces, and polite discouragement. If I invited someone to my rooms for a meal, she always had another place she absolutely *had* to be.

If I offered to entertain a woman's children, she insisted that they *never* got along with anyone except her and their regular nursemaid. If I overheard one of the ladies complaining because she'd misplaced a particular pot of perfume or jar of paint for her eyes and I volunteered to let her have some of mine, suddenly she'd remember *exactly* where she'd left the missing item.

I became very used to hearing "Thank you so much, Nefertiti. You're so nice, but this just won't work out now. Another time, yes? I'm so glad you understand!"

Oh, I understood. I so-so-*so* definitely understood. Aunt Tiye's hand was in this somehow. Her rivals in Pharaoh's household might hate and envy her, but they were also wise enough to fear her. She had found a way to let it be known that I was not to be befriended unless the person fool enough to do so wanted to feel the wrath of the Great Royal Wife.

No one did. There were times I saw a look of commiseration in the faces of some of the palace women, especially those who weren't that much older than I, but that was all they dared to do. Many of them had children to protect from the never-ending intrigues of palace life. Could I blame them for lacking enough courage to open their hearts to me? I was no one. Aunt Tiye ruled their world from the shadows.

I began to spend more and more time in my own rooms, playing listlessly with Ta-Miu. Each morning I would eat breakfast, give my maids a few small chores to do, then dismiss them until it was time to bring me my dinner. I gave them so much free time that they must have thought they'd tumbled into some sort of wonderful dream.

I soon found myself falling into an odd routine, sleeping more and more during the daylight hours and straying from my rooms only after sunset. Ta-Miu decided that this was a great improvement and trotted along with me everywhere. Sometimes I took my scribe's kit with me. It may sound strange to say this, but there were many times that I'd see something in the abandoned halls or gardens or great rooms of the palace that would touch my spirit in a way that begged to be put into words. Without the turmoil of Pharaoh's followers, servants, and attendants distracting me, I could see that the walls held ghosts. Who had walked in my steps over these stones a hundred years ago? Who would walk here when the sacred river's waters had risen and fallen a hundred times more? There was no way for me to know their names or their fates, but I could let my mind weave tales about who they *might* have been and let my pen write them down.

One night I took a route that was unfamiliar to me and couldn't find my path back to the women's quarters. I blundered through the halls, hoping to come across one of the night guards, but I seemed to have wandered into a part of the palace that wasn't worth patrolling. My confusion was made worse by the fact that even though these halls were deserted, they were as well lit as if Pharaoh himself would come striding through them at any moment.

Ta-Miu's ears perked up at the scuffling sound of mice going about their business, though we never saw a single one. I dropped to one knee and petted her. "If you were a hunting hound, I could ask you to find us a scent trail to lead us out of here," I joked.

"Mrow!" Ta-Miu replied with so much resentment that she must have understood me. She switched her tail peevishly, jerked her sleek head out from under my hand, and walked away.

"I didn't mean to insult you, O daughter of Bast," I said, following her. "Now what am I going to have to do in order to earn your forgiveness? A fish? Two? Some roast duck? A new cushion? That would be a waste: You always sleep at the foot of my bed. How about—"

Ta-Miu made a sudden bound through a narrow doorway. I gave a small cry of surprise and leaped after her.

Soft starlight soothed my eyes. The crescent moon above gleamed like the graceful horns that crowned Hathor in her beauty. I smelled rich earth, fresh greenery, and the inviting perfume of many flowers. "What a lovely garden," I said to Ta-Miu in a hushed voice. "I don't think I've ever seen this one before."

"Then I'm glad you're seeing it now," said a woman's husky voice from a place under one of the sycamore trees. There was the sound of a linen dress whispering over stone, a few footsteps, and she was standing before me. Her beautiful face, broad and dark-skinned, and her tightly curled hair were Nubian, and her smile was more dazzling than the array of gold and jewels adorning her neck, ears, and arms. I had to stare. Who wore so much finery at this time of night, in such a lonely place as a silent garden?

She saw how my eyes were fixed on her adornments,

and her teeth flashed when she laughed. "Why shouldn't I?" she said, answering my unasked question. "I love these pretty things. Why can't I wear them even when I am the only one who'll see them? Don't *I* count as someone important enough to impress with all these treasures?"

She tapped the heaviest bracelet on her arm. "This one was given to me by Pharaoh himself. Well, they *all* were, but this one he gave to me with his own hands, on the morning after he took me for his wife. Your aunt didn't like *that* at all, but she was still just another one of his women. There wasn't a thing she could do about it . . . then."

"You know that I'm Queen Tiye's niece?" I was astonished.

The woman nodded and her earrings jingled. "I've known her for years, and I've known who *you* are from the first day you arrived. You might not have noticed me, but I was there, just another face in the curious crowd who saw you enter the royal palace. I remember thinking, 'Isn't she a pretty girl! Is she going to be someone's new toy or one of Tiye's handpicked tools? But you surprised me: You were no one's plaything, and when your aunt tried using you to build her older boy a throne, you became the ax that slips through the workman's hands and chops his foot off!" She laughed so loudly that a pair of owls roosting in the tree above her head took flight, hooting angrily. Ta-Miu followed their path, paws drawn in close, tail lashing, then launched herself after them, her claws slicing thin air.

"Look at her, will you?" The woman chuckled over Ta-Miu's antics. "Ready to take on two owls at once when even *one* could probably carry her away. I don't remember her being this feisty when she belonged to Thutmose." She saw my renewed expression of surprise, and it amused her mightily.

"Yes, yes, I know that this is—was—Thutmose's cat. I know a great deal about that boy." She clucked her tongue. "A pity, what he's become. He was such a sweet child, so affectionate! I loved him dearly. He liked to come visit me and my boy Khenti until Tiye put a stop to it. That child couldn't have been more than five years old when she began filling his head with the notion that his life was just a race to the throne, that every one of his brothers was a rival, and that nobody would ever befriend him because they *liked* him, only because they wanted something in return."

"It sounds like you've known my aunt a long time," I said.

"Oh, from the very beginning! She and I arrived here within a few seasons of one another, the daughter of a prince and the daughter of a commoner."

"You're a prince's daughter?" I asked. I could believe it. She carried herself with the easy elegance of someone used to being obeyed.

"Oh, I beg your pardon, Lady Nefertiti; I know you, but you don't know me. My name is Tabiri, and my father— may his soul live on—was a prince of Nubia. Well, you can imagine how surprised *this* princess was to find that my chief rival for the position of Great Royal Wife wasn't royal at all! We were both beautiful girls, but Tiye was also single-minded and clever. I counted on my good looks and my princely blood to bring me the honor I thought I deserved.

She counted on nothing being *brought* to her; she would *take* it. And she did!" She chuckled.

"You—you don't seem to mind what happened," I remarked.

"What good would it do me to resent her victory? If you spend your days chewing over your old grudges, you'll soon have nothing but a mouthful of poison and no room on your tongue to taste life's sweetness. Besides, I didn't lose to your aunt because of something she did, but because of something that just . . . happened." She paused and looked to the stars. "Sometimes I like to sit out here and pretend I see the spirits of my father and my son shining up there together, laughing with the gods."

"Your son . . . I'm sorry, Princess Tabiri."

She shrugged. "At least Khenti left this world knowing that he had my love and that he never needed a crown to keep it. And when he died, Tiye mourned almost as much as I. I can't say she was *un*happy when I couldn't bear any more children, because that removed all chance of Pharaoh naming me Great Royal Wife instead of her, but I know she never wanted to achieve that title through my Khenti's death. She is not a *bad* woman, Lady Nefertiti; it's only that she's built a brick wall in front of her eyes, and she refuses to believe there's anything worth seeing on the other side."

She's built another around me, I thought. I felt very tired. "Lady Tabiri, I think I want to go back to my rooms now, but I don't know the way. Will you help me?"

"It would be a pleasure, my dear." She linked one arm through mine and led me out of the garden by a different doorway. As we strolled through the silent palace, she told me stories about her lost son. "That Khenti. He was born with a warrior's spirit. Even before he was born, how he kicked! When Pharaoh first saw him, he said to me, 'Tabiri, this one won't wait to be given the crown; he'll snatch it from my head!' That was the day I received this." She pointed proudly to her heavy collar of gold, turquoise, and lapis beads interwoven with at least twenty scarab amulets carved from a host of precious stones. It was beautiful, and massive enough to cover half her chest.

"That's breathtaking," I said.

"And I would throw it into the sacred river in a heartbeat if that would bring Khenti back to me. I'm pleased to be able to show it to you. I'm giving it away tomorrow as a sacrifice to Hathor."

"I hope you're praying for love and not because you need her healing powers," I said.

"I'm praying for both, but not for me. I don't need anything from the goddess. I'm making the sacrifice for Thutmose's sake."

I stopped in my tracks. "Princess Tabiri, do you know what he *did*?"

"I have lived in this palace almost as long as Tiye. My ears are sharp, and the servants know I pay generously for information. If a fly lands on Pharaoh's forehead, I know about it. Thutmose drew a weapon and utterly blasphemed in the Palace of Ma'at; *then* he tried to kill you. His father had him imprisoned in his rooms and wouldn't even speak *about* him, let alone *to* him." She raised her arms to admire her collection of bracelets and bangles as she added, "That changed twelve days ago. Tiye was able to convince Pharaoh to temper the boy's punishment."

"My aunt could convince Isis to pardon Set," I muttered.

"Thutmose is still forbidden to step outside the palace walls, but inside, he can go where he likes."

"Anywhere?" My head spun. A serpent was at large in the halls of the palace. He had been freed to prowl wherever he liked for twelve days, and I'd heard nothing, seen nothing, just as the mouse fails to see the falcon's shadow or hear a rush of wings until the talons strike. How could I ever hope to sleep soundly again?

She heard the rising note of panic in my voice and put one arm around me. "Is this the little girl who stood up so bravely in the presence of Ma'at? I tell you, child, you have no worries. Thutmose has been given liberty, but the gift lies untouched. He has not stirred from his rooms. From what I hear—and I hear everything—he has not even stirred from his bed."

"Is he ill?" *That would explain the sacrifice to Hathor.*

"In body, no. But some fevers don't burn the flesh. Tiye sent her best physician to the boy's rooms, but discreetly, to keep Pharaoh ignorant."

"She's good at that sort of thing," I said tartly.

"When her doctor reported that there was nothing physically wrong with Thutmose, she sent a magician to sniff out any evil spells or curses." She looked at me closely. "From what I learned, *you* were very lucky that the man was too honest to tell Tiye what she wanted to hear."

"She thought *I* was at fault?" I shuddered. My enforced

solitude had made me miserable, but suddenly I realized that the ignorance that came with isolation could be a very dangerous thing.

"She *hoped* you were at fault," Princess Tabiri said. "For as long as I've known that woman, she's only felt secure if she could heap the responsibility for her problems in another person's lap. It makes everything so . . . tidy for her. You are safe for now—a goddess spoke for you—but I have a bad feeling that Tiye won't rest until she finds someone else to blame for her boy's illness. She's desperate to drag him out of this unnatural behavior, one way or another. She literally tried to drag him out of his bed with her own hands, but he was too strong for her. What's worse for Tiye is that in spite of all her schemes to keep Thutmose's condition secret, Pharaoh has taken notice. He's not pleased. The way he sees it, Thutmose is deliberately defying him. When Pharaoh moderated the boy's punishment, instead of appreciating it, Thutmose turned his back on such a gracious gift. Six days ago, he ordered the boy to leave his bed and his rooms, but as his Pharaoh, not his father."

"But Thutmose still refuses?"

"Oh, no, he complies with the royal order, in a way. He rises from his bed, walks once around his private garden, and lies down again. Then he summons a scribe to write a letter testifying that Pharaoh's command has been fulfilled. I hear that Pharaoh is furious, and Tiye is distraught. It's as if the boy wants to bring doom on himself." She unfastened her collar and held it at arm's length to admire it. "That is why I make this sacrifice to Hathor: for healing *and* for love. Thutmose needs both."

She took my arm a second time and we walked on. Ta-Miu took turns rushing ahead of us, trailing behind, and sometimes doing her best to wind through our feet and trip us. I gave up the battle and gathered the little cat into my arms for a scolding. She just purred and rubbed her head on my chin.

At last we came to a part of the palace that I recognized. "Oh! Princess Sitamun's rooms are nearby," I said. "I can find my own way back from here."

"Do you dislike my company so much, Lady Nefertiti?" Princess Tabiri's ready laugh warmed the night. Before I could protest, she patted my hand and said, "Now that we know one another, you will come back and visit me, yes? And I will come to the women's quarters and visit you."

"I'm surprised your rooms are so far from that part of the palace."

"If Tiye does not live cheek-by-jowl with the rest of Pharaoh's women, why should I? Private apartments befit my rank. I may be childless, but I am still a prince's daughter, and not some *junior* wife. And Pharaoh is still sometimes fond of me." She tapped another heavy gold bracelet.

"I hope you will be able to come see me," I said. "But Aunt Tiye might find a way to prevent that."

"I'd like to see her try. Really, I *would* like to see that. The two of us haven't butted heads in a while. My life these days flows peacefully, but there are times I miss the thrill of a lively clash with a worthy opponent."

"Princess Tabiri, with all due respect, I don't think you realize how good your life is without that sort of thing."

"Does anyone ever appreciate the life they have? Good

night, Lady Nefertiti." She smiled, kissed my cheek, and went back to her rooms.

I started to do the same when I heard new voices coming from one of the corridors. They sounded agitated, and I noticed that the hall from which the voices came was far more brightly lit than the one where Princess Tabiri had left me holding Ta-Miu.

I wonder what's going on? I thought, peering curiously toward the light. The cat meowed and stuck her head under my arm. "Tsk! Where's your sense of adventure?" I said, tickling her neck just under the gold collar she wore. "Let's investigate. Something important might be happening. If it is, won't it be grand for me to be the first person in the women's quarters to know about it? That will teach them to play keep-away with me, even if Aunt Tiye's the one forcing them to play that game! And if it's nothing more than a servants' quarrel, at least I can ask one of them to bring a lamp and light us all the way home."

It was not a servants' quarrel. As I approached the source of those raised voices, I could hear what they were saying and it had nothing to do with any sort of squabble between them. Both voices belonged to young men, both were on the same side, and both were deathly afraid.

"—not even one bite this time! See for yourself, the food's all untouched."

"Even the bread?"

"The bread *and* the meat *and* the fruit *and* the beer. What are we going to do? If the queen finds out—"

"We'll do what we did yesterday, except this time you'd

better share the beer or people will start asking questions about your morning 'headache.' "

"We can't! Didn't you hear what he told us tonight? He suspects we've been eating his rejected meals, and he's sent word to the chief cook to notify him at once about how much food the man finds left over on the prince's dishes."

"That's crazy."

"What, have you forgotten who we serve? Of course it's crazy! *He's* crazy! But he's still sane enough to cut down anyone who gets in the way of his insanity."

One of the speakers groaned. "What are we going to do? The queen threatened to get rid of every servant and slave in Prince Thutmose's household if we can't make him eat and drink like a normal person."

"I know, I know." A mighty sigh reached my ears as I moved nearer to the voices. "When that woman says she's going to get rid of you, she doesn't mean she's sending you to a new master."

"Unless it's Osiris."

"Gods, what are we going to *do*? My wife is trapped in that madman's household, too. What will become of our children if both she and I are taken from them?" The words turned to sobs, answered by murmured sounds of attempted consolation.

"Good evening," I said as I turned a corner and stepped fully into the light. My sudden appearance made one of the young men drop the laden dishes he was carrying. They smashed when they hit the ground. A loaf of bread came rolling up to my feet. Ta-Miu uttered a happy yowl and kicked free of my arms in order to pounce on a flight of roasted quail that had gone tumbling over the floor. The servant responsible for the mess fell to his knees, buried his hands in his face, and moaned.

"Lady Nefertiti?" The other young man stared at me in disbelief. "Why are you here this la—? I mean, may we serve you?"

I looked past his ashen face to the towering door that dominated the hallway. The wall above it was painted with a glorious image of Horus in his hawk form, blue, gold, and red feathers spread wide in a protective pose. Its frame was adorned with pictures of Isis and Hathor as well as the cobra-goddess Wadjet and the vulture-goddess Nekhbet, protectors of every pharaoh. The door stood between two seven-armed lamp stands, their carved stone cups all aglow. The pleasant scent of burning olive oil arose from the wicks. Someone had decided that the pungent reek of common castor-berry oil was not suitable for the nostrils of a crown prince.

Except he's not the crown prince anymore, I thought. I gestured toward the door. "I am here to see Prince Thutmose. Take me to him."

"Uhhhh . . ." The man squirmed. "Yes, my lady, at once. Er, that is, I'd better see if he is willing to, um—" He scratched the back of his hairless head. "Are you sure you want to see him now? If it would please you, I can carry any message you like to him and bring you his reply right away. Right away *tomorrow.* Or if you'd rather—"

"*Enough.*" The word of command echoed like a blow. I was not Nefertiti; I was once more the awesome goddess whose voice was enough to put would-be tomb robbers to flight. "Since you can't decide how best to serve me, I will do it myself." I started for the door, pausing only long enough to snatch Ta-Miu away from her impromptu feast. She was *not* happy.

Neither were Thutmose's servants. They scrambled to get ahead of me and bar my path to the door. "Please, *please,* Lady Nefertiti, don't go in there. If Prince Thutmose doesn't want to see you, he'll kill us for letting you in."

"Then don't let me in," I said reasonably. "Weren't you on your way to the kitchens?" I indicated the smashed dishes and the scattered food. "If you were busy cleaning that up, you never noticed me." I laid my free hand on the first man's shoulder and gently guided him out of my way, then treated the second servant in the same way. "Did you?" They were too stunned or too confused by my self-assurance to put up any further resistance. I smiled into their anxious faces as I opened the door and slipped inside.

I stepped into Thutmose's apartments expecting gloom and shadows. Instead, I entered a grove of seven-branched lamp stands all filling the place with light. A flock of maidservants were tending the many lamps. They gasped and squealed in alarm when they saw me.

"Lady Nefertiti?" A tall, angular man hastened up to meet me. He had the well-fed, well-dressed look of a high-ranking servant. He bowed as if he was doing me a favor, then said, "Ah, it *is* you. And Ta-Miu, too?" He raised his eyebrows so high that they were swallowed up by the wrinkles on his forehead. "She's looking well. My lady, I am Uni, the prince's Master of the Household, at your service. I will be overjoyed to help you go where you *want* to be. Please don't feel embarrassed by this mistake. Even those of us who have lived all our lives in the palace sometimes get lost. If you will be good enough to wait on *that* side of the door, I will conduct you to your own rooms personally as soon as I let my assistant know that I am leaving." He made an elegant wave at the entryway to the prince's apartments. I was being thrown out in the most gracious way.

"You're mistaken," I said crisply. "I'm not lost; *this* is where I want to be. However, if you feel you *must* escort me somewhere, take me to your master. Now."

"Ah, um, er—" Uni's bewildered reaction to my announcement was comically similar to the one I'd gotten from the servant in the hallway. "My lady, the time is late. The prince is not receiving visitors; the circumstances are—"

I raised my chin almost too high, trying to look dignified, and had to look a long way down my nose at him when I responded, "You have a simple choice, Uni: Bring me to Prince Thutmose, force me to find him on my own, or pick me up and carry me out of these apartments with your own two hands. I promise you, any consequences you might suffer for the first choice will be much less painful than for the second or the third—*especially* the third." I held his gaze steadily until he understood I meant everything I'd said.

Uni sighed. "This way, my lady."

He brought me to one of the inner rooms of Thutmose's apartments. As we walked, I noticed lights burning everywhere, a fortune in olive oil going up in flames, but when we came to the prince's bedchamber, all was darkness.

Uni positioned himself in the center of the doorway so that I had to stretch on tiptoe or duck my head to see around him, but it was all the same: I could peer into that room for as long as I wished and I'd still see nothing. It was so pitchy beyond the threshold that I couldn't even make out the shape of a bed, a chest, a chair.

"My lord Prince Thutmose, I beg of you to forgive me for this intrusion," Uni said in a wheedling, submissive tone. "There is one here—a young woman—who has insisted on seeing you. You have only to say the word and I will have her escorted from your apartments, but if there is some small chance that you might find her company agreeable—"

A dull, cold reply came from the blackness: "A young lady? Huh! Mother is getting creative. Give her a pair of gold earrings and send her away."

"If I wanted a pair of gold earrings from you, Thutmose, I'd get them directly from Aunt Tiye and save time!" I called out over Uni's shoulder.

"Nefertiti?" The dull voice sparked to life. "Oh, gods, I *have* lost my mind."

I nudged Uni. "Bring a lamp into that room."

"My lady, I can only heed my master. If you can persuade him to call for a light—"

I made an impatient sound and stalked over to the nearest lamp stand. Snatching one of the stone vessels, I cut past Uni into Thutmose's lair. The lone flame was enough to illuminate that small space. While Ta-Miu wriggled in the crook of my arm, I looked around briefly, perplexed. The only piece of furniture I could see was a bed, and not even a bed fit for royalty, but a simple, undecorated wooden frame holding a thin mat of woven reeds. Thutmose lay on it, his gaze on the ceiling, his arms at his sides.

"So it *is* you," he said without looking at me. The lamplight fell on his face, still extraordinarily handsome but now a little gaunt and haggard. His eyes were unpainted and red, his cheeks and scalp covered with stubble. "Why are you here? Don't tell me you've come to gloat, not you, not the darling of Ma'at, the perfect girl, the pure, *pure* heart."

"First tell me why *you're* here, Thutmose," I said.

"Me?" His laugh was ghastly. "Stupid question. In my bed, in my bedchamber, in my apartments—where else should I be after my own father ordered me sealed away as if I were already dead?"

"Don't be ridiculous," I snapped. "This isn't your bedchamber. It looks like it belongs to one of your servants."

"Ha. Still so smart. Smarter than Uni." Thutmose rolled onto his side and propped his head on one hand. "You hear that, Uni?" he shouted. "Maybe if you weren't such a mealymouthed foot-kisser, you'd have had the intelligence to tell me my visitor's *name* instead of letting me make a fool of myself."

"Ah! Pardon me, my lord, pardon me." A flutter of apologies came from the doorway. "I am your *most* unworthy servant. I will do better in the future, I swear by Ma'at that, uh, I mean, I swear by Amun—"

Thutmose laughed until he was wheezing. "Swear by Ma'at, if you like. Swear by a dog's backside, for all I care. What does any of it matter? Vows, promises, oaths, they're all dust and dung." He let his head drop to the mat. "Go away, Uni. Go, and see to it that none of the other servants come anywhere near this room. If I catch the faintest whisper of their presence, I'll whip them with my own hands and then I'll guarantee that your career in the palace is over."

"Ye-ye-yes, my lord prince! Just as you desire! At once!" I heard feet running away and the distant sound of a very harried Master of the Household yapping out commands to his underlings.

"Thutmose, why are you doing this to yourself?" I asked. "You aren't a prisoner in these rooms any longer. Your father changed his mind; you have the freedom of the palace and you know it."

"Scraps," Thutmose rasped. "They give me scraps and they want me to pretend that it's a banquet. Everything else has been taken away from me. Nothing to live on but scraps, until the day I die." He closed his eyes. "Leave me alone, Nefertiti. I don't want your company. Go throw your scraps somewhere else."

I perched on the edge of his bed and braced myself for him to object, but he had sunk himself too deeply in his own misery to notice or care. A single tear trickled from the corner of his eye, a droplet that the lamplight turned to gold. I took a breath and was surprised to hear it turn into a tiny sob.

Am I crying for him? For Thutmose? Lord Thoth, give me wisdom: Why? I must be as mind-sick as he is. I let go of Ta-Miu so that I could wipe the tears from my own eyes and still hold on to the oil lamp. She leaped lightly onto the bed and planted all four paws on Thutmose's chest, purring madly. With his eyes still closed, he reached up and began to pet the little cat with so much tenderness that it made me smile.

You do *love her more than anything, Thutmose,* I thought. *When you forged charges of sacrilege against me, you created false evidence to show that I'd spilled her blood, but you refused to allow any real harm to come to her. A heartless man would have ordered one of his underlings to kill her outright. You kept her alive because you loved her, even though she was the living proof of my innocence.*

I made a choice.

I can't say exactly why I did it. I had lived long enough to know that most people—highborn or low, male or female, poor or rich—would think I was a fool. I could hear their scornful voices calling out, "Aren't you the same girl who was dumbstruck when Princess Tabiri told you she was praying to Hathor for Thutmose? Aren't you the one who shrilled, 'Do you know what he did?' Where has your outrage gone, Nefertiti? He wanted to crush you. He tried to kill you. He's made his brother's life an unending procession of mocking words, contempt, and humiliation. Has he shown one flicker of remorse for any of that? Let him live and die with his scraps! They're more than he deserves. Let him suffer; it serves him right."

No, it doesn't, I thought. *It serves no one.* I recalled the sorrowful look on Amenophis's gentle face as he said, *"Forgive me, Nefertiti—I still love my brother."*

I watched as Thutmose continued to stroke Ta-Miu's fur. She uttered happy sounds that were a curious mix of snarls and purrs when she drew back her lips, and he rubbed her gums with the edge of his thumb. Her forepaws massaged his chest with a motion like a baker kneading dough. Anger and despair melted from his face. He looked as if he had finally found peace.

"You asked me why I'm here, Thutmose," I said quietly. "I want you to have Ta-Miu."

"*What?*" His eyes shot open. He sat up so fast that the cat went flying in fright from her safe haven on his chest and shot under the bed. He seized my arm before I knew it and brought his face close to mine. His breath smelled sour and stale as he demanded, "Whose idea was this?"

"Mine."

"Why? What are you up to? Do you give such wonderful gifts to everyone you hate?"

"I don't hate you, Thutmose."

How he laughed when I said that! "If only you'd spouted such a lie on that accursed day in Ma'at's house! Then a *thousand* goddesses could have howled your innocence to the skies for nothing."

"It's true," I maintained. "I don't think I *can* hate you anymore. These past days, I've been forced to live cut off from anyone who's ever been important to me, anyone who's ever cared about me for who I am—not for my rank or my future or my face. The loneliness—it's awful. No one should have to suffer that. No one."

He hadn't been eating. He had spent most of his time lying inert in a darkened room. It wasn't so hard for me to twist my arm out of his grasp, but once I'd done that, I slipped my fingers through his and held his hand because it was what I wanted. "I met a woman tonight who knew you when you were a child and who still loves you very much:

Princess Tabiri. Her son, Khenti, was your playmate, remember? She does. She wants you to be well and happy and *not* alone. So do I."

He pulled his head back and stared at me. "You met Tabiri?" I saw the start of a fond smile on his face before the old, hard glare of suspicion clamped down over his features again. "You watch yourself around that woman, Nefertiti. She's a worse liar than you. I haven't seen her face since her son died, and I don't want to. She resents me for being alive."

"Oh, who told you *that* nonsense?" I burst out. "Your mother?"

He refused to answer. Jerking his hand from mine, he sprang from the bed and turned his face to the darkest corner of the room. "You want me to believe that you pity me for being alone? Don't. I don't want your pity, not even if it is real. I know better than to trust you. All your sweet talk is honey poured over a dish of scorpions. You're not offering me my Ta-Miu because you feel sorry for me; you're trying to deceive me the way you've always done! A simple, heartfelt good deed, a gift from the heart." Sarcasm made his words ugly. "What a clever way to lead me on, to let me feel *safe* with you. Safe as a sheep feels the moment before the butcher cuts its throat."

"Thutmose, listen: All I'm trying to do is let you have Ta-Miu again." I spoke slowly, as if explaining things to a man who'd cracked his skull in a fall. "I have no hidden reasons for it."

"Not you," Thutmose said, turning sharply. "Amenophis. He's heard that Father's made my unfair punishment milder, and now he's afraid it's just the first step to bringing things back to the way they *should* be. He's trembling because he thinks I might win back my rightful place as crown prince. And I will! Then I'll show him what Pharaoh does to traitors."

I could hardly breathe, listening to the madness pouring from Thutmose's mouth. "Amenophis isn't a traitor; he loves you! He doesn't want the crown."

"More lies! He envies me. He's always envied me. He's always wanted everything I have. Why else did he work so hard to turn *you* against me? We should have been married by now, Nefertiti. We would have been man and wife, if not for his disloyalty, and Father would have made me his coruler. Amenophis couldn't let *that* happen. He's a sly one. He doesn't love you any more than he loves me. He saw that you're a stupid girl who likes to rescue broken creatures, so he played on your weak-minded ways and shaped your soft heart to suit his plans. He only won your devotion to keep it away from me."

He leered as if challenging me to argue the point. What would be the use of that? It would be like trying to empty the sacred river with a cracked cup.

"What will it take to convince you that Amenophis cares about you, Thutmose?" I asked. "What does he have to do for you to treat him like a brother, not an enemy?"

"You want to give me back Ta-Miu," Thutmose replied. "Tell *him* to give me back *you*."

"He can't—"

"Ha!"

"*Can't,* not *won't*," I said fiercely. "Do you think I'm a gift or a reward or the prize that Amenophis has to drop into your hands if he wants to buy your heart? No one has that power over me."

"Not even you, O beautiful one?" Thutmose smirked. "Just think of all the good that you could do if you stopped your stupid games and accepted the fate that was always meant for you. Come with me tomorrow to my father's council. Declare before Pharaoh and his most trusted men that we are husband and wife. From that moment on, I swear by the crown of the Two Lands, I will love, cherish, honor, and respect my brother Amenophis above all other men. I will raise him up as high as he cares to go among the powerful of my realm. There will be everlasting peace between us, and I will make his life so sweet that the most gifted poets and singers of the Black Land will be left mute when they try to describe it."

"All you would need to do is call him *brother*," I said.

"Fine. I don't mind getting off cheaply." He laughed at me. "Does this mean you agree to my terms? I must warn you, though: Once I wear the crown, you won't be my queen. You've been a public spectacle and an embarrassment to me far too often. How would it look if Pharaoh Thutmose rewarded such unwomanly behavior? But don't worry, you'll live a very comfortable life as one of my junior wives. I'm sure your family will be pleased. Come, let's seal the bargain." He tried to take me into his arms.

I thrust the oil lamp between us at eye level and he recoiled, calling me a stream of revolting names. I waited until he had to catch his breath, then spoke:

"Let me go, Thutmose," I said. "Let me return to

Akhmin. I can never be your wife, but if you consent to heal the break between you and your brother, I promise that I will never be his."

"Fresh trickery." His lip curled. "You both want me dead; you both want to wear the crowns of the Two Lands! He'd never let you push him aside, and you'd never give up the chance to be Great Royal Wife to a man you could lead around like a tame baboon."

I made such a loud noise of sheer frustration that it was a miracle Uni didn't risk his master's displeasure and come running to see what had happened. "Which *is* it?" I exclaimed. "With one breath you say Amenophis is a mountain of strength who won't *let* me leave him; with the next, you insist he's mine to control. What will it take to reach you, Thutmose? Say the word and Amenophis and I will stand in the house of Amun, Isis, any god you care to name, and publicly swear that we mean you no harm, that we've never betrayed you, that we've never coveted the throne of the Two Lands, and that your brother loves you faithfully, truly, and much more than you deserve!"

"An oath." Thutmose's snicker made my skin itch. "An oath before the gods. We both know what that's worth, don't we, Nefertiti? Empty air. Why go to the temple when you'd accomplish the same thing by shouting your words into a jar? The houses of the gods house *nothing*."

"You don't believe in them?"

"You do?" he countered. "If they exist, they don't dwell in the piles of stone we build for them. If they can hear us at all, their voices are too weak to answer us. Perhaps they used to touch the lives of men, once upon a time, but now they've grown old and weak, too weak to raise their voices or their hands when the priests claim they can buy and sell divine favor or displeasure. Fools and children may still believe in them; I am neither."

"Then I must be a fool, Thutmose," I said. "I believe that something greater than myself exists in this world." And in my thoughts, I added, *I just don't know if that power belongs to the gods I've known since childhood, or to Nava's faceless One, or to something—some*one*—else entirely. But I feel that presence as surely as I feel the sacred river's flow, the winds from the south, the life-bringing rays of sun. It's there; my heart tells me it's there.*

"Oh, what fine, solemn words! 'Something greater than myself' indeed." He mocked me in singsong. "Of *course* you can believe in something greater than yourself. Look at you! You're a mere girl. Nearly everything I can name is greater than you."

"Then I suppose I'm right to believe," I said.

My calm reply annoyed him. "Why so much faith? Because Ma'at spoke to you? Don't you know her so-called voice is a fake? A priest speaks for the goddess! A priest *I* paid"—he scowled—"though obviously not enough. The loathsome insect took his bribe and hasn't been seen since."

He doesn't know who replaced that priest as the voice of Ma'at, I thought. *Good. Amenophis did it to save me, but Thutmose would just see it as more evidence that his brother is against him.*

"Why don't you worship *me*, Nefertiti?" he went on. "When I'm pharaoh, I'll be the god-on-earth, and I'll have more real power than the so-called gods. When someone offends me, I will strike them down. But the gods? If Ma'at was more than an empty image, surely she would have punished me by now for having invaded her sanctuary with a dagger! Yet the only penalty I've suffered has come from my father's hands. Even that is slowly being withdrawn. Why should I believe in something I don't need to fear?"

"All right, Thutmose, I tried," I said. "You won't accept a sacred oath as proof that your brother's not your rival. You won't accept my offer to give him up and leave the court so you can reconcile. Will you even accept Ta-Miu, or will you choose loneliness and isolation because you're determined to spite me? It's late and I'm leaving. Just tell me whether I should take her with me when I go."

"Leaving?" he echoed, anger rising in his voice. "It's more like you're running away. That's all you can do, run."

I snorted. "You'd have liked it better if I hadn't run from your dagger in Ma'at's house, or if I'd stayed in my prison and waited for someone to send in another viper. But if you were honest, Thutmose, you'd admit that you're not half as annoyed by all the times I've run from you as you are by the fact that you've never been fast enough to catch me. And you never will." I started from the room, taking the oil lamp with me and leaving it up to Ta-Miu to decide whether she stayed with Thutmose or came with me.

"Nefertiti, wait!"

— 14 —

THE HOUND AND THE GAZELLE

Thutmose called out for me to wait, and so I waited to hear what he had to say, at least for Amenophis's sake.

Some time later, I was waiting again. I stood under the stars and looked for the moon, but the night had grown old and Hathor's horns had sunk behind the walls of Thutmose's private garden. One of his many maidservants was by my side, ready to fetch me anything I might want to eat or drink. She was a thin, shy girl who would look me in the eyes for only the briefest instant before turning away as if she'd been caught committing a crime. I wanted to ask her what it was like working for Thutmose, but I doubted she'd tell me. Most people don't like being made to talk about unpleasant things. Besides, she was probably terrified that anything she'd say against Thutmose would get back to him and earn her a severe punishment.

"Do you think he'll be much longer?" I asked. We had stood there in silence for a noticeable while, and my unexpected question made her jump. I tried to calm her by lightening the mood. "He did tell me to wait, but I didn't think he meant forever."

"Yes, Lady Nefertiti," she replied much too quickly. And then: "I mean, no, Lady Nefertiti. My lord Prince Thutmose will be with you soon. He told us all that he wants to look his best for the contest."

The contest . . .

"The race, Nefertiti, will be twice around my garden."

"A race between us—I still can't believe you're serious about this, Thutmose."

"Then call it a joke, if you like, something to amuse me. But you've heard the stakes I've set on it, and I promise you, I was not joking about them. I'll have the slaves hold torches to light our course. My servants will be our witnesses, so you can't cheat."

"You won't have to worry about that."

"Won't I? You claimed that when you ran, I could never catch you, but I know I would have been able to do it easily if not for all your tricks. Remember how you forced me to drink poppy juice that night? And in Ma'at's temple, how you . . . Well, I don't remember precisely what you did to outdistance me, but you won't have any such chance now. It will amuse me to have us run an honest race, speed against speed, no tricks, no cheating. Agreed?"

"Yes, if you'll let me send for my own witnesses, people who don't have to read their futures in your smile or frown."

"Tsk. You think the only way for me to win this is to coerce my servants into lying? I should feel insulted. You claim to believe in the gods, yet you doubt the word of your future god-on-earth!"

"But—"

"No. I set the terms of this race, and you are free to take it or

*leave it. If you win, I go to my brother and ask his forgiveness for
everything you claim I did to him in the past. I free him from all suspicion and offer him friendship. If I win—"*

*"If you win, I'll kneel at Aunt Tiye's feet and tell her that I'm
ready to be your wife."*

*"What a lucky girl you are, Nefertiti. You win this race either
way."*

I remembered how animated Thutmose had become
when he spoke about this strange and terrible contest he'd
devised. It transformed him from the listless man sprawled
in a darkened room into a whirlwind of energy, issuing commands, sending slaves and servants running to obey. He
seemed to have cast aside his life-haunting belief that traitors surrounded him and was actually *enjoying* himself. I
would have rejoiced to see such a healthy rebirth if not for
the feeling that he'd only transferred all of his mistrustful
nature to me.

*What is he planning? How will he twist this "honest" race
into a snare?*

I sighed loudly and fidgeted, then decided to put my
nervousness to good use. Back home in Akhmin, in the days
when my greatest worry had been mastering an intricate
dance so I wouldn't look foolish or clumsy, I'd always prepared myself by stretching my arms and legs, to limber
them. I began to do so now. Ta-Miu watched me from her
place on the rim of the long ornamental lotus pool that took
up the center of the garden. She yawned.

The maidservant attending me took more interest.
"Lady Nefertiti, are you all right? Do you need anything?
Are you in pain? When one of us has a backache or stiffness

in the shoulders, one of the other girls is very good at kneading away knotted muscles. I could fetch her for you."

Her eagerness to help made me smile. "I'm fine. I'm just getting ready to run." I stuck my right leg out behind me and tried to bend my left knee, but my dress got in the way of a full stretch. "Hmm. This was *not* intended for running," I said, standing straight and plucking at the tightly fitting linen. "I'd better go back to my rooms and find something I can move in more easily. Look after the cat for me; I'll be back right away." I started for the doorway out of the garden.

"Oh, no, you mustn't go, Lady Nefertiti!" The little maid ran after me and grabbed my arm, then squeaked over her own boldness and held up her hands as if to proclaim *"I never touched you! Never! And I didn't mean to do it!"* "My lord Prince Thutmose will be angry if he doesn't find you awaiting him here."

"Then tell him I haven't gone far and that I'll return quickly," I told her. "He can wait for *me* for a change."

She shook her head and looked miserable. "He won't believe me. When he gives a command and it looks as if it hasn't been obeyed, he won't listen to explanations or excuses. If you try to tell him anything about it, he turns the matter over to Uni, and then—" She said no more but discreetly held out her left arm. The wrist had the crooked look of bones that had been broken and not healed well.

I gritted my teeth. I knew that slaves were beaten, even servants. The more powerful and high-ranking a master was, the freer he felt to treat the common people of his household worse than his hunting hounds and chariot horses. It infuriated me.

But what could I do about it here and now, for this one frightened girl, except comply with Thutmose's orders so she wouldn't suffer for my disobedience?

That *really* infuriated me.

"Never mind, then," I said, putting on a pleasant expression. "I'll wait until he arrives; then I'll get a different dress. Ha! Maybe I'll see if I can cut one of my dresses short enough to be a tunic and that's what I'll wear to run. I'd love to see the face Thutmose—Prince Thutmose—will make when he sees me like that!"

"Yes, Lady Nefertiti," the girl replied. She looked deeply relieved.

I rested my hands on my hips. "What is taking him so long?"

"He . . . I heard . . ." The maidservant sidled nearer and spoke in a nearly inaudible whisper. "I heard that he wanted to bathe and to have his head and face shaved, and that he's called for the finest scented oils for his skin, and a fresh kilt, perfectly pleated, and then he wanted Uni to lay out all of his best jewelry so that he could choose what to wear."

"Hathor save me, he sounds like he's getting ready to be married." One corner of my mouth quirked up. I lifted the hem of my dress and wiggled my toes in the dirt. "He's going to be very disappointed."

There was a stir from the prince's apartments and a chain of torches emerged. The line of slaves moved slowly around the garden, dropping off individual light-bearers at regular positions, like a broken necklace slowly shedding its beads one by one. I crossed the garden to follow their course from the doorway, all around the raised stones bordering the lotus pool, under the rustling leaves of a line of sycamores, around the corner of the pool where willows grew, past a magnificent doum palm crowned with fronds like daggers, and through a stretch of the garden where small white myrtle blossoms glowed like stars in a sky of lustrous, dark green leaves. I wanted to examine the path I'd have to run, studying it step by step for any places where it might not be level, where I might discover large stones or loose pebbles underfoot, or where a wayward root, snaking its way out of the carefully maintained beds, might become a hazard.

I had nearly completed my walk around the garden when I heard Thutmose calling my name. He stood outlined in the doorway to his apartments, and the change in him was stunning. There was no denying what a handsome man he was. Even when he'd lain unwashed and unkempt in his self-imposed prison, anyone could still see the perfection of his face and the strong yet graceful shape of his body. Now that he had regained an interest in his appearance and was bathed, scented, groomed, and adorned with a wealth of gold and polished gems, he did look fit to be called a god-on-earth.

If I didn't know what he was like behind that thin layer of beauty, I would have called myself crazy for rejecting him as my husband. But I *did* know better, and I thanked Isis it was a lesson I'd learned in time.

The future god-on-earth was eating a pomegranate. When I approached him, he spat out a mouthful of pulpy red seeds at my feet.

"Oh, *that's* nice," I said, taking a step backward and

making a face at him. "Does your nursemaid know what a rude little boy you are?"

He laughed, took another bite of the scarlet fruit, and this time spat the seeds well to one side. "Pardon me, Nefertiti, but I've been confined to these rooms for so long that my manners have gathered dust. We'll begin our race soon. I just want to finish this. I didn't realize how hungry I was. I haven't eaten properly for a long time."

"Who are you planning to blame for that?" I couldn't help myself; he had no right to keep up the pretense of being the eternal victim. "A royal prince doesn't go hungry in the palace unless that's what he wants to do." I tried to push my way past him through the doorway.

He sidestepped to block me. "Where do you think you're going?"

"I'm not *running away,* if that's what you think," I replied. "I'm going to my rooms to change my dress for something with more room."

"No, you're not. You'll run our race in what you're wearing now. I don't have the time to wait for you."

"You mean you're afraid that if I'm free to run at my best, you won't have a chance against me."

He glowered at me so viciously that there was no denying I'd hit the target. Then he smiled stiffly and said, "When you consented to let this contest decide things between us, you agreed to the conditions I set for our competition. My race, run under my terms, or no race takes place at all. If you leave now to return to your rooms, you can stay there. Nothing will change from the way things are now. Is that what you'd like?"

Nothing would change. The walls Aunt Tiye had built around me would remain in place, keeping me apart from Father, Mother, Bit-Bit, Nava, Henenu, and, above all, my beloved. The days and the seasons would pass, and Pharaoh's heart might soften toward his oldest son and re-instate him as his heir. Aunt Tiye would work toward that goal with every grain of strength and willpower in her being.

And when Pharaoh Amenhotep dies, Thutmose will have the double crown on his head, the crook and flail in his hands, and his brother's throat under his heel. The thought of how Thutmose would use his unchecked, limitless powers against Ameno-phis terrified me more than any notion of how he might use those same powers against me.

If I let nothing change tonight, a day would come when *everything* would change.

"Fine," I spat. "Have it your way. I'll still win." I walked back into the garden, head held high, and motioned for the little maidservant who'd been attending me. "See if you can find some pins to help me hold up this skirt," I told her.

"Yes, Lady Nefertiti."

"*No,* Lady Nefertiti." Thutmose folded his arms across his chest and defied me to object.

"You said I was to run the race in what I'm wearing now. And I will! Do you think that *one pin* will be enough to defeat you?"

"But you're not wearing that *one pin* now."

I pointed at the gaily colored sash that bound my waist. "I'm wearing *this* now. Do you have a good reason why I can't use it to shorten my dress, or do you need time to patch one together?"

He shrugged. "You can do anything you like to prepare yourself for our contest as long as you do it quickly and you add nothing to what you've already got on."

I tore off my sash and handed it to the little maidservant. "When I pull up the fabric, tie this tightly around my—"

Thutmose snatched the sash from the girl's hands. She cringed. "I said *you* can do anything you like to get ready for our contest," he said. "You *alone.*"

"And I suppose *you* did all that yourself?" I waved one hand up and down, indicating Thutmose's splendid appearance.

"None of it was done *after* I set foot on our racecourse," he said smoothly. "Now that I'm here, I'll abide by the same rules as you. You can see for yourself that no one will lift a finger to help me." He removed his sandals with two casual kicks and showed me his teeth. "There. All by myself. Satisfied?"

I refused to rise to the bait of another exchange with him. He was getting too much pleasure out of taunting me. I was no sorceress, but there were times I could make certain people invisible by ignoring them so thoroughly it was like they'd never existed. I banished Thutmose's wickedly grinning face to oblivion and spoke to the still-shivering maid as if we were alone.

"My dear, I won't need your help with my dress after all. Will you please do me the favor of catching Ta-Miu and holding her until the race is over? I'm afraid she might get too excited or take fright and wind up in the pool. There must be a basket you could use for her."

"Why are you giving orders to *my* servant about *my* cat, Nefertiti?" Thutmose knew he was being ignored and barged in to put an end to it. "Have you forgotten that you gave her back to me, or were you hoping I'd forget?" He clapped his hands in the maid's face. "Find Ta-Miu and keep her safe, but not in a basket, as if she were a load of figs. Let her watch the race and bring me Bast's blessing."

"Yes, my lord Prince Thutmose." The girl hurried away. Soon she had Ta-Miu in her arms and was standing next to Uni and a group of three torch-bearers at one end of the garden pool. The little cat seemed content to cuddle into the maid's arms and purr herself to sleep.

I couldn't resist shooting a small barb at Thutmose: "It looks like Ta-Miu would rather watch dream-mice than witness your performance. So much for Bast's blessing."

He gave a disdainful sniff. "As if I needed it!"

I did the best I could to fix my dress, rolling up the material at the waist until the hem was halfway up my calves. I passed my sash under this clumsy ring of fabric, tied a double knot, then began removing the few pieces of jewelry I wore. They weren't too heavy and wouldn't weigh me down, but I didn't want to feel them slapping against my skin as I ran. *No* distractions!

"I'm not *adding* anything to what I'm wearing!" I called out to Thutmose, in case he wanted to come up with a new twist to his rules.

"I never said a word," he replied, all innocence. "I'm simply waiting for you to begin."

We walked to the spot he'd picked for the start of the

race, at the short end of the lotus pool that lay closest to the doorway back into his apartments. "Twice around, remember, and we end there," he said, pointing to where Uni stood, his shaved head shining in the light of three torches. Dropping to one knee on the raised stone border, Thutmose stretched his hand over the glittering waters of the pool and plucked a single blue flower. "When it touches the ground, we go." He tossed it into the air.

We watched intently as the handful of fragile petals came to earth and then—we were off! I ran as fast as I could, my eyes focused on the path ahead of me. Torchlight cast some shadows that could be mistaken for obstacles and others that might conceal a hazard on the ground. My feet crunched over earth and crushed stone as a breeze lifted my hair. Thutmose was only a few strides ahead of me, running with a weird, uneven gait. Once I thought I saw him stagger and veer to one side, then catch himself and put on a short, sharp burst of speed just before I caught up.

What's the matter with him? I thought. I remembered the servants in the hallway who'd spoken about his lack of appetite. His own words came back to me as well: *I haven't eaten properly for a long time.*

Was that it? Had his self-imposed hunger weakened him too much for any last-moment meal to repair the damage? If that was so—O merciful Isis!—I was sure to win this race. I pushed myself to run faster, and as we turned the corner of the pool where the doum palm grew, I left him behind.

Five of Thutmose's servants were gathered near Uni at the spot where the race would finish once Thutmose and I had circled the pool one more time. They were the ones he'd chosen to play witness—four broad-shouldered men and an older woman who looked strong enough in her own right to pick up her fellow witnesses and shake them like wads of wet laundry. As I rushed past her, she shouted, "Well done, little gazelle!"

The men with her laughed; then one of them called out, "Don't let the hound catch your scent!"

A second joined in the spirit of things: "Leap, little one, leap! Over the thorn bush and you're safe!" The third and fourth men had their own jests to add, and I smiled and waved my appreciation as I turned the next corner of the pool, flew past the entryway to Thutmose's rooms, and trampled over the lotus that had signaled our contest's start. I'd begun the second and last round of the race and Thutmose hadn't even finished his first circuit of the course. I wanted to spread my arms like wings and laugh.

Another voice laughed first. I heard running feet coming up rapidly behind me, the drumming of their bare soles drawing closer and closer, faster and faster, until Thutmose shot by me like an arrow. "Did you like my little dance, Nefertiti?" he called over one shoulder. "But *now* I run!"

So do I, I thought grimly, and put fresh power into my pumping legs. As I tried to catch up to Thutmose, to my horror I felt the rolled-up dress material at my waist begin to come undone. First on one side, then the other, the thin linen slid down in spite of the sash securing it. I tried yanking it back in place as I ran, but without the time to gather it patiently and evenly, I wound up hampering myself even more. The narrow bottom of my dress became a noose that tightened around my legs. I stopped fighting it when it threatened to become a tangle that was sure to send me sprawling.

Thutmose must have heard something of my struggles because he paused for a moment at the far end of the lotus pool and peered back to see what I was doing. When he finished laughing, he started running again, but *toward* me.

If that braying jackass gets within arm's reach, I swear by Bes that I'll slap the gloating grin off his face, I thought. With my hem now back around my ankles, I couldn't break into a wide stride and had to work twice as hard to keep up a good pace. Sweat trickled down my spine. I ran with my hands bunched into fists and felt them become damp. I wasn't fighting for breath, but it was harder to draw the air in easily. Oh, how much I would have given for the one pin Thutmose refused to let me have!

He overtook me near the place where the willows grew. "Is *this* the direction we're supposed to run, Nefertiti?" he asked in an irritatingly childish voice. "Or should we be going *this* way?" He ran around me twice, tittering, before sprinting onward.

I was still only halfway along the far end of the lotus pool when he reached the myrtles growing beside the last stretch of the course. Though there wasn't that much distance between us, he stopped to make fun of me once more. He knew he had the advantage, and he couldn't keep from flaunting it in my face.

"You're doing better than I expected, little *gazelle*!" he called out. "Too bad your hooves are tied, or else you might have had a hope of beating me. What luck that hounds are smarter than their prey! Ah well, cheer up. You can teach our sons how to run." He fell into an easy stride. I could only see the back of his head, but I'd have wagered my life he was grinning like a fully fed hyena.

Then I heard his voice raised in anger. "No cheers for my victory? Not even you, Uni? You shout for your precious *little gazelle,* but not for your master? Curse you all, if you don't fill the air with your voices, I'll—!"

They cheered for him before he could finish the threat of what they'd suffer otherwise. Slaves and servants, everyone who feared Thutmose's wrath, sent up a roar of celebration as loud as it was false. It burst out suddenly, a shock of sound so startling that even I gasped and recoiled in midstride.

Somewhere in that eruption of noise, Ta-Miu woke in fright and bolted from the little maidservant's arms. The panic-stricken cat dashed blindly across the garden path, her flight directly under Thutmose's feet. She yowled when he tripped over her and desperately tried to keep his footing. Arms flailing in the air, he went stumbling and lurching in a zigzag pattern until he lost the battle and went sprawling over the rough, rocky border stones, face-first into the lotus pool.

I waited until I'd run well past Uni and the witnesses before I drank in a deep, deep breath and drenched myself with laughter.

"What is going on here?"

The voice of Pharaoh turned all of us to stone. Uni looked ready to collapse. The maidservant who'd lost her hold on Ta-Miu broke the silence when she began to weep in dread. From the lotus pool, Thutmose groaned, then cried out in pain.

Without thinking, I rushed to help him, kneeling on the stone border and letting him sling one arm over my shoulders so that I could help him stand. He was a soggy mess, his body streaked with water and slime. A deep, nasty, bleeding scrape ran down one leg from thigh to ankle. When he tried to step away from me, he yelped again: He'd done some damage to his right foot and couldn't stand unaided. His eyelids fluttered as he blinked furiously through the water still dribbling down his face. He had the empty, bewildered expression of someone who has seen the bottom fall out of the world.

When no one else seemed able to do so, the sturdy female servant who'd first called me "little gazelle" approached Pharaoh and touched her forehead to the dust at his feet. "O my lord Pharaoh, eternal and mighty, I beg for permission to speak."

"Then rise," he said tersely. "Tell me what all this means. I heard the uproar from my bedchamber."

I wondered why he hadn't summoned guards to investigate what might have been a perilous situation. Then I saw that Pharaoh Amenhotep was holding a massive war club. If the health and strength of the Black Land depended on the health and strength of its ruler, we were safe for many years to come.

The woman got to her feet and told Pharaoh everything. When she spoke about what Thutmose and I had wagered on the outcome of our race, she was wise enough to omit all mention of my forced marriage and to change my prize to "a great feast that my lord Prince Thutmose will give for Prince Amenophis, to celebrate the bonds of love and brotherhood between them."

"So, an altogether friendly wager." Pharaoh nodded, pleased. "My son, I'm glad that you've made peace with Nefertiti, but above all, I rejoice to find your spirits restored. I've been deeply concerned about you." He signaled for one of the male servants to take his war club, then moved toward Thutmose and me. He tenderly slipped Thutmose's other arm over his own shoulders. "Let's get you inside. It's a shame that your game ended so badly, but we'll soon mend that. Cats! If they weren't protected by Bast herself, perhaps they'd treat us with a little more respect, eh? Now, don't be afraid to lean on me, my son." He glanced down at Thutmose's injured foot. "Hmph. That looks broken to me, but I'm no doctor. I'll send for my physician. Let's hope he proves me wrong. You'll be better in no time, and then I insist on helping you arrange that feast."

Uni recovered his professional poise in time to rush through the doorway ahead of us and see to it that a proper bed was prepared in Thutmose's real bedchamber to receive the injured prince. As the torch-bearing slaves from the garden began trickling back indoors, the Master of the Household began barking commands in every direction. Pharaoh watched the resulting commotion and chuckled.

"My son, I was going to send one of your people to fetch the doctor, but I think we'll have him here sooner if I bring him myself."

"I can do that for you, if you'd like, my lord Pharaoh," I offered.

"Thank you, dear. That would be—"

"No!" Thutmose made a grab for my hand. "Please, Father, I want her to stay."

The urgency in his voice put me on edge, but it only made Pharaoh's brows rise in speculation. "Is that so? Well, I won't deny a sick man such a simple request." He left us.

As soon as his father was out of earshot, Thutmose bawled an order to the rest of his servants: "Get out! I want to speak with Lady Nefertiti alone." They didn't wait for a second command.

When we were by ourselves, Thutmose shifted his body on the bed and winced in pain. "I think I did break a bone." He looked up at me with a twisted smile. "Aren't you going to say 'Serves you right' or 'That's what happens to those who deny the existence of the gods' or 'I'm sorry it wasn't your neck'?"

"No, I'm not," I replied. "I might have wanted to push you into the pool, and I definitely wanted to slap you for all of your stupid teasing during the race, but I never wanted you to suffer something like this." When I saw the skeptical look on his face, I added, "I'm not asking you to believe I'm your friend, Thutmose, but the fact is, I'm not your enemy."

Uni entered to announce the arrival of Pharaoh's chief physician. It was time for me to go back to my own quarters. I wanted nothing more than to find my bed and go to sleep, but as I headed for the main door of Thutmose's apartments, someone called my name. It was the female servant who'd called me "little gazelle."

"Lady Nefertiti, may I speak with you?" she asked in a low, confidential voice. "There's something you should see."

I followed her into the now-unlit garden. The stars above us were losing their light with the waning night, but the woman knew her way. Her work-hardened hand closed on mine as she brought me to a place by the wall where the myrtles' perfume was heavy on the air. Here I heard the sound of crying and peered into the dark. The maidservant who'd dropped Ta-Miu crouched there, curled up into a ball of tears.

"Why are you out here alone?" I asked.

"He'll kill me," the girl whimpered. "I tried to hold the cat, but she kicked and she clawed and I couldn't do it and the prince fell because of *me*. I can't go back, I can't get away, and I don't know what to do. He'll *kill* me!"

I knelt beside her and rested my hand on her curved back. "I won't let that happen. You're going to come to my rooms and serve me." She raised her head and looked at me, a tentative glimmer of hope in her eyes. "I'll send word to Uni and give my *two* maids in exchange," I went on. "I doubt he'll make a fuss over such a good bargain. He won't have time: He'll be as busy as everyone else here, looking after Prince Thutmose. And if not"—I smiled at her and shrugged—"it's something we'll resolve tomorrow."

— 15 —

THE HORIZON OF HEAVEN

As I'd hoped, Uni was still too upset by his master's accident and too stressed dealing with the aftermath to block the exchange of servants. My maids were thrilled to be joining the prince's household—they saw it as a promotion. I sent them off with best wishes for their future and promptly received a rather confused note from Uni, acknowledging the trade. Somehow he'd gotten the impression that it was all his idea. He closed by reporting that Ta-Miu had been found and was a marvelous comfort to her master, who was resting as well as he could with a broken ankle.

I'll miss you, Ta-Miu, I thought. *But Thutmose does need you more than I do. I'm glad he bears no grudge against you for tripping him. Thank Isis, he's capable of love.*

After Uni's letter arrived, I spent the rest of the morning letting my new maid get used to my rooms and the women's quarters in general. Her name was Teti, and she was the daughter and granddaughter of royal servants, though her family's long history of loyal service had done nothing to protect her from a bad-tempered master. She was a hard worker, but she did her chores with one eye on the door, as if fearing the imminent arrival of a messenger from Thutmose, demanding her return. When I told her that there was no need to be afraid of that, she dutifully agreed with me, but her expression said "I know better."

If I don't convince her that she's safe, she'll never be able to enjoy her new life, I thought. It will be as if Thutmose still owned her. I considered how I might prove to her beyond all doubt that she was in my household now and finally came up with a plan. "Teti, please come here," I called. "I need you to help me prepare for a visit."

"Yes, mistress," Teti said. "Where will you be going?"

"*We* are going to see Prince Thutmose."

"Ah!" His name nearly sent Teti running back into my rooms, but I grabbed her hand before she could bolt.

"Listen to me: I pledge by the sacred Feather of Ma'at that if I bring you back into the prince's apartments, I will bring you out again. I want you to know, once and for all, that I will always defend you, my life for yours. Do you trust me?"

She nodded, but again I saw doubt in her eyes and the absentminded way in which she cradled her left wrist, the one that had been broken. I could imagine her asking herself, "Who made such promises to mere servants?"

I do, Teti, I thought. *I do.*

Teti alone did a better job of helping me bathe, oil my skin, and paint my eyes than my two former maids had ever done. As she slipped a fresh dress over my head, she asked where I kept my jewelry. My laughter at the question baffled her.

"Oh, Teti, this is perfect," I said. "I was wondering what excuse I could give for going to see the prince, and now I have one: my jewelry! I took it off last night in the garden and left it there."

"You—you don't have more?"

"Someone else needed it. If Hathor is willing, I'll have more someday. If not, we can make me some ornaments from flowers."

"I can do that, Lady Nefertiti!" she cried eagerly, and dashed away.

We arrived at Thutmose's apartments as the Aten's bright disk was just beginning to descend from the highest point in the heavens. When Uni opened the great door and stared at Teti, my new maid retreated so closely behind me that I felt her breath on my back through the thin linen of my dress.

"I'm sorry if she is not working out for you, Lady Nefertiti," Uni said pompously. "But we can't undo the exchange."

"That's not why I'm here," I said, making my voice twice as haughty as his. "I have come to visit with Prince Thutmose. I want to be certain that he is being well cared for and is resting comfortably. Teti has come as my attendant."

"I can assure you, my master is receiving every attention."

"And I can assure you, I will leave as soon as I've seen him for myself."

"As you will, my lady." Uni bowed and stepped to one side so that we could enter.

Prince Thutmose was not in his bedchamber. He had been moved, bed and all, to the doorway that looked out on the garden. Ta-Miu was snuggled against his side, butting her head under his hand to demand more and more petting. When Uni announced my presence, the prince jerked his head as if waking suddenly from a deep sleep.

"Nefertiti? Why are you here?"

"It's good to see you, too, Thutmose," I joked. Tilting my head to one side, I added: "You're looking much better than last night."

"They cleaned the mud and blood off me, if that's what you mean, but you can see for yourself I was right about the broken bone." He gestured at his right foot, splinted and bandaged with clean linen. There were other bandages wrapping the scrape higher up his leg. A strong smell of honey and acacia gum hung over everything. "I'm going to be trapped like this for a long time. So many long, empty days." He sighed.

"There's nothing you can do to fill them?"

He lifted his hands, helpless. "I loved to hunt, and to train for war, and to drive my chariot. Do you know a magician with a spell that will let me do such things from my bed?"

I thought about it. "Maybe not a magician," I said.

I never did remember to ask for my jewelry back, not even after more than fifteen days had passed.

If a passing stranger somehow gained access to the

prince's apartments and saw us together, he would think we were childhood friends. I came to see Thutmose every morning and sat beside his bed until midafternoon. Uni told me that was when Aunt Tiye paid her visits, and I didn't want her jumping to the wrong conclusion about Thutmose and me. It was bad enough that she was continuing to keep Amenophis close to her in order to keep us apart. If she found out I was getting any enjoyment out of Thutmose's company, she might be mean enough to put an end to that, too. She wanted our marriage or nothing.

Thutmose and I almost did have nothing. At first he regarded my visits with suspicion. When he spoke, his words were often mocking or bitter. More than once, he asked me outright what I hoped to gain by coming to see him so often.

"I'm keeping an eye on you, waiting to catch you dancing around the room when you think no one's looking," I said dryly. "You're only pretending to have a broken ankle because you won't have to give that feast for Amenophis until it's healed."

"Ah, so my evil plan is discovered. A thousand curses on all clever girls!" he exclaimed, and for the first time, I heard him laugh with warmth and pure joy.

Things were much better between us after that. It became my pleasure to keep him amused with jokes, entertained with songs, enthralled with the same sort of stories I used to tell my little sister, Bit-Bit. Sometimes I had Uni bring us the game board for playing Senet. We tossed knucklebones to see how many spaces we could move our pawns around the course, and when he tired of that, we turned the board over for a match of Twenty Squares. We soon agreed that the winner would be whoever was farthest ahead at the moment when Ta-Miu pounced into the middle of the game and scattered the pieces.

One day, Thutmose refused my offer of a game. "I don't feel well," he said. "I'm too tired to play."

I studied him closely. "You do look a little flushed. You might have a fever. I'll get the doctor."

"No, don't. I just want to rest a bit. Why don't you go out into the garden? I'll have Uni bring you back when I'm ready to beat you at Dogs and Jackals."

"Since when do you have a Dogs and Jackals board?"

"Since I remembered what an excellent player I am. Now go and prepare for your doom."

I did as he asked, though I would have rather made sure that Pharaoh's doctor came to check on him. To take my mind off my worries for Thutmose, I turned my thoughts elsewhere as I walked along the garden path. He did love the tales I told, so I began creating a new one, resting my sight on the tranquil ripples of the lotus pool as I waited for fresh ideas to come to me. A bird was singing in the willows, and I tried to seize that thread of song and weave it into my story. Was the bird a messenger from the gods? An enchanted princess? A wandering spirit that could not enter the afterlife until a curse was broken or an incomplete task was fulfilled? I decided that the bird was an ordinary girl, a farmer's daughter who had done something to please the dwarf-god Bes. Bes offered to grant her one wish, and so she wished to be able to fly, but before her wish was granted, she did something to annoy the god and so . . . and so . . .

"And so what *did* she do to anger him?" I asked the sky. "It would have to be something awful. Bes is very kind and patient, especially with children. Would he get mad if she laughed at how short and ugly he is? Oh, I know! The evil one, Set, *disguised* himself as Bes, in order to play tricks on mortals, and—" I lowered my voice as I wrestled with the problems of my story.

"That's not fair, Nefertiti. Now I can't hear you, and you were getting to the best part."

My heart beat faster at the sound of the voice coming from the green shade of the willows. The singing bird took flight as Amenophis emerged through the delicate, drooping branches, his arms held out to me. I rushed into their circle with a cry of pure happiness.

"So *this* is why you sent me into the garden, Thutmose?" I said, pointing at Amenophis as we came back into the prince's room, arm in arm. "The next time you claim to have a fever, I'll simply dump a jar of water on you." I tried to sound severe and angry. I was a total failure.

The three of us gathered around the Dogs and Jackals board, but we talked more than we played. My spirit sang louder than any bird as I saw how well the brothers were getting along. It all felt so much like a happy dream that I was afraid to ask how such a thing had come to be, in case asking that question would break the spell and wake me.

Luckily, Thutmose didn't want to wait for my question before telling me everything. He took mischievous delight in playing the storyteller for once: "You know Mother came to see me every day at first, and she brought *this* old papyrus stalk along." He jerked his thumb at Amenophis. "But as soon as the doctor told her I was in no danger, she found other business to mind. Think of how surprised I was on the first day she didn't come here, but he did!"

"I can't say I got a warm welcome," Amenophis added. He glanced at a place on the wall where the painted pattern was marred by a dark, irregular stain and some chipping. "I hope that wasn't a special goblet you threw at my head."

"It was made of glass." Thutmose looked sulky, remembering how his temper had led him to destroy something so rare, precious, and costly. "I don't know why you came back after that."

"Come back? I *stayed* that first time!" Amenophis chuckled. "I was safe enough. As soon as you realized what you'd destroyed, I reckoned you'd think twice before hurling another treasure at me."

I gave Thutmose a hard look. "You threw a glass goblet at him? What about our wager?"

He was visibly ashamed. "I forgot, for a moment."

"Nefertiti, let's not argue about pebbles and forget to look at the mountain," Amenophis said. He sat beside his brother on the bed and put his arm around him.

Thutmose resumed his story, telling me how Amenophis came to see him loyally, day after day, sometimes bringing him small, special gifts, always sharing the news of the palace. Aunt Tiye was content. As long as Amenophis stayed away from me, she didn't need to come up with more and more excuses to separate us. She never knew how much Amenophis welcomed this chance to be with his brother.

But Thutmose did, in time. The brotherly friendship I'd tried to force on him had come into being on its own.

When he finished his tale, Thutmose clapped his hands together with satisfaction and announced, "Now that you see where we are, Nefertiti, we can all plan our next step together."

I glanced around the room uncertainly. "How much longer do you think we will be able to meet like this?" I asked. "Your mother's agents are going to tell her that Amenophis and I have been under your roof together, and she won't like it."

The charming smile that had once attracted me to Thutmose was back. "My mother's agents aren't paid enough to tell her things that I pay them to conceal."

I breathed a little easier. "All right. What's this 'next step' we need to plan? The feast for Amenophis? Doesn't that have to wait until your bones are healed?"

"That will be soon enough, but, no, we have bigger plans to set in motion. I want to see you and Amenophis married, Nefertiti. That will be something worth celebrating with the greatest banquet Thebes has ever seen."

I squealed with joy so loudly that I embarrassed myself, and when I tried to throw myself into Thutmose's arms to thank him, Amenophis had to grab me and hold me back.

"Watch out, Nefertiti, you're going to land on his bad leg!"

I pulled back and gave him an insulted look. "I know enough not to touch his broken ankle."

"Yes, but the scrape farther up his leg still hurts, too."

"In that case"—I steered Amenophis out of my way and

gently put my arms around my new friend and kissed his cheek—"Isis bless you, Thutmose. I pray for the day when Amenophis and I will see you standing at your father's side as coruler of the Two Lands."

I did more than pray. I wrote a letter to Pharaoh, filling it with just enough praise for his oldest son for him to notice but not so much that my words rang false. Whatever else she was, Aunt Tiye was crafty when it came to knowing how her royal husband's mind worked. She saw my marriage to Thutmose as the only way to persuade Pharaoh that his son's past offenses were forgiven and that he could reinstate Thutmose as his heir. I showed her that there can be more than one path to any goal.

The first news I received to let me know I'd succeeded did not come from Pharaoh or Thutmose or even Aunt Tiye, but from Sitamun. Teti came running after me as I headed out for my morning visit with Thutmose (and another sweet, secret afternoon with Amenophis).

"A messenger came to your rooms with this after you left, Lady Nefertiti," she said, panting for breath as she handed me the small papyrus scroll. "She said it was *very* important."

I unrolled the message and read it, then read it again, and a third time before I could believe it. "Teti, bring my sandals and my oldest dress to Princess Sitamun's rooms," I said as I rushed away down the hall.

Soon after that, I found myself holding on to the rail of a chariot driven by one of Sitamun's menservants. I don't know how much gold changed hands for her to provide me with that transport. I do know that the driver was unskilled and was distinctly relieved when I told him to give me directions to our destination while I took over the reins. We must have made a very odd picture, even if I hadn't been the one driving. We were passing through the poorer sections of Thebes, and because I'd followed Sitamun's suggestion that I dress as humbly as I could, I appeared to be of the same rank as the servant with me. But if my friend had hoped we wouldn't attract notice, she'd forgotten that a royal chariot's presence in such a neighborhood was the same as arriving crowned with gold.

On a street lined with run-down houses, my escort indicated the one we sought. I threw the reins to him and leaped down from the chariot while he struggled to control the horses. A crowd of curious onlookers gathered around the vehicle at once, but I never looked back or even bothered to announce my presence before barging through the badly hung wooden door. It swung back with a loud crash that instantly commanded the attention of the three people gathered in that one-room dwelling.

"Nefertiti!" Nava was in my arms.

At first all we could do was laugh and cry and hug and laugh again while the tears poured from our eyes. I don't know how long we would have carried on in that way if I hadn't heard another voice say, "Let her breathe, little sister. I don't think you were this happy when you saw me."

"Oh, that's not true, Mahala; you know that's not true!" Nava sprang away from me to embrace her sister fiercely.

It was Mahala's turn to laugh, with Henenu joining in. The scribe held up his hands as if he stood before the gods. "I am here to bear witness that Nava is right. When the priest of Ptah agreed to our offer and ordered Mahala to come greet her new 'owners,' this child threw herself on her so violently that I could just imagine that man telling himself, 'I should have asked for double the price.' "

I faced Mahala and Nava, then deliberately knelt and pressed my forehead to the ground at their feet. "You saved my life, Mahala," I said. "Not a day passes when I fail to thank you for that wonderful gift. May your god and mine bless you forever."

"Lady Nefertiti, you mustn't bow to me!" Mahala dropped to her knees and forced me to lift my head. "You cared for my sister, you made her free, and you redeemed me from slavery. The debt is mine."

I held out one hand to her, one to Nava, and drew the sisters into my arms. "You're alive and well. All debts are paid."

We emerged from the hovel to see my escort fighting a losing battle against the street children who were determined to swarm all over the chariot and the horses. He looked both worried and relieved when I told him he was free to drive back to the palace at once.

"We can't all fit in the chariot, so take Henenu and we will come along on foot."

He helped the dwarf scribe mount, fumbled with the reins, and let the horses run. Mahala, Nava, and I watched his hectic, ungoverned departure. I looked at the Habiru sisters. "Do you think we'll reach the palace before he does?"

"Do you think we'll ever see Henenu again?" Nava asked plaintively.

Mahala and I both assured her that Henenu was not

going to be carried halfway back to Memphis by his hapless driver. Then I asked the sisters, "How long have you been here in Thebes, and why didn't you come to me in the palace?"

Nava didn't know, but Mahala said, "We came as far as the gates, but when the guards heard who we were, they told us that there had been reports of a great sickness in Memphis—perhaps even plague—and no one who'd been there could enter. It wasn't until later that I realized they hadn't bothered to ask us if we'd come from Memphis; they just *knew.* Henenu grew angry and asserted his rank as a respected scribe. He demanded to speak with a higher authority. It didn't do any good. We were brought to the house where you found us and were warned to stay away from the palace unless we wanted to see the inside of a prison cell. We had to give in."

"I'm surprised Henenu never tried to send word about your situation."

"He did! He wrote at least three messages each day and found reliable men to carry them to the palace. The local children used to fight each other for the job of getting him fresh papyrus for all of those letters. I know that at least some of them were meant for you. Didn't you receive them?"

I hadn't, and I knew whose hand had barred Henenu's messages from reaching me. It was the same hand that had pushed my friends away from the palace gates with false reports of sickness in Memphis. It was the same hand that, until today, had kept me unaware that they were in the city, that had stood like a wall between me and Sitamun, that had curved itself around Amenophis to draw him far from me. It was probably the same hand that had crushed all letters between me and my family in Akhmin. Now, suddenly, those unyielding fingers had loosened their grip, letting my life come trickling back to me like a flow of golden sand.

I remembered the first lines of Sitamun's message: *Your words on my brother's behalf have reached Father's heart. Mother is satisfied.*

She didn't need to specify the source of Aunt Tiye's contentment. It could only be the fulfillment of her dearest desire—to see Thutmose named crown prince once more.

It was early afternoon by the time we reached the palace. The first thing I did was bring Nava and Mahala to Thutmose's rooms. Poor Nava! She found it impossible to accept that the "bad prince" of her nightmares had changed. She refused to cross his threshold.

"There are all sorts of healings, dear one," her sister said, soothing the child's fear. "How can you believe that the One has power to mend the body but not the spirit?"

"You never met Prince Thutmose," Nava replied stubbornly, but she consented to enter his apartments if her sister and I promised to hold her hands the whole time.

It was a promise we didn't need to keep for long. The first thing we all saw when Uni led us into Thutmose's presence was Amenophis, sitting on the floor beside his brother's bed and making Ta-Miu dance for a bunch of feathers on a string. Nava's greeting struck him like a war-club blow. The cat rose straight up in the air, hissing, and shot out into the garden. Thutmose laughed so hard he complained he'd split open the bandages on his scraped leg.

"It's not right for the crown prince of the Two Lands to tell lies," I said primly, which made him laugh even more.

With Nava and Mahala in my household, my daily visits to cheer Thutmose's convalescence became miniature parties. With Sitamun's help, the Habiru sisters were provided with the musical instruments they played so well, and I could play the sistrum while I danced to their lively tunes. Ta-Miu often tried to be a part of our performance, and once she succeeded in catching my feet so that I hit the floor on my backside.

"Why couldn't you do that during the race, you treacherous cat?" Thutmose joked. "You must suffer for your disloyalty! I condemn you to eat a plateful of fish and a cup of fresh milk at once!"

"You spoil her," Amenophis said. "She's getting as fat as a castor bean."

"If you think *I'm* to blame for how fat she's getting, we need to have a talk, brother," Thutmose replied. He turned his face to Nava and said, "How would you like a kitten, little bird?" Her dance of joy was so boisterous that Uni came in to see if anything was wrong.

Nava was still bouncing madly as we returned to my apartments for the evening. All she could talk about was her kitten, what to name it, when she might have it. "The kittens aren't even born yet, sweet one," I told her. "Worry about tomorrow when the sun rises."

I should have slept peacefully that night. My heart was filled with contentment; my life floated on calm waters. No doubt Aunt Tiye still resented me for not having been the docile little rag doll she thought she'd taken from Akhmin, but at least we were no longer at war. I was just as happy to have her ignore my existence as I would be to hear her offer a thousand words of thanks or apology. All that remained to make my joy complete was to be recognized as Amenophis's bride. The royal brothers assured me that this would happen very soon, but I didn't believe them. They were having too much fun conspiring over ways to outmaneuver their mother if she objected. Once their plot succeeded, the game would be over.

Was I being too greedy, wanting to have all of my wishes fulfilled? Was that what was disturbing my dreams? They were crowded with half-formed sounds and images, winding paths that turned into bottomless pits at my feet, skies that swirled with plumes of smoke that were either murky green or dull crimson, sinister whispers from unseen creatures in the branches of dead trees with twigs as white as bone. To escape those visions, I would have welcomed the return of the lions that had been my childhood night-mares, but I was held fast in their awful grip until dawn.

How happy I was to see the Aten's bright disk bring the day's first light! It had never looked so beautiful. I raised my arms and called out a prayer of praise.

That morning, as Mahala, Nava, and I approached Thutmose's apartments, I became aware of a faint tension in the air. Without knowing why, I doubled my pace until I was almost flying through the palace halls. My friends were carrying their instruments and couldn't hope to keep up with me, and so I was the first to reach the prince's door. It stood wide open, and the sounds coming from inside were not good to hear: shouting, wailing, the desperate sound of many people running as if from some disaster, scuffling, and uncounted voices calling on the gods for mercy.

I crossed the threshold into chaos, dodging the slaves and servants who seemed to be coming from every direction at once. I soon saw that this wasn't true, and my heart fell as I realized that the source of all that tumult and confusion was the doorway to Thutmose's bedchamber.

"Lady Nefertiti, what are you doing here?" A very disheveled Uni staggered toward me and blocked my way. "You mustn't stay."

"Think about your words," I told him as calmly as I could.

"Oh! Pardon, pardon me, I should not have said—" He gulped for air. "I meant that you will not *want* to stay here this morning. My lord Prince Thutmose can see no one. Last evening he complained of a dizzy feeling, and he spoke harshly to the servant in charge of changing the bandages on his leg. He hasn't acted like that for—for—well, since your visits began. Toward dawn, we heard a crash from his bedchamber and found that he'd tried to get up and walk."

"His ankle hasn't mended enough for that," I said. "He knows it. Why did he try such a foolish thing?"

"He—he—I think he did not know anything when he made the attempt."

"Sleepwalking?"

Uni shook his head. "When we came to pick him up off the floor and settle him on his bed again, his skin felt like fire. His eyes were open, but he didn't recognize any of us, his loyal servants, and he was babbling. I fetched Pharaoh's own physician at once. He is with the prince now." He glanced at the commotion still boiling out of the bedchamber door and sighed. "My lady, there is nothing anyone else can do."

"I don't know if I can do anything more than the doctor," I said. "But I *will* see my friend."

No one stopped me from entering Thutmose's bedchamber. The room was brightly lit by the daylight streaming down from the high, narrow windows as well as from a grove of lamp stands, all ablaze. A brazier smoldered in one corner, perfuming the air with sweet incense. Slaves carrying water vessels, bowls, and clean linen strips came and went, their eyes wide with apprehension.

I saw a tall, dignified man standing at the head of Thutmose's bed and guessed this must be the doctor. I was glad to see he was not old Master Ptah-Hotep. Bitterly I recalled that other physician. On Thutmose's orders, he'd tricked me into swallowing a potion that had made it impossible for me to speak in my own defense when I was tried for Ta-Miu's "death." I had forgiven Thutmose for the past, but I dearly hoped that old man was no longer practicing the art of healing. A doctor who could be corrupted was no doctor at all.

The physician's keen eyes flashed when he caught sight of me. "You are Lady Nefertiti?" he asked crisply. I nodded. "We have never met, but I have heard you are a very beautiful girl. I see that the gossips are right, for once. Come here. He's been asking to see you."

"Is he—is he better?" I asked.

"Stop wasting the doctor's time with silly questions, Nefertiti. I can speak for myself." Thutmose waved at me from his bed and propped himself up on his elbows.

Oh, how happy I was to see that provoking grin of his! His face lacked healthy color and his cheeks were a bit sunken, but otherwise he looked like himself. I came close but remained standing at his bedside instead of taking a seat on the edge the way I often did during my morning visits. His hand shot out, closed on my wrist, and pulled me down to my usual place.

"You can stop acting as if I'm made of flower petals," he said. "I had a bad night, that's all. It was caused by a sudden fever, but the doctor had my attendants wash me with cool water and crushed herbs and now the fever's gone."

"*Almost* gone, my prince," the physician corrected him. "It burns low, like an ember. I will deal with it so that it is completely quenched."

"While you're at it, do you have any remedies for pain? The place where I cut my leg is hurting more than usual."

"I am told you fell on it last night. You are lucky you did not do additional damage to your broken bones. Does your ankle hurt as well?" He looked pleased when Thutmose shook his head. "Good. That means the broken bones will soon be whole. As for the pain, I will make you a compound of willow bark for that and poppy juice later, if something stronger is needed."

"You should talk to Nefertiti. She's got experience prescribing poppy juice." Thutmose's smirk became a long, loud yawn. He lay back on the bed and closed his eyes. "I'm sorry, Nefertiti. I'm worn out from last night's fever-dance. I wanted to see you this morning, but I think I'm too tired to appreciate your songs and stories. Come back tomorrow?"

"I will," I said, leaning over to kiss his brow as I rose to go. "I promise."

I found Nava and Mahala waiting for me just inside the door to the prince's apartments. I explained to them what had happened and they made sympathetic noises.

"The doctor said his ankle will soon be healed," I told them, wanting to keep our minds on good things.

As we walked down the hall, Uni came hastening after us, carrying a basket. It was meowing loudly and irritably, in a familiar voice.

"Ta-Miu!" Nava cried, beaming.

The Master of the Prince's Household bowed to me, holding out the basket like an offering. "Lady Nefertiti, Prince Thutmose requests you look after his cat until he has made a full recovery. He asks you to recall that she has a history of getting underfoot. He is afraid that with so much fuss going on, she might be injured if someone stumbles over her, and given her condition . . ." He shrugged.

I took the basket from his hands. "Tell the prince that I will be honored to take special care of Ta-Miu but that I hope it won't be for long. We all look forward to his swift recovery."

Nava was overjoyed to take over the responsibility of minding Ta-Miu. That evening, after feeding the cat a mound of shredded duck and half of her own dinner, she ran through my rooms trailing a string behind her for our furry guest to chase. They made so much noise that Mahala finally put a stop to it.

"The cat should rest, and it's time you were asleep," she said. "You can play with Ta-Miu tomorrow."

Later, I was awakened by a great commotion coming from beyond my bedchamber doorway. *Is it morning already?* I thought drowsily as I sat up, wiping sleep from my eyes, but the room was still dark. *That child! Couldn't she wait for dawn before playing with Ta-Miu?* I swung my feet out of bed and felt my way carefully toward the noise.

It wasn't coming from the outer room, so I stumbled into my courtyard. That was where I found Teti, Mahala, and Nava huddling together, their eyes fixed on the portal that connected my rooms to the rest of the women's quarters. The disturbance came from there, an unearthly wailing heard over the sound of pounding feet, screams, and children yowling.

"What is it? Oh, what's happening, mistress?" Teti cried, clutching my arm.

Before I could answer, someone came lurching through the entryway, into my small garden. With streaming eyes, Amenophis stood shaking like a willow leaf for a heartbeat before the dreadful words rasped from his mouth:

"My brother is gone."

— 16 —

THE BOOK OF THE DEAD

For seventy days, the palace waited while Thutmose lay in the House of Beauty, the place where the priests and embalmers would prepare and preserve his body to last for eternity. Beyond the walls, in the workshops of many artists and artisans, there was a great surge of activity as many hands worked to create and assemble all of the possessions the dead prince would be taking with him into the afterlife. Coffins were being carved and painted; boxes were being filled with tools, clothes, and jewelry; and the goldsmiths labored to provide the shining mask that would cover Thutmose's face.

I didn't want to think about any part of what was unfolding around me. When the first shock of the news struck, I threw back my head and cried aloud with grief. Thutmose had begun as my foe, but that day I had lost a friend.

Amenophis held me, and Mahala and Nava linked their arms with his to form a circle of consolation around me.

Even timid little Teti dared to join us. Amenophis's tears mingled with mine, but at last we had no more to shed. I was the first to break the embrace and turn back to my rooms.

"Where are you going, Nefertiti?" he called after me.

"To dress," I answered. "And then to the queen's apartments. My aunt has lost her firstborn son."

Just as I had gone to visit Thutmose every morning, now I arose each day and went to sit with Aunt Tiye. She said nothing the first time I crossed her threshold, only staring at me with empty eyes. She didn't bid me welcome, but she didn't order me to get out of her sight, so I chose to approach the gilded chair where she sat flanked by six maidservants and attended by her four daughters. I knelt at her feet and pressed my face to the floor, reciting a prayer to Anubis, the god who guides the dead, then one to Osiris, asking his mercy when the time came to judge the heart of Thutmose. When I was done, I didn't wait for her permission to stand. I understood that there would be no words between us this day.

Other days came, and I went to her apartments every morning. Sometimes all of her daughters were with her, sometimes a few, sometimes none. In time, on a morning when I was her only visitor, she spoke to me. I had just turned to one of her maids to ask if the queen had been eating enough to stay well when I heard Aunt Tiye's hoarse voice behind me grumbling, "I can speak for myself."

Her words echoed those I'd heard Thutmose speak on that last morning. When I burst into tears at the memory, she questioned me, cried with me, comforted me as I comforted her. From then on, her sorrowful silence was broken.

We spoke about many things during those seventy days of waiting. She shared stories of Thutmose's childhood, her dreams for him, her regrets. At some point, she found the words to apologize to me for the heavy hand she'd tried to lay upon my future, and I found the heart to forgive her. She was no longer the scheming queen, using me like a pawn in a game of Senet: She was only a mother who had lost her child.

"Thank you, dear one," she said, hugging me. "I'm going to send for your family. You haven't seen them in far too long. That's my fault, too, and the letters—" She was weeping again.

"That's past," I told her. "Past and pardoned. I'll see them soon, won't I? That will make up for everything."

Since Thutmose's death, there were no longer any bars between Amenophis and me, yet we still spent most of our time apart. He had been called away to study the funeral rites he would have to perform for his brother. Everything had to be done perfectly to ensure that Thutmose's spirit would reach Lord Osiris's court in safety. The rituals at the tomb were only a part of that. There were many charms, spells, and incantations to be placed on the prince's body. Above all, he needed to be buried with the Book of Going Forth by Day.

I had never seen a copy of the Book of Going Forth by Day, though like everyone else in the Black Land, I knew all about it. That sacred scroll described every step of the journey that awaited Thutmose's spirit. There were many perils on the path to his rebirth in the afterlife, but the book provided all the knowledge he would need to triumph over them. Of all the things being made ready for Thutmose's tomb, the book was the only one I could stand to imagine without tears.

On a morning halfway through the time of preparation, I entered Aunt Tiye's apartments to find that she had a number of other callers. Princess Tabiri sat next to her, holding her rival's hand and urging her to have one more sip of wine, one more nibble of bread. Henenu was also present. I hadn't seen very much of my friend and teacher since the day I'd overseen his return to the palace. Now he was in deep conversation with my aunt over the piece of papyrus in his hands and didn't notice me come in.

"—describe the collar you would like him to wear as he approaches Osiris?" I heard him say just before he glanced in my direction. "Nefertiti, how good to see you. Come and look at this." He let me have a good look at the document he'd brought, a masterpiece of art. Even before I read a line of the writing on it, the parade of exquisitely painted gods told me I was looking at part of the Book of Going Forth by Day.

"This will be my son's," Aunt Tiye said, and this time it was Princess Tabiri who held her while she wept.

"Henenu?" I murmured, tapping him on the shoulder. "Henenu, can we speak privately?" I drew him aside and told him the idea that had come to me as I'd looked at the portion of Thutmose's scroll.

He listened attentively, and when I finished, he said, "Come with me."

He brought me to the room where many men bent their backs as they worked on long strips of papyrus, creating the scenes Thutmose's spirit would encounter. Thutmose himself was there, accompanied by Anubis, led by Horus, kneeling in the presence of Osiris, awaiting the final balance to be struck between his heart and the Feather of Ma'at. Some of them were so intent on their work that they didn't even look up to acknowledge my presence.

Henenu brought me a scribe's kit, a worn piece of papyrus covered with clumsily scrawled lines. "Copy this text *here*," he told me, setting down another piece that was adorned with fresh paintings.

I read the words before me: " 'I have risen, I have risen like the mighty hawk of gold . . . ' " I would copy these words and many, many others into the Book of Going Forth by Day that would accompany my friend into his tomb and beyond, to a life that would be as eternal as the stars. I said a prayer to Thoth and Seshat, She-Who-Writes, and began.

On the day before Prince Thutmose's body emerged from the House of Beauty—wrapped in linen, guarded by countless amulets, masked with gold, sealed in many coffins—my family arrived from Akhmin. Because of Father's rank and his relationship to Aunt Tiye, they were to be welcomed formally by Pharaoh himself in one of the finest audience chambers in the palace. I was brought into the room just as they were paying homage to the royal couple and their children. An attendant announced me, but before I could say anything to Father, Mother, or Bit-Bit, Aunt Tiye summoned me to her side on the low platform where her husband sat enthroned.

"The gods take much from us," she said, smiling at me with genuine affection. "But they also give us many blessings. When I took Nefertiti from Akhmin, I hoped to see her married to my son." She spread her arms to either side and took Amenophis and me by the hand. "When our time of mourning is over, I will see that hope fulfilled." She placed our hands together, cradled between her own.

I looked at Amenophis; he was as stunned as I. Aunt Tiye squeezed our united hands and leaned close enough to whisper in my ear, "You have become a true daughter to me, Nefertiti. You shared my grief. I won't forget it." Then she turned to Father and called out, "Don't fret, Ay. This marriage is *her* idea, too."

I looked to my parents and sister. My second mother, Mery, had tears of joy in her eyes. Father looked bewildered and pleased at the same time. Only Bit-Bit's face was unsmiling. Why was she glowering at me that way? In the midst of my happiness, I thought I heard the scorching winds of the Red Land bringing Set's mocking laughter.

If Ma'at herself were to demand that I testify to everything that happened on the day of Thutmose's funeral, I would have to bow my head before the goddess and confess that I could not. I remember the strident cries and lamentations of the professional mourners, women who tore their hair, beat their breasts, and knocked their heads against the ground as the procession escorting the prince's body went through the streets of Thebes. I also recall how the coffin was placed on a canopied sled drawn by oxen and by a small army of the highest-born men in Pharaoh's court. Father was among them, wearing the white sandals and headband of mourning.

Beyond that, I have only a blur of images as the sled was loaded onto a boat and ferried to the western shore, then carried on into the valley of the tombs. My head was a tangle of that day's memories and those belonging to the time that Amenophis, Nava, and I had been fugitives in that same valley. While Amenophis and the priests performed the rituals that would let Thutmose begin his journey to Osiris, I saw apparitions of Samut and his little boy, of Kawit and her erring brother, even of Idu and his devious uncle.

As soon as the last of Thutmose's belongings were placed in the tomb, masons sealed the entryway with stone, and priests sealed it with words of power. Several tents were set up nearby, each sheltering a royal feast. We were supposed to honor the dead by taking pleasure in the plentiful food and drink, but I was so exhausted that I might as well have eaten handfuls of flour.

All I wanted was the chance to speak with my family. That didn't seem like much to ask for, yet from the day of their arrival until the day of Thutmose's funeral, all of our meetings were brief, distracted, formal, or all of those together. As the recognized bride-to-be of Prince Amenophis, I was herded here and there like a prized cow. Oh, it was all done with perfect politeness by adept, tactful servants and officials, but it was still *herding*.

"How do you do it, Ta-Miu?" I said, gazing down at the little cat and her five babies. "How do you manage to go your own way and escape all the go-here-go-there-your-regal-presence-is-requested?"

Ta-Miu cocked her head at me as if considering a reply. Her basket was kept in the room where Nava and Mahala slept. If it had been placed in my bedchamber, Nava would have been in and out all night, doting over the kittens, and I never would have gotten any sleep. The cat had given birth in the middle of the time of waiting, and her kittens gave me stronger faith in the renewal of life than the chants of a hundred priests. At last, having reached a conclusion, Ta-Miu closed her eyes as the kittens nursed and purred expressively as if to say, "It's your own fault for not having been born a cat!"

She was probably right. I'd just have to make the best of being who I was.

I hoped that with Thutmose's funeral over, I'd be able to spend more time with those I loved, but I was wrong. Now the palace bustled with preparations for the magnificent banquet at which Amenophis and I would be presented as man and wife to all the most important people in the Two Lands. Because this was to be a royal event of the highest significance, countless details had to be arranged. In all the uproar, a foreign army could have invaded Thebes and no one would have noticed. In fact, I'd wager that the head cook and chief steward would have grabbed the soldiers and put them to work.

Nava and Mahala were seldom around. The master of the royal musicians had whisked them away to be part of the entertainment. They came back to my quarters very late every night, and it was making Nava cranky.

"Why does this stupid feast have to be so *complicated*?"

"Because it's the one event that tells everyone Amenophis and I are married," I told her.

"We just have a ceremony. Mama told us about it, right, Mahala?" Nava asked. When her sister confirmed this, she went on: "It's short and there's wine and then it's *over.*"

"Yes, but that's a ceremony for Habiru people," I said, doing my best to humor a tired child. "We don't have any wedding ceremonies except for this feast. I'm not Habiru."

"You *should* be."

"And Ta-Miu thinks I should be a cat."

Nava nodded thoughtfully. "That would be good, too."

Seven days before the banquet, I received a message from Aunt Tiye, inviting me to her apartments for a meal. When I arrived, I was overjoyed to find Father, Mother, and Bit-Bit there. Aunt Tiye beamed as I embraced my parents.

"It's about time," she stated. "Ay was making my life miserable. 'Why bring us here to see our daughter if we never *get* to see our daughter?' he said. Well, now here you are. See her all you like. I have banquet arrangements to supervise." She swept out of the room gracefully, followed by all the servants.

We didn't need them. A fine meal was spread out on several small tables. Within moments of Aunt Tiye's departure, we were laughing and talking and taking deep pleasure in each other's company just as if I had never left Akhmin.

Or perhaps that was only what I wanted to believe. The truth was, the longer I sat feasting and chattering with my family, the more a sense of *strangeness* seemed to creep over me. As I recounted all that I'd experienced since leaving home, Father and Mother reacted to my adventures with astonishment, sympathy, fear, praise, even scolding. They seized some parts of my story as opportunities to tell me what *they* would have done and others as moments to sternly order me never to do that again!

Bit-Bit stayed silent. Her face was stone, and the only time her lips moved was when she ate or drank. Even then, she avoided the delicacies laid out for us, taking only a few mouthfuls of bread and a few sips of beer. There was no sign that she was glad to see me again. What had happened to my loving little sister? My heart ached to know.

Father leaned back in his chair and patted his belly. "I don't know if I will ever be able to forgive Tiye for intercepting our letters for so long, but I will say this in her favor: She knows how to order good food."

My second mother, Mery, leaned over to take his hand. "We are together now, and Tiye is truly repentant for what she did. If that won't let you forgive her, then try to do it for your own sake, or for the sake of the son she lost."

"I'll think about it."

"I've forgiven her, Father," I said.

"Have you, little kitten? Well, you're still young. Wait until you have your own children and someone keeps *you* from knowing if they're well or happy or even alive!"

"Not knowing if *you* were all well was just as bad," I replied. "But it's over."

He snorted. "I'm not the kind of person who can forget the past, Nefertiti, and my sister has a hand in too many sad memories for me. I'm not ready to forgive her, but for your sake, I'll try to concentrate on how well she's treating you now. I hear that Tiye has commanded that Princess Nefertiti be moved out of the women's quarters into more spacious apartments, with rooms for those Habiru girls you've taken into your household."

"She's done *what*?"

It was so. Aunt Tiye had recovered some of her old spirit. She didn't bother to ask for my opinion or consent; she simply assigned me a new place to live. There are worse surprises.

I liked my new rooms very much. They were lighter and airier than the old ones, and they were connected to a huge garden with many small pools filled with fish and flowers. The only problem was how empty they felt, even with Mahala, Nava, Teti, and a new contingent of royal handmaidens sharing them with me.

As the time for my wedding banquet drew near, I became more and more uneasy. Mery had spoken to me about what I should expect from my husband, but that wasn't the source of my distress: It was Bit-Bit. The distance between us was very real and very cold. Several times since our family feast, I'd tried to reach out to her, but all I met with was a wall.

My feelings must have shown plainly in my face. On my last evening as a bride-to-be, I invited Father, Mother, and Bit-Bit to my new apartments. The silence between Bit-Bit and me was still there and sharper than ever. It left me with very little appetite. Mery noticed this, and while the servants cleared away one set of dishes in order to bring in the next, she gently asked me to show her the garden.

"But it's dark," I protested, confused.

"We won't go far, and the moon is high. Please, my dear."

It didn't take her long to get me to reveal the reason for my sadness. When I finished, she said, "I thought something wasn't right between my girls. You need to talk to her."

"I've tried. *She* won't talk to *me*."

"You'll try again, and I will find a way to help this along."

Mery's "way" was to return to the table and tell Bit-Bit she was going to sleep in my bedchamber that night. "Your sister will be a married woman before the sun sets tomorrow, *and* a royal princess. This is your last chance to be together as you used to be." Bit-Bit greeted the news with the same face of stone she'd worn since her arrival.

Mother's plan could have worked better. When Bit-Bit and I were by ourselves, I might as well have been alone. No matter how hard I tried to draw out my sister, she never responded beyond a few terse words, a grunt or two, and some very exaggerated shrugs. Finally she announced, "I'm tired," lay down on the bed I'd had brought in for her, and closed her eyes so tightly that her whole face looked like a fist.

I tried to sleep after that, but it was no use. There were too many things on my mind—not just my sister's coldness, but thoughts of what was waiting for me in the new life I was about to start. I gave up and got out of bed, padding through my new rooms and out into the garden. I knelt at the edge of one of the small pools and gazed at the reflection of starlight on the water between the fragrant lotus blossoms.

A rustling in the bushes to my right turned out to be

Ta-Miu. The little cat's family had grown to the point where she could leave the kittens on their own more and more. I scratched the star-shaped marking on her brow and said, "What am I going to do, Ta-Miu? Tomorrow I become Amenophis's wife, and a princess! I don't care about the princess part, but—this scares me—with Thutmose gone, Amenophis will be crown prince. He will, I know it. His father recognizes his worthiness, and besides, Aunt Tiye wants her son on the throne. Oh, it's going to happen! And when it does, I won't be just a princess: I'll be *queen*.

"To be a queen—to be Great Royal Wife, like Aunt Tiye." I hung my head. "No, not like Aunt Tiye. Like myself. I'll have the chance to do so much good! Amenophis shares my heart. He'll want me to be more than a wife and a mother, as long as that's what I want, too. What I want . . ." My words drifted away as I thought about the future.

"I know what I want," I said at last. "I want to share his dreams. I want to help him become a stronger man, a pharaoh who governs with justice. If we rule together, maybe we can put a stop to those who buy and sell the word of the gods. I want to help him use his power to clear away schemes and corruption, and to heal . . . Oh, Ta-Miu, it's too much! I want to help Amenophis be stronger, but will I be strong enough, too?"

"Don't be silly; you know you will." Bit-Bit knelt by my side, put her arms around me, and pressed her cheek to mine. "I'm sorry for how I've been acting. I missed you so much!"

"I missed you, too, darling Bit-Bit."

"Yes, but I think first I envied you even more than I

missed you. You were going away to marry a prince! You'd have gorgeous jewelry, and wonderful clothes, and all kinds of servants to wait on you. You'd be *Princess* Nefertiti, *Queen* Nefertiti, and I'd always be nothing more than plain old Bit-Bit." She was regretful. "I told myself I was being a bad sister, envying you your good fortune. I decided that I was being foolish, because even if you became Great Royal Wife, we'd always be sisters and you'd never forget how much we love one another, but then . . ." She looked away from me, but not fast enough. I saw the shining trail of tears.

"But then you didn't hear from me," I said softly. "Not one letter, not one message, nothing. You couldn't have known that Aunt Tiye was intercepting my letters. And you must have thought I was so wrapped up in my splendid new life that I'd forgotten I ever had a sister." I hugged her with all my might. "Never, Bit-Bit. That will never happen, as long as I live. No matter what I am or what I may become, you are *always* my beloved sister."

We sat under the stars all that night, talking, shedding happy tears, even teasing one another in our old way. Then, as the sky began to lighten with the coming dawn, Bit-Bit said, "Wait here a moment," and dashed back into my apartments. She came out holding a small piece of papyrus.

"I have something special to give you, Nefertiti," she said, kneeling beside me once more. "It's a charm of great power, blessed by Isis herself. Actually, it's not mine to give. You made it. You didn't see me, but I was secretly watching you that last night before you left Akhmin. I saw you put this at the goddess's feet. It's stayed there ever since, for such a long time, and no matter what the weather. Even though

I was angry at you, once I learned we were going to see you again, I knew you should have it. Whatever spell you wrote on it must be very strong if it protected you enough to see this day." She handed me the papyrus as she added, "I wish I could work so much magic. I wish I could read what it says."

I looked at the familiar writing, the characters carefully formed with a piece of charcoal rather than a scribe's pen or brush. It was the oath I'd made to Isis, promising to live my life as bravely as I could and recognizing that it was not enough to be born free if I didn't have the courage to *live* my freedom.

I put my arm around Bit-Bit's shoulder and rested the papyrus on the ground between us. "If this is magic, I want nothing better than to share it with you." As the first gleam of the Aten's disk showed on the horizon, I began to read aloud the vow I'd made—the vow I hoped my sister would take for her own: to give no one power over my life but myself.

— Epilogue —
WAKING THE QUEEN

"Nefertiti? Beloved?" Amenophis peeked around the corner of my doorway in the temple's guest quarters, a lamp held high in his hand. "Are you almost ready?"

"I would be, except my braids have come undone." I grinned at my husband. "I must look more like a market woman than a royal wife."

"You look beautiful."

"You always say that."

"It's always true. And it's also true that you said you wanted to do this before dawn, though I don't know why."

I rolled my eyes as if I'd explained the whole matter to him a hundred times. "Ever since your father named you coruler, everything we do becomes a royal *occasion*. We're swarmed by people everywhere we go. What I've come here to accomplish is simple and personal. That means getting up before anyone else knows about it."

"Including the priests?"

"Especially the priests."

"Getting up and sneaking away," Amenophis mused. "It reminds me of our courtship." I glared at him so hard he threw his free hand up in surrender and cried, "What? What? I'm ready to go."

"So am I."

I tossed on a cloak in case the air was chilly and took one of the oil lamps from my room. Together we left the temple guesthouse in perfect silence and made our way to a place that, until now, I had only seen in my dreams.

The Great Sphinx loomed above us, his human head framed by a scattering of stars, his massive lion's paws outstretched. I bowed before him. I gave my lamp to Amenophis to hold and stepped forward, holding out the scroll I'd brought with me from Thebes, the same one that my sister, Bit-Bit, had brought to me from home.

In the days since the celebration of our marriage, Amenophis had opened his heart to me, revealing all the plans he hoped to achieve when it was his time to reign over the Two Lands. His ideas were astonishing, world-changing, dangerous, and noble, even if there would be many who wouldn't see matters that way. More than ever, I wanted to be a part of his dreams, but I also wanted to be his shield and his shelter. More than ever, I would need to be brave.

I laid my written oath of courage at the feet of the Great Sphinx, the one who'd first showed me that I could master my fears and live my life truly free. I gave my thanks in silence, prayed for new strength, then turned to take my husband's hand and face the east where the Aten dawned in beauty.

AFTERWORD

In my previous books, *Nobody's Princess* and *Nobody's Prize,* I wrote about Helen of Troy, a woman of legendary beauty whose life was mythical but very well might have been historical, too. Many people believed that the Troy Homer described in his epic poem *The Iliad* was purely the stuff of myth, until nineteenth-century amateur archaeologist Heinrich Schliemann used that same epic poem to help him uncover the remains of a real Troy that had been attacked, conquered, and put to the torch at the time Helen would have been living.

Now I'm writing about Nefertiti, another beautiful woman, except this time she's a historical person who very well might have been mythical!

There's much that we know about Nefertiti and much that remains a mystery. One of the most wonderful parts of this puzzle is the world-famous statue of this fascinating Egyptian queen, a carved and painted bust that has preserved her beauty through the centuries. Much of ancient Egyptian art depicting members of the royal family was formalized, which is to say that if Pharaoh or any of his relatives had physical imperfections, the artist did not show them. Think of it as the great-great-great-to-the-nth-degree-grandfather of Photoshopping.

Nefertiti lived during one of the most interesting and dangerous periods in ancient Egyptian history, the Amarna Period. It was a time of new ideas and concepts, which is especially exciting when you remember that we're talking about a millennia-old civilization that did not handle change well (to put it mildly). One of the changes of the Amarna Period was Pharaoh Akhenaten's decree that artists should portray him and his family realistically. This says a lot about Akhenaten, since his surviving statues show him with a potbelly, an oddly shaped head, and numerous other physical characteristics that might lead some people to describe him by saying, "But he has a *great* personality!"

It speaks highly of Akhenaten's character that he was willing to be immortalized in art warts and all (even if he didn't have warts). It also tells us something about Nefertiti: If the famous bust of this Egyptian queen shows us a beautiful woman, she really *was* a beautiful woman. Amarna Period art was honest.

I suppose it was lucky for Nefertiti that she was beautiful, since her name means "The beautiful woman has come." Imagine having to live up to a name like that! And everyone would know, because her name was in the language used throughout Egypt. Modern names have meanings, too, but they often come from foreign or dead languages. If you're named Hope or Brooke or Heather, everyone knows what your name means. But what about Alexandra ("man's defender") or Madison ("son [yes, son!] of the mighty warrior") or Emma ("embracing everything")?

Nefertiti was as beautiful as her name, but aside from that, we don't know a lot about her before she became Egypt's queen. The name of her father is known, and her stepmother, and her half sister, but what was her *mother's* name? There's further debate about her ancestry, too. Did Nefertiti come from a purely Egyptian family, or was she of foreign blood? Was she born into the nobility, or was she a commoner?

We do know that there was more to her than just her looks, because she is portrayed many times on walls and monuments acting not merely as Pharaoh's wife but as an independent ruler, a monarch in her own right. Some evidence suggests that she might have ruled Egypt for a time when her husband could no longer do so. What's more, it's theorized that she didn't rule as regent but as Pharaoh, using a male name. There is even one carving that shows her destroying the enemies of Egypt with her own hands! (All right, maybe Amarna Period artists sometimes did stretch the truth just a bit.) But whether she acted alone or with her royal husband, she challenged many powerful men who didn't want to give up even the smallest bit of their wealth and influence. Even for a queen, that took courage.

Then . . . she was gone.

There are no official records of her death. Her tomb has never been found. Recent discoveries in Egypt have raised hopes that her mummy has finally been located, but this has not yet been confirmed to the point where we can say, "Yes, that's Nefertiti, no doubt about it."

That's the historical Nefertiti, a flash of beauty, bravery, and wisdom who stepped out of the shadows of mystery and back again. We still don't know where she came from or why she vanished, but we can look at the exquisitely painted image of the-beautiful-woman-has-come and let our imaginations supply those parts of her story that history still conceals.

Above all, we can remember that she was much more than just another pretty face.

ABOUT THE AUTHOR

Nebula Award winner **Esther Friesner** is the author of 31 novels and over 150 short stories, including "Thunderbolt" in Random House's *Young Warriors* anthology, which led to her novels about Helen of Troy, *Nobody's Princess* and *Nobody's Prize*. She is also the editor of seven popular anthologies. Her work has been published in the United States, the United Kingdom, Japan, Germany, Russia, France, Poland, and Italy. She is also a published poet and a playwright and once wrote an advice column, "Ask Auntie Esther." Her articles on fiction writing have appeared in *Writer's Market* and other Writer's Digest Books.

Besides winning two Nebula Awards in succession for Best Short Story (1995 and 1996), she was a Nebula finalist three times, as well as a Hugo finalist. She received the Skylark Award from the New England Science Fiction Association and the award for Most Promising New Fantasy Writer of 1986 from *Romantic Times*.

Ms. Friesner's latest publications include the novel *Temping Fate*; a short-story collection, *Death and the Librarian and Other Stories;* and *Turn the Other Chick,* fifth in the popular Chicks in Chainmail series, which she created and edits.

Educated at Vassar College, receiving a BA in both Spanish and drama, she went on to receive her MA and PhD in Spanish from Yale University, where she taught for a number of years. She is married and the mother of two, harbors cats, and lives in Connecticut.